PAK SIX

Mission in Pak Six

I yanked the wings level in the dive, the nose pointed steeply down, the afterburner spouting flame and rocketing me toward the earth. The ground was alive with winking, flashing glints. Guns. Three black puffs erupted next to me and were gone instantly. I stopped looking at anything but the sixth span of the huge bridge. The glowing gunsight crept up to the span, I made one quick correction, paused, then pickled. Bombs away. The lightened plane leaped forward, and I heard, "Wildcat leader is hit!" That was Smitty.

The view ahead narrowed to a small hole surrounded by grey fuzz as my aching hand pulled the stick into my gut. My vision cleared, coming out of the dive, and I saw a flicker of a warning light on the console. *Not now . . . too busy.*

We were low to the ground and doing better than 700 knots and everybody was shooting at us. The light flashed again and stayed on. I looked . . . a low fuel warning!

Suddenly, the entire sky became overcast! It was incredible! A speckled, blue-grey overcast just happened. It was 57 millimeter fire all going off at once and exploding above us . . .

PAK SIX

G. I. BASEL,
Lt. Col., USAF (Ret.)

A STORY OF THE WAR IN THE
SKIES OF NORTH VIETNAM

JOVE BOOKS, NEW YORK

PAK SIX

A Jove Book / published by arrangement with
Associated Creative Writers

PRINTING HISTORY
Associated Creative Writers edition published 1982
Jove edition / June 1987

ISBN: 0-515-09005-0

Jove Books are published by The Berkley Publishing Group,
200 Madison Avenue, New York, NY 10016.
The name "JOVE" and the "J" logo
are trademarks belonging to Jove Publications, Inc.

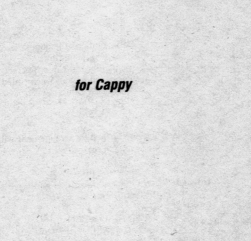

for Cappy

CONTENTS

FOREWORD

by Larry Pickett
Colonel, USAF (Ret.)

G.I. Basel tells it as it was. He gives specifics of experiences, both physical and emotional, so that a reader often feels that he is there (again), flying with him in the cockpit. To some, the stories in this book may be hard to believe, but those who were there will believe, because the experiences ring true. They are true. The skill with which the story is told quickens the pulse and gives an insight into the emotions felt by the courageous pilots who flew the missions in Pak Six, living with the fear and controlling it, and getting the job done. This is the true meaning of bravery. The pilots who were there were brave men.

It has been stated many times, and few disagree, that the defenses against air attack massed in North Vietnam during the war years, especially in Route Package Six (Pak Six), were the most awesome in the history of aerial warfare. The supplies needed to maintain this defense system were enormous and had to be shipped in—through rail yards, over roads, by air, on the water. Those shipping lanes were our targets.

In many instances, the North Vietnamese shipped their supplies into the area without opposition, for we were prohibited from bombing many critical and strategic targets. Probably the best example of this was the restriction against striking targets in the Haiphong area, where a large amount of supplies arrived and were unloaded.

For this reason, the North Vietnamese always seemed to have plenty of guns, shells, missiles, and MiG fighters to throw at the Strike Forces that were taking the war into their heartland.

But the book isn't about restrictions and defenses. It's about the strike missions a group of men had to fly, right into the teeth of the dragon. It's about flight plans and mission tactics and refueling in the air and diving through flak and outmaneuvering missiles and more.

This, then, was the arena in which this unique group of fighter-pilots operated.

In this book you will find humor and sadness. Humor in the funny things that always seem to happen when a bunch of fighter guys get together, sadness when a comrade is lost.

This book leaves a clear understanding of how it was in Pak Six and introduces some of the great people who were there.

PAK SIX

PAK SIX, A PREFACE

The war in Southeast Asia had been going along for several years while I watched my Air Force career being slowly eaten away to nothing. I knew there was no future for a professional military pilot without actual combat experience.

I was a soldier with wax bullets, a fraud in uniform, a warrior who had never met the enemy. I wrote letters and made phone calls, knowing all the while the war would finish before I could get there. Then, in the year 1967, I went to fight my war at last.

It was a ghastly, unredeemable horror with no glory, no sense, no worth to it. It just went on and on with nobody winning and nobody losing, except maybe all of us who were fighting; for we were dying.

After eight months of it, my plane was slammed from the sky, my bones broken, and my war was over. I was immensely grateful to be alive.

Since that time, I've been haunted by the friends

left behind in the steaming jungles of that place. There were many.

The contract is fulfilled. I've fired the gun in anger and the cordite is still bitter in my nostrils. Life is sweet, because it was so nearly taken, but I live in a shadowy world of familiar ghosts and grey, persistent loneliness.

The all-important career is over. It became unbearable, insignificant, petty.

Here's my story, here's my war.

THE WARRIORS

Sixteen of us came to Takhli Royal Thai Air Force Base to fight the war. Though we were experienced fighter pilots, we were fresh from special training at Nellis Air Force Base in Las Vegas, Nevada. At Nellis, we were checked out in the F-105 "Thunderchief" and given some practical training in how to use the plane in combat. The experience was an excellent preparation for us. The instructors were pilots just returned from the war, and the vast airspace over Nevada gave us a chance to really get to know this superior airplane.

Four of us were from the same former unit and were close friends. We volunteered together, trained together, and went to war together.

Tom Kirk was our leader. We called him "Superball" because he was always bouncing off the walls. It was easy to tell when Tom was in the Operations shack; you could hear him barking. He played saxophone like I've never heard before or since. Tom's lady, Yolanda, was from Italy and sang like an angel. They were a remarkable musical team. The two of them often treated us with some of their music after a few drinks at the club.

Tom insisted that we learn to eat rice (he hated the stuff); he badgered us about getting our teeth fixed; he insisted we make out a will. It was prophetic. Yolanda would have a long wait.

Gary Olin was the youngest of the four. He was a recent graduate of the Air Force Academy and had a truly beautiful wife he called "what's her name." Her name was Patty, and they were in love. Still are.

Tall and moustached, Gary was full of the spirit fighter pilots are sometimes rumored to possess. His energy level was nearly always critical. At a party, for instance, Gary could often be found on the roof.

Ed Cappelli had been my immediate boss; Gary's too. Ed had been commander of "A" Flight, one of the four units that make a full squadron. His career had been placid until he joined us. Though he had been flying fighters part time, his primary job was more cerebral and kept him on the ground most of the time. When we met and began to work together, it was immediately obvious that Ed's limited experience in fighter tactics was not a problem. He could make an airplane talk.

Cappy was a quiet and kind man. My children preferred to sit on his lap, rather than mine. We were very good friends, as were the two families. There were picnics and parties. We knew each other well enough to talk into the night about things such as the universe and what it all means.

He had a bad neck, went to civilian doctors on the sly. Exactly what was wrong, I don't know, but it gave him a lot of trouble. I wrapped it with stretch bandage more than once. He was always afraid someone would find out and ground him.

I worried about that neck—if he ever had to eject...

He seemed kind of frail to me. I guess B.J., his soft-spoken wife, knew more about Cappy's strength than I did. She has more than her allotted share, too.

As for me—I was the "wildcat" of the group; that is, up from the ranks and into Aviation Cadets to learn to fly and become an officer. I didn't care one way or the other about the officer bit, but I'd always wanted to fly. In the third grade, when the teacher had us stand up one at a time and tell what we wanted to be, I proudly announced I was going to be a pilot. It never changed. It's a trauma to reach...at age 19!...the only goal you've set for your life.

I had been flying fighters a long time, flying while the other guys were getting smart. I had a lot of experience and the others respected that, even though they had to teach me to write.

Being a terribly nervous type, I spent much of my time trying to find a calm niche from which to view the chaos around me. The nervousness had its good side; it made me very quick in those days. Probably saved my life.

My lovely wife waited in Italy, her native country, while I played at war. Tina and Yolanda saw each other frequently and comforted each other when Vietnam news frightened them.

A fifth member of this close-knit group, Gene Smith, was from another part of the military world, the Air Defense Command. He won our respect and admiration by quickly adapting to tactical fighters and giving us a run for our money. He was tall, blond, and crew-cut, and loved to play the guitar and sing folk songs. We spent hours of off-duty time trying to perfect our act (I play some guitar, too) as if we were about to be on the Grand Ole Opry.

It was a jovial and talented bunch of pilots, the five, and the sixteen. We worked and watched each other grow brown in the Thailand sun. Many sprouted gigantic moustaches. We began to appear tough, mean and dangerous.

We had it good at Takhli . . . that is, if you must fight a war, fighting a few hours a day and being safe the rest of the time is the way to go. We had good food and drink, and a bed. We were clean.

Our attitude about the rightness of the conflict was probably a good cross section of American opinion. We were not draftees, but not truly professional soldiers either. We trained and honed our skills, hoping never to use them.

War came and we put our lives on the line. It was part of the contract. There was more . . . a personal thing, a moral issue. I struggled with myself for a while and held counsel:

"I've flown these wonderful, expensive, agile airplanes for years. I've taught other men to fly them. Now, war is here, and war is what I've been trained for. I hoped it would never happen, but here it is. I must do this thing because any other action will be an admission of ongoing fraud. Only after it is done can I question it."

Many of the others had the same feelings.

The American people questioned. The reason for this war was not visible enough, and the method was no-win.

If the enemy had been coming over the back yard fence, raping our daughters and killing us, all Americans would have fought.

Now, all of Southeast Asia is held by those who vow to bury us. Millions have fled; many thousands have died fleeing rather than live under the conditions in the land now.

I can't help but be saddened by my own personal conviction that my grandson is going to have to fight and die to correct a wrong that I wasn't able to handle. I wasn't allowed to.

When the whole thing comes back to haunt us, I'll be the tiresome old man on the end of the bar with a glass of burgundy, who says, "I told you so."

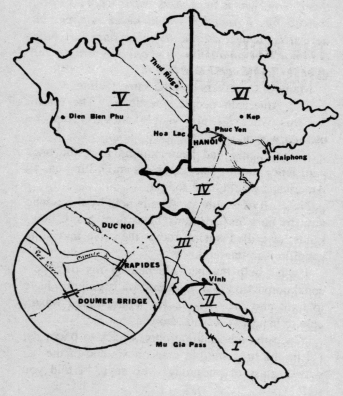

V

VI

● Dien Bien Phu

Thud Ridge

● Kep

Hoa Lac ● Phuc Yen

HANOI

● Haiphong

IV

DUC NOI

III

Red River

Canals R.

RAPIDES

● Vinh

DOUMER BRIDGE

II

Mu Gia Pass

I

North Vietnam

THE AIRPLANE
AND THE ARENA

Republic Aircraft Company built the airplane we flew and named it the "Thunderchief," but we called it a Thud, and so did everybody else. How the name got started is not clear. It just evolved. In the early days, the F-105 was plagued with a number of serious design problems. It crashed a lot. It didn't have a good reputation with fighter pilots . . . at first.

Some liked to call it the iron "Squat Bomber." To employ the Squat Bomber, one simply drives it along an enemy road until reaching a vital link, such as a bridge. On the bridge, you raise the landing gear and the Thud will squat there forever, gallantly blocking the way.

The enormous size and weight of the airplane provided the notion it had been built at the Republic "Foundry," rather than a proper aircraft factory. It was billed as the world's first flying locomotive.

The Thud had one engine and one seat and was the largest single-seated fighter ever built. The thing was built like a tank, but was deliciously graceful in flight. Sixty-four feet long, with a wingspan of thirty-five feet, it was an enormous dart with a needle nose and sharply swept back wings.

The Thud had speed. She could outrun any airplane in the world at that time, provided the race was run at medium or low altitude. I found I could urge even more speed from her when I was scared spitless.

It was this remarkable speed that earned the machine its mark on the history page. Speed was needed to get in and out of the arena. The Thud had it.

The arena, of course, was North Vietnam.

Looking at a map of the country, you see it resembles a Colonel Sanders' drumstick, original recipe. To simplify navigation and planning, we divided the drumstick into sections we called "Packages." Being Americans, we quickly reduced "Package" to "Pak."

From south to north, the country was sectioned into Pak One, Two, Three, and Four. The fat part, up north, was split in two—Pak Five in the west and Pak Six in the east. Pak Six contained all the good stuff—the airfields, the headquarters, the main industries, and the capital city, Hanoi.

Pak One was our training area. The new pilots flew missions there before graduating to Pak Six.

Ten missions was the standard criterion for qualification, the ticket to Hanoi.

This training area was a dangerous place, with plenty of determined enemies to deal with, but it seemed permissive in comparison to the chaos of the area around Hanoi. There was a tendency to be less watchful there.

The sky of Pak One was not always full of bursting flak, the dirty puffy explosions from anti-aircraft guns. The SAM was absent most of the time. SAM is our name for Surface to Air Missile —a frightening thing, guided by radar to self-destruct against my airplane. MiGs couldn't fly that far south. MiGs were the Russian-built fighters we had to tangle with in Pak Six.

None of this stuff was apparent in Pak One. The enemy was hidden, ready; waiting for one mistake, one slip. They were well disciplined and well trained. Led by men with 20 years of actual fighting experience, they were good at their work.

They were directed by bugle call. When a flight began to circle, began to get ready for an attack, a bugle sounded. The gunners for miles around manned their hidden guns, and waited. As the planes made their bombing runs, the gunners watched intently with expert eyes. Let one plane go too low, or too slow, or make a second pass, a bugle call set the guns to firing, and the sky filled instantly with explosions and tracers. They only fired when the chances were excellent for a kill. We lost many planes there.

• • •

I flew into Pak One for the first time in mid-August, 1967. It couldn't have been a more dramatic day to go to war: one of those dark, misty overcast days that never gets brighter than twilight.

Getting ready for that first mission was like walking in a surrealistic world. Zipping up the tight, anti-G suit with my wooden fingers, I could think only that I was about to do violence to another human being. This was not a cloth target to practice on; this was a tough, angry adversary. He was going to try to kill me, as I was determined to kill him. As I put on the net survival vest, all the items in the many pockets screamed, "You are going to need me!" This was ugly reality crashing into my storybook, TV, John Wayne world.

The reality was further emphasized when I came upon my flight leader, standing in the dark morning air, alone and silently smoking a last cigarette. I knew it was better not to speak to him.

At sunrise, we crossed the border into North Vietnam. I was all eyes and pumping heart as I peered at the landscape.

The face of the moon.

Raw earth, torn and scarred, with thousands of craters.

The war was over, the land was dead.

The terrain below me was devoid of roads, trucks, buildings, trees, or anything. There was no enemy. There couldn't be, not there on the face of the moon.

There were four of us, going like hell as we crashed across the border. I was flying woodenly, my natural skills reduced to automaton jerkiness. I missed the leader's call to switch radio channels. His voice showed a hint of irritation when he came back to my frequency, "Bear Four, go to strike freq . . . Now." I switched and checked in.

Then I began to learn about the enemy. From out of a crater on the moon came the stuttering yellow flashes of gunfire. There were people down there! Not only were they there, they were shooting . . . at me!

"Watch it, Bear. They're shooting." It was John Piowaty, Bear Three. The words filtered calmly through his huge, carefully folded moustache. He sounded bored. Just a little annoyance.

We went into a jinking, weaving pattern to complicate their aim. While we were in this aerial disco, I pondered the people whose bullets we were dodging, pondered them living there on the face of the moon.

We went in, piercing the mist, weaving and going fast. My headset crackled with the indolent tones of Bear Leader calling a Forward Air Controller (FAC). There was a lot of static on the air, as if we were being jammed. My ears felt swollen.

The white wing of the tiny FAC plane was stark against the dark landscape as he fired a smoke rocket to mark a suspected target. The rocket struck the earth and left a tiny white balloon of smoke.

We swung in a wide arc, all eyes on the smoke.

"Green up, Bear." I flipped two switches, and a light said a green READY on the armament panel. We climbed as one, banking left, angling toward the target.

"Lead's in."

I watched Bear Leader plummet toward the white smoke. Number Two followed, then Number Three. I took a deep breath and rolled inverted, hurling my plane at the ground. The leader's bombs were exploding, casting great chunks of dirt into the air, blowing the smoke away. "Aim south, Bear!" the FAC yelled. Which way is south? I thought as I pressed the bomb release button on the control stick. Six bombs rippled from the bomb rack.

I hauled the stick into my lap and the big Thud began to recover from the steep dive. Heavy G's tugged at my eyes, and I tried to raise my head to search for Bear Leader. The rush of increasing speed and the strange squeezing feel of the G's in my head gave me a dizzy drunken fix as I struggled to raise my 150 pound head and look around. Little fireflies flickered around the edges of my sight, and I squinted.

The worst thing a new pilot can do is lose his leader. It's a no-no. I began to panic as I searched the mist . . . my career was on the line, the enemy forgotten.

I came out of my dive level and the G-force eased off, restoring my ringing head to normal. The fuzzy fireflies went away. I saw him then, a tiny gnat on the horizon, a fly-speck on the canopy. My hand relaxed on the control stick. I thanked God for being spared the stigma of being a lost wingman.

I had already dicked-up this mission royally, missing the channel change, gawking at real estate, and probably missing the target. I was fervently thankful that I didn't have to call, "Lead, where are you?"

I slid into formation with professional silence. I was now a combat veteran, with one mission to mark on my hat. I had dignity.

Ninety-nine to go.

SNAKE SCHOOL

Before flying any missions at all, we had to go to Jungle Survival School. Normally, pilots arriving at Takhli were fresh from the school, a product of what was called "Pipeline" training. En route to your new assignment, you received the training required. It was written right in the orders.

I thought I had cleverly sidestepped this unpleasant task. Instead of joining the masses on the ocean crossing to Thailand, I had flown a Thud across, one of a flight of five replacement birds.

I was enjoying my one mission, getting ready for my second, when Jack Hart came to me and said, "You haven't been to Snake School . . . Go!" He was pissed. Jack didn't like cute little tricks performed by junior officers.

His steely blue eyes bored into mine and the toothy grin on his swarthy face suggested he would gladly do violence on me. The iron grip on my frail shoulder confirmed this.

I may have bypassed the assembly line in Cali-

fornia, but none could bypass the bear-trap mind of
my new boss. I went.

My trip to Snake School took me through Saigon on my way to Clark Air Base in the Philip-
pines. The terminal in Saigon was a total mess.

There were lines for tickets, lines for passports,
lines for shots. There were lines to get in line. The
terminal was teeming with people from all over the
world, going everywhere.

I was surprised when an official took my arm
and ushered me gently out of line and into a small
clearing room reserved for dignitaries.

He spoke no English, but answered my questioning gaze by pointing to the patch on my flight
suit. (We wore flight suits everywhere.) It was an
arrowhead patch that announced I was a Thud
pilot.

I was soon to learn; all of the Far East, native
and visitor alike, held the F-105 and its pilots in
the highest esteem. It was similar to the love affair
England still has for her fighter pilots since the
Nazi blitz.

There were no more lines, no hassle. I moved
through the big, crowded terminal without effort
and boarded my plane for Clark.

It was dark when the plane landed, and I was
thirsty and hungry. A taxi whisked me from the air
base to an inn just outside the main gate. There
was no room on the Air Base. It seemed everyone
in the world had decided to come to the Far East to
see the war.

The mirror behind the reception desk showed I hadn't changed since my one muddled trip into combat. The green eyes were semi-innocent, the glance level and mild. The five foot, nine inch frame and slightly greying hair suggested something less violent than my actual occupation.

"Where you go, Captain?" The young clerk smiled.

"Jungle school."

"Okay. Bus leave out front nine o'clock. No wait for stragglers."

"Thanks."

He handed over a key with a green plastic tag on it. "Room 27. Dining room close in 35 minutes. Better hurry."

I went straight into the dining room and ordered a martini to sip while I looked at the menu. I chose a big steak, rare. While I waited, the dining room turned into a party room. The waitress saw my shoulder patch. Another martini arrived quickly, only bigger and colder than the first.

Everyone was in a strange sort of euphoria, a kind of non-existence that people involved in war seem to have. The whole place was in that kind of mood. A couple of Special Forces troops sat down, just wandering through. The fact that I was a Thud driver, even with only one mission, was good for two more big martinis. Three more guys sat down. They were all from the same outfit.

The steak came, and I ate it . . . or part of it. I gave some away, I think.

I can remember sitting at the bar and not being

able to remember if I'd eaten or not. I was talking to this morose guy who was going to be killed and buying him a drink because of that. He flew some sort of secret missions, and I suppose he's dead now.

This good-looking blonde broke in between us and tried to get the bartender's attention. She had no trouble. I turned on the charm, and she showed some interest. She was a big girl, and nice . . . mountain climbing type. I included the guy in the conversation because he was going to be killed and all, but kept up a good steady patter with the blonde.

They left together, the blonde and the doomed guy. He sure looked happy.

Back at the table, the troops were getting on with it. I bought them all a round of drinks—and found that I had four more martinis lined up. The one I bought made five, not counting the two or three I'd drank . . . or was it four?

"Pick one!" The Sergeant was feeling no pain. His hand swept the room. I looked around. The place was full of very enticing young ladies. "Pick one, Captain."

"Where'd they all come from?" My eyes were drooping badly.

"Town's closing, but not this place."

"There! That one." I picked an especially exotic creature and chuckled evilly.

"Done!" he said.

I struggled to my feet, just about a minute from passing out. "Hah!" I said, slapping him on the back; "don't joke 'bout that to horny, drunk Captain." I managed to grip my bag without falling and somehow shuffled off to bed. I fell on the bed still in my flight suit and was instantly asleep.

Some time in the very early hours, the door burst open. "Captain?"

I opened one eye.

"Here she is."

"Juz put her over there . . ."

I looked out the smudged window of the battered Air Force bus that pulled out of the parking lot that morning. Many of the survival students were late, and some were barely surviving. I was one. It was a full three hours of a bouncing, jolting ride to the camp. I vowed abstinence a dozen times, but the pain continued on and on.

The camp was disheartening. I wanted to be air-conditioned and bathed. Not to be.

There was a wooden shack for lectures and a yard full of tropical animals (for lectures). That was it. We were given lunch, preserved in a box from World War II.

That afternoon, we sat in hot, grey metal chairs and dozed through lectures on snake bite, insect bite, animal bite, and jungle rot. Flies buzzed and the lectures went on.

We were issued only what we would have if we entered the jungle via parachute, fresh from a burning fighter. They put us in the jungle just as it was getting dark.

It rained all night. Even in the driving rain, big,

voracious mosquitos dined on our blood while we sweated in the soggy night. I strung my parachute between two trees and lay in the rain swatting at the giant, flying things. Once, I dozed for a few minutes and fell out of the chute into the spongy, gooey jungle floor. That was enough. I joined the growing crowd of miserable pilots under a giant tree. We had a small fire and brewed coffee through the night.

The next day, we stomped through the jungle, cutting likely vines and sipping the bitter water they produced. We became generally scratched up, tattered, and more or less hostile.

This went on for three days. It rained the entire time. We were finally pronounced miserable enough to graduate. I was given a ticket that said I could survive, and I left for Takhli to fight the rest of my war.

BAK GIANG

On easy missions (our term for anything other than Pak Six) the enemy fired at us enthusiastically, and some of us were shot down. The rest of us became pretty excited, our minds and hearts racing. Being shot at is stimulating. We became invigorated, but everything in the system remained under some semblance of control. Not so in Pak Six.

There, the pilot often reached another, higher level of stimulation, one just short of coma. It's called "Hydraulic Lock," a terrible state of the circulatory system in which the left and right ventricle pump together instead of alternating. Everything locks up. Heroes are made from this, flying through a hail of enemy fire with total disregard for personal safety. They don't care.

Some ex-Thud drivers carry the effects today.

The bridge at Bak Giang was in Pak Six. Since it was just a little bridge, it seemed kind of silly to send so many fierce airplanes to bomb it. But Bak Giang was important because it was on the main road from Hanoi to China, a link in the life-line. The North Vietnamese were "proud" of it. They ringed it with guns of all calibre, giving it a status few little bridges have.

One thing about the bridge at Bak Giang; it wasn't really a bridge. It was a road across the water with dirt under it instead of air. How do you knock down a bridge that isn't up?

My position in the big formation that went to Bak Giang was Tail-End Charlie, the last one in. Though our formation was designed so that, as nearly as possible, there was no last man, there is just so much space to put 16 to 20 airplanes into. We played One Pass-Haul Ass, but, no matter how hard you try, somebody's got to be last. I was the newest; I was it.

The way it usually worked . . . the leaders wake up the enemy gunners (if you've achieved surprise) and they are ready to shoot by the time Charlie flies by. Poor Charlie gets hammered.

I'd heard about all this, and it didn't help my state of mind as we nosed up to the tankers over the Gulf of Tonkin to take on a load of much-needed gas.

It was a sight to see. Five big KC-135 tankers (Boeing 707s) and 20 Thuds, four to a tanker. We all filled up, and it was Twelve O'clock High all over again when we joined together, heavy with fuel, and set out for the Bak Giang bridge. We dropped to a lower altitude to pick up speed, and the force commander sent the "Weasels" out ahead.

Wild Weasel is a term for a flight of two-seated Thuds with special equipment on board. They were able to "see" the enemy missile radar, and the gun radar, and were able to home on it and destroy it. Each strike force that went into Pak Six had a flight of Weasels to help protect it.

The Weasel missions were demanding. The pilots that flew them were specially trained, and the officers in the back seat were highly skilled in electronic warfare.

In a nutshell—the tactics were cat and mouse. A SAM (Surface to Air Missile) site takes a "look" at the Force. The Weasel sees the look and turns as if to fire a Shrike (a radar-homing missile). The SAM site shuts off (if he's smart). Another SAM site takes a look, and the Weasel responds. This goes on for a while until the Strike Force gets closer. Soon they are in range of many SAMs and the show is on. The SAM sites begin launching missiles in spite of the danger from the Weasels. It is, after all, their job. They attack in great numbers and hope not to be the one the Weasels will attack.

No SAM site ever looked like a SAM site. They were most often innocent villages, sometimes patches of woods, but never the classic Star of David pattern scraped on the ground. The easiest way to find a SAM site was to get him to fire. There was no mistaking that cloud of dust and smoke with a flaming missile rising from it.

The Weasels got good at faking a SAM into firing, so they could turn on the site and strafe or bomb it, saving the Shrike for later surprises in the heat of battle.

I felt a great deal of confidence, hearing the Weasels at their work. Their capabilities were quite awesome; the task for the Force would have been impossible without them.

The Weasels were already hard at work, well into Pak Six when Tail-End Charlie turned inbound at the Isle of Madelene, just north of Haiphong Harbor.

I could see a group of islands, jutting black rock out of green water. They had a crazy look about them, fake. Ebony rock with sparse, blue-green vegetation, cracked and splintered rock sitting at crazy angles. A Walt Disney fantasy, peaceful and lovely and fake. I would like to see the Isle of Madelene someday . . . up close.

Passing over this place of dreams meant we had entered North Vietnam. We increased our speed and spread out to a more defensive formation.

"Bandits, Bandits . . . Bullseye!" There was a big voice in the sky announcing enemy fighters taking off from Hanoi. The voice sounded like God talking.

The Welcome Wagon was on the way.

Forty miles to go, less than five minutes to target.

"SAM, ten o'clock, sweeping guns out of Kep . . . No threat to the Force." The calm voice of the Weasel was a comfort to me on that first one.

"Bandits, Bandits, Bullseye! 270 for 15." The MiGs were coming out to meet us.

We were hastening along at 520 knots. I was slewing the tail of my plane out of the way so I could look back every few seconds. I looked back and saw four silver delta-winged airplanes high and to my rear, MiGs sliding smoothly into the sun, getting in position to dive down and ventilate my flawless body.

Hydraulic Lock.

I looked again . . . they were white, not silver, and I saw the drooping tails of the F-4 Phantoms, our MiG cover. Funny, ugly, drooping tails! Beautiful! Breath returned to Tail-End Charlie.

"Bandits, Bandits, Bullseye! 090 for 30." There were MIGs out, alright, and much closer.

"Disregard the launch light, not a valid launch, no threat to the Force." The Weasels were getting more business. The SAMs were sending false signals to spice the stew.

"One minute, Bear Force. Green 'em up." The Force Commander's voice was crisp and tight. Each of us glanced inside the cockpit, making sure the six bombs we had were armed and ready to go. I saw a small green sign . . . READY.

Suddenly, we rolled in. I was caught by surprise; it was too soon for me; I wanted to stay where I was, safe for now. But I didn't want to be alone, so I went with them. All sixteen Thuds were in a steep dive at once. From my position, I could see the whole Force as a unit, 16 big fighters plummeting earthward and the Bak Giang bridge below.

I hurtled toward the earth, speed winding up fast; 600 . . . 640 . . . 700. I saw the leader pulling off, and my element leader just ahead (below) and to my right. The bridge grew bigger in the bomb sight. The sky was dirty . . . full of fleeting shapes, debris, trash. As I allowed my sight to settle on the thin bridge, I sensed the guns around it ringing off. Big, ugly cat-eyes flashed fitfully all around the bridge, guns hurling lead up at me.

I smashed the button and felt the bombs ripple off. The bridge was forgotten instantly; now it was my time, time to get out of there. We came off the target about the speed of heat, tailpipes spouting fire as we kicked in the afterburners and shot eastward. I brought the big nose up to level flight and jinked hard left. The sky was dirtier now, full of smoke and flying junk.

Out ahead of me, the force was a weaving, dipping, high-mach calypso, all afterburners blazing, and vapor trails streaming from the fleeing, maneuvering planes. We plunged into a big cloud bank together.

The guns had unnerved me, but this was terrifying! There were 16 airplanes in this cloud, all blind, all going like hell and all jinking madly. I grimly pulled hard on the stick, climbing sharply to get above them all. I tensed for the impact with a friendly fuselage, one that I probably wouldn't feel. We popped into the clear together. They were all above me!

We joined up in a ragged weaving formation and blistered out to the coast and safety. Over the Gulf and safe, we slowed to a mad gallop, but I couldn't stop breathing hard. I wanted a cigarette bad. I ate one and felt better.

It seemed to me, as we languidly cruised toward home, that this sort of thing could replace jogging, but could be hazardous.

Two hours later and back at Takhli, I reported the ground fire I'd seen. I was explicit about the number of guns firing, how many sites I had seen, and what it had looked like to me. I was receiving some polite but doubtful looks from the other members of the flight. They hadn't seen much ground fire. Did I have the New Guy Deliriums?

We moved to the big auditorium where we always hashed over the mission with the whole Force and the Weasels.

Again the ground fire was reported as light by the members of the force. I was doubting my sanity until it came time for the leader of the Weasels to speak. He was tall, and sandy-haired with a well trimmed moustache.

"There wasn't much fire at all . . . we must have caught them napping for once . . . but they woke up just as the last Thud rolled in. I thought they'd got him! They really hammered him."

The Force commander looked around the big room. "Who was Tail-End Charlie today?"

I raised my hand.

"Oh! Basel. First Pak Six, eh? How did you like it?" There was some laughter.

"How do you get out of this chicken outfit, Sir?"

More laughter.

I was exonerated. For a few minutes, my comrades had thought I was one of those squirrelly new guys that see things that aren't there. A burden, a problem. Their smiles showed their relief.

I marked the eighth mission on my Sierra Hotel Hat, my first red mark. Only 92 to go.

Jack Hart handed me a black and red patch.

"What's this?" I said.

"You're a Rat. You've crossed the Red River in anger."

"Just like that?"

"Yeah, just like that."

SIERRA HOTEL

This story can't be told properly without introducing a new term. It became part of the language in the early years of the war. Pilots used it to express a particular state of excellence. No other term could handle the concept. Even though I've coined some pretty bad phrases in moments of weakness, this expression was offensive to me at first. It sounded meaningless and was overused disgracefully. Now it is an indispensable part of my vocabulary.

Everybody was calling everything "Shit Hot" in those days. There were shit hot people, shit hot airplanes (and the Thud was the shit hottest), shit hot drinks, shit hot missions, etc., etc., etc.

Some small sensitivity in us caused an alternate term to evolve. This was for use when the situation seemed to warrant discretion. "Sierra Hotel" was born, the military phonetic expression of S, H, which stands for Shit Hot.

In 1967, our squadrons were all Shit Hot. Each

pilot in each squadron was Shit Hot, for the whole is equal to the sum of the parts, and each part is as good or better than that which it is a part of . . . Hmmm. No pilot was any less than Shit Hot.

Our hats were Australian Bush Hats, wide brimmed with one side tacked up, revealing a crescent patch that said "TAKHLI RTAFB," (Royal Thai Air Force Base). The hats were all Shit Hot, for they rested on Shit Hot heads, but we called them Sierra Hotel.

The Thud pilots at Korat, our sister unit, had Sierra Hotel hats, too. They had a distinct advantage in the Shit Hot word game. It didn't rhyme when someone shouted, "I'm Shit Hot from Takhli!"

We marked our accumulated missions on the front of our hats with a stroke of a ballpoint pen. This caused each hat to be a personal and valuable thing. The marks told each man's story.

We used a red pen to specify missions in Pak Six. We put a dot over the marks that were especially hairy and heavily spiced with enemy fire. (Oh yes, there were missions that were wonderfully void of that kind of excitement.) We took to drawing small symbols instead of marks for significant missions. A mission that had caused the demise of a SAM site might be represented by a tiny, carefully-drawn missile.

The hats that displayed numerous red marks drew more respect than either rank or age. I remember my first day at Takhli, staring at a hat with 72 marks on it, and I whispered "Jesus" to myself. Oh, I wanted those marks! My hat held none then, and I couldn't buy marks, steal them, or even get extra ones for good work. I had to go get them, one at a time.

Somewhere, my hat decorates someone's wall. It has 78 marks on it that came very dearly indeed. If you have it (it can be positively identified by the symbol of one MiG, three SAMs, and 78 marks, 34 of them red), you can keep it, and good luck to you. Do me one favor . . . add another ½ mark — and a Thud — to make it complete.

PHUC YEN

Alonzo Ferguson is a name that suggests an Associate Professor of Chemistry at a small university. In truth, the man is a soft-spoken philosopher and an utterly Shit Hot fighter pilot. I'll not embarrass Fergy with any other heavy words, I'll just tell about the day he led us on a raid of the Phuc Yen rail yard.

We wanted to go to Phuc Yen, but not the rail yard. We wanted the Phuc Yen airfield in the worst way, but some unexplained high level restraint kept us from hitting the airfield. This caused a lot of pilot anger, because MiGs were taking off from there and giving us fits. It was the primary fighter base in the north and was operating with immunity. It made sense to us—bomb Phuc Yen, the air base, not the rail yard.

Our target was the rail yard, and we were about as happy as mashed hornets about that. Fergy's plan of attack had a nice twist to it that tickled me and improved my attitude.

We were going in just like a normal force, but the last eight planes carried no bombs. They were clean as a whistle, aside from the nasty little Sidewinder heat-seeking missiles nestled on each wing tip. MiG-killer missiles. The Phuc Yen MiGs would get a surprise if they jumped this formation!

There was a lot of bargaining going on, pilots trying to get into the last eight planes of the Force, hoping to bag a MiG and experience the thrill of a victory in the air.

Fergy didn't let it go at that. He had another little trick he wanted to try. This one involved just him and me. The plan was to come down from the north, along a landmark called Thud Ridge. The rail yard would be on our right, and the Force would roll right to bomb it. Just at the roll-in point, and to the left of our course was a newly active SAM site. Intelligence had uncovered its presence just that morning. Fergy was not going to let that site go unmolested.

We came down Thud Ridge as planned, the Weasels working west of us. "Lead 14," the code word for our SAM site, didn't come on the air. He was waiting, sitting safely to the east, hidden and watching for his chance to lash out at us. We were at the roll-in point when the Weasel called, "Fourteen's up!"

"Rodge," said Fergy. Ho-hum.

The Force rolled right, but Fergy and I, the first two planes, continued to roll over on our backs and around until we were headed the other way, noses down, pointed right at Lead 14.

I had a life-sized picture of the SAM crew happily sighting on us, calling range and azimuth to each other cheerfully as we rolled away from them. An easy kill, this. Then the change of heart as two of the planes somehow flipped around and came at them. Lead 14 became a very bad place to be!

Finding the site in the few seconds we had was not easy, but we'd done our homework. One small dirt road intersected another, and to the left of that was a green field with a dark green spot in it. That was our target.

The site launched a missile in a cloud of white smoke and dust. The missile didn't guide, just lofted by us ballistically. I think they (the SAM crew) were all running about that time. We let our bombs go, and 12,000 pounds of TNT turned Lead 14 into a hole in the ground. We pulled up hard, the lightened planes accelerating, heading back to Thud Ridge.

The Big Voice in the sky droned, "BANDITS, BANDITS, BULLSEYE." MiGs were on the way.

Fergy and I streaked north, eager for the safety of the ridge and hoping to join again with the force. I hung with Fergy, weaving and jinking and looking over my shoulder for MiGs. I reached over and armed my Sidewinder missile. No green light. I looked out at my left wing and discovered why no green light. My wing tip was missing, and so was the missile. I never felt a thing.

I kept an eye out for MiGs. The Big Voice kept saying they were coming, and Fergy and I were still alone.

A bunch of small missiles zipped past us from the rear. Maybe twenty of them. They weren't even close, and it surprised me too late to get tensed up. They had to have come from some sort of ground launcher. I could see no MiGs.

The MiGs never found us that day. Our would-be MiG-killers had been cheated, or perhaps they had been lucky. We'll never know for sure, but I think they were lucky. Thuds shouldn't play with MiGs.

Back at Takhli, I taxied in, wearing my "Red Badge of Courage," a mangled wing tip. Crew Chiefs stopped to look and held their heads. Pilots shook their heads in mock rebuke. One must not allow bullets to strike the aircraft.

In truth, with this little charade, we were all celebrating my return. It was a stronger, and more meaningful way of saying, "I'm glad you're back, glad you made it."

WILD WEASEL

September flew by in a flurry of missions of little note. Each mission was a geography lesson, places I'd never heard of and probably never would again. Enough of the enemy took angry potshots at me to keep my attention. A routine developed, and I counted missions with detached confidence, not to say cockiness. A Superman complex was growing. I was exempt, they just couldn't hurt me. I was too good.

My past experience drew respect from the others, especially the older leaders. I was happy. Respect from your peers is a heady thing, especially when they are the best in the world.

I became an element leader (two airplanes), then flight leader. No more Tail-End Charlie.

I was beginning to realize I was a member of a well organized team, much larger and more complicated than I'd imagined. The strike force was part of an intricate and invincible machine that was capable of settling this thing quickly, once and for all.

On October the 13th, Friday, I sat at the Squadron Duty Desk answering the phone, making coffee, and feeling good. It was a great day not to be flying. None of us were superstitious, you understand; it just does not make sense to tempt fate.

We wore Buddha pins, a curious Thai butterfly pin, a rabbit's foot, shark's teeth, and any other thing that might help. I had a gold coin that helped me get through some bad times.

I was thinking about how horny I was getting and wondering how to make it through the months ahead without doing some disgusting thing like getting laid in town. The signs were beginning to alarm me . . . the cover of Redbook had sexual connotations . . .

Bob Huntley, our senior Wild Weasel, came up to the desk. "Ever fire a Shrike, G.I.?"

"Of course not. I'm a strike pilot, a breaker of bridges, a hero; not a Weasel Puke like you."

"Well, that doesn't matter."

"What are you trying to get at? What's a Shrike?"

"Quit clowning, I'm serious." Bob was grinning.

"I'm serious too, serious as a heart attack!" I stared at him, my pleasant little Friday the 13th world crumbling around me.

He leaned both elbows on the desk. "A Shrike is a missile designed to seek and destroy Surface to

Air Missile sites. It homes in on the enemy radar..."

"Yeah, okay..." I held up a hand.

"...has a range of..."

"Hey! You might as well come to the point. What's this all about?"

He straightened. "We can't get four Weasel birds together for this afternoon's strike. The Boss has agreed to let a single-seater go with us. He chose you. It's an honor." He grinned evilly.

"Shit," I murmured, seeing Jack Hart appear behind Bob, grinning like a wolf and nodding.

"Briefing in twenty minutes, get suited up."

Heading for the Personal Equipment shop in the back, I saw a headline on the second page of the Seattle Times:

LAKE CITY AIRMAN LOSES ASS
ON FRIDAY THE 13TH

I talked to myself as I zipped up the G-suit and checked the emergency radio. *It's a counter, a step toward home.* I stuffed the extra rabbit foot in a leg pocket and zipped it up. *It's Bak Giang...I don't like Bak Giang.* A memory appeared; dozens of guns hurling lead into the sky while I dove through the dirty air on my first Pak Six mission. *This would be number 23...lucky? Do 23 and 13 go together? Mmmmm...36. Doesn't bring any vibes. Single-seat Weasel? Shit.*

Back in the small briefing room for my per-

sonal, quicky Weasel school, Bob briefed me:
"Just stay about 45 degrees back, cover my six,
keep nose-tail clearance so we don't run together."
He was all business now, no funny grin. "When we
get ready to shoot, I'll tell you. Be on the right,
stay on the right side of me. I always break left
after firing. Got that?"

"Right."

"Right?"

"Right, right."

"Right."

He laid out a map that showed the SAM sites we
were likely to have dealings with. He pointed his
pencil at names and positions, hundreds of them it
seemed. I began to panic; there was no way I could
remember all I had to. The map was obviously
used daily, for it was earmarked and had many
erasures and scribbles. Intelligence kept the Weasels informed about the positions of each and every
site.

So, there I was. It was Friday the *&%! 13th,
and I was rocketing along at low altitude, under an
overcast, out in front of the Force, and wondering
why I'd let them do this to me.

The Isle of Madelene was far behind. I was seeing North Vietnam from lower than ever before,
and I didn't like it. Without a heavy bomb load,
carrying just Shrikes, we were able to get a lot
more speed from the airplanes. The green country-
side whipped by at dizzying speed.

High above us and far to the rear, the Force was

turning inbound to Bak Giang. They were above the clouds and unable to see the ground.

"Otter, this is Bear. How does it look?" We were Otter.

"Not good, Bear. Don't see any openings yet." Bob's voice was muffled as if the heavy clouds were deadening the sound.

"SAMs at twelve; sweeping. No threat to the Force." Bob's back-seater, reading his scope, was keeping us informed.

"Think we'll have to abort, Otter." Dale Leatham, leading the Force, sounded disappointed. "We'll press in one more minute."

"Roger, Bear Lead. Otter's got you covered."

On the instrument panel in front of me, a large red warning light suddenly flashed. At the same instant, a loud squeal filled my headset. I flinched. The word LAUNCH screamed in the middle of the light. A SAM was up!

"Valid Launch! Valid Launch, Bear! Take it down!"

Bob had already turned toward the missile site. We started down to build more speed while Bob sent the second element up to fire. "Otter Three, get him!"

"Rodge, three's up to fire."

Down we went, turning left. I could hear Dale, "Bear! Hard left turn, take it down!"

The big armada of airplanes maneuvered in controlled alarm, diving toward the overcast and turning hard left, knowing a blazing missile would soon burst from the clouds below and seek one of the struggling airplanes. It was escape time.

Bob and I swung left and down to the deck, then back hard right to head toward the SAM site. I was all hands and elbows trying to stay in close formation. Vapor streamers poured from the wing tips of Otter Lead as we pulled around to the right. No sooner had we lined up on the telltale strobe of hostile radar, than we began a hard pull straight up. Streamers again.

"Ready Otter Two?"

"Ready." My Shrike had been ready for many minutes, gibbering and squeaking in my headset at random signals in the air. It now began to squawl and squeal at me as it sensed the radar energy from the enemy site. "Set me free! Let me go! Want eat!"

I was pulling hard on the stick, following Bob upward in a steep climb. We punched through the layer of clouds together. The sense of speed was startling as we shot skyward in the clear air.

"Otter Two . . . fire now!" My thumb punched the button. The missile left the wing with a swoosh, freed at last to seek and gobble radar food. Predatory!

"Breaking left!" Bob yelled.

The trouble with that . . . that's where I was—on the left. I was supposed to be on the right, but I wasn't. Nobody's perfect. I had no place to go but up. I pulled hard and missed a collision by a few feet, but now I was going nearly straight up and a SAM missile, another one, was on the way.

No airplane, especially a Thud, would go

straight up without losing speed very quickly. When you are flying an anvil, the loss of speed is a disaster.

The Thud wouldn't turn; the controls were loose and ineffective. I pushed hard rudder, trying to roll left. The nose slowly came around. The big plane shuddered, near a stall. "Come on, come on!" I urged. And the Thud and I turned a nice cartwheel in the sky.

Bob's next radio transmission was like a bad dream.

"G.I., it's after you! Take it down, fast!" The second and third missiles had been launched on us . . . me.

Bob's use of my name instead of the call-sign was really unnerving, implying total disaster.

I was still hanging there, rotating in slow-motion stop-action, when the missile exploded. It was an instant ugly orange spider in the sky, one thousand feet behind me. Further away, another spider grew. Our Shrikes had found the mark, knocked out the site, detonating the missiles in flight, and saving my dumb ass.

I recovered control of my airplane. With nose down and afterburner blazing, I gained speed fast, and we were quickly back in our element. "Not your fault, old girl; mine, all mine." I dove through the overcast, muttering thanks to some-one, hearing lots of yelling on the radio from Bear force about something, and looking very hard for Otter Lead. I popped out below the clouds and spied Bob making streamers as he pulled out, turning back for another attack on another site.

"Do we really have to go back, Bob?" I whispered. No one answered, because my thumb had refused to push the mike button.

"Three's up!" Our second element was taking his turn in this strange eggbeater pattern we were making.

Back at the Force, Dale had his hands full. His wingman was losing power. The two of them were gently sinking into the overcast while the rest of the Force was retreating (under Dale's orders). It was an impossible situation. They were too far north to hope for any rescue, but were calling for help just in case. We all knew one simple fact of life about Pak Six. Rescue is not possible. Just jump out and be captured, and don't whimper about it.

We were still doing our nip-ups, harassing the SAMs, covering the Force as they retreated, and I was really getting tired from all the G forces and all. We had lost sight of the other element, Otter 3 and 4, while zipping in and out of the clouds. I was just thankful I still had sight of my leader.

The situation above the clouds took a turn for the better. The sick Thud suddenly began to run normally again. Perhaps it had been having its own version of Pak Six lock or something. You could hear the relief in Dale's voice. "Let's get the hell out of here!"

I was very happy when Bob finally called it off, and we too began our getaway. We had come in fast, but we went out a full-fast-reheat plus adrenaline boost. I had my foot in the carburetor and couldn't keep up with Bob.

"Otter Lead, I can't catch you. What's your speed?"

"A thousand miles an hour."

"Oh."

We didn't get the bridge that day, but we think we knocked out two SAM sites. Bob thought it was a good mission. I thought it was time for a vacation. Flying with the Weasels had been an education—hairy, exciting, and demanding. Everything I'd ever wanted. It was definitely a strong boost for my budding Superman complex!

I marked my hat with the 23rd mark. It was in red, with a big dot over it. When I got home that night, there was a SAM SLAYER patch on my pillow, something to sew onto my blue party suit. I was proud to wear it.

THE CLUB

Between missions, there was always a lot to do. A squadron doesn't run itself, and though there were various clerks and the First Sergeant handling much of the reams of paperwork required to keep everything going and recorded and legal, there were dozens of essential tasks that only the officers could handle. These were things that dealt with the very essence of the business—tactics, techniques, codes, flight discipline, search and rescue, escape and evasion, enemy aircraft capabilities, recognition of enemy tanks, boats, planes and men . . . and more. All these things were the necessities required to keep a pilot certified "Combat ready."

The ironclad requirement for weekly ground training was never neglected, and it had to be conducted by us. No one else knew anything about that kind of stuff. Each pilot was given one or more "Additional Duties" when he entered the squadron. From then on, he was the expert on that particular subject. He was responsible for keeping the rest of us informed on everything pertinent that came along in his particular specialty. I was lucky enough to get the job of weapons officer, something really close to the real job of flying and blowing up bridges.

It was nothing new to us, for the peacetime Air Force had been the same. We were often astounded at the tremendous faith headquarters had in our abilities. Somehow the Generals knew we were so smart and tough, that we were perfectly capable of logging 40 hours of ground training in one day, and still fly a combat mission!

I remember Ed Cappelli saying, and I quote, "It seems to me, if we must log 40 hours of training today, they ought to cancel the mission, give us the day off. Doesn't that sound only reasonable?"

We were continually updated by wing Intelligence on any new development in the enemy war capability. We had to know what They were doing, and we had to know before we met The Thing head-on in the air. Being surprised and baffled in the air was a good way to get hurt.

The rules and restrictions imposed on us were both complicated and extensive. Before anyone flew at all, he was given hours of instruction and a comprehensive test on the ROE, the Rules of Engagement. No errors were allowed . . . 100% was the only passing score. Anyone not completing this test once a week with a 100% score, was decertified and not allowed to fly until the training was accomplished. The bosses were paranoid about the Rules of Engagement!

This was time-consuming and a headache to the scheduling people, for the hours were long, the tasks complicated, and there was never more than half the squadron available for training at any one time. Everything had to be done at least twice.

A great deal of our time was spent trying to comply with some of the impossible red tape imposed on the squadron by the support element of the Air Base. Pay checks didn't arrive, or were sent to Bangkok or Tokyo; baggage went to the wrong base and new pilots had to live with one flight suit and a change of underwear; mail didn't come, or was sent to another mail room on the base, and pilots were ordered to retrieve it no later than . . . now.

I was trying to get plywood and boards to make briefing consoles to put in the bare briefing rooms. The material was there in the supply section, but there was no way to get it. We did finally get it, but it practically took blackmail and larceny.

Even though there were plenty of things like this to keep up the morale and keep us busy, we had time off. Most of this time was spent in three places. The hootch where we lived had a radio and magazines, and a bed for each of us. Some just sacked out the entire time.

Another attraction was the Base Exchange, where cigarettes, cameras, film, magazines, and shoe polish were for sale. There was a theater near the Exchange, but we seldom went there. It wasn't air-conditioned, and the large crowd in the building made it unbearably hot and aromatic.

The only place to spend time on purpose was the Club. That was where we ate, where we partied and sometimes slept, but mostly we ate there. Breakfast, lunch and dinner.

The food was ordered by number. D-6 was hamburger steak, J-9 was chili with weenies. K-4 was a thing called "Cow Pot" and it looked like it. Cow Pot could be ordered by name because it was a Thai dish, the only one offered. It was a mushy plate of rice with hot sauce on top. D-4 was my favorite, a small steak that was kind of oily, but tender and tasty.

If you ordered weenies by name, you were likely to get anything from a pack of Winstons to a bowl of Wheaties.

The waitresses, lovely little dolls, were the daughters of the Thai officers on the base. They spoke little or no English. Because of this, we ordered food by number.

The system worked well, but there were times we had difficulties.

You order D-6 and you get D-4, so you say, "I no want D-4. Want D-6." We talked like that after a few weeks in the country.

"No hab D-6, I bring D-4."

"No hab?"

"No hab."

And you eat D-4, or you don't get lunch and the waitress will cry.

• • •

Thai people, among all the Eastern people, are unique. There is a certain strength and respect for tradition that baffles the average Westerner.

Some of the tradition is expressed in taboos. One taboo is never, but never, say anything even slightly bad about the King and Queen. Don't even joke about them. There are pictures of them in just about any building in the country—bars, cafes, everywhere.

Thai legend has it that a Queen of Thailand drowned centuries ago when her Royal Barge capsized during a parade on the Grand Canal. None of the attending boatmen were able to save her. They treaded water and watched in agony as she drowned. They were not allowed to touch her.

Whether connected or not, the no-touch taboo was in full effect in the Club at Takhli. The little waitresses were a breath of spring in an ugly, tiresome world. Many Americans are touching people, the expression of greeting or agreement or friendship being by hand or arm or shoulder.

A new arrival had misinterpreted the friendly smile of one of the girls and was about to make a wrong, if innocent move. I risked death to prove a point to him. As the girl placed a napkin at the table, I touched the back of her hand with one finger.

She exploded with such fury that tables all around looked to see what had happened. She harangued in Thai for a while, off in the corner where the girls gathered to gossip. It took a personal and sincere apology from me for her to go back to serving. I drew long frowning looks from her for a week after that.

The Club was open 24 hours a day, and it had to be.

Three in the morning might find four tables of silent pilots eating breakfast before going out into the dark sky to wage destruction, and another table or two of long-gone, bleary-eyed whiffenpoof singers on their way to three days of rest somewhere. The first would be diving through ground fire at bloody-fingered dawn's first light, while the last would be on a train to Bangkok. It was an unreal life and an unreal place to be.

We spent evenings in the Club, for there was no other place to go. The people who ran the place were marvelous. We could do no wrong. Some of us developed habits that were to get us in trouble in more dignified and controlled Officer's Clubs. The night I drove my Honda 90 through the dining room and into the bar, nobody even looked!

Lunch at the Club was a circus, especially for those that sat at the big round table on the raised portion of the dining room. It became the place where the combat pilots ate. The noise was near the threshold of pain. Jokes flew back and forth in Thai and pidgin English. Pilots yelling for food and greeting each other. Some back from a bad mission, glad to be alive, or trying to cover the sorrow of a lost friend. Others going on the next mission, burning up nervous energy in the ritual of eating noisily.

I finally started eating in the hootch—beans and bologna sandwiches. The noise in the Club at lunch drove me bug-nuts.

It was especially difficult to stand the confusion when feeling the need for some quiet contemplation. I always felt that need before going on a rough mission.

Ed, Gene Smith, and I were trying to take some nourishment in the midst of this noisy lunch scene. The food wasn't going down.

Somehow, learning I was about to pay my first visit to Hanoi took the edge from my hunger.

Gene, too, pushed his plate away and lit a cigarette. To this day, I think he knew what was coming.

HANOI

There were no cheers in the big briefing room when it was announced the target was Hanoi. Hollywood would have had us on our feet, clapping each other on the back, glad and eager for a shot at the capital at last. Not so; the room was coldly silent. There was a tangible determination and resignation in the air.

The area around Hanoi had been restricted until just before we, the sixteen, arrived. Our pilots couldn't even fly through there. Now, we were ordered to bomb it. It's almost as if the White House was waiting for them to get enough guns and SAMs in place to warrant our attention.

Among all the places to bomb in the country, Hanoi had become the worst. Some experts argue it was the worst in the world, and in history. We all knew this. It had been common knowledge to pilots everywhere... legendary. Some of us weren't coming back. The question was: how many?

• • •

Today, the town's not what it was . . . oh, the city itself was never bombed; but the Paul Doumer Bridge, the rail yards at Duc Noi, the underground Military Headquarters, the Canale di Rapides bridge and the Northeast Railroad were rearranged.

Years ago, the place was the world leader in fireworks and aerial displays. Almost daily, one could witness high altitude explosions of crimson and black, the sky laced with the squiggly trails of soaring SAMs, blazing aircraft tearing across rooftops, dog fights on a grand scale—MiGs and Thuds and Phantoms, locked in a dazzling death struggle.

Being a North Vietnamese pilot then must have been interesting. Hunting every day for the human game bird known as Thud, the one with iron wings and guns that shoot back, must have been a thrill. I'd call it a quantum jump from shooting birds in upstate New York. The hunting in the skies of Hanoi was serious.

Our target was the Paul Doumer Bridge, the big bridge next to the city. It had several lanes of vehicle traffic and a rail line crossing it, Hanoi's main link to the supply line out of China.

Intelligence held big charts before our eyes, charts that had the positions of gun and missile sites marked carefully in red. The number was mind-boggling. The city and surroundings were wall-to-wall guns. The railroad out of the town had a picket fence of guns on either side . . . all the way to China. SAM sites were overlapped, looking like a thick ring of red bubbles, with a thick splattering of single bubbles out to 75 miles from the capital.

The tense Captain briefing us took a deep breath and began to point out locations and numbers of MiG fighters we were likely to encounter.

I wrote, "Ain't no way," on my knee pad. Cappy nodded. Our eyes met. He was not afraid. I envied him.

Cappy faced it head-on. I still don't know how he did it. I played a game in my mind and was able to hedge reality and get the job done.

The weather is bad in Hanoi. Too bad for airplanes to fly, too bad to see the bridge. We'll have to go home, retreat to friendly skies, return safe to fight another day. Any number of other things could cause me not to fly over Hanoi; mechanical problems crop up all the time, fuel transfer, engine vibrations . . . anything. Chances are good, I won't be going to Hanoi today.

I'm convinced the pretence (different versions) was going on in many a head as we readied for Hanoi. At least, I found it an effective way to prod my body into the breech.

We took off in the afternoon heat, our planes struggling to get airborne in the wet and heavy air. We carried two big 3000 pound bombs each. Ed Cappelli was leading Bear flight, the second flight in the Force. I was on Ed's wing.

Behind us, Gene Smith was leading Wildcat flight.

Minutes from the target, Bear three got into trouble. Jerry Evert was flying an already notorious airplane, number 385. That Thud had gremlins, bad ones. The mechanics had torn that airplane apart over and over, had all but replaced every component of the flight control system, and still it went crazy on nearly every mission— usually at a critical point.

We were approaching Hanoi from the west at about 500 knots. Jerry began struggling with his cursed airplane as it rolled and pitched violently. He just about took me with him when he shot out of the formation, out of control. His speed brakes opened and the plane slowed enough to regain some control. Jerry turned back and number four followed him for protection.

That left Cappy and me exposed on our right. We squeezed in close to the lead flight, hoping for some protection. Then the SAMs came up.

The Weasels had been crooning, "No threat to the force, no threat to the force." Then they changed their tune.

"Valid Launch! Valid launch! Heads up in the force! One's on the way; twelve o'clock!" I was looking till my eyes stung, but I wouldn't see anything. It's the one you don't see that will get you. Twenty-eight eyes peered ahead anxiously.

Two lazy flaming missiles rose high in the blue sky several miles ahead. I was awestruck. Here was the dreaded SAM in person. They flew together at incredible speed, impersonal and magnificent, arching over above us. Then they exploded together; two big yellow splashes rained down on us.

Fireworks.

We flew through the smoke they'd made. It was spent and harmless. Why they exploded so early, we could only guess. The operator probably had to try and guess when to detonate them; his judgement was wrong, thank God.

The gunners around the city went to work. Flak began to blossom here and there in groups of six. Big red flashes grew in an instant to thick black puffs that lingered as if marking the spot.

The air became filled with sound. The big voice yelled about MiGs, and the Weasels had gone to work.

"Bring it around, Barracuda, let's fire now!"

"Take it down, Two—SAMs on you!" I sympathized.

"Shark, burner now, climbing . . . target 11 o'clock, rolling left in thirty seconds." Our leader was hardly visible through the heavy black clouds that splattered the sky around us. Fourteen Thuds belched fire and leaped ahead, angling toward Hanoi. I could sense our speed as we whipped past the ugly black puffs dying and reappearing instantly.

Everyone was weaving. It's an automatic thing, you don't learn it. I was good at it when I was born. You can't help doing it when they are shooting. My gloved hand was trying to squeeze the control stick to pulp. I waited for the shattering explosion that would come any moment.

The Force rolled in. I looked at the bottom of Cappy's Thud for a split instant, then planted the stick hard against my left knee.

The world, flak and all, spun right and tilted up as my nose swung downward. There it was: the Doumer Bridge . . . Jesus!

I yanked the wings level in the dive, the nose pointed steeply down, the afterburner spouting flame and rocketing me toward the earth. The ground was alive with winking, flashing glints. Guns. Three black puffs erupted next to me and were gone instantly. I stopped looking at anything but the sixth span of the huge bridge. The glowing gunsight crept up to the span, I made one quick correction, paused, then pickled. Bombs away. The lightened plane leaped forward, and I heard, "Wildcat leader is hit!" That was Smitty.

The view ahead narrowed to a small hole surrounded by grey fuzz as my aching hand pulled the stick into my gut. My vision cleared, coming out of the dive, and I saw a flicker of a warning light on the console. Not now . . . too busy.

We were low to the ground and doing better than 700 knots and everybody was shooting at us. The light flashed again and stayed on. I looked . . . a low fuel warning!

Someone screamed, "Get out! Get out! Get out!" Gene Smith's wingman. Gene's airplane was a tumbling torch in the sky.

Suddenly, the entire sky became overcast! It was incredible! A speckled, blue-grey overcast just happened. It was 57 millimeter fire all going off at once and exploding above us. My jaw tightened, a filling cracked. I punched the mike button. "Cappy, I've got a low fuel light."

I could picture Cappy, mind racing. What can you say—"Tear up some sheets and boil some water" or "Be quiet and die like a man, I'm really very busy"?

The radio was full of the noises of war. The beeper sounding Gene's misfortune was a monotonous, mournful wail: an automatic signal activated upon ejection. I had no time to dwell on that. I was about to join him, floating in the sky over Hanoi, if I didn't find another couple of tons of fuel quick.

We were almost to Thud Ridge, going as fast as we could, jinking and weaving wildly. Every bad guy in the valley was still shooting. Then my mind began to work again. I'd forgotten to turn on my belly tank! I quickly turned it on and anxiously shot glances at the fuel gauges, waiting for that sickening surge that announces impending flameout.

Agony. The fuel gauge went down and down . . . then stopped and slowly began to increase. Six hundred gallons of beautiful, smelly JP-4 flowed into the internal tanks of my plane. I could almost see Cappy's plane sigh when I told him I had solved my difficulty. No more problem, except for being target in the biggest shooting gallery in history.

We passed Thud Ridge at the speed of sound with MiGs giving chase. They didn't have a chance. We had that extra edge of speed they lacked: adrenaline. Once the Red River passed under my nose in a blur, the panic of escape left me. I could breathe again.

Gene's beeper was still sounding, weaker now, telling us he was still floating over the city, not yet in the grasp of his tormentors.

Wildcat three checked the flight in and reported one missing. Good-bye, Smitty.

That night there was an impromptu wake for Smitty. Cappy and I sat quietly watching as a thing I called the "Hanoi Dodge" began.

The "Shooters," armed with beer bottles were at one end, while a group of pilots, flight suited and still wearing mask marks on their faces, lined the wall near us. The trick was to make it from the near wall to the far, about 40 feet, without getting hit with a beer bottle.

Bill Grieger broke from the line, dashing one way, then darting quickly the other, alternately bending low and stretching to tiptoes as he ran. Bottles flew, one set colliding in mid-air without breaking. The red exit sign at the far end disappeared in a shower of glass. Bill made it unscathed. He stood proudly with his drink, watching as two more set out to run the "Valley," boots crunching on new-broken brown glass. There were cheers as they, too, found safety on "Thud Ridge," the far wall.

Cappy sat with twinkling eyes and a slight grin, watching the show. His face broke into a broader gleam and the blue eyes almost closed with humor when another made the run with awkward body movements, holding a sloshing drink.

"How do you do it, Ed?" I asked.

"What, Geno?"

"Hell. We brief and go to the airplanes; you could be on your way to the 7-11 . . ."

There was a loud crash as one fleeing figure went out of control through the back door without opening it. There were cheers. Out under the street light, the figure could be seen getting up and checking the beer in his hand. The shooters laughed in relief.

"It's an act," Cappy said.

"You . . ."

"I'm scared spitless."

"Hm." I took a drink.

"You let it out, one time, and it can get to you." Cappy was looking out the shattered doorway. The bartender was cheerfully calling for carpenters.

"God, that makes me feel better. A lot of the time, I've got a bowling ball in my stomach . . ."

"It doesn't show, though." He looked at me. "Those young guys . . . [he waved] they've got to follow us."

Larry Pickett sat down with us. The room quieted. Larry was the Vice Commander of the wing. Incredible man. Grey haired, dignified, in charge of life and death—should have been in a cushy executive office, air-conditioned and chauffeured; but he was still flying a single-seat fighter into the fray, right along with the teen-agers.

"We lost a good one today." He raised his glass. "Cappy . . . G.I., we'll see him, after this is all done."

We drank, and some of the pilots near us raised their glasses and nodded solemnly.

"He knew," I said quietly. "He knew it was coming."

"Did he tell you?" Larry asked.

"At lunch today . . . it was in his eyes." I wanted something stronger than bourbon, something to dissolve the ball in my gut. Would I know? Would it be tomorrow?

"You all get on with the game, boys," Larry yelled, waving for another drink.

There were smiles. The shooters lined up. The wake began again.

THUD RIDGE

The Red River runs diagonally from the Northwest, through Hanoi, and out to the Gulf of Tonkin. The river and the city make up two of the three major landmarks of Pak Six. The third is Thud Ridge. Situated some 20 miles north of Hanoi, it is a narrow, 15-mile-long finger pointing to Hanoi. This way, boys.

The peaks and crevasses of Thud Ridge were largely inaccessible, unless you happened to be a mountain goat. The Ridge was a logistics problem to the North Vietnamese. They couldn't get any guns up there, 5000 feet into the misty air of the Red River Valley. Escaping Thuds hugged the "lee" slope of the ridge and were masked from pursuing SAMs, gun radar, and hawk-eyed MiGs. Thud Ridge was our haven, our first full breath of air, the first step to safety.

We entered the arena often by way of Thud Ridge. More times than not, our escape was north to the Ridge. We tried to mix up our routes in and out of there to keep them off balance, but there was really no better way to go. To enter the valley from the west, south, or east was to face miles of table-flat plains infested with SAM sites. No friendly hills or mountains jutted to block the view.

There was a place on the Ridge we called the "Rest Camp." It looked like a hot bath resort and was easily seen from the air. The Weasels, who spent a lot of time working around Thud Ridge, used the Rest Camp as a reference point.

Gus was a Wild Weasel and a good one. I don't remember where he was from, it was deep somewhere, and he wasn't always easy to understand on the radio. "Whar in thee Hayal er we gowin' nayow?"

One day, Gus was leading his Weasels up the Ridge and the Force Commander asked him where he was. Gus was a little irritated since he had been playing tag with some angry MiGs, and his tone of voice sounded excited, something Gus never got. "Ahm hettin' up the reeidge ht' th' Res' kep!"

There was a lot of immediate excitement because it sounded like he had said, "I'm hit, at the Ridge, get the ResCap." (ResCap is Air Force talk for Rescue Forces.)

He had simply stated, "I'm heading up the Ridge at the Rest Camp."

The Thud was incredibly tough. We grew to expect five to seven minutes of high-speed escape from the magnificent old bird, even when it was a blazing torch in the sky. It just kept going, a truly remarkable piece of machinery. It had heart, and we loved it.

We always headed for the Ridge when we took a hit or ran into mechanical trouble. A good many Thuds made it to the Ridge and then came apart or went out of control. A considerable tonnage of Thuds was deposited on Thud Ridge.

Not only was the Ridge a haven, it added the proper setting to the war. Like the Isle of Madelene, it didn't appear real. Unlike the Isle, it wasn't beautiful. It was a dark and ghostly place. Mist hung in its highest crevasses even on sunny days. It looked like a colossal dragon, lying there in the Red River Valley.

In late 1967, the dragon grew teeth. They began to put guns on the Ridge. The logistics problem had been solved; giant choppers began carrying guns to the Ridge. The door to our safe escape route slowly closed.

There was a throng of Thuds that didn't make it to the Ridge. Gene Smith didn't. Without comment, he jettisoned his burning plane and floated down into the center of Hanoi.

The same day, we finally went to bomb the Phuc Yen Airfield. Ray Horinek, one of the unlucky sixteen, went down on that raid. He didn't make it to the Ridge either. Ray calmly said, "See you later," and punched out. We weren't prone to histrionics.

• • •

The silver screen is full of twisting, diving, turning aircraft. Smoke is pouring from one as we zoom the camera into the cockpit and see a young, helmeted face . . .

"Skipper! I'm going DOWN!"

"Pull out, RICK, pull out!"

"No use, (gasp), tell Julie I love her!"

There is eerie silence as the battle still rages, and the Skipper circles while gazing profoundly at the burning hole in the ground. There is a crescendo of music that nearly drowns the sound of tracers flashing by as the enemy refuses to take a break.

"Damn shame, damn shame," *mutters the Skipper. A look of grim determination grows on his chiseled features, and you know he is going to turn around and shoot down all them bastards!*

CANALE DI RAPIDES

It was O-dark-hundred hours when we waddled out to our airplanes, laden with all our gear. The sun was an hour away and the dark flightline was silent. Sleek hulks crouched in the darkness, waiting for pilots to give them life and movement.

Our bodies were wrapped in G-suits from the waist down, corseting our sleepy flesh into pseudo-firmness. Fifty pounds of parachute was strapped on the back, and a bulky survival vest held a minihardware store: a two-way radio, 2 knives, a flashlight, some flares, a fishing kit, a gun and ammunition (to fight our own, one-man war), water, K-rations, and a saw. Yes . . . a saw.

We also had a first aid kit (an absolute marvel; it seemed the entire prescription counter from Walgreen's was compacted into a 4 inch cube).

Each of us carried a $500 helmet in a nylon bag. I always thought of Icabod Crane when I picked up my "head" to go fly.

Cappy found his plane first and waddled over to

the sleek monster. He was calm and cool. I felt my
butterflies subside as I watched him.

Then I was in front of my bird. I eyed the big
Thud squatting there in the dark. She had two red
stars painted on the fuselage just below the canopy.
A MiG killer. It was not comforting to realize I
was flying into Hanoi with butterflies in my stomach and stars on my plane. The two don't match.

The name painted on the nose of the plane was
"Mary Kay." I wondered who Mary Kay was and
hoped I could bring her back safe and sound.
Soon, I was to get a plane of my own, and I could
paint a name on it. "Ho's Horror" . . . no, something less juvenile . . . "Tina Ann" or "Tiny Tina"
maybe. Plenty of time to think about that.

I walked around the bird and climbed in. No
need for a detailed inspection on this flightline.
Peering at every nut and bolt would be an insult to
the Chief who had been up all night fondling this
machine.

As I strapped into the monster, I began to feel
better. It was just too good an airplane, too tough
and well built to ever let you down.

I looked around the cockpit. It was more like
the inside of a tank than an airplane. It seemed
impossible that any bullet could ever penetrate all
that iron around me. I felt snug and safe, securely
strapped in this cocoon of iron. (It was actually
mostly aluminum and some steel, but seemed to
me to be constructed of cast iron).

"How do you read me, Chief?" My voice
sounded muffled over the interphone.

"Loud and clear, Sir." The voice was cheerful, crackling into my headset from the end of a long cord out in the dark ramp somewhere.

"Ready down there?" I peered into the darkness.

"All set, let 'er rip."

The second hand on my watch jittered past 12 and my finger poked the start button. The silence burst into sound as the four planes in Bear flight started engines in unison. Grey smoke, invisible in the dark, stung my eyes, as the big J-75 engine came to life. Gauges dithered and the cockpit glowed with a dull red light as the generator came on the line. I sat in a pulsing world of machine, ready to go.

"Chocks out." The chief pulled the wooden chocks that held the tires.

The glare of the floodlights sent patterns of refracted light bouncing around my glass canopy, and the early morning mist gathered on the windscreen. I nudged my airplane forward and turned to follow the flashing lights of Cappy's plane. Even with the helmet and mask on, the noise was loud enough to hurt. The roar was primarily from my own airplane, shrieking along in idle.

We taxied to the arming area, pulling in the parking places in turn, like big sleek convertibles at a drive-in.

Our canopies were open and our hands in sight. It was always like being frisked, while the crew on the ramp armed the bombs and the gun.

I sat there with my gloved hands sticking out in the dark. My movie camera was taped securely to the side of the gun-sight. I told myself not to forget to turn it on when things started happening. It might be a million dollar home movie. It had been taped there two days before, ready to film the Paul Doumer Bridge.

You guessed it . . . I forgot to turn it on.

When the arming was done, we lined up on the long black runway and ran the engines up to full power. Standing on the brakes, I scanned the instrument panel for any sign of trouble. Good bird. I switched off my taxi lights, indicating I was ready to go. When all four lights had gone out and the runway ahead was pitch black, Cappy called, "On the roll."

I closed my eyes to keep from being blinded by the flash from Cappy's afterburner and punched the clock. The airplane next to me lurched ahead, its tail section opening up and belching a fifteen-foot plume of beaded blue and yellow fire. (I always had to sneak a squint . . . it was such a fantastic sight.) I squinted at the clock. When the second hand stuttered past 20, I let my feet slip off the brakes. The light from Cappy's afterburner was still nearly blinding.

My left hand slammed the throttle to the outboard position. There was a second delay and then I felt that familiar kick in the butt as my plane lunged ahead. Gauges still looked good. One more switch to do; water injection. Everything increased, temp, RPM, exhaust pressure, respiration, cooking right at the limit.

The engine growled meaner, and I was on my way to Hanoi . . . again.

Fifty . . . ninety, one-twenty. Don't look outside. There is nothing but black out there. Believe that or die. Read the gauges and live. Hold the heading pointer exactly on, steer the rudder with delicate toes. One-ninety, time to fly. Pull the stick back easy. Up comes the nose . . . keep heading exactly, main gear still rolling on concrete. The glowing artificial horizon shows ten degrees up. Good . . . hold that. Vertical velocity needle moves, we're airborne, check it again to be sure . . . gear up.

Hand goes from throttle to gear handle and back. Speed, 250; flaps up. Now comes the vertigo. Read the gauges. The big bird sinks and instinct goes bananas. No doubt about it, plane is going straight up. Instinct says push forward on stick, nose down, gain speed; but the gauges say all is well, hold what you have. Flaps are all the way up now, and the sinking stops. Speed 300 and building. We're on our way.

The light of dawn is ahead, a faint line. Cappy's afterburner looks like a star on the horizon.

I left it in burner and cut into the inside of Cappy's turn, angling to join up with him. The throb of sheer brute power was all around me, quiet in my cocoon, but tearing the air apart outside with an awesome shriek. I shut off the afterburner, and soon eased into close formation with Cappy.

The big plane next to me was just a silhouette in

the dim light as numbers three and four slid slowly into formation. It was spooky. Four iron sharks, bound for Hanoi with 6000 pounds of bombs under the wings of each, and a gun in each needle nose, a gun capable of sawing a truck in half instantly. Deadly monsters, these sharks.

It was a beautiful morning over Thailand. The mist from the night heavy in the valleys, a snow-white blanket with black rocks jutting through it, and the feeble pink sunlight filtering through here and there.

We climbed away from the mist and the light grew stronger. I longed for a cup of coffee.

Ahead, I could make out the fat tankers winging north to the rendezvous point, a school of mammoth bass in the misty sea of air. They grew in size as we approached, and soon I could read the tail numbers and see the big blue ribbon painted on the side.

We slid smoothly behind the lead tanker and Cappy nosed up to the hose for some gas. The remaining three planes nestled in formation with the huge tanker, waiting our turn for a drink.

Aerial refueling is one of the most demanding tasks a pilot must accomplish. It requires very precise formation, while enduring the trauma of metal to metal contact in the air, a thing most pilots are violently opposed to. It somehow smacks of air to air collision.

It takes something like 6 minutes to fill a Thud with gas. In that time, the others in the flight burn 100 to 150 gallons. Once the leader has finished,

he must wait until the other three have each taken
their 6 minutes. The leader has now consumed as
much as 450 gallons, so he must return to the nozzle to "top off." Yes . . . it takes a lot of gas to keep
a locomotive in the air!

Once refueling was complete, we began to join
together to go to war. The big tankers turned south
and the fighters dropped off and shuffled positions,
getting into the proper formation. The sky was full
of airplanes moving about and settling down.

It is to our credit that, with nervous hands and
distracted minds, we didn't have any collisions
during this time of shuffling the Thuds.

With everyone together in position, a gigantic
formation heading for Hanoi, the radio became silent. Each man, alone in his tiny world of gauges,
switches, and turbine whine, sat silent with his
own thoughts. There is a lot to think about when
you are going to Hanoi.

"Bison Force, channel two." Twenty hands left
twenty throttles to seek the flat wafer switch on the
UHF radio. Three clicks to the left, and the
number two danced in the little indicator window.

We all checked in and the leader said, "Spread it
out, music on." Criss Lawrence was leading us
today.

We turned on our jammers and spread into a
wide, sprawling formation. Otter, our Weasels,
began to edge out ahead of us. They looked like
four tiny minnows meandering away from the main
school.

"Spares, go home." A Thud from each of Bison

and Zebra flights dropped down and reversed course, joining together in a flight of two.

"Bison, green 'em up." I flipped the red Master Arm switch on. A green light glowed. I was ready. The thick jungle and karst below us was hostile, we had crossed the NVN border. The mist was thinning to reveal large patches of rich, green jungle torn by huge slabs of grey rock jutting skyward.

It looked as if the earth had wrinkled and cracked here when the whole business was being formed. I could imagine an ancient Tonkin giant stumbling around knee-deep in jungle, stoned out of his gourd, trying to landscape his poppy garden with these stones. That's what it looked like to me.

The jungle and karst gradually dwindled to gently rolling hills as we bore down on the Red River Valley. We turned right at the Red River and headed for Thud Ridge. Our speed increased and things began to happen. The time for daydreaming was over.

Sam Adams, leading the Weasels, was hard at work over the Ridge. The air was filling with urgent voices.

The Force rushed on toward Thud Ridge, our final turning point. Other voices were on the air now. "BANDITS, BANDITS, BULLSEYE!" MiGs were out.

Our heads swiveled like owls.

We turned at Thud Ridge and headed south to Hanoi. Seven minutes would pass before we would be over that famous death trap. These were the well known (to us) minutes that made Thud jocks into old men.

Flak blossomed in clusters off to our right. Out of range, no threat. A SAM was on the way. The pace went up another notch. The SAMs were coming.

Twenty minds went into passing gear, slowing the actual events to a workable pace. Everything was in slow motion. Mental fine filter set in, and the useless thoughts of minutes ago were not allowed to get through. There was no room for fear and uncertainty. Whimpering was banned.

The flak to our right edged closer, still no problem, not worth a glance. We warily eyed a SAM glowing bright in the morning sun and lifting slowly out of the valley south of the Ridge.

"SAM! Two o'clock!"

"Hold formation, look for his mates."

The missile, glowing like an acetylene torch, picked up speed and carved an immense arc in our direction. Another lifted from the same spot, following the first in nonchalant splendor.

"Bear Four's got trouble!" I tore my eyes from the SAM in time to see Bob Kennedy literally swapping ends, up and down in a gigantic porpoise movement. His speedbrakes popped out and the bombs and fuel tanks tore from the plane and tumbled out of sight.

I looked back at the SAM and watched it flash overhead. A second later, its cousin whizzed past, and another two were rising into the sun.

Bob broke formation, out of control, turning

violently left and down to the deck. Then I remembered; he was flying good old 385, the wonder Thud.

I sincerely hoped Bob would get home alright, but instantly forgot him as more SAMs came tearing out of the sun from the left, out of the glare of the eastern plains.

The sky was fast filling up with flaming missiles. We were caught in a massive crossfire. They came through the formation from both sides, from ahead. They were passing very close and individual planes jinked to avoid them.

The Weasels were going crazy. Against this attack, the most savage to date, they could do little. All their Shrikes were gone. They had killed three sites, but they could kill no longer. The SAMs knew it. The missiles flew and we dodged them. Several went behind me, almost flying formation with each other. I could hear someone was hit and going down. Zebra leader, Bob Stirm.

It was useless to call out the deadly things, for they were everywhere, but we tried to warn each other anyway: "Three more out of the city!"

"Two from the left . . ."

"Three o'clock! Watch it!"

"Dead ahead, Bison!"

More missiles than we'd ever seen sailed through the morning sky. The entire Red River Valley became a huge launching pad for SAMs. They filled the sky with their peculiar splattering explosions. They came from the east, out of the glare of the morning sun, and from the city, left and right, salvos of two and three—guided missiles, each a kamikaze intent on our destruction.

We had to descend. Like a wounded colossus, the Force started down, ragged but still together, still heading for the bridge over the Canale di Rapides.

The sky suddenly erupted with red explosions in and around the formation. We were now in range of the 85 millimeter guns on the outskirts of Hanoi. All I could think of was that we needn't worry about MiGs for a while.

As we neared the target, the flak grew in intensity, bursting very close. I could glimpse the bridge ahead. Near it, a missile had just launched. All along the river and on the edge of the city, glaring, ugly red rings grew and faded. Flak sites spewing death into the morning sky. The sun was being blotted out by a growing cloud of smoke and debris over Hanoi.

A flaming missile streaked straight for my head. I ducked and shoved the stick forward. The missile passed above and exploded orange and angry. I pulled back into formation just as Cappy veered left to avoid hitting someone in Bison flight. We were all weaving and bobbing wildly now. I pulled up and over to miss Cappy, yelling, "Let's get out of here!" to myself. Things were getting out of hand.

I completed a nice aileron roll, right there over Hanoi, and saw the Force suddenly diving away from me toward the bridge! My gloved hand slammed the stick into the rear right corner of the cockpit, sending me hurtling down after them.

The sky was too crowded, no place to go. I'd gotten right in trail with Cappy and was about to eat his bombs. I could hear explosions near my canopy. When you can hear them, they are close.

It wasn't possible to do anything about any of this. The thing was happening and I was in it. Cappy's bombs came off in my face and I flew through them, settled the sight on the bridge and pickled mine off. The stick was in my gut and my vision dimming on the pullout, but I could see the gunners clearly, working furiously pumping lead at us at point-blank range. I was turning hard left, belly up, afraid I might run into Cappy. The air was filthy with debris and explosions and smoke.

"There just ain't no way!" I gritted. My hands and feet punished the controls, sending the plane left and right, up and down in a drunken, broken-wing, jinking pattern. I flew like a wild man, muttering insanely to myself and heading generally south. Vapor clouds skittered over the windscreen as the big Thud hammered through the moist air. Then, I was out of it. There were no holes in my jacket, or the canopy, or the plane that I could see. One thing was wrong; I was alone.

I peered around, looking for Cappy or anyone at all. The mist was heavy at this low altitude. Then I saw them, off to my right and ahead of me a mile or so. I turned to intercept them, but suddenly a silhouette popped into my peripheral vision to the left.

A single . . . no there were two of them.

I'd never seen a MiG before, and I had always felt it would be hard to identify one quickly. Not so; the high swept-back tail and blunt nose left no doubt. They were MiG as MiG could be, zipping along, trying for a shot at the fleeing Thuds ahead of me.

It wasn't a memorable aerial battle. They didn't see me. I whispered "Jesus" and filled the sky ahead with 20 millimeter bullets. It didn't seem fair, I wanted to honk or something. The big gattling gun spat bullets so fast that it sounded like a big burp, rather than a gun. The leading MiG flew into the barrage and flashes of light glimmered and winked on his tail section. When he felt the hits, he did the swiftest reversal I've ever seen. I tried to keep the gun pointed at him but it was impossible. I flashed past close by, my eyes wide with the nearness of this alien creature, beautiful in green battle dress, standing on its wing in a hard left break; flaming, and mortally wounded.

My speed was considerable. It allowed me to keep turning west without worry from the second MiG. I'm sure he was busy with his stricken leader anyway.

My headset crackled with a strange voice. "SAMs coming in low! Heads up!" I dove for the weeds, scanning the sky anxiously, looking for missiles, forgetting all about MiGs. At zero altitude and with full afterburner cooking, I blistered out of there gratefully.

On the way home and away from danger, I thought about the MiG pilot. I wondered if he'd been able to eject. It was a personal thing, my thoughts were mixed. I had the same feeling one time before, a long time ago.

The bird on the beach was so far away, there was no way to hit it with a .22 pistol; but now there it was, tiny and still in the wet sand at my feet . . . The tail section was the only part on fire; he probably had made it okay, chances were good.

And I wondered about myself . . . where was the elation? The sweet smell of victory?

SUPERBALL

I was groggy and wiped out. It had been a hellish week, going to Hanoi every day. We were losing men and airplanes at an alarming rate, soul-searching every night, trying to devise ways to reduce losses, falling into bed and tossing for three hours to get up and do it all over again.

The brutal facts were: our tactics were good, the planes were good, the pilots were Shit Hot; it was just the most heavily defended area in the world, and to attack it by air meant losses, lots of them.

A General in Saigon demanded an explanation for our "Unacceptable" losses.

"We are going to Hanoi every day," we reported. This was an unacceptable answer. We agonized and searched for a better answer. There was none.

Another time, we received an angry order to "find that sonofabitch that bombed an innocent village." I sat all night looking at strike film, trying to find who had done the dirty deed, or rather, trying to prove we hadn't done it.

Finally, one good sequence turned up that told the story. It clearly showed a missile emerging from the center of a village, climbing straight up for a few feet, then falling back and exploding. With but a split second delay, the "village" disappeared in a blinding flash of light.

The village had been a cleverly disguised SAM site, chock full of stored ammunition and missiles. It was no more, but there were hundreds more just like it, shooting down our planes with immunity . . . immunity provided by our own leaders with their "Rules of Engagement."

And we sat sleepless through the night, searching for evidence to hang one of our own, and went out during the day to kill commies gently and in an absolutely humane manner.

It was saddening, disheartening work; trying to find a way to do what we were ordered to do, not get dead, not get hung. It was impossible.

Disillusionment began to seep into my young, wide-eyed mind. I hung tenaciously to my belief in a just and knowledgeable leadership of my country; but, in all its wisdom, it was doing a better number on me—destroying my ability and will to fight—than any enemy could do. The enforced lack of sleep, the conflicting orders (kill the enemy, but only the ones we point out from 12 thousand miles away), the open mistrust of our motives and ability and constant intent to intimidate and punish our own warriors: All this was straight from the enemy's bag of tricks.

It was five in the morning and the planning room was full. Maps were being torn, cut, pasted, and lines were being drawn. Fresh from two hours of lying on my back, I scanned the flight lineup for my name.

The target was Hanoi again, the Rapides Bridge. I felt a twinge of guilt. The bridge must be still standing, I thought. I wanted to join the appropriate group to help with the planning.

This time, I couldn't find my name anywhere. Jack Hart saw me looking over shoulders and asking questions. In his most kindly and tactful manner, he said, "Basel, get the Goddamn Hell out of here!"

Then I remembered . . . it was my turn for three days OFE (Off the Face of the Earth). I wasn't going to Hanoi today, I was going to Tokyo! Trying not to show any elation, trying not to hurry, trying not to whistle, I made for the door.

I ran into Tom Kirk near the door. He was intently dissecting a detailed map of Hanoi. We hadn't talked in a few days, and I was surprised at his appearance. Tired is the word. We were all tired, but Tom really looked bad.

"Hear you nailed a MiG, G.I., Shit Hot!"

"Thanks, Tom. He sort of flew into my gunsight."

"Old modest G.I." Tom grinned, his eyes wandering back to the map.

"Got to get going, Tom. Good luck."

"Check six, and all that pilot talk."

Pedalling along on my five dollar Thai bike, I wondered if Tom had taken any rest trips, any OFE. The minute I wondered, I knew. Tom doesn't rest. It's not in his check-list. He'd been at Takhli two weeks by the time the others had arrived. He had 11 missions before I had one. Tom was in overdrive all the time, and the rest of us had just three forward speeds.

I loved Tom like a brother, but never was able to quite understand where he was rushing. He made me nervous when we spent a lot of time together: I never had time to collect my thoughts and feel I had control of anything. I was content to be in a squadron other than the one Tom was commanding.

When I arrived at the hootch, the phone was ringing. I tried to ignore it. Time was racing and Tokyo beckoned. I had to pack. It was already 5:30, and the shuttle plane left at eight.

The phone wouldn't shut up, so I grabbed it by its scrawny black neck and squeezed, "Yeah?"

"Basel, this is Colonel MacDonald..." (Pregnant pause.)

"Yes, Sir?"

"Better get down here and fill out a claim for that MiG, if you want credit." I looked at my watch.

"Sir..."

"The squadron deserves credit as well, Basel."

"Yes, Sir, on my way." I put down the phone and climbed aboard the rusty old bicycle. There was still time for Tokyo. The planning room was empty when I walked through to the Wing Intelligence office. Five fifty-seven, just about time for the morning time hack. They would be sitting silently in the big auditorium eyeing their watches, waiting.

Intelligence was excited. An enemy plane destroyed was not a usual thing for us. We were bombers, we knocked down bridges and avoided the enemy fighters if we could. The sergeant had the forms ready. I filled in the blanks and wrote a short narrative in the space provided and headed for the door.

Speedy Gonzales from the Information Office headed me off, asking for a statement for the newspaper.

What do you say about such a dazzling aerial duel? "I hosed him down."

"Awe! Come on, Captain. You got more to say than that. There was fire blazing and chit coming off the other plane . . ."

"Well, there was a little fire . . ."

"You've always wanted to choot down one of these bastards, right?"

"Speedy, I . . ."

"Okay, I never can get two cents out of you guys. I'll just have to make up something." He took off his glasses and rubbed his eyes. "This chob is killing me."

I paused and looked at Speedy for a moment, and then looked at my watch; six-forty, still time.

"The sky was like grey blood. I could see him lunge at me from the murk, guns blazing, his gog-

gled head visible, hunched over the gunsight . . ."
Speedy had begun to write. "The tracers tore at my
wings, scribbling a jagged tattoo along my empen-
age. I jinked right and left . . ." Speedy was looking at me, his head nodding gently, a tiny smile
playing at the corners of his mouth.

"At least, let us take your picture."

"Okay, there's time." Speedy was on the phone
and the photographer was there in a few minutes.
We went outside and I stood pointing at a chart of
North Vietnam while they took a picture.

Speedy finally shamed me into writing the es-
sentials of the "Victory." He looked like death
warmed over as he scanned the stirring account. I
headed for my bicycle. Seven-fifteen. They were
probably leaving the tankers about now, heading
for Hanoi.

Throwing clothes in my B-4 bag, I visualized
the Thuds leaving the tankers and settling into the
strange box-kite formation for the run into Hanoi.
Tom would be way out in front, leading. I called
for a taxi, knowing that "ten minutes" meant
twenty—and allowing for that. I was trying to
hide a month's pay in my bag when the taxi drove
up, five minutes late, or five minutes early, depending on the way you looked at it.

As I hefted the bag, the phone rang. Determined
to let it ring, I hobbled to the door. Someday, they
are going to invent a phone ring that's not a ring. It
will say,

"This phone call is urgent, better answer it,"

or, "This is just a nuisance call, forget it."

Anything to replace that urgent sound of the phone yelling at the room. I answered it, bag in hand, vowing not to spend any more time on that damned MiG. It was quite enough that I knew what had happened there over Hanoi. No one else need know or care.

It was Tom's Operations Officer asking for Tom's home address. By his voice, I knew Tom was down.

I wanted to know where and how and what and how did the message get through so fast and did anybody see a parachute and what got him, but none of these questions could be asked, let alone answered.

I looked at my watch again, this time for another reason: it didn't seem possible there had been enough time for them to get to the target. Seven-thirty. Time enough.

Communications from the arena was incredibly fast, relayed from plane to plane and into a central phone system.

Tom had kept his address a secret in order to protect Yolanda from the misguided do-gooders that like to harass and hurt wives of warmongers. I knew she was in Trieste, Italy . . . that's all. (Tina was in Italy too, in a town called "Castello di Aviano." The nearby Air Force base knew her address, so she was treated to the sight of a blue-suited Colonel stepping out of an Air Force staff car, a sight that means only one thing to a pilot's

wife ... He's dead. They had come looking for
Yolanda. It took them quite a while to get Tina
calmed down.)

I hung up the phone and stared at the cab outside. The driver was gazing calmly at my open
door. Tokyo called my name, louder than before.

All those girls know me, I thought. They all
say, "Hey, G.I." ... they know me. I closed the
door and got in the cab.

The rickety C-47, "Gooney Bird" got me to
Bangkok by ten that morning. I was ready for a
drink. I was in a frozen think-tank, and the
thoughts couldn't do anything but just recycle over
and over.

Tom's dead, I'm alive. I didn't knock down the
bridge, too busy shooting down MiGs, glory
game. Tom got the bridge and died doing it. I'll be
a hero, Tom will be dead. Tom's dead ... Yolanda
will be understanding.

I was so tired.

The wonderful town of Bangkok was right
there, and I almost checked into one of the plush
hotels, but my stubborn mind would accept nothing but Tokyo. It was my original plan and I had
spent some good hours there with Tom. And, be-
sides, the girls know me there.

I jumped a KC-135 tanker bound for Okinawa.
The flight route would take us over Tokyo on the
way. Knowing airplanes and their ability to get
sick over good places to land, I took a chance that
this tanker might just have to make a stop in one of

the many air bases around Tokyo.

Ah So . . . not so. Tokyo was spread before my eyes as I peered from 37,000 feet through scratched plexiglass. The vastness of the city was horizon to horizon . . . dwarfing Los Angeles. I was searching for a parachute when Mount Fujiama went down on the misty horizon. We were on our way to Okinawa.

It was late afternoon when I walked into the Base Operations at Kadena Air Base, Okinawa. Even in Okinawa, word was out about Thud pilots. My 105 Patch started a conversation with a Master Sergeant who looked me in the eye and decided I wasn't an imposter. He knew of a flight into Tokyo that evening, one that wasn't logged on the big board, secret. Would I sign a waiver? For Tokyo, I would have sold one of my children, just then.

Yokota Air Base is near Tokyo. The officer's club is big and plush. The place probably hosts everyone remotely connected with the military that comes into the Tokyo area. It endures transient pilots from all over the Orient.

The fighter pilot tradition lives there. The bar is in the shape of a big V. In those days, there was a bell at the tip of the V attached to a cord that was strung along both sides of the bar. Anyone sitting at the bar had only to reach up and pull the cord to ring the bell. The rules were posted:

HE WHO ENTERS HERE

HIS HAT UPON HIS HEAD

SHALL BUY A ROUND OF CHEER
WHEN RINGS CONDITION RED

There was another sign, just below the first:

HE WHO RINGS THE BELL IN JEST
BUYS A ROUND FOR ALL THE REST!

Wearing my best wrinkled sports coat, and my grey slacks, and feeling a rush from two fast shots of bourbon while showering, I walked into that bar and sat right under the bell. Not drunk yet, but determined to get there, I reached up and grasped the cord. The man on my right, who apparently had been dozing over his beer with Cuddy back, grabbed my arm and pointed to the big sign. I nodded philosophically and pulled the cord.

Oh, that bell! It had such a fine tone!

As I remember, it was first stolen from the bridge of the Enterprise when it was on maneuvers in the Mediterranean. It was then stolen by an Air Force fighter pilot that loved those Navy Jocks, but had to have that bell.

It had been stolen and recovered time after time, showing up in clubs all over the Orient until it was stolen back by a Phantom pilot from Yokota and sealed in a marble pillar there in the bar.

I entered the place alone, but quickly became popular. The bar was about to close, but this bell-ringing provided ample reason to keep it open. The mood for a party was definitely in the air. Even the bartender had a drink. I was gulping bourbon.

Standing unsteadily on the bar with one hand on the cord (all eyes followed), I said, "This one's for Tom Kirk, shot down today over North Vietnam!" I rang the bell and they cheered.

The mirror behind the bar showed I was decomposing nicely. One eye was drooping and the nose was almost gone. I belted another bourbon with grim determination. There was too much noise suddenly. I turned on the stool and spoke loudly, "Hey!" No one noticed. "This boy is getting too drunk . . ." The din swelled. "When I was his age, I was . . ."

"Son . . . To get ahead in the service, you have got to get a specialty . . . keep it confidential, tell no one." Everything was backwards, nothing made sense. I looked into the lifeless eyes of the speaker, a forty-year-old Captain. The eyes were focused on my earlobe. I have to rejuvenate, had to get out of there.

Kay's Massage Parlor, famous all over the Far East, was just down the dusty, narrow street. The buildings tilted and swayed because the road wouldn't remain still. Once, they touched at the top and I feared for falling stones.

Safe inside Kay's, I was in the hands of the Dragon Lady. She washed me all over and put me in a hot bath the size of a small swimming pool. Water swirled and caressed my tired muscles.

After nearly dozing off in the bath, I was soaped and washed again and given an ice-cold Asahi beer. The steam cabinet cooked me for ten minutes, during which the frosty bottle was lifted to my lips periodically.

I lay dreamily on a padded table while her expert hands manipulated my body with oils and scents. More ice-cold beer. Soon I began to glow with health. I was loose and clean and *hungry*.

One huge birdbath martini, hurting cold, and an almost raw New York steak (no potato, salad or vegetable), and I was ready to try and recapture better days; days when friends didn't die, and times were simple and the biggest problem was getting a date with the girl that worked over at Howard J's.

It was a smuggler's hideaway. Beads of light touched her face from a million-sided mirror. She was infinitely soft and fragile and liquid. Electricity from her smooth shoulder burned mine, setting fires where ice had been. My eyes went out of focus when she turned her face to me and her pale, full lips bade me follow.

We went out the back way.

The new day was gentle and soft, subdued light filtering through the rice-paper wall. There was an aroma of cherry blossoms, and the girl next to me was truly beautiful, but she was all dirty. So was I. We were covered with a light film of soot: candles had been burning all night. Very romantic, but sooty.

She had one clean breast.

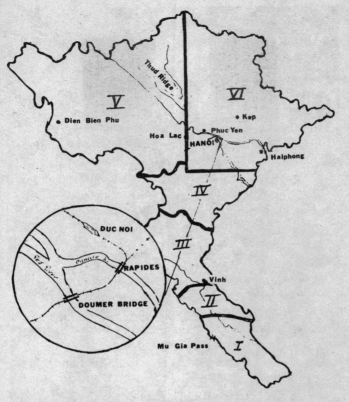

North Vietnam

The Packages.

Joe

Gl

Gary

Cappy

Tom

Five friends pose on the ladder of a Thud. From bottom: Tom Kirk, Ed Cappelli, me, Joe Grimaud, and Gary Olin. (Joe served at Korat Air Base.)

Back in the saddle.

The Doumer Bridge, a painting by
Keith Ferris.

the warriors

The warriors.

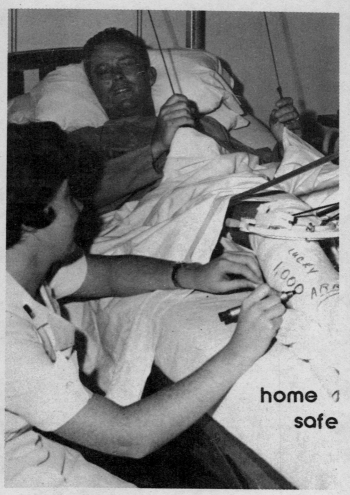

home safe

Safe in the hospital. Nurse Sherry Gahan scribes "Lucky 1000" on the cast. Who was counting?

KEP AIRFIELD

Bill Grieger turned at the Isle of Madelene and eased the throttle forward, edging his flight of Weasels out ahead of the Force. The weather was misty, but there were no clouds.

Erick Koch sat in the back seat, scanning the scope for signs of enemy activity. The equipment was silent and blank. He shrugged and keyed the mike button. "No signals, no threats to the Force," he droned.

Later on, there were still no signals. Erick shifted in the seat and keyed the interphone. "Something's up, Bill. It's too quiet."

"When we get closer..."

"Yeah."

High and to the rear of the Weasels, I flew on Cappy's wing. We were Bison flight. The target was Kep Airfield, twenty miles northwest of Hanoi. The Weasel song had just broken the heavy silence. We dipped down and picked up speed. We were coming in from the east, the long way around.

"Bear Force, green 'em up. Music on." Bear flight was leading the force today. Sixteen gloved hands flicked 16 switches and 16 green lights glowed softly. Ready.

"Tonight you die, Yankee Dog."

The phrase was spoken without emotion in a singsong voice with all the inflections in the wrong places. There was a thick silence. Then it came again.

"Tonight you die, Yankee Dog."

It might have been worth a laugh, had the voice said something else. It was eerie, otherworldly, that impersonal, robot voice broadcasting on our frequency. Ice water crawled up my back.

Then the Weasel broke the silence, "No signals, no threats to the Force." He sounded slightly puzzled.

Kep suddenly became visible. A big cloud of flak appeared five miles ahead, right over Kep. It was as if they were saying, "We know you are coming, here we are. Come on, if you dare."

They did know we were coming, and they knew what the target was. It wasn't just good radar. There were indications, time after time, that they had detailed information about when, where, and how we were coming. We suspected a leak in Laos.

About that time, Bill made a prophecy. "Hummm. No SAMs. No radar. Looks like a MiG day." Erick nodded.

The flak continued to burst over Kep, a strange bubbling cloud of explosions, a crazy waste of ammunition. We flew over it and the Force rolled in, plummeting toward the seething cloud. Then it suddenly stopped!

I plunged down toward the grey airfield, squinting into the bombsight. Bombs from the first flight were hitting right on the runway. I let mine go and began a hard pullout. Alarmed voices filled my headset.

"MiGs! Bear!"

"Weasel's got MiGs! Look out, leader! Six o'clock . . . SIX!"

"Bison! Check six . . . MiGs!"

Bison, that was us!

"Bear, move it aro—"

"Git him off me, two! . . . Eating me alive!"

"Bison! MiGs at two o'clock!"

I caught a sun-glint at two o'clock high, sun glancing off a pair of swept silver wings, just a wink as he turned, coming in fast. I turned to meet him, stabbing the emergency jettison button, cleaning the wings for battle.

I looked back quickly, nothing on my tail. The headset was a yelling, hollering thing, hurting my ears. There were a dozen voices cutting each other out. There were MiGs everywhere.

The MiG was bearing down on me, cutting me off in the turn. I lit the burner, and he fired two missiles at me. I came out of burner—heat seekers. The missiles flashed by, wide by several hundred feet. He closed for a gun kill, but his angle was still too high. He couldn't turn hard enough to point his guns at me. I kept turning hard and he finally overshot. My neck was aching and my eyes dimmed as I watched him sliding behind me and to the outside of my turn; a shining little jeweled flying machine; a deadly and beautiful thing!

I craned my neck, the G's pulling at my eyelids. I spotted him, finally, on the other side, *turning away*. I jammed left rudder and stick and whipped around to the left. The big Thud shuddered but kept turning.

"My turn," I whispered.

The radio was chaos. Everyone had a MiG or was being had by a MiG. I couldn't talk, there was nothing to say. My MiG was in front of me now— running away.

The universe narrowed to just me and the MiG pilot. My hand was like deadwood as I switched from bombs to guns. The glowing sight slowly settled on the fleeing fighter. I carefully squeezed the trigger. The plane shuddered as the gattling gun spat out a barrage of bullets. The MiG was untouched. I eased the sight a little ahead of him and fired again. No dice.

Down we went to the deck, he twisting and turning in an insolent and leisurely spiral, while I fired at him and missed. I aimed behind him, to each side, right on, ahead of him, everywhere. I expected him to explode, disintegrate, or smoke, or something. He didn't.

By this time, we were very low, right on the deck and heading back to Kep. The MiG led me through a hornet's nest . . . grey bursts began ripping the sky all around me. I broke a filling and kept shooting.

Something told me to quit. It said, "Git, *now!*" I broke hard right just as a torrent of bright orange tracers flashed past, inches from the left side of my canopy, right where my head had been an instant before.

I horsed the plane wildly to the right, away from the stream of tracers coming from behind me, announcing vividly the presence of another, very hostile MiG on *my* tail. I turned with every ounce of strength I had and jammed the throttle outboard to light the burner. Looking back, I saw the MiG turning away, going home. For a long moment, I just breathed deeply and then tried to figure out where I was. My afterburner was still belching fire, so I played rocket ship for home. The radio was still full of calls but was quieting down.

The Thuds—one by one—were able to get away from their attackers. They began to assemble in two's and three's, heading east in a ragged, high-speed gaggle.

Scant minutes later, we were safely over the Gulf of Tonkin and the leader called for a check-in.

Everyone checked in! Everyone had made it! You could hear the cheerfulness in the voices as we nuzzled up to the fat tankers for the precious gas to get home . . .

"My! Doesn't he look pretty without any tanks! Whazamatter? Did some MiGs scare your tanks off?"

"Hey, G.I., I got a shot at one."

"Hit him?"

"Nope."

"Man! Was that something? Woooee!"

Full of fuel and with nothing to do for two hours, except gently guide a docile airplane home, I sat back and thought about the fight. What a hassle! Just like in the story books. Hop Harrriii-gaaaan!

The event ran through my mind, time after time, from beginning to end, as I sat in the cockpit droning toward home.

I had been so sure I had my second MiG. The ghostly fighter twisted and turned in front of me again, eluding my guns miraculously. I could see myself lighting the afterburner, closing to point-blank range, and blowing him out of the sky. Why hadn't I done that? Afraid? No, didn't want to overshoot. It wouldn't be too smart to pass him up and give him another shot at me.

Sound argument, but more like an excuse. I could have taken him; no doubt about it. Lacked the basic ingredient, killer instinct.

How lucky (and foolish) I'd been! Allowing a MiG to nearly put me away. It had been a very close thing. What told my hands to turn hard right at just that particular instant?

I lit a cigarette and thought about that.

It occurred to me that my plane had been a big

factor in my survival. She had turned beautifully, outmaneuvered that first MiG, and maintained speed, allowing me to get away. Oh, that beautiful speed! It was like an insurance policy.

The coast slipped under the nose and we headed west for Takhli. The late afternoon sun glared in the windscreen, highlighting tiny scratches that were usually invisible. My eyes fell on the gun camera. The counter showed I'd used all 50 feet of film. It should be an interesting movie, I thought. It was!

We were a jovial bunch at dinner that night. We were veterans of the classical dog fight, a true rarity for Thud pilots. None of us was dead, and we'd had one Helluva good time. I laughed and shouted with the rest, but occasionally found myself trancing into the glass.

I saw the MiG twisting and turning in front of me, sun glinting from the bubble canopy that housed a human head; I wanted that MiG, it was my ticket to fame . . . I didn't want to hurt that MiG. My back hurt in several hot spots as I thought about the other MiG, the one on my tail, the one I didn't see, the one who should have killed me.

I did wrong, not pressing in for the kill, and I survived because of it, would have died if I had had the killer instinct.

And who told me to get out? Right at that instant?

• • •

Cappy leaned forward. "You look like somebody just handed you a turd on a silver platter."

I smiled. "Oh, doing some very rare thinking."

"Don't let it get out of hand. Ruin your reputation." He grinned. "I got a shot at one, too."

"You did? I kind of lost track . . ."

"Boy! Join the club, Geno, things went Tango Uniform, for sure."

"Did you hit him? . . . the MiG?"

"No. I looked at my film, just a wing tip flashing by. It happened so fast. You see your film?"

"Yeah; scared me all over again."

"It was scary as hell, but, I don't think I've ever had so much fun!"

"I know what you mean, I just can't stop thinking about it. Don't know what it is. I guess it's got to be the Ultimate Hunt."

"Something like that."

The Weasels had tape recorders on board. They taped every mission, and the tapes were used to recap what happened and to identify "lessons learned."

We sat in the quiet hootch that night and listened to Bill's tape. We marveled at his prophecy and heard again that robot voice, "Tonight you die, Yankee Dog."

That was mission number 32. Sixty-eight to go.

THE NUMBERS GAME

We were all there for the big prize, 100 missions. Once this goal was reached, we could sew on the coveted red white and blue patch and go home with honor. He who wore it was immune, homeward bound. He would live. He was honored by those of us who still bore the stigma of death.

One Hundred Missions was the goal. We marked them on our hats religiously, each one a step toward home. The first ten marks were won in relatively safe places like Mu Gia Pass in Pak One or Dien Bien Phu in Pak five.

The theory was, a new pilot should have time to adjust to the concept of being blown away by a real enemy bullet. He was given ten missions to think about it. In reality, ten missions was not enough, 100 missions was not enough. But, being a qualified combat pilot didn't prepare the man for the shock of what Pak Six had to offer. It was well that he had time to learn the jargon, the people he was to fly with and the control agencies he would have to deal with before entering the realm of Pak Six.

I'm not sure anyone really adjusted; most of us just slipped into a sort of calm resignation to the inevitable. It didn't take but a few missions to realize, this was war, war of an intensity that guaranteed injury or death. The phrase was, "Ain't no way."

I realized the enemy was courageous, resourceful and determined; no bumbling fools, nothing like those on the silver screen of my youth. I think I'd known it all along, knew even as I watched dozens of Japanese fall dutifully dead under the fire of a single American on a bicycle, that it was a gigantic hoax. Suspicions confirmed. Only one thing to do, shrug and get on with it.

"Ain't no way." I could see it in their eyes, the "older" ones. It just wasn't that big of a deal to be dead. Once that was established, the job was much easier.

New priorities shuffled around with the old: numbers became jumbled, then lined up in a new order. It was necessity, reality barging in.

The counting of missions was important to us, like the score of a ball game, only more vital.

There were frustrations in the Numbers Game, places we had to go that didn't count.

Laos didn't count.

A war was happening in Laos. It was a hot, vicious war, but it didn't count. We went to Laos and knocked down a bamboo bridge or tore up some roadway and they shot at us and knocked some of us down. It really killed me, and literally some of my friends, to fly a "Non-counter" in Laos.

After X number of missions, human nature being what it is, the pilot suddenly realizes he has made it this far alive and it seems that there is indeed a chance that life may be possible. It becomes utterly priceless again, and the warrior becomes a Candy-Ass. He starts planning to survive the terminal disease of war, and his courage leaves him. He is now vulnerable and a hazard to himself and his compatriots.

The bosses recognized this phenomena, and declared the number 90 as "Golden." After reaching 90, you went only to the easy ones again.

The Numbers Game didn't work well. Each man established his own time of usefulness, and most based it on the number 90, I think, instead of 100. So, you see, it could have been an endless thing.

There were some pilots that didn't adjust at all. They lived a pure hell through all 100 missions. Their courage is greater than that recorded about heroes. Certain they are going to die, acknowledging the fact that they were unable to view themselves with proportion, to see insignificance in their own lives and to accept their own death on reasonable terms, they flew every day, and did the job.

Then we had our Heroes. There were very few, thank God. I can only guess as to what went on in their minds. They may have been fighting a life-long feeling of cowardice, and overcompensating wildly—the proof of bravery taking priority over the mission, common sense, and life itself. They were desperate to become a legend and get promoted. They were usually leaders with experience and confidence. They took chances, hung it out a mile. It was usually their wingmen that didn't come back.

The majority of the pilots who flew the Thud into North Vietnam were reasonable, sensible people, capable of feats above and beyond—if crowded—but possessed of a healthy fear that accelerated the mind and aided in the sane completion of the mission.

I like to think I was one of those.

BAK MAI

Somehow, Intelligence had located the headquarters and nerve center of the North Vietnamese Air Force. It was underground, bunkered, and well camouflaged. They had photographs of an entire fake city at Bak Mai, a suburb of Hanoi. Rows of barracks with trucks and bicycles parked outside, streets strangely empty, a Star of David SAM site (unoccupied) and even a field with some kind of orchard. (Infrared photography showed the trees to be the unalive kind.)

Under all this was the center of the air defense system for all of North Vietnam. Coordination between the SAM sites, the MiG bases and the guns of Pak Six came from here. Land lines from thousands of visual outposts in the hills terminated in this elaborate command post. Early warning radar sites reported directly here. To destroy it would mean a major victory at last.

There was a bright air of optimism in the planning room. This looked like progress at last, a target of real importance, one that would make a difference. The Force was being loaded with special, deep-penetration, 2000 pound bombs—big bangs that would get down into the command post if we could put them on target.

We busied ourselves with careful planning. Cappy and I worked together. It was his turn to lead the Force.

The orders directed a route of flight straight in from the west. We didn't like that, but we knew it couldn't be changed. There were tankers, jammer ships, MiG cap, radar warning ships, and many others working and planning from that same order. It was too big an operation to change now, hours before takeoff.

Coming in from the west meant 20 miles of open country infested with SAMs and guns all the way. So be it. We got on the hot line and worked out a few tricks with the jamming folks that would cause confusion in the enemy radar vans. Cappy also put a five mile jog in our course that might fake them out. We felt it was a good plan, not too fancy, just right.

I was on the schedule as airborne spare. For once, I wanted to go to Hanoi, wanted to be in my customary slot on Cappy's wing. But I would go only if someone had mechanical problems and had to turn back.

Planning finished and the briefing complete, we were back in the squadron getting ready to suit up, when Cappy did a no-no. We were in Jack Hart's office talking about a task Cappy needed to complete within a few days. It had to do with searching more film, and recording estimated bombing accuracy.

Cappy said, "I'll get to that when I get back this afternoon." He stood, wearing a sky-blue scarf, hat cocked neatly over the left eye. Ice crept between my shoulders. He looked at me, eyes twinkled as if to say, "It's okay, Geno, just a small breach of etiquette."

I smiled, but fingered the gold coin in my pocket. It's not done. You don't talk about coming back.

An hour later, we met with the tankers high over the hills of Northern Thailand. The rendezvous was smooth and without incident. I waited my turn, flying as Number Five in the second flight. I also waited for someone to develop a gas leak, or rough engine, or anything that would put me on the first string.

My turn came for fuel, and I reached down and pulled the yellow handle that opened the little doors in the nose of the Thud. I slid in behind the trailing probe and held the plane steady a few feet aft of the shiny, worn nozzle. I could see the helmet and dark visor of the "Boomer" peering from the tiny window in the tail of the tanker. He telescoped the boom steadily out, flying it with precision until it slid into the receptacle. The Thud jittered slightly at the contact. A little light in front of me said CONTACT. The airplane soon began to gain weight as the probe forced 12,000 pounds of fuel into it. I held the bird rock steady, advancing power slowly every few seconds to compensate for the weight. Suddenly, the probe was pulled away. Another light said DISCONNECT.

Jet fuel sprayed on my windscreen. I backed slowly down and to the left, my eyes stinging badly as the fuel got into the cockpit vents and misted in my face.

Clear, and again on the outside of the formation, I pulled a handkerchief from my G-suit and wiped my poor, streaming eyes. It occurred to me, for the hundredth time, that the people who designed these systems—this air refueling system in particular—had it in for pilots. I wondered if periodic doses of jet fuel have a permanent effect. I coughed and let the cockpit pressurization clear the air. My hand pushed the refueling handle in. The doors slammed shut and the lights went out.

Still, there was no one experiencing any kind of difficulty. I waited.

"Zebra Force, check in." Cappy was giving us all a last chance to abort. The Force checked in quickly, no aborts.

"Spares, go home."

"Roger, Boss. Luck." I eased out of formation slowly, looking around for the other spare. He was detaching himself from the last flight, dropping low and angling to get on the inside of my turn, joining up with me.

We headed south. Our job now was to avail our firepower to anyone in Pak One that needed us. I lit a cigarette for the trip, and settled back. My wingman flew loosely off my left wing. I was grateful to be headed away from Hanoi, but a guilt trip struggled in my gut.

A bored controller cleared us into Pak One and gave us authority to attack any hostile force we encountered on a certain section of road.

We followed the specified road segment, looking for trouble. We found none.

I checked with the controller again as we exited Pak One. He had a road along a mountain that he wanted cut. We dropped our 2000 pounders just above it, and the mountain fell down on it. Quite a sight!

We headed for Takhli. As we climbed to altitude, I heard a call on Guard channel. "Uh, this is a Mayday . . . (garbled) is down at coordinates (garbled)."

I looked at the fuel gauge and turned north. We had plenty. I called the controller for the north sector, offering assistance. We still had a full load of 20 millimeter bullets.

"Zebra lead is down, stand-by; we may need you."

Cappy.

We continued north and waited for more word. Not wanting to use the radio, I made a drinking motion with my right hand. My wingman showed five fingers. He had about 5,000 pounds of fuel left; still enough. I pulled the throttle back to maximum endurance. We hung in the sky at 300 knots.

Then the word came. "No rescue, Bear flight. Zebra is Downtown . . . copy?"

I copied. Cappy was in Hanoi. No rescue. The

radio was silent. I pictured hundreds of silent men, wanting to say, "Can you verify that?" but not saying it because they all knew it was confirmed. No rescue.

I wanted to do something, push the time button and make it 45 minutes ago. I would say, "Cappy, fuel is streaming from your airplane; I'm taking over," or "Hanoi has surrendered, Zebra. Return to base. This is God. That's an order."

Push the time button again, and it's five months ago. I wrestle Cappy to the ground and whisper in his ear, "We are going to quit, right now, open a Buick agency, we're not cut out for this!"

"Uh, Bear Lead..." It was my wingman. "Shouldn't we turn south?"

"Rodge, turning south." I watched the compass swing reluctantly around to indicate 180 degrees. My hand moved the stick and the compass stopped. Funny how you can turn the whole world around with your hand. The sun, bright and bald, shone on the rolling hills of Thailand, sliding slowly under the nose, so green and lush, stately.

Bob Kennedy had been on Cappy's wing. I cornered him after the debriefing, and he told me all he could. He sat across from me and patiently answered all my questions.

"We started out across the plains east of Hoa Loc, and the SAMs came up early. It was one Intel hadn't charted that got us. Right under our nose, and out of sight. We never saw it until it blew up. They must've moved it in there last night; nobody knew it was there." Bob waved a hand.

"Cappy took it directly under the nose. His bird was on fire instantly, from the nose all the way back. I picked up a bunch of holes from the explosion. I went with Cappy, down and to the right. Jack took over."

He looked at me. "They got it. The whole thing is a big hole." There was a hard gleam in his eye. I felt a twinge of pride, of grim joy, or something.

"We got turned just about south when the canopy came off and the bird pitched over, controls burned through. That's when Ed got out, I think . . . there was so much flame, hard to see anything. I circled back and followed the chute down. I could see him. He didn't move or wave . . . anything. I stayed around after the chute hit the ground. It was in a gully. Never got an answer on Guard. I tried to see him, got too low and they hammered me, had to get out of there."

"Do you think he was hit . . . I mean, do you think he was hurt?"

Bob thought a moment. "He was moving when he was still in the cockpit, and was flying the plane . . . he was able to eject; what more can I say?"

"That really scares me, not moving in the chute. He had a bad neck . . . always worried about ejecting. You didn't hear anything from his radio after he was on the ground?"

"Well . . ." He paused. "This is just my opinion, no real reason, except I'm sure it was Ed's radio . . ."

"Yes?"

"There was a guy talking on Ed's radio. It was senseless junk, Chinese or something; and laughter each time I called. They were trying to imitate me. Like a child's game."

I stared; I saw Ed lying on the ground and a group of smiling North Vietnamese tossing the radio back and forth . . .

"Bob, can I buy some drinks at the club?"

"Thought you'd never ask. Bad weather tomorrow, bad day today, time for some 'mission whusky,' don't you think?"

"Oh yes . . . I'm ready."

The usual crowd in the back bar knew that Bob and Cappy and I had spent a lot of time together. They left us alone.

Bob got philosophical. "This kind of thing has existed since the beginning of recorded history. There have been many Ed Cappelli's and G.I. Basel's killed; war has no favorites, and it goes on."

"Yeah. That's true. I knew that all along, but this is awful close to home. I'm not taking it well."

"Well, I guess a person has to just get into a hypnotic state to get through some of this." Bob took a sip and I took a long pull. The whiskey was raw and good, burning the gut bomb deep inside.

"Trouble is, no matter how distant you remain, something grows when you are flying and fighting together. It's stronger than an ordinary friendship, has a new dimensh . . . dimension. God, I've got the hiccoughs." I guzzled some more of the double whiskey.

"You okay?" Bob looked at my watery eyes.

"No. Got a toad in my throat."

"Frog."

"Okay, frog."

"I'm going to sit down and write B.J.; they'll notify her, but a personal letter..."

"Let me tag on a paragraph... God, waddu'ya say?"

Later, Bob brought a pizza to the table. I'd been showing signs of permanent brain damage.

I swayed in my chair. "Hell, s'bad enough just to be alive, ledalone get dead! That's th' pits!" I pushed the pack of Winstons across to Bob and waved for more booze. "There were 16 of us came here, and how there are..." I held up my hand and counted, "Eight!" I was triumphant. "Don't you see? They are after us!"

"No, G.I...." Bob was trying to get my attention.

"Got our number..."

"You guys were a crop of experience that was needed here. You were put out in front." He grabbed my arm. "That's where the flak is."

Bob was talking from two faces. It was funny to see him talking in stereo. I was trying to say, "What about Tail-End Charlie?" when things got all wormy.

They tell me I was carried out of there.

DUC NOI

The weather in North Vietnam got pretty bad for a few days. We didn't fly at all for three days, and the rain came down. My mood was ugly, matching the downpour outside the quiet Operations shack. I busied myself making charts to hang in the briefing rooms. They provided a graphic, quick method of adjusting the sight picture while in the bomb run. We had been getting some problems with bombing accuracy because we'd been forced into shallow bomb runs by varying circumstances, mostly MiGs, SAMs, and guns. These charts were supposed to help.

It was good to have something to do, something to keep my mind off the sadness that was a physical pain gripping me.

Then the rain stopped and we prepared to launch again. Now, it was my time to lead the Force. It was my check-out as Force Commander. If I came

back, I'd be one. Jack Hart, old "Magnet Ass,"
was the Deputy Commander and my check pilot.
He was flying as Number Three in my flight. Bob
Kennedy was on my wing, flying as Number Two.

We were Bear Flight. I was thankful for that—
sort of thought "Bear" was my own personal call-
sign. Not to seem superstitious, you understand,
but no less than five Zebra leaders had been shot
down in the last month. Coincidence, of course,
but . . .

I pulled the same old tricks on myself as we
approached the tanker, trying to convince someone
inside me that this wasn't happening, that I wasn't
really going to Hanoi, again.

*"Air refueling is a very, very tricky business.
The fuel intake manifold could be cracked and the
cockpit could fill up with JP-4. I'll have to go back
to Takhli, then Jack will have to take the Force
into Pak Six. Let Jack do it."*

I tried hard to break these thoughts and concentrate on the job at hand. My mind raced, trying to
think ahead, to anticipate any problem, large or
small. I had to be ready.

*"Don't think about the sky over Hanoi, the
soaring missiles, the instant overcast, the black 85
millimeter stuff that keeps creeping up and up, as
the gunners feel for your altitude . . . or the idea
that you could get hurtled into cold space, alone;
to be captured, tortured or killed. Killed."*

The refueling was half over. I could see that the
Force was converging on the point in space just
about on time. Nothing was going wrong.

"It could happen right in this snug cockpit, it's happened before. A fragment could penetrate the canopy, shattering the glass and making an awesome noise. It could penetrate the left eye and probably exit at the back of the head, fracturing the camouflaged helmet and ending all thought."

The last of the Thuds were topping off. Everything was on schedule. We would be at the drop-off point in thirty seconds.

"Or . . . much worse, the plane could be hit and burning, and you could be sitting there burning with it and unable to do anything about it . . . and you would finally know what they thought . . . what Cappy thought, then."

I shook my head roughly. Enough of these thoughts! Think about the mission, you are leading this whole shiteree, for Christ Sake! Get it together.

"And, worse yet . . . don't think about your wingman, who is more vulnerable than you—and probably more scared. He is hit and needs your help. He's burning and calling, but your duty is to bomb the target and leave him. Don't think about what you might do."

I took off my mask and rubbed my nose. Did I smell gas fumes? No. Well, don't you worry. The weather is terrible up there.

The Force was congregating behind me, an odd feeling—having nothing ahead but air. I adjusted the throttle gently and took up the planned heading, watching the tankers disappear in the mist to the south.

"Bear Force, strike freq—Go!" My voice sounded calm, authoritative, and slightly laconic. Just a lovely day for flying, gang. See this lovely overcast below us? It goes all the way to Hanoi. We'll just fly up there and take a look, from a safe distance, and then turn back. Weather abort, boys, that's the ticket!

My various electronic companions in the cockpit told me we were crossing the border into North Vietnam. The clouds covering the ground below allowed no visual clue.

"Bear, green up, music on."

I had no sooner spoken than Jack said, "Verified." His electronics agreed with mine. We had indeed crossed the border.

We raped the NVN air. Uninvited, we rammed along, twenty tiny minnows dwarfed by the vast white rug below us.

The Weasels moved out ahead, four barbed bullets holding eight tense men.

"No signals, Bear. No threats to the Force."

Twelve minutes to the target. We were coming in from the west, the same route Cappy had taken. I didn't like it, but was stuck with it.

It was five minutes of flat lowland into Hanoi while the missiles had at you; five minutes of target practice all the way from Hoa Lac to Hanoi. We were to roll in directly over the city, hitting the big rail yard at Duc Noi, two miles north. Our exit was north to Thud Ridge and out.

The thick, heavy carpet of white clouds below us stretched ahead. It looked more and more like a weather abort. I had briefed carefully how I wanted to do it. Too many aborts had been a fire drill, every man for himself. Somehow, it was the hardest time of all to keep discipline and integrity, when the urgency of escape suddenly takes over.

It would be a hard right turn, in afterburner, diving to gain speed. Each flight would keep defensive formation, just as if we were under missile attack. We, the leading flight, would hang back to cover the Weasels' exit.

Ahead, the clouds appeared to break just a little. Nothing serious, just a "sucker hole."

"Guns, sweeping twelve o'clock. SAMs at two; no threats, Bear." The Weasels were five miles ahead of us. "Weather looks bad, Bear."

"Rodge, one more minute."

My hand was beginning to creep to the mike button for the abort order, the call that would send us all scurrying for home, when I saw the Red River and that damnable Y that marks Hanoi.

From my higher altitude, I could see what the Weasels couldn't. There was a hole in the clouds over Hanoi.

"Bear, target is clear at ten o'clock! Afterburner . . . Now!"

The Force acted as one and jumped ahead. The 85 millimeter flak began dirtying the soft, white undercast, and I eased back on the stick, nursing us to a higher altitude.

"One minute, Bear."

Then came the missiles, out of the north at first,

then from the east and some from behind. The flak was getting heavier and was moving up toward us a layer at a time. They knew we were coming and were probably as unhappy about it as I was.

Suddenly, we flashed into the clear, the sprawling black city was just below and glittering from muzzle flashes everywhere. The Red River Valley turned into the Fourth of July just for me.

An angry orange SAM whipped underneath from the left and I called, "Comin' through ... heads up!" A useless call, but absolutely necessary. Two more zipped by and then the sky filled with them.

Most flew high overhead and came down on us, while the flak kept exploding in groups, upward, at ever increasing altitudes, nearer and nearer. It always seemed to work that way, SAMs starting high and squeezing down, flak starting low and squeezing up.

Soon, you were in a corner with no place to go, and, oddly enough, it usually happened at the roll-in point.

I was mesmerized, watching the soaring SAMs. It was unbelievable! The distances and speeds involved defy description. A SAM lifted leisurely off the pad at Phuc Yen, fifteen miles away, and slowly increased speed. In about ten seconds, it flashed by at twice the speed of sound. I watched them and gauged the distance to the target.

"Any second now, don't rush it. Let's get the right dive angle for once. Jeezus, look at the mis-

siles! Flak closer, climb a little more. Look at the Goddamn SAMs!"

"Bear's in." I rolled hard left and pulled the nose straight down. Too steep.

Wham! Something hit the plane hard. The sky was dirty, just like before and the target rotated sharply in my windscreen as I rolled out and began to track.

My target was the SAM site next to the rail yard. The rest of the Force was going after the yard. The yard was full of cars—a bonanza—big ones, little ones, red, black, and brown.

I was diving much too steep, 70 degrees at least, and going like hell. I popped the speed brakes to give me a second more of time.

My world closed to the few inches of bombsight. I knew I'd been hit on the roll-in and some warning lights were on, but I didn't know which ones. I couldn't take my eyes from the bombsight. The SAM site had fired on me . . . straight up. The missile didn't get but a few feet in the air before it turned sideways and exploded, an ugly yellow splash of fire raining on the heads of the controllers.

I pickled my bombs and pulled off just in time to see my three wingmen flash past me. I'd forgotten to retract my speed-brakes! I was amazed then, when I saw all three open speed-brakes. I call that camaraderie—to stop over downtown Hanoi and let me catch up.

The sky was filled with grey and black explosions as we folded our speed-brakes and shot north toward Thud Ridge. I took one quick look over my shoulder. Devastation.

The entire rail yard was blowing up and spewing debris and thick black smoke into the sky. Those boxcars weren't loaded with rice. We must have caught a year's supply of missiles and ammunition in that yard.

My Thud kept acting up as we jinked our way to Thud Ridge. The warning lights were not serious, just irritating, sitting there glaring at me. The fuel gauges were frozen, and the speed-brakes opened and closed at their own whim. There was some black box damaged, but the important parts of the airplane were okay.

The Weasels were having some trouble. They were still under fire covering our exit. Erik Lunde, strike pilot flying with the Weasels, was losing part of his wing. The lead Weasel offered, "Slow down, Otter Two."

"No thanks." Erik was doing about 800 knots.

I called them, reporting that we were out of the package, and they took off for home. Once they slowed down after they crossed the Red River, Erik's wing stopped trying to peel off.

I called the Force over to another frequency for a check-in. All twenty checked in, sounding like a troop of singing seals. They all had made it.

The Big Voice called me personally as we approached the tankers, "Bear leader, you guys really did a helluva thing. The place is still blowing up. Korat had to turn back because their target was obscured by smoke. Good job!"

I gave him a calm "Roger, thanks." It wouldn't do to show any elation or surprise, but I had a hard time masking it.

On the journey home, there was time to rejoice. It had been a good one. I'd been tested and wasn't found wanting. Helluva job. I patted the instrument shroud of the big old Thud and looked out over the big nose, scarred with hundreds of scrapes and scratches from refueling probes.

"Good job, steed."

I tasted the feeling of success. I was a live Force Commander. It was good.

It was just a little hole, about six inches long and one inch wide. A fragment had gone into the electronics bay just behind the cockpit and torn up some wiring.

Intelligence was very pleased. All our sources of information reported that we'd truly wreaked havoc in the rail yard. The SAM site was a goner.

I was just happy that we'd all come back. It was the first Hanoi raid in which we had not lost anyone. Hanoi Hanna reported "Nine Yankee Air Pirates, lost in Duc Noi raid."

Bob Kennedy cornered me and stuck out a hand of congratulations. "How does it feel to be a Force Commander?"

"I don't know!" I laughed. "I made a lot of mistakes . . ."

"Hell! It was a great mission!"

He was right.

THE DOUMER BRIDGE

The end of November brought heavy clouds and rain to Pak Six. We spent our days cutting the trails in Laos and the South, that complicated network of roads and trails known as the Ho Chi Minh Trail. I was working hard and the days went by, wonderfully exempt from death. We were shot at, but it just wasn't the same as Hanoi.

Because of the bad weather, it seemed I wouldn't ever seen Hanoi again.

I wrote in a notebook: "MSN 42—Dien Bien Phu—A nice one in Pak Five. Cut a road through a hole in the weather. Old 'Magnet Ass' Jack Hart led it. They shot at us from the hilltops around Dien Bien Phu—shooting down at us. It was 'different' getting shot at from that angle, scary, since it is so much more visible, and the feeling that the bullets are going to come through the glass at you, instead of up from the bottom armor. Scary. My wingman was elated. He thought the flak was beautiful. That will change. Flak is ugly!"

123

And so it went, relatively easy missions, checking out new flight leaders and wingmen, and the count slowly mounted. We flew into Pak Six two or three times a week, only to abort and to drop bombs on an alternate target in Pak Five or Pak Three.

"MSN 47—Led a happiness job into Pak Three. Easy. Got good hits on a road segment and truck park."

Mother Nature flooded Pak Six, washing away her runways and roads, wiping out her little bamboo bridges and generally doing my job. I rejoiced.

Christmas arrived and I flew into Pak Six singing "Here comes Santa Claus" to myself. We weather aborted and dashed South to cut another of the trails in the jungles of Laos.

Several in the wing finished 100 missions. We had a celebration each time, wearing gaudy flight suits and making humorous speeches. I passed the 50 mark and had my own celebration. "Halfway!" I wrote.

I was getting ready to throw away my red pen when Hanoi broke into the clear. Mother Nature had taken a late Christmas leave.

We had Intelligence briefings each morning, keeping us up to date on the situation in the north. Just as in each bombing halt, the enemy was busy.

In our absence, the North Vietnamese had built the Doumer Bridge back just like new. There was only one thing to do; knock it down again.

• • •

Twenty of us came across the mountains west of Hanoi, weaving at near the speed of sound. Twenty Thuds, each carrying 3 tons of explosives and a busy, watchful green-clad pilot. I was in the third flight. My good friend, Ken Thaete, was on my wing.

The voices on the radio were calm and business-like, but with that certain note of urgency that sparks the senses, sends the adrenaline flowing. It was the kind of talk that is heard in the operating room, each order spoken clearly, and only once. Each member of the team must hear and understand the first time. No second chance.

I was flying my own airplane at last. "Terrible Tina" was her name, and her tail number was . . . 385; that's right, the Wonder Thud.

The SAMs started early. We were still 5 minutes from the bridge when the first lifted out of Phuc Yen. I watched them come, first streaking high and then starting down, gaining speed. Some went under us but most were sailing overhead, not even close. Then they got the range. Other sites joined in the fun and games. Some came in from the target area, head on. One of the Phuc Yen missiles singled me out personally. A great honor.

He was headed right for me. I dipped down slightly, and the missile dipped down slightly. No doubt about it, I was it. I leveled off, and the glowing missile leveled off. I watched it come, a bright yellow dot growing bigger every second. My hand tightened on the stick. When I couldn't stand it any longer, when the fiery dot appeared to be entering the cockpit, I yanked on the stick. The plane shuddered and shot skyward.

The missile tried to follow, but aerodynamics were on my side. Its wings were too small and its fuselage too long. The front canards rotated sharply and served only to stall the missile. It tumbled and began to break apart—and then exploded.

I shoved forward on the stick and floated back down into formation, my map and checklist floating around in the air in front of me. As I settled back into formation, the leader called, "Bear, burner . . . Now!" We shot ahead and started a slight climb, edging up away from the creeping bursts of flak that were beginning. I could see we were too far south. The bridge was 3 miles to our left, too far away for a decent dive angle. Here we go again, I thought.

We rolled in; a disgracefully shallow run. Our sights were set for a 40 to 60 degree dive, and we were only at 20 degrees or so. I wanted to be someplace else. We were hanging it out again.

I was having trouble with Terrible Tina. I kicked rudder and she kicked back! The nose swung around and the wings dipped back and forth in an awkward "Dutch Roll." She wasn't responding to the controls. I managed to horse the bird around and into the bomb run, but couldn't get the sight on the target. The wings were rocking drunkenly and the nose was doing a calypso. I finally stomped both rudder pedals hard, just stood up on them, locking the controls, and she settled down.

Down we came in all our ridiculous glory, twenty screaming fighters strung out on a shallow "glide-bomb" attack on the bridge at Hanoi. I could see the sprawling, grungy city to my left, spewing lead and shrapnel into the air. I was reminded of the famous level run on the bridges at To-ko-ri. It was all wrong. Somebody was going to get hurt.

I had to go lower than planned; much lower. Down I went, lower than common sense allowed, down into the altitude where little old ladies with rocks are lethal. I had to wait for that right combination of airspeed, dive angle, and altitude that would put the bombs on the bridge. It was instinct, not dedication, at work. Ten years of practice had "loaded" my personal computer with certain data. The computer was working in my head, and it was right, except for one small thing. There was a minimum altitude for "safe" delivery of a 3000 pound bomb, and I was already way below it.

The bombs from the first flight were hitting the water. Short. Just so many waterspouts. That proved I was right but, as my thumb touched the bomb button, I knew just how wrong I was. I was way below the minimum altitude. My stubborn thumb refused to abort. It smashed the bomb button even though I was saying "No!"

Whether it was my bombs or the ones ahead of me didn't matter. A gigantic explosive force was pushing, wrenching me to the moon. There was violent buffeting, but I continued to haul on the stick. I wanted altitude.

It felt like I was crashing through rocky hilltops, one after another in quick tattoo. The G-meter pegged and all the other instruments were acting so erratic that it was impossible to read any of them.

Soon it was over, and I was still flying. The gauges looked normal; speed 720, altitude 2400 feet and climbing fast, heading north. Thud Ridge loomed ahead, just minutes away.

I knew the plane was damaged, but it was flying just fine and there were no red warning lights, so I just pretended nothing had happened and jinked my way out of there.

I kept a wary eye on the gauges, especially the hydraulics. They were steady and in the green. Thud Ridge swept under the wing and there were a few flashes of gunfire from one of the peaks as we sailed past, and then we were out of it. The Force was together as we turned west and crossed the Red River, and we spread into individual flights for the trip home. Once we were on our own discreet frequency, I was able to say, "Ken, give me a visual; think I've got holes." I looked over at him. He was close on my wing. I saw his olive-drab helmet nod. He slid down, out of sight below and behind me. I felt the surfing effect as he edged up close to check me over. Soon, he reappeared on my right wing. I could see him shrug.

"No holes, G.I."

I looked away, relieved.

"Uh . . . how about giving me a check?" I looked back. It was impossible, of course, but his visor and mask took on the appearance of a sheepish grin. I knew he had gone all the way. I dropped down, shaking my head, and eased up close to his tail section. The rumble of his engine was loud and I could feel the jet blast from his plane on the rudder. There were no holes!

We were lucky that day, Ken and I. It was a dumb thing we did, but we got away with our skins, and we got the bridge. Sometimes, almost never, but sometimes, it pays to be ignorant.

I told the crew chief that Terrible Tina still had gremlins, bad ones. His grey eyes rolled back in his head.

I put a red mark on my hat, Number 54. Forty-six to go.

In the bar afterwards, I was kidding Ken, "I'm going to put you in for a medal. Anybody that does a dumb thing like we did, deserves a medal."

Almost a year later, GHQ in Hawaii gave us each a D.F.C.

VINH AIRFIELD

MiGs had been increasingly aggressive and numerous. We lost several Thuds to them, and some of our guys were reporting they'd seen Chinese markings. What was more disturbing, the MiG attacks were messing up the missions. It's not easy to bomb a target with a MiG on your tail. We began a concentrated campaign against the Phuc Yen Airfield, and Kep, going there almost every day.

The SAMs were conspicuous by their absence, but the flak continued to be heavy.

I like to think that our successful cutting of the Doumer Bridge, the final dumping of the Rapides Bridge, and the holocaust at the Duc Noi Railyard had deprived our enemy of the SAM missile. They had been firing hundreds of them daily for two months and had finally run out. It looked like progress. If they couldn't get missiles, they probably couldn't get ammo and fuel to their fighting armies in South Vietnam. That, after all, was the reason we were bombing the North, our reason for being there.

We blew up Phuc Yen several times, and we raised havoc with the Ty Nuyen rail yard and industrial complex. The missions mounted, and the marks were all red. Two of our wild Weasels shot down MiGs. Bob Huntley was one of them. It's too bad that they didn't get credit for the victory, because there were no witnesses and the gun film wasn't conclusive.

I led a small Force into Hanoi, but we had to weather abort because of heavy clouds. (That's the ticket, boys!) We went in with eight airplanes and came out with ten! Radar reported our extra buddies, so we stoked the afterburners and ran away from them—MiG 21s out of Gia Lam.

That was my last Pak Six. The weather finally closed in, blanketing the area solid. I had 67 missions, 34 of them in Pak Six. I was bone tired, wiped out. I was desperate for a rest but couldn't get away. Uncle Sam needed a few more drops of blood before I could have a break.

It runs in cycles. No matter who is in charge, no matter how intelligent and talented, he is unable to prevent a dumb historical ailment from recurring. The many lessons learned from yesteryear must be learned over and over again.

In 1965, the boss sent a bunch of Thuds into Pak Three at very low altitude, on the deck. Needless to say, they were at high speed, the fighter pilot's Linus blanket. This is a tactically sound

concept if the target isn't surrounded by 50 miles
of observers with telephones and guns and sharp
eyes and ears. But sneaking under the radar net
does no good if you are picked up and reported by
a thousand eyes. The raid was a disaster. We lost
three or four out of eight planes, and the others
sustained enough battle damage to put the planes
out of commission for months.

A special team, headed by a General, came to
Takhli to investigate and to try and determine the
cause of such losses. The answer jumped out readily: you can't go low enough and fast enough
through a thunderstorm to keep from getting wet.
Most of the targets in Paks Three through Six were
lead storms. The only possible way to attack these
targets was to stay above the magic altitude of
5,000 feet. Below that altitude, the sky was full of
flying lead of all calibres.

But, in late 1967, somebody new came into the
planning shop at Headquarters, someone who
hadn't been around in 1965, someone who had
read a lot of old books from World War II. He was
enthralled with the old concept, liked the picture of
F-105s streaking in on the deck, surprising the pale
Hell out of the enemy and wreaking havoc. In
breathless tones, he sold the General on a daring
attack on Vinh Airfield.

Vinh isn't Hanoi, that vast shooting gallery in
Pak Six, but Vinh was possibly more dangerous
than Hanoi. The density of guns at Vinh probably
surpassed that in Pak Six, even though they were
all in one place.

Vinh was being prepared as a MiG base. This would put MiGs within range of many of our bases in South Vietnam. The Boss didn't want MiGs shooting F-4s in the landing pattern at Danang. Vinh had to go.

Erik Lunde and I were sleeping while all this decision-making was going on in Hawaii. We had done a few hours of planning, drawing lines on maps and taking note of frequencies and code words for a target that was routine. No big deal. Erik was Force Commander and I was Deputy.

We received a call at two in the morning. Wiping sleep out of our eyes, we stumbled down to Flight Planning to see what was going on. The target had been changed to Vinh.

That wasn't all. We were ordered to use an entirely new type of bomb, a low altitude, high drag device that none of us had ever dropped. In fact, the Thud didn't even have the right wiring for the bomb.

As if that wasn't enough, we were to perform the attack under a 700 foot overcast, low level, high speed, with sixteen Thuds. Our bloodshot eyes met over the map of Vinh, and we knew somebody had gone stark mad.

We had about a half hour to plan a route to a new target, get a semblance of an attack plan in mind, and try to dig up some sort of weapon setting that would allow us to drop these bombs somewhere near the target. It was awfully quiet in that room as we discussed the best way in and out of Vinh and began to draw lines on the map.

The only way to get in was from the sea. Vinh was near the coast, and the mountains to the west were impassable. You can't get under a 700 foot cloud layer when you have 1,500 foot mountains. Ain't no way.

So, it was the water. That killed the element of surprise. Coastal radar can pick up fishing boats out in the gulf. They would be ready for us.

From the sea, there were only a couple of ways to go in. We picked the one we thought had the best chance of success, and tried to think positively. Heavy rain was forecast and a visibility of less than two miles. It was going to be wild!

Erik and I felt we'd be lucky to lose only half the third flight, and probably all of the fourth. In the first flight, we might have a pretty good chance to get in and out before they could zero in, but the guys behind us would really catch hell.

The WORD came down in the usual dramatic way, just a few minutes before we were to brief. It was firm, we were going to Vinh.

Erik is a cool one, both on the ground and in combat, but today his coolness was thawed. He briefed well, but his usual manner was marred by a certain tension discernible only by the movement of the pointer and the excessive clearing of the throat.

Under the circumstances, we had come up with a pretty serviceable plan. By use of our radar, not too shiny in the Thud, and plain old "dead reckoning," we intended to let down through the weather over the water and arrive at a point 25 miles south of the target and in the clear. It was going to be a mess, with 16 Thuds in the weather in formation, but there was no other way.

If we were able to accomplish that without running into each other, we would be in a position to set up a low-level attack without too much milling around.

With the basic plan outlined, the Force broke up into individual flights for the detailed briefing. It was impossible to brief our flight. Every Colonel in the world, it seemed, wanted to talk to Erik or me on the long distance phone from Headquarters. There must have been some kind of confusion going on there about this mission! Most of the calls were just anxious inquiries . . .

"Did you make a good plan?"

"Yes, Sir."

"Y'all be careful now."

"Yes, Sir."

It seemed to me (that day) that Hawaii was fanatically determined to cause a failure of an already impossible mission, issuing a nearly impossible order, and then, by harassing the doers unmercifully, making sure there was no time to implement it.

Time came to go to the planes, and I was very unhappy. We hadn't had time to brief the flight properly. We were going to have to "wing it," play it by ear. Bad business.

Then we got the first good news of the day. The third and fourth flights were cancelled. There was a spark of sanity there after all. It was still going to be rough, but it wouldn't be a slaughter.

The rest of the story of this first raid on Vinh is very short.

We didn't go.

We had just finished aerial refueling when we received word that we were diverted to another target. There was no flak, and no damage to the target, because the new bombs failed to detonate. Just so many lumps of iron lying there in the jungle. We would have gone to Vinh for nothing.

This wasn't to be my last round with Vinh Airfield. I was soon to become convinced that Vinh, of all places, was to be my undoing.

I marked a black 76 on my Sierra Hotel hat and packed a bag for Bangkok. It was my turn to get lost for three days.

BANGKOK

I was on a motorcycle, going like the wind, and there was a bus approaching the intersection from the left. I twisted the throttle hard trying to increase speed so I could cross ahead of it. The front wheel came off the ground and wouldn't come down because, impossibly, the throttle was now somewhere out of reach over my head. I accelerated wildly toward the rise of the crossroads, out of control. The motorcycle became airborne as I hit the intersection.

The people on the bus watched and whispered, and I could hear them, "He's going to die." As the ground rushed up, I tensed, trying to will myself back into the air.

I awoke, soaking, in the cool hotel room. Soft music hissed from a hidden speaker. The sun slanted across the room through the gauge at the window. I poured ice water. My mouth was dry and sandy, eating gravel. I was in Bangkok.

The dreams had been coming too frequently. I had died four times in the last week. Obviously, I had a problem. I had come out of my trance, and bright, hoped-for possibility loomed ahead. Twenty-four more times, twenty-four more exposures, and I could go home. Twenty-four more small deaths. The self-hypnosis, the shark's teeth, the lucky coin; it had all run out. I was on my own.

I had come to think I was immune, had a curious sort of ignorance that allowed me to escape real fear. Seventy-six missions and I had used it all up. I had become a candy-ass.

I thought about the people I'd trained with, the sixteen. Seven were gone. Not good odds. There were plenty of other losses in the wing, but our group had really taken a hit, the unlucky sixteen.

Scotty had been picked up and was back in time for dinner. Bob Stirm probably hadn't made it. His shattered aircraft had spun lazily into the soggy ground near the Rapides Bridge.

Ray Horinek might be a prisoner. Jerry Evert couldn't possibly have survived that fiery dive into Phuc Yen. Bill Bennett was a big, smoking hole in the ground. Cappy might have made it, but it didn't look like it. Tom Kirk. He could have made it.

Gene Smith, how about Smitty? Do you survive parachuting into downtown Hanoi?

Brave men, talented and vitally involved in this life are dead or imprisoned, leaving budding families to mourn and struggle alone. A high price has been paid.

For what?

I looked out at the happy people splashing in the pool; some Americans, some Swedish, and mostly Thai. The people of Hanoi are not like the people I see here. They are evil and ugly, so it's okay to be killing them. Right?

Wrong.

And, if it means anything at all, weren't those beautiful people in "South Pacific"? Weren't they "Tonkin"? Tonkin, which is now called North Vietnam?

If we are doing this thing to stop the spread of tyranny into the south, why in God's name are we going about it in such a timid and hesitant manner, like an inept thief, guilty as charged.

Surely, the losses on both sides warrant a bold and speedy execution of this war, not this endless mess with nobody winning.

What justifies the bombing restrictions (Phuc Yen), the "Rules of Engagement" that send us to war with one hand tied behind us? Where is the little grey, bearded man with a stone tablet under each scrawny arm, carved with the complete and final justification of my grisly task?

I moved to the dresser, where the bottle of Early Times and some melting ice waited. The sound of ice against glass was familiar and comforting. It promised a few hours of wisdom and peace.

• • •

Office of People's Rep
NVN Privileged Doc

Mr. President,

Both our countries are beset by an extremely grave situation. In the next decade, there will be no food or energy for our peoples. This is a harsh fact that must be addressed. All shall perish if nothing is done. Some must sacrifice that others may live.

I can't unleash my military on my own people, but military action by an outside power would reduce the population and bring my people together with a single purpose.

Mr. President, your situation is equally grave, and the solution is the same. A small war now will spark your failing economy, strengthen your sadly undisciplined military, test and perfect your new weapons and reduce the population of the productive force.

If this meets your approval, I shall create an incident in the Gulf of Tonkin to get things started.

I await your reply

Ho Chi Minh

The whiskey warmed going down, and I again formed the fictitious letter in my mind's eye. One of the guys had joked about such a letter, but claimed things like that have been done in history.

It was ridiculous, yes, but seemed less so as the

whiskey warmed and more pieces fell into place. It filled the gaps, farfetched as it was. It was so off-the-wall, it would remain forever beyond suspicion, and it Does the Job.

I hooked back the rest of the whiskey and built another, stronger one.

With another amber drink frosting over, standing ready, and chill water of the shower pummelling my body—the answer came like a bolt.

Celestial Madness! Of course! God was held hostage, and we are all patsies in this ugly, screwed up game, manipulated by evil powers who chortle hideously to each other as they view the senseless carnage and the mindless, panic-stricken leaders trying to convince each other and themselves that this, too, is in the name of a higher purpose.

I stood naked and dripping on the cool tile floor and took a long pull on the cold whiskey. It was good to have finally found the answer. Now, with the Answer tucked neatly away in my mind, I was free, and it was time to see the town.

Though it was mid-February, Bangkok was balmy and festive. I wore a light jacket only in case I wanted to visit one of the places that required a tie. Baht was the currency, and I had a fistful of it in my pocket next to my carefully folded tie. Baht would get you anything, and I wanted it all.

Two Baht got me all the way across town in an open-air cart. Six Baht got me a one hour massage and two frosty Thai beers and an almost love affair with an exquisite girl named "Crazy Charlie."

Charlie said my face reminded her of a movie star. Which one, I never discovered. I was pushing for a Steve McQueen, but her jumbled words came closer to Hyvanis Disquat.

Seventeen Baht got me some super food at Nick's Number 1, a converted chicken coop. Candles were in tin cans and the tables were rough wood plank with matching benches. My steak was rare filet mignon cooked inside another lesser cut. I ate them both and learned later that I was supposed to leave the outer steak for the help. I left a big tip.

Riding along in my Baht cab, I saw towering temples everywhere. Bangkok is a forest of temples. The Temple of the Dawn can be seen from miles away, a golden shining needle piercing the skyline. I came close to it, had to see its beauty and touch it.

I was shocked and angry when I found it was made of fragments of coke bottles, saucers, cups, marbles, bottle caps, and every kind of cheap glitter imaginable. Tons of downtown USA glued carefully into a masterpiece.

Once I thought about it, I completely changed my mind. The myth of real gold leaf covering these temples was not nearly the wonder of trash turned to glory before my eyes!

Another four Baht took me to a place where the music was Spanish and the drink was tequila. The large polished dance floor was ringed with dozens of pretty girls, each with a number pinned over her ample breast. The most ample of all was number 4. I danced with number 4 many times. Her name was "Nit Noi," Thai for small. She was tiny and delicate, but small she wasn't. I was going to ask her to marry me, when I recalled that, somewhere back in the real world, I had a wife and two children.

It was such a sobering thought that I went directly to the hotel and went to bed. I slept dreamlessly.

I was up very early, eager to see the Farmer's Market. To see the real Bangkok, you have to get down to the Grand Canal early in the morning. Then the name "Venice of the Orient" can be appreciated.

Farmers from all around gather with their produce. The canal banks are lined with peculiar flat bottomed wooden canoes laden with everything that can be grown or carved or fashioned by hand. Buying and trading goes on at a furious pace. The one who comes late will find that all the bananas or yams or the green whatsitz are gone.

Shoppers cruise in tiny one-person barges and the vendors range from small boats to big jobs with whole families living on board in comfort. Never in my life have I seen cooked food being served from a 10 foot boat equipped with a small charcoal broiler. To me it was a marvel; to the Thais, it was simply a matter of everyday commerce.

Cruising down the canal, the tour-boat sounding

like the "African Queen," I saw an old man, soaped from head to toe, slowly submerge himself in the canal.

Somehow I envied them all, those people of Bangkok, though I knew most of them had very little of anything. I had a feeling they had something I could never have.

Back on shore, I Baht-cabbed over to the Chao Phiya, the big military contract hotel, and found some fellow Thud drivers there. They had been up all night and were having a fine drunk.

Yawning, I sipped an Irish coffee, trying to wake up, and listened to the stories.

One of the guys had totally baffled a hostile MiG pilot the previous day, by stalling his Thud and going into a crazy inverted spin.

After two more stiff coffees, the world took on a warm neon glow. I told about running out of gas over Hanoi with Cappy, adding a few extras for spice.

One big guy from Korat was trying to tell a joke, but nobody could understand him, and he kept collapsing under attacks of laughter.

Strangers gathered around to listen. (We were making quite a lot of noise.) We lazily sprawled on big plush leather couches around a huge glass coffee table. Smoke hung in a blue stratus about head high.

Billy Sparks, our favorite Weasel, was wearing a bright gold flight suit with black insignia and several embossed, embroidered patches. On his left shoulder was a black Jolly Roger that identified him as a "Yankee Air Pirate" in white letters. On his right shoulder was *the* red, white and blue patch declaring "100 missions, North Vietnam, F-105," crowned by a red triangle stating "50 plus Pak VI" (over 50 missions in Pak Six).

Sparky is a master storyteller as well as a crack fighter pilot. Gaudy and impressive with his giant handlebar moustache and waving a silver mug full of whiskey, he was telling about the time he was shot down in Pak Six.

Billy had been hit in a bombing run at Phuc Yen. "I was going like stink and couldn't see a daa-um thing. Smoke so thick I couldn't see the fricking compass, so I blew the lid." His eyes got as big as robin eggs, as he gestured, daintily waving the smoke away from his face again. "It was windy as hell in that damned convertible at 800 per. But, you know, there was still too much smoke to see the compass." He pantomimed taking off his glove, leaning far forward, and flapping furiously at an imaginary compass. "I loosened my shoulder straps and put my nose right on the compass. It said two seven zero, and that's what I wanted."

As Billy stood there, his palm to his nose and his moustache wobbling up and down and his eyes wide with drole concern, the tale of sheer terror and imminent death was causing whoops of uncontrollable laughter.

Billy didn't crack a smile. He looked fierce and

dangerous. "I was so damn mad, that Thud didn't dare quit on me. It just kept on going, burnin' and churnin'."

"How long . . . ?"

"'Bout a year. Damn near to Dien Bien Phu. Then it got awful mad, put its head between its legs and started grazin'. Since I stopped eating dirt years ago, I jettisoned the whole burning mess.

"Y'know? That damn thing turned around and took a swipe at me before it blew up against a rock. Didn't even bounce once."

Billy sat down. "Rubber bumper in the nose didn't work." He took a sip.

The laughter was destroying me, and so was the coffee. I ordered a stinger in a stemmed glass. Stingers have a special elegance for me, ever since I saw Cary Grant take over a hotel and order stingers all around, "and keep them coming." I thought that was a good line. We all had a drink in our hand.

The room became quiet, as if we all had the same thought at once. Billy looked all around and raised his mug. "To those who didn't make it."

"Hear, hear," we chanted.

VINH AGAIN

The misguided but articulate planner at head-quarters had been working hard to get my innocent body over Vinh. We had briefed twice more and flown once, trying to get to Vinh. One was weather aborted before takeoff and the other was a real fire drill as eight Thuds thrashed around under the weather trying to get to Vinh through a canyon in the mountains to the west. The clouds were on the deck.

I never got to Vinh, thank God, but did so much planning for it that I feel I have been there. I can see the runway, partially complete, the stacks of construction materials, the SAM radar vans, the control tower. I even dreamed about going there, and it was so real, it deserves to be told here:

We were the second flight of four, loaded with six bombs each. The weather was right down to the water, 200 feet or so. It was ragged, and we were popping in and out of it as we raced toward Vinh at 500 knots. We didn't think about MiGs.

147

They have more sense than to fly around in that kind of weather.

The water was grey and peppered dull with rain. We couldn't see more than a mile in front of us. I was using the radar to navigate. On the radar scope, I could see the coast ahead and the river inlet that I'd selected as my timing point. I had the timer set for 4.2 seconds. At the river, my thumb would hit the pickle button, and I would hold precisely 500 knots until the bombs came off. If the map was accurate and if I could hold exactly the right heading and exactly 500 knots, and if the timer was right, the bombs would fall on Vinh Airfield.

The plan then called for a hard right turn, descending to absolute minimum altitude, 50 feet or less, and on out east to the water. No one was to enter the clouds under any circumstances. That was certain death. It's not possible to dodge an unseen SAM, and SAMs can see through clouds.

We could hear the first flight crossing the river...

"Zebra lead's pickling...now!"

"They're shooting, lead."

"Can't help that."

"Two is hit!"

The flight ahead was already in trouble.

"Bombs away...Break right!"

"Zebra three is in the weather...!"

The river loomed suddenly in front of us. I punched the button as we flashed across it. I held

200 feet altitude and exactly 500 knots. Tracers were flying everywhere and there were two big fires burning off to the right of us. I froze, waiting for 4.2 seconds to elapse. My peripheral vision caught sight of a tumbling, splashing fireball to my left. One of mine, no radio call.

The bombs came off.

I was in the weather. The Thud just jumped up 200 feet when the bombs came off. I desperately tried to decide which way was up as I scanned the instrument panel. The gauges meant nothing to me . . . Just so many blank, glassy eyes, staring at me. "Oh boy, here we go!" I thought. Vertigo was there, and I was upside down. Then the gauges made sense.

I was turning right, altitude 600 feet. I kept turning and tried gently to ease the Thud back down out of the clouds. Vertigo was still with me . . . telling me to go up, which was really down. A form flashed by, brilliant and golden. SAM?

Suddenly, I was out of the weather going down. Too steep. The ground came up fast and I pulled hard on the stick. The airplane swapped ends, out of control, and I broke a filling but didn't feel the impact as I hit the ground. My brain switched off.

I awoke as before . . . soaked. It took many minutes before my breath came in even packages. I'd always heard that a person can't dream of his own death. Aren't you supposed to wake up just before it happens?

MU GIA PASS

Khe Sanh was hot. There was a full-scale war going on there, and we had become a part of it. The weather in Pak Six had become consistently unworkable, and the struggle at Khe Sanh had become crucial. It was first priority for everyone.

The Thud would go farther, faster, and carry more bombs into the enemy heartland, than any other fighter we had. But it wasn't designed to perform "close in" like the work required at Khe Sanh. The mission required fast turning and quick response. It was like sending a locomotive to compete in the local stock car races.

We abandoned our One Pass—Haul Ass tactics and changed our sight setting and dive angles to "get down amongst them." We were going to enter a racehorse in the roping event.

Armed with our revised tactics, I leaped off with a flight of four, headed for Khe Sanh. We were Bear flight, my usual call sign. On my wing was Colonel McKinney, my new Squadron Commander. Flying Number Three was Colonel Pickett, the Vice Wing Commander. Number Four was Captain Don Harten. I was flying Terrible Tina.

We were refueling when Colonel Pickett had an electrical fire in the battery compartment. There's no need taking an already screwed up airplane into combat. Colonel Pickett headed for Takhli. I sent Don with him for protection. That left two of us.

We filled up with gas and Tina behaved like a lady. No tantrums. We went to an orbit point and waited for instructions. The orbit point was like the holding pattern for Los Angeles International Airport. There was no shortage of air power at Khe Sanh. Dozens were orbiting and waiting, just like us.

After an hour, we began to get short on gas, so we were sent north to a place near Mu Gia Pass. A "Misty" had a target for us. The Misty FACs were Forward Air Controllers piloting F-100s.

Misty pilot Eben Jones had been working this area for months. He knew the territory well. Jonesy knew there was some fuel oil hidden in the jungle near a dirt road. He directed our eyes to a particular patch of jungle, then wheeled his F-100 around to pinpoint the target with a smoke rocket.

We had Jonesy's smoke in sight. "Bear Two, take spacing."

"Roger that." Colonel McKinney zoomed high and to the outside of my turn, getting distance between us so he could watch my bomb run and have time to adjust his for better accuracy. There was no need for mutual protection here. It felt strange, rolling in from such a low altitude, and rolling in alone. I pressed in and rippled off the bombs. Bingo!

Large black secondary explosions tore great holes in the jungle. I'd hit pay dirt! Number Two got the same results.

We had two more bombs each, loaded on the wingtips where the jammers had been in more exciting days. No need for jammers here.

"Misty, Bear's got some more bombs. Need another pass?"

"Sure can use it, Bear. Put 'em just 100 feet west of the last bunch. There's more stuff in there than I thought."

I rolled in for the second run, feeling almost guilty. No ground fire. There hadn't been many milk runs such as this. It didn't seem fair, bombing without opposition.

My sense of fairness was served in less than a heart beat, for as the bombs came off, a hidden gunner opened up and hammered Tina with bullets. The impact was sudden and violent. Instantly, both fire warning lights glowed red on the panel in front of me. I knew I wouldn't be having dinner at Takhli that night.

I pulled off and turned left, heading for safe territory 80 miles west.

"Lead's off with a hit."

It was a dumb radio call. It sounded like I had commented on my bombing accuracy.

"Roger, lead. Bear Two, drop your bombs a little south of lead's."

"Will do, Misty."

My rearview mirror showed a blazing inferno immediately aft of the cockpit. The airplane was a torch. It was time to get un-calm.

"Hey! This is Bear lead. I'm hit, heading west; got me?"

Colonel Mac looked up then and saw me, a white-orange fire, heading west. "Got you in sight. You're on fire; better get out!"

I didn't answer, for my problems were compounding by the second. The temperature gauge was pegged at 1000 degrees, and smoke began pouring into the cockpit. What really got my attention was the RPM gauge. It was winding toward zero. My precious engine, my transportation out of there, was a clanking, banging mess, grinding to a halt. That was not fair.

I could smell the acrid smoke and my eyes stung. It had become very quiet.

Suddenly the stick had no effect. Then the nose pitched down. I had no choice. I gulped a breath, took up the fetal position, and pulled the ejection handles.

Nothing.

I was still seated in the burning plane; the seat had failed. I was supposed to be out there, not still in here. My thoughts were a classic. Zero, zip. Just sat there squeezing the triggers, feeling cheated.

Suddenly, the universe ripped in half!

Fifty thousand pounds of burning fighter plane exploded into aluminum and steel confetti. A noise louder than I ever knew a noise could be hammered me. I could hear it in my pores. I was being mauled and pounded by a gargantuan animal and my arms and legs were being yanked in every direction at once. The parachute wasn't opening . . . if there was a parachute.

It seemed like forever that I twisted and spun and flailed through the sky. I felt calm, but sad. At last, it had come true; no more need to worry.

Then everything stopped with a jolt. I was jarred and stretched from shoulder to toe when the chute opened. I didn't mind at all. I was momentarily suspended level with the horizon, and there was a beautiful orange and white umbrella behind me, slowing my swift dash across the sky. My speed diminished and finally I hung peacefully in the harness.

I could see what was left of my plane, just a sky full of fluttering pieces of metal. A loud report sounded from the land below, an echo of the explosion, Terrible Tina's swan song. I saw the seat sailing merrily away from me at unbelievable speed.

It took several minutes to descend. During that time, I discovered that the explosion had broken both legs. They hung lifeless from my body. The armored seat had probably saved my life, but it was also the reason for my fractured thigh bones.

The jungle was rushing up to me, and I was headed for a towering jagged karst. If I slammed into the side of it, or landed on top with two broken legs . . . forget it!

I pulled hard on the rear shroud lines, trying to slow my forward motion and land short of the rock. The chute spilled and swung wildly; I almost had a cardiac arrest. I let go and looked at the rock rushing up. Gingerly, my hands reached again for the lines. As I reached, I could see that four lines were broken and some panels of silk were blown out.

I was going to hit the rock. I had to do something. Gently, I tugged on the lines and it seemed as if the forward motion slowed. I pulled some more and held my breath as the trees came up fast. I'd made it.

Just before entering the jungle, I caught a glimpse of a soiled and tattered parachute hanging from the side of the karst. Someone hadn't made it.

I crashed through the tops of the tallest trees at a slant. I was spun around, my legs flailing crazily over my head. I plunged into thicker, darker jungle, banging and crashing, falling through foliage and vines and branches and slowing down all the time. Finally, the chute snagged, and I came to rest, suspended fifty feet from the jungle floor.

It was quiet, very quiet. I sensed the creatures had stopped what they were doing and were waiting, listening for what this noisy intruder might do next. Slowly, my head turned, directing my eyes to peer into the dense jungle. I examined my surroundings politely and discreetly. Each second, I expected a pair of brown and hostile eyes to meet my gaze. None did. I was alone for the time being.

My helmet was gone, many of my flightsuit pockets torn away, the survival kit was lost, and there was a lot of blood coming from the side of my head. Now was the time to be calm. I thought about what to do next, and that made me sleepy. I passed out.

Reality came and went. I hung in the tree for an hour and a half. I passed out and revived many times. During the times I was conscious, I made contact with the rescue planes on the small emergency radio. The helicopter was on the way, and it was a race against darkness, just two hours away. Each time I awoke, I felt worse. Shock was setting in. My dreams were always that I was dreaming I was hanging in a tree in a hostile jungle. Each time I opened my eyes, the jungle was still there.

The radio was hanging at the end of the cord. I could see it down below, dangling into the darkening jungle. I had no idea now long I'd been out. It crackled.

"I haven't heard from him in 20 minutes."

"Keep trying."

"Roger. Looks bad, it's almost dark."

My hands were working furiously, pulling the radio up to me.

"Hello, Bear Leader, Bear Leader, come up voice, Bear." The voice had a hopeless note to it, as if he'd gone through this sort of thing before.

The little squawking box was three feet from me when I dropped it. My hands were feeble and baby weak. Finally, the radio was in my hands, hissing. I wrapped the cord around my left hand and the radio, bonding them together. I punched the mike button.

"Bear Leader here, I'm here." My voice had a weird hollow sound.

"Roger, Bear! We got a little worried there. Don't go to sleep now, you hear? We have a chopper on the way; he'll be over you in five minutes. Hang on!"

"Okay, thanks."

Strength pumped through me when the "whap-whap-whap" of the "Jolly Green Giant" filtered down through the tangled jungle growth.

The chopper hovered over me, creating a small hurricane that sent branches flying around and me tumbling merrily out of the tree. The chute snagged again about ten feet from the ground and I hugged a big grey tree trunk for dear life.

Down came a long rope with a young man dressed in striped jungle fatigues, hanging on the end. We stared at each other while leaves and dirt and branches flew around. It was a sort of slow motion, nightmare scene. He was reaching out, and I was reaching out, but our hands lacked five feet of touching. He was on the rope, and I was in the tree. Finally, he radioed something, and the line was let down to the jungle floor.

I know I probably looked like a madman, with flying hair and a bloody face and wild eyes. Those hanging legs were a feature that added to the over-all effect. I wonder to this day if I may have scared him, just a little.

His name was Joe Duffy, and he was 20 years

old. I'm sure it occurred to him (as it did to me) that if we kept fooling around down here, there was a good chance that some alien people would come and kill us both.

Joe was getting ready to scale the tree when I motioned I was coming down. I swung away from the tree trunk and pulled the emergency release. Down I went, like a giant rag doll, and damn near landed on top of him.

We both scrambled onto the folding jungle penetrator at the end of the rope. Then Dale Oderman, the chopper pilot, began to ease us out of the jungle. Slowly, up five, left three, with Joe radioing instructions. I was so weak that my pale hands would hardly grasp anything. I was in danger of slipping off. Even though I was trying with all my might, gritting my teeth, my hands wouldn't grab. Joe kept a white-knuckle grip on my sleeve, as we agonized our way slowly up through the trees and vines.

Then we were free, and I heard Joe shout, "Let's get out of here!"

Dale gunned the big Super Jolly, and the jungle fell away. Joe and I were on the end of 200 feet of swinging cable, and I should have been scared and nervous about the ever increasing height, but I just hung there and watched the jungle whirl and recede, and I muttered "Good-bye" over and over again in a senseless and primitive chant.

POSTSCRIPT

I lay in traction in the hospital at Korat. The war was over for me. I was enveloped with a wild appreciation of being alive. The nurse closed the blinds, and I begged her to open them again so I could look out at the world. She understood. The view was nothing. An open field with a lamppost in the center, growing out of a small pond of light. I stared and stared through the window.

I hurt all over, especially in the legs, but the hurt was good. Dead guys don't hurt.

A postcard lay on the bedstand, signed by all the men in my squadron.

Jack Hart wrote, "Who's the Magnet Ass now?"

The last signature was Colonel McKinney's, my recent wingman who had witnessed my swift departure from the world of flight.

"Lost every one in the flight on my 4th mission. Only 96 to go!"

• • •

Later, they came all at once, the entire squadron, dressed in festive blue flight suits. They crowded into the hospital room, filling it with animated movement, the 354th Fighter Squadron, my squadron.

It was an honor, being visited like that. I was embarrassed.

They were upright, walking around with the fine edge of survival lighting their eyes. They told me of things that were happening, and I hardly listened, for I was no longer one of them. That was no longer my world. Safe, content, and going home, I was a lesser being. The fine edge was gone.

The Boss presented me with the Purple Heart, pinned it on my pillow. I should have made a speech, but I was empty, burned out. They filed out finally, calling good wishes, and suddenly I wanted to go with them.

They left me a patch to wear, should I ever put on a flight suit again. It was red and blue, with white letters:

It's been many years since I went down and was lucky enough to be rescued. Those years have been dear, but vaguely unhappy. Part of me was always with my friends, suffering an unknown fate. Then, a few years back, some came home. The reunion was fantastic!

Tom Kirk, Gene Smith, Bob Stirm, and Ray Horinek made it home. Jerry Evert and Bill Bennett didn't. Neither did Cappy.

I walk the streets, and still I grieve for those that didn't return, and for those that did. For all the others and for myself.

We are all permanently changed, and not for the better. We ask a collective question: What was it all about? This magnificently orchestrated endeavor that accomplished nothing.

Casualties of this monstrous charade, we ask: for what?

TRUE ACCOUNTS OF VIETNAM
from those who returned to tell it all . . .

___PHANTOM OVER VIETNAM: FIGHTER PILOT, USMC John Trotti
0-425-10248-3/$3.95

___MARINE SNIPER Charles Henderson
0-425-10355-2/$4.99

___THE KILLING ZONE: MY LIFE IN THE VIETNAM WAR Frederick Downs
0-425-10436-2/$4.99

___AFTERMATH Frederick Downs
Facing life after the war
0-425-10677-2/$3.95

___NAM Mark Baker
The Vietnam War in the words of the soliders who fought there.
0-425-10144-4/$4.50

___BROTHERS: BLACK SOLDIERS IN THE NAM Stanley Goff and
Robert Sanders with Clark Smith
0-425-10648-9/$3.95

___INSIDE THE GREEN BERETS Col. Charles M. Simpson III
0-425-09146-5/$3.95

___THE GRUNTS Charles R. Anderson
0-425-10403-6/$4.50

___THE TUNNELS OF CU CHI Tom Mangold and John Penycate
0-425-08951-7/$4.50

___AND BRAVE MEN, TOO Timothy S. Lowry
The unforgettable stories of Vietnam's Medal of Honor winners.
0-425-09105-8/$3.95

THE BEST IN WAR BOOKS

___DEVIL BOATS: THE PT WAR AGAINST JAPAN
William Breuer 0-515-09367-X/$3.95
A dramatic true-life account of the daring PT
sailors who crewed the Devil Boats—outwitting
the Japanese.

___PORK CHOP HILL S.L.A. Marshall
0-515-08732-7/$3.95
A hard-hitting look at the Korean War and the
handful of U.S. riflemen who fought back the
Red Chinese troops.
"A distinguished contribution to the literature
of war."—New York Times

___THREE-WAR MARINE Colonel Francis Fox Parry
0-515-09872-8/$3.95
A rare and dramatic look at three decades
of war—World War II, the Korean War, and
Vietnam. Francis Fox Parry shares the
heroism, fears, and harrowing challenges of
his thirty action-packed years in an
astounding military career.

234

6TH
EDITION

FIND IT FAST

Extracting Expert Information From
Social Networks, Big Data, Tweets, and More

ROBERT I. BERKMAN

CyberAge Books
Medford, New Jersey

Information Today, Inc.

First printing

Find It Fast, Sixth Edition: Extracting Expert Information From Social Networks, Big Data, Tweets, and More

Copyright © 2015 by Robert I. Berkman

Library of Congress Cataloging-in-Publication Data

Berkman, Robert I.
   Find it fast : extracting expert information from social networks, big data, tweets, and more / Robert I. Berkman. — Sixth edition.
      pages cm
   ISBN 978-1-937290-04-7 (paperback)
   1. Information retrieval.   2. Research.   3. Internet searching.   4. Search engines.   5. Information resources—Evaluation.   I. Title.
   ZA3075.B47 2015
   025.0425—dc23

                                                                        2015019680

Printed and bound in the United States of America

President and CEO: Thomas H. Hogan, Sr.
Editor-in-Chief and Publisher: John B. Bryans
Associate Editor: Beverly M. Michaels
Production Manager: Tiffany Chamenko
Indexer: Nan Badgett

Interior Design by Amnet Systems
Cover Design by Alison Gallagher-Rehn

infotoday.com

To Sol, Pat, Budd, and Don

Contents

Part I: Sources

Part II: Searching

Part III: Experts Are Everywhere

List of Figures

Tables

Acknowledgments

I'd like to express my gratitude to the many people who in one way or another played a big part in making this book come to pass, from the first edition published in 1987 through this one, the sixth.

My wife, Mary Walsh, gave me encouragement at the most critical moments—without it the book would not have been written. George Finnegan has been a true mentor. I'll always be thankful for the chance to have worked for him which was a once-in-a-lifetime learning opportunity. Janet Goldstein, my first editor at HarperCollins, believed enough in the book to give it a chance and always provided support and great ideas.

Nancy Brandwein, Ken Coughlin, and Lilli Warren all offered critical insights, suggestions, and critiques of the original manuscript. Those who assisted with past editions include Sandy Gollop, Debbie Cohen, Ginny Fisher, Leigh Woods, Hella Rader, Cindy Pereiri, Jeff Goodman, Pam Goodman, Marie Kotas, and Trisha Karsay. Thanks are also due to Sasha Mishkin for her valuable help with the new edition.

I'm very appreciative of my colleagues at Information Today, Inc., particularly my editor John B. Bryans for helping get this 6th edition published after a 15-year hiatus from the 5th. I've been fortunate to have a helpful and encouraging team to work with for many years, publishing my books and the monthly research journal I co-edit, and supporting my other professional endeavors. I also want to note my appreciation for the excellent work of Beverly Michaels for her careful reading of the latest manuscript and her vital observations and questions that helped shape it into a better book.

A special thank you goes to everyone in the Norris family for providing me with such a beautiful and relaxing spot in which to write the first edition, in North Truro on Cape Cod.

Finally, thanks to my parents and brothers for their love, support, and invaluable ideas.

Preface to the Sixth Edition

It's simple to go on the web and find information. So why would you need a book about doing research?

Perhaps if you Google that question you'll find the answer.

Actually . . . no. Googling that question won't get you a good answer. There are, in fact, still countless queries and information problems for which the answer won't be found via Google. Or Wikipedia. Or Twitter. And that's one of the points of this newly revised book on how to find credible information and perform good research.

Find It Fast, first published in 1987, was last revised for its fifth edition in the year 2000. That's eons ago in the information world, and an awful lot has happened in that world since then. For example Web 2.0, Wikipedia, Twitter, citizen reporting, sentiment detection, real-time search, social media, Google+, Pinterest, Instagram, Tumblr, YouTube, Vine, tagging, cloud collaboration, the wisdom of crowds, collaborative filtering, LinkedIn, Klout, Siri, Snapchat, social media monitoring, Facebook, Foursquare, and Flickr—and more!

Back in the year 2000, all those concepts and sites were either not around or barely emerging. That's an enormous amount of change in the information world.

But a lot has *not* changed—specifically, the elements of doing good research. For example, understanding how sources differ, knowing which resources to use, finding and evaluating experts, verifying information, understanding surveys, controlling one's biases, asking the right questions, assessing source credibility, disregarding the noise, understanding what's truly significant, and knowing when to conclude a project.

The More Things Change . . .?

Can we say, then, that doing good research has not fundamentally changed, but that the sources, tools, and strategies have changed?

Well, not quite. Not only have the sources, tools, and strategies clearly changed, they have, in fact, changed *so* dramatically that they have produced a revolutionary rethinking in many aspects of what constitutes good research.

Why are these changes truly *revolutionary*? We have to start by looking back to the mid-1990s, with the arrival of the internet, of course, which demolished the high barriers to entry for becoming a publisher. The last time we had a change *that* revolutionary for creating and distributing information was over 600 years ago when a German by the name of Johannes Gutenberg came up with the concept of movable type.

By the early 2000s we saw the emergence of the social web—or Web 2.0 as it was then known. Initially, interaction on the web was primarily in the form of blogs, but this innovation was quickly followed by an explosion of other two-way information-sharing platforms: Flickr, YouTube, Tumblr, MySpace, Facebook, and many others. The social web permitted anyone to share his or her opinions, knowledge, and content, and to become part of a larger global *conversation*. As a result, we have all had to rethink some fundamental assumptions about what constitutes a credible source and, therefore, what it means to do "good" research.

Who's an Expert?

Who counts as a trusted source today? Before the social web, an individual established his or her authority on a subject through credentials (e.g., a PhD in history, an MA in design, etc.) or with their published works, professional presentations, or other means that demonstrated recognition by institutional gatekeepers such as universities, publishers, and editors.

If a person could manage to clear those hurdles—write the dissertation, get a presentation approved, have an article published, be quoted in a news story—then he or she was given the mantle of legitimate authority. The rest of us could then feel certain that he or she was in fact a credible source of expertise.

The internet and, more recently, social media have forced us to reconsider, or at least expand, our criteria for who should be considered an authority and whose views and knowledge are worth taking seriously.

Today we live in an information-rich environment, where the views of countless people without any formal—or even informal—credentials, who have never been peer reviewed or quoted in a newspaper, never presented at a conference or even created a piece of work, are given a great deal of credence. Consider, for example, the popularity and sometimes even prominence of certain bloggers, "citizen-journalists," YouTube producers, prolific Wikipedia entry writers, or just someone with a high "Klout" score. These people are sometimes trusted as credible sources. Should they be given that recognition just because they are popular? Should popularity really confer authority and expertise?

These critical questions will be discussed later in this book.

And what about the whole "wisdom of the crowd" meme: that, in certain circumstances, a larger group of ordinary people is smarter and more likely to come to a more accurate decision than any one individual—even if that individual is an expert?

These are the kinds of questions that are creating major—in fact revolutionary—changes in how we all create, find, and assess information sources, and they will be treated in detail.

Big Data and Big Challenges

The question of expertise—who currently deserves to be considered a legitimate authority and credible source—is not the only dramatic change faced by information searchers today. Of course, there is little difficulty these days in finding a simple fact or answer, or even turning up a good description of a place, person, or thing. Link to a search engine, key (or speak) a few words into Google, and get matching results instantly—that's as easy as it gets.

But significant challenges are still faced by those with more involved research tasks. One is simply how to sort through and make sense of the countless streams of incoming real-time data continually washing over us. The fact that we are *all* becoming publishers and broadcasters means that more and more data is generated—from tweets to video clips—making it that much harder to discern what truly deserves our precious and limited attention.

One increasingly popular approach for making sense of the growing ocean of information is to rely on "big data," perhaps the hottest buzzword in the business and technology world. The term describes the use of super-powerful computers to collect, crunch, and analyze the enormous and ever-increasing quantities of information being produced these days. There are countless sources of data, ranging from people's social media profiles to sensors on household objects, supermarket scanners, weather station reports, and smartphone geolocation data.

The promise of big data lies in its ability to deeply analyze so much disparate data, find correlations, and surface previously hidden patterns to provide new insights and drive more informed decisions. The big data phenomenon also presents challenges for the researcher, described later in this book.

The Value of *Find It Fast* in the Digital Age

Finally, you may be wondering about the value of some of the items included in this book or even the concept of the book itself.

Why, for instance, have I bothered to include certain seemingly old-fashioned print directories and indexes in the library chapter? While there are a few reasons print is still valuable, as discussed in Chapter 2, one subtle but quite important reason is that using these types of sources serves as an important check on your internet searching, which generally gives the highest rankings to the most popular sites. This is fine as far as it goes (much more on that process in Chapters 3 and 5), but what it means is that while you are likely to get a lot of results published by the best known and most used news and information sources, such as *The Huffington Post*, *The New York Times*, *CNN*, the *Guardian*, *TMZ*, etc., you are much less likely to turn up articles published in very small, niche, and lesser-known journals and news sites. And sometimes these turn out to be your best sources.

By adding an old-fashioned print index and directory to your set of research tools, you can at least complement this search-engine ranking method by using a source with a different mechanism for discovery, and thereby override the built-in biases of the search engines. You then have a more rounded set of results than you would receive from a Google search alone—and that's a good thing.

Given the speed of change in this arena, you may also wonder how long a book like this can remain relevant and useful. That's a good question.

It is certainly true that the websites and search tools referenced in this book are bound to change, so I've addressed this issue in two ways: first, by including only sources that have been around—or are most likely to be around—for a long time. But even more importantly, the heart of this book is not a list of sites or the technologies of the moment. It is all about cultivating a deeper understanding of the critical principles of research and what it means to be a good researcher in the digital age.

Finally, a few more words on the journey this book has taken since its first edition in 1987.

The introduction to that initial edition began with the remark that "it may come as a surprise to you, but for virtually any subject, facts and information are out there—by the truckload." The book promised to provide the necessary know-how so the reader would "be able to get the kind of information that's normally available only to a select few."

But by fifth edition, published in 2000, the power of the internet—as a source of an unfathomable amount of information to anyone, anywhere, anytime—was becoming more fully realized. And that edition of the book concluded with some thoughts on the potential of this amazing new technology:

> The internet provides explanations for problems or concerns that may have stumped us for years . . . The sum total of all of our knowledge and thoughts, in fact, is increasingly being made public, linked and accessible. All sorts of artifacts of knowledge are being digitized, made searchable and available . . .
>
> Of course, the internet will never answer the deepest human questions . . . or will it? And finding answers to one set of questions allows for, and even compels, the emergence of a new set . . . and so our questioning will surely continue.

And so it continues today.

Here's to getting your questions answered—and then generating new and even better ones!

Introduction

Who's in Charge of Your Research, Anyway?

If someone were to ask you who's in charge when you do some casual searching on the web, your response would likely be something like, "Well, I decide what I'm looking for online. Most of the time I go to Google, enter the words for what I want to find, and I get my results. So I'd say that *I'm* in control."

Well, not to get too Matrix-like on you, but there are a whole host of hidden entities that are jockeying for your attention and working to control what you are able to do, how you are able to do it, and what results you will view. Among the most powerful behind-the-scenes forces are the following.

Google Itself

As will be examined in detail in Chapters 3 and 5, Google prioritizes the pages that are most popular—these are the ones with lots of incoming links. It also prioritizes web pages that, according to its calculations, are supposed to be of highest interest to you personally, based on your past search history, geographic location, and other individual factors.

Search Engine Optimizers (SEOs)

SEOs use a variety of techniques—some approved by Google, others more iffy, to try to drive their clients' pages to the top of the returned list. This means that what you see from your research not only reflects your search statement and Google's own ranking algorithm, but also the skill and intent of other entities trying to get their pages ranked highest.

Clickbait Creators

Clickbait is the term used to describe those ridiculous yet oddly alluring headlines crafted just for the purpose of getting you to click and read the story. Unfortunately, research shows that these absurd techniques often do work, due to creating what's called a "curiosity gap" in us, causing our minds to seek the missing information.[1]

So what's a good researcher to do?

First we might ask, Why is any of this a big deal? Haven't there always been external forces directing how we do research?

No, not really; at least not in the same way.

In "the old days"—let's put that before the mid-1990s or so—when a researcher went to consult his or her sources, whether it was an encyclopedia, reference book, journal, magazine, primary document such as a letter or photo, or a traditional searchable online database, the primary forces that determined what the researcher would find included only the following:

- The scope, content, and timeliness of that resource (archive, timeliness, quality controls, etc.)

- The methods and limitations of the tool employed for searching a set of data or sources (ability to find a citation vs. abstracts vs. full text; ability to do advanced keyword searches, etc.)

- The researcher's own skills and abilities to construct an effective research strategy and search statement

- The method selected by the publisher/database to define what constitutes a relevant result (keyword match, recency of item, etc.)

But now we all must contend with external forces whose larger goals don't necessarily coincide with our own as researchers.

The fact is, unlike a library database or other traditional information provider, these entities do not have the same overriding goals as we do. They include a larger mission that typically means attracting more users, luring in paid subscribers, selling advertising, collecting data, and ultimately turning a profit. And so what we ultimately end up seeing as searchers in some manner serves those overriding goals.

A primary purpose of this book is to help put you back in control of your own research. This means having a level of digital information literacy so you are aware of the various forces that impact what you find and why, and enough knowledge and understanding of today's information environment so you are in the driver's seat—finding what you need and seeing and working with sources that are going to best fulfill your research needs.

What can you do to ensure that you are in charge, that you're steering the ship and finding the best—most relevant, insightful, timely, and credible—information?

That's where this book comes in.

What's Inside This Book

A preliminary section, "Getting Started," will help you define what information you're really after and organize your plan of attack. Part I consists of two chapters that identify specific information sources and provides tips on how best to find and use each of them. Chapter 1 is a compilation of my favorite all-purpose and powerful "super sources," ranging from associations to museums to government data, which are among the best resources for virtually any research endeavor. This chapter also identifies some of my favorite open access sources. These are scholarly books, journals, and other resources that were created to be free and available to anyone, reflecting the goals of the open access community to make information more freely available and outside of expensive and restrictive paywalls. Chapter 2 explores how to find the right library, why libraries are still valuable in the age of the internet, some of the best ways to use your library, and even when it is most effective to use print sources.

Part II looks at what it really means to be an effective information searcher on the internet. Chapter 3 examines the birth and development of search engines: how they work, getting the best results out of your search, alternatives to Google, and a discussion of lesser-known internet discovery tools that are not even search engines at all. Chapter 4 explores the recent rise of "social searching"—using your social network as a source of information, when it makes sense to do so, and practical search strategies you can employ for the most popular social networks including Facebook, Twitter, and LinkedIn. Finally, Chapter 5 takes on the particularly tough and perplexing issue of source credibility, examining both traditional scholarly and journalistic methods for assessing a source, and also the latest thinking and methods for verifying citizen journalism and social media posts. This chapter also analyzes the notion of the wisdom-of-crowds, explaining how that principle works, under what circumstances it can be relied on, and when it does not apply.

The last major segment of the book, Part III, is about finding and interviewing experts. In Chapters 6 through 8 you'll discover how to locate the best type of experts for your research, and the pros and cons of each type. You'll also learn how to make contact with the experts and how to get them to open up and share their knowledge.

Finally, the last chapters offer advice on how to tell when it's time to wind up your project and some tips on writing up your results. Chapter 10 includes a "Researchers Road Map," a guide to choosing and understanding the varying types of information sources.

At the end of this book are two appendices. One lists useful research and verification tools, and in the other I share my favorite books, journals, and other resources on doing research and understanding how to better leverage knowledge in the digital age.

Note

1. For a detailed analysis on how the site Upworthy refines this process of creating the most attention-grabbing headlines possible, see this piece in *New York* magazine: nymag.com/daily/intelligencer/2014/03/upworthy-team-explains -its-success.html.

Getting Started

Before plunging into your project, take a few minutes to consider your endeavor. Try to determine for yourself exactly what kind of information you need and why. What are your reasons for wanting to find this information? What are your overall goals? Try to be as specific as possible, even though it may be difficult to do so at the earliest stage. The more you can narrow your scope and break your task into subprojects, the easier your search will be and the more likely it is that your project will be a success.

> **TIP: Deciding What to Research**
> How do you decide what to research when the research topic is up to you? The best guide that I've come across is called "Identifying Your Interests and Establishing a Research Plan" (http://tinyurl.com/p8w8sjp) written by Professor Shannon Mattern at the School of Media Studies at the New School for Public Engagement. While geared for media studies students, Mattern's inspiration and advice is invaluable for any researcher.

For example, say your goal is to find information on how newspapers are rethinking their business models in the digital age. With a little reflection, you can break that topic into its major components: What were the traditional business models before the internet? What elements provided revenue, and how much? Which of those elements are no longer viable? What new methods are being tried out to generate revenue? Who are the leaders in creating a workable business model—what did they do, and how did they do it? Are there differences in other countries or lessons that can be learned—what are they? What do readers say they want and like in a newspaper today? Will they pay for those features, and if so, under what circumstances? And so on.

Now you have some specific and concrete subtopics to zero in on. If during your research you discover that your subject is too broad for you to adequately handle it within the strictures of your plan, you can decide whether to choose one or more of your subtopics instead. And if you are not familiar enough with your subject at the outset to identify the subdivisions, you'll find that you will discover them once you begin your research.

The first step in the information-gathering process is to find the best "nonhuman" published sources—whether in print, in databases, or on the web. Although some of your best results will eventually come from talking to experts, you don't want to begin your project by contacting them. It's much better to first read and learn about your subject, and then speak with the experts. This way, when you do eventually talk to the authorities in the field, you'll be knowledgeable enough to ask the right questions and get the most out of your conversation.

Before you actually start your research, you should also come up with a method for capturing the information you'll be gleaning from your published and expert sources. Your approach to note taking and organization is important because it will affect the course of your entire project. If you need advice on this, see Chapter 9. If, however, you feel confident enough to jump right in to the information search, continue on to the first chapter.

Sources

Chapter 1

Super Sources: The Cream of the Crop

The resources described in this chapter are the cream of the information-source crop. They range from museums to the federal government, from the state business filing registry offices to other storehouses of information, but they all have a few things in common. Each contains information on an enormous scope of subjects. Each can easily be tapped for answers and advice. And each provides answers either free of charge or nearly free.

I've organized these sources into the following broad categories:

- The Best of the Library Sources
- The Best of the U.S. Government Sources
- Business Super Sources
- Statistical Sources
- Scholarly Databases, Theses, and Journals
- Open Access and Public Data Sets
- Other Super Sources

The Best of the Library Sources

In Chapter 2, I examine the continuing value of libraries in the digital age and how to make the best use of libraries when doing research. Here I'll simply list a handful of the very best individual libraries and library-oriented resources that you can turn to in order to find information on virtually any topic you are researching. This section is broken up into two subcategories: "The Best of the Best" and "The Rest of the Best."

The Best of the Best

Source: *Library of Congress*

The U.S. Library of Congress in Washington, D.C., is the largest library in the world. Its collection includes millions of volumes and pamphlets, technical reports, maps, manuscripts, photographs, negatives, prints, and slides. The library is also known for its collection of rare books and foreign publications.

Using the Library of Congress's vast resources can be tricky—not only because there is so much information available but also because the library's policy discourages extensive reference usage when the same materials are available on a more local level. However, it does assist users in researching topics unique to the library (such as copyright, legislative research, and international law).

There are also certain services and sections of the Library of Congress that are set up specifically to help the public find and use its resources:

- Ask a Librarian. Click on a specific subject area and see a page with the range of the Library of Congress's resources, and have the opportunity to pose your research question to a librarian. You should receive a response within five cases. In some cases, you can even have a live chat.

- Virtual Reference Shelf. A list of sites and resources recommended by the Library of Congress on topics ranging from architecture to statistics.

- Searchable databases. While many of these powerful databases are available only for in-library use at the Library of Congress itself, others are free and available remotely.

There's a lot more—spend time browsing and searching the site and you'll see for yourself!

Source: *WorldCat (OCLC)*

Do you have need to find the library closest to you that has a copy of a particular book (or music CD or DVD)? Just enter the name of the item and your zip code into WorldCat and you'll get an immediate listing of which libraries nearest you have that item on their shelves. (You can do a lot more on WorldCat too, including finding journal articles and downloading ebooks, but its fundamental purpose is to seamlessly search about 10,000 of the world's library catalogs to help people find the books or other content they seek.)

> **TIP:**
> Remember that WorldCat only surfaces titles and other bibliographic information about a book or content, so you'll need to track down the original item yourself. However, Hathi Trust, a consortium of major leading research libraries around the world, is another excellent resource that not only allows searching across millions of public domain and private books, journals and other resources, but also permits a certain amount of free fulltext searching as well.

Note that when you find a book on Google Books, the dropdown menu under "Get this book in print" includes a "Find in a library" link to the WorldCat entry for that title.

Source: *The New York Public Library*
The New York Public Library (NYPL) is a tremendous source of all kinds of information. The library's mid-Manhattan branch is especially rich in its holdings and regularly answers inquiries from around the country via its ASK NYPL reference service, which accepts phone calls at 917-ASK-NYPL from 9:00 AM to 6:00 PM, Monday through Saturday. Email requests are also accepted. Its collections cover the fields of art, business, education, history, literature and language, and science. In addition, the library contains an extensive image collection.

Specialized research collections of the NYPL include the George Arents Collection on Tobacco; Berg Collection of English and American Literature; Dorot Jewish Division; Jean Blackwell Hutson Research and Reference Division, which focuses on peoples of

African descent throughout the world; Jerome Robbins Archive of the Recorded Moving Image; Lionel Pincus and Princess Firyal Map Division; Rodgers and Hammerstein Archives of Recorded Sound; Schomburg Center for Research in Black Culture; Science/Industry and Business Library; Spencer Collection of illustrated word and book bindings of all periods and all countries and cultures; and the Theatre on Film and Tape Archive. There is also the Performing Arts Research Center, which answers inquiries regarding music, dance, and theater at no charge.

Here are just a few of the ways you can start learning about the resources of the NYPL:

Research Guides. The NYPL has created detailed step-by-step instructions on how to begin research in the library on many different subject areas, ranging from historical photographs to maps to patents.

Digital Collections: The NYPL has digitized over 800,000 items from its holdings and made them available online. There are digitized photographs, audio, and other formats, on topics ranging from the arts to maps, birds, immigration, and social conditions.

Articles and Databases: All of these are free to use when visiting the NYPL in person; online, there are a mixture of free and fee-based databases.

The Rest of the Best

Source: *The Center for Research Libraries (CRL)*
The Center for Research Libraries (CRL) is an international consortium of university, college, and independent research libraries headquartered in Chicago and it makes its catalog of holdings available for free searching on the web. Documents themselves are available on loan free to member libraries or to nonmember libraries for a fee. CRL's holdings include international newspapers, doctoral dissertations, and much more.

Source: *CiteSeer*
CiteSeer is a digital scientific literature library that focuses primarily on computer and information science.

The Best of the U.S. Government Sources

The U.S. government is a gold mine of information. Although some government resources and information services have been eliminated over the years, an awesome amount of advice, data, and information is still available—and since the mid-2000s or so the focus of the government has been to make much of that information freely and easily available over the internet. Information is available from the government on a vast number of topics. The following table of departments and agencies, along with selected topics each covers, should give you a good feel for what's available.

Department/Agency	Topics
Department of Agriculture	animal and plant health; consumer affairs; family nutrition; food safety and inspection; human nutrition; veterinary medicine
Department of Commerce	business outlooks; economic and demographic statistics; engineering standards; imports and exports; minority-owned businesses; patents and trademarks; technology; travel; weather and atmosphere
Department of Defense	atomic energy; foreign country security; mapping; military history; nuclear operations and technology; tactical warfare
Department of Education	adult education; bilingual education; civil rights; educational statistics; elementary and secondary education; handicapped services; higher education; libraries; special education
Department of Energy	coal, gas, shale, and oil; conservation; energy emergencies; fusion energy; inventions; nuclear energy; nuclear physics; radioactive waste; renewable energy
Department of Health and Human Services	AIDS; alcohol abuse; disease; drug abuse; drug research; family planning; food safety; minority health; occupational safety; smoking; statistical research data; toxic substances; veterinary medicine; NIH institutes for cancer; eyes; heart, lung, and blood; arthritis and musculoskeletal and skin diseases; dental and craniofacial research;

Department/Agency	Topics
Department of Health and Human Services (cont.)	diabetes and kidney diseases; environmental health; neurological and communicative disorders and stroke; human development services; aging; children, youth, and families; developmental disabilities; Native Americans
Department of Housing and Urban Development	block grants; elderly housing; energy conservation; fair housing; urban studies
Department of Homeland Security	border security; citizenship and immigration services; civil rights and civil liberties; cybersecurity; disasters; economic security; human trafficking; immigration enforcement; terrorism prevention; transportation security
Department of the Interior	archaeology; fish and wildlife; geology; mapping; minerals; Native Americans; natural resources; water
Department of Justice	antitrust; civil rights; drug enforcement; immigration; justice statistics; juvenile justice; prisons
Department of Labor	employment training; labor-management relations; labor statistics; occupational safety and health; pension and welfare benefits; productivity and technology; veterans' employment; women
Department of State	African affairs; arms control; Canadian and European affairs; East Asian and Pacific affairs; human rights; inter-American affairs; international environmental affairs; international narcotics; Near Eastern and South Asian affairs; nuclear and space arms negotiations; passport inquiries; prisoners of war/missing in action; refugees; visa inquiries
Department of Transportation	automobile safety; aviation safety; aviation standards; boating; hazardous materials transportation; highway safety; mass transit; National Highway Traffic Safety Administration; railroad safety; shipbuilding; vehicle accident statistics; vehicle crashworthiness
Department of the Treasury	coin and metal production; currency production; currency research and development; customs; saving bonds; Secret Service protection; taxpayer assistance; tax return investigation

Department/Agency	Topics
Consumer Product Safety Commission	burn hazards; product safety assessment; mechanical hazards; injury information; electrical shock hazards; safety packaging; chemical hazards
Environmental Protection Agency	air and radiation; pesticides and toxic substances; acid deposition; climate change; environmental monitoring and quality assurance; solid waste and emergency response; water; noise control
Federal Communications Commission (FCC)	cable television; broadcast stations; radio regulation
Federal Trade Commission (FTC)	advertising practices; competition and antitrust matters; consumer protection; financial statistics
General Services Administration (GSA)	consumer information; government audits and investigations; fraud hotlines; federal property; purchasing of equipment and supplies; information management; public buildings management
National Aeronautics and Space Administration (NASA)	aeronautics and space technology; life sciences; astrophysics; earth sciences; solar system exploration; space shuttle payload; Mars observer program; microgravity science; upper atmosphere research; solar flares
National Archives and Records Administration	naturalization records; census data; military records; land records; passenger lists; passport applications; selected vital statistics; presidential documents; audio and other media
National Endowment for the Arts and Humanities	literature; museums; folk arts; visual arts; music arts; theater arts and musical theater; opera; media arts; history; language
National Science Foundation	atmospheric/astronomical and earth–ocean sciences; mathematical and physical sciences; Arctic and Antarctic research; anthropology; engineering; biology; genetic biology; chemistry; computer science; earthquakes; economics; ethics in science; meteorology; galactic and extragalactic astronomy; geography; geology; history and philosophy of science; nutrition; linguistics; marine chemistry; metallurgy;

Department/Agency	Topics
National Science Foundation (cont.)	minority research; nuclear physics; science and technology to aid the disabled; small business research and development; sociology
National Transportation Safety Board	accident investigations involving aviation, railroads, highways, and hazardous materials
Small Business Administration	women's businesses; veteran affairs; disaster assistance; financial assistance; management assistance; minority small businesses; statistical data; export advice

Table   U.S. Government Sources by Topic

To get connected to the best research resources for each of these departments or agencies, access their website (a simple Google search with the name of the department or agency will bring you there) and look for assistance right on the homepage.

The government is so huge that it is impossible to describe in a single chapter (or an entire book for that matter) the full range of information available. However, to give you a taste of what you can find, I have listed below a selection of my favorite clearinghouses and all-purpose resources for locating the most broadly useful information. Note that none of these is completely comprehensive, and many federal search sites are disappointingly subpar when it comes to navigation, design, and interface. But I have found that the following sites represent the best of what the federal government offers today to help ordinary people find the resources, documents, reports, or other sources of expertise they need.

One-Stop Government Clearinghouses

Source: *Data.gov*

Data.gov is an open-site source with a collection of tools and data sets for researchers who want to use government data to inform their own research or create new types of applications. There are over 100,000 data sets from dozens of agencies, which can be searched on topics such as weather, the economy, health records, international trade, civil rights, criminal justice, geographic data, and much more.

Source: *FedStats*
FedStats offers researchers access to the full range of official statistical information produced by the federal government without having to know in advance which federal agency produces which particular statistic. You can search and link to more than 100 agencies that provide data and trend information on such topics as economic and population trends, crime, education, health care, aviation safety, energy use, farm production, and more.

Source: *GPO Federal Digital System (FDSYS)*
FDSYS provides free online access to official publications from all three branches of the federal government and permits users to search for, browse, and download documents and publications. Sample documents include *The Federal Register; The 9-11 Commission Report; The Budget of the U.S. Government* (by year); congressional committee reports; congressional bills and hearings; Supreme Court decisions; and historical documents such as the *Wilderness Act of 1964* or *The Surgeon General's Report on Smoking and Health.*

Source: *MetaLib*
MetaLib lets users search across a set of dozens of U.S. federal government resources, including agencies, data sets, and reports, and retrieves actual documents and links to the original source material. I have found it to be one of the most powerful and advanced search sites created by the federal government.

Source: *USA.Gov*
This clearinghouse is geared for consumers and small businesses that need general information and questions answered. It includes information on making a consumer complaint, starting a business, and similar topics. One particularly useful part of the site is its Business Data section, where you can find data on banking, earnings data/statistics, labor data, economic analysis, regional business information, trade statistics, and more.

Source: *Contact Your Government, by Topic*
A browsable directory of contacts for key government agencies and departments

Source: *Demographics*
A listing and links to the most comprehensive sources from the federal government that provide demographic data

Searchable Databases

In addition to the one-stop clearinghouses we've just considered, look for government sites that don't merely provide general information about the relevant program, its scope, and links to resources, but actually offer free searchable databases. Such sites allow you to conduct advanced, precision keyword searches across large amounts of data, reports, findings, and the like. Following are a number of agency databases, listed by broad topic, that I recommend.

Agriculture

Agricola: U.S. Department of Agriculture, National Agriculture Library
Library of Agriculture Decisions

Banking/Financial

FDIC datasets: Federal Deposit Insurance Corporation
Federal Reserve Board materials: Federal Reserve Board
Home Mortgage Disclosure Act: Federal Financial Institutions Examination Council
Credit Union Data: National Credit Union Administration

Country Information

U.S. Bilateral Relations Fact Sheets: U.S. Department of the State
CIA Factbook: CIA
Country Studies: Federal Research Division, Library of Congress

Economy/Economic Data

Economic Report of the President: Council of Economic Advisors
Federal Reserve Archive System for Economic Research: Federal Reserve Bank
Federal Reserve Economic Data: Federal Reserve Bank
Economic Indicators: Council of Economic Advisors

Employment/Labor
Bureau of Labor Statistics Search: Bureau of Labor Statistics
National Labor Relations Board Search: National Labor Relations Board
O*Net Occupational Requirements: U.S. Department of Labor

Energy and Environment
ADAMS Nuclear Information: UN Nuclear Regulatory Commission
DOE Research and Development Project Summaries: Department of Energy
Energy Citations Database: Department of Energy
EnergyFiles: Department of Energy
Envirofacts: Environmental Protection Agency
International Energy Annual: Department of Energy
National Climatic Data Center Search: NOAA, Department of Commerce
Superfund Site Information: Environmental Protection Agency
The Information Bridge: Department of Energy

Government Procurement
Federal Business Opportunities: General Services Administration

Health
CDC Wonder: Department of Health and Human Services
Entrez: National Institutes of Health; National Library of Medicine; National Center for Biotechnology Information
Household Products Database: National Institutes of Health, National Library of Medicine
Medline Plus: National Institutes of Health, National Library of Medicine
National Center for Health Statistics Search: Centers for Disease Control and Prevention, Department of Health and Human Services
National Library of Medicine Databases and Electronic Resources: National Institutes of Health, National Library of Medicine
National Toxicology Program: National Institutes of Health, National Toxicology Program

PubMed Central: National Institutes of Health, National Library of Medicine

TOXNET: National Institutes of Health, National Library of Medicine

---

TIP: PubMed

Be sure to try out PubMed Central for virtually any medical- or health-related research (or even personal research query) you may have. It's one of the most comprehensive and valuable free government databases available anywhere.

Import/Export/Trade

Exporter Database: Department of Commerce, International Trade Administration

Foreign Trade Statistics: Census Bureau

Interactive Tariff and Trade Database: U.S. International Trade Commission

Market Research Library: Department of Commerce, U.S. Commercial Service

Trade Compliance Center: Department of Commerce, International Trade Administration

Trade Data & Analysis: Industry Data: Department of Commerce, International Trade Administration

TradeStats Express: U.S. Department of Commerce, International Trade Administration

Virtual World Trade Reference Room: Department of Commerce, International Trade Administration

Patents, Trademarks, and Copyright

Search Copyright Records: U.S. Library of Congress

Trademark Electronic Search System (TESS): U.S. Patent and Trademark Office

USPTO Search: U.S. Patent and Trademark Office

Transportation

Fatality Analysis Reporting System (FARS): U.S. Department of Transportation, National Center for Statistics & Analysis

TRIS: Online Transportation Research Information Services: U.S. Department of Transportation, Transportation Research Board

Miscellaneous Searchable Federal Databases
Federal Trade Commission: Search: Federal Trade Commission
Global Legal Information Network: Library of Congress

The Rest of the Best

Source: *Census Bureau*
Do you want to know which neighborhoods have the highest concentration of people over 65 years of age? How many women work in the medical field? Which sections of Florida are the wealthiest? The U.S. Census Bureau can supply you with figures on these and countless other data-oriented questions. Major areas covered include agriculture, business, construction, foreign nations, foreign trade, geography, governments, housing, manufacturing, mineral industries, people, retail trade, service industries, and transportation.

The U.S. Government on Social Media

What about finding information from the government via social media? Is that a good option for researchers? While some agencies, such as the Census Bureau and the U.S. Department of Commerce's International Trade Administration, among others, do maintain a presence on Twitter and Facebook, these sites are not necessarily the place to do in-depth research. However, if your research requires keeping up with breaking news, announcements, and information on the latest reports and data releases, social media can be a useful source. You can find a listing and a source for a regularly updated list of government agencies on social media from a regularly updated wiki simply called "Federal Agencies" created by Josh Shpayher, an attorney and partner at Shpayher Bechhofer LLP in Chicago, IL and founder of GovSM.com—see the appendix for the URL.

If you link to the Bureau's main page you'll get a good sense of the wealth of information available at your fingertips. Some of my favorite all-purpose sections of the site are the American Fact Finder and the American Community Survey, State and County Quick Facts, its A to Z topic listing, and data from the 2010 Census. If you're looking for business data, be sure to check out the sections on economic censuses, state trade data, the industry statistics portal, USA Trade Online, and Statistics of U.S. Businesses.

Source: *Statistical Agencies*
The government is an enormous creator of all kinds of statistics, including tons of data related to business, industry, and trade. Many, though not all, of these sites are part of the Census Bureau. Here are a few of my favorite all-purpose sources:

- USA Trade Online
- U.S. Bureau of Labor Statistics
- U.S. International Trade Center DataWeb
- U.S. TradeStats Express
- U.S. International Trade Administration: Trade Statistics
- U.S. International Trade Administration: Data and Analysis

You may have come across a prominent book that has sometimes been called the "bible for statistics" of all types, the *Statistical Abstract of the United States*, an annual compilation published by the Census Bureau with tens of thousands of statistics ranging from the number of eye operations performed to the amount of ice cream consumed, and so on. Unfortunately, the Bureau stopped publishing the guide in 2011 due to budget cuts. On the bright side, a private information and publishing company, ProQuest, picked up the job of compiling the data and continued publishing new versions beginning in 2012, in both print and digital versions. So you can still find this ultimate government statistics source at many libraries.

Finally, there is one "catch-all" government super source that is worth mentioning: Congressional Research Service (CRS) reports. These are in-depth, objective, fact-filled reports undertaken by

> **TIP: What About Finding International Statistics?**
> While the above Census sources focus on providing statistical data about the United States, there are several sites on the web that specifically link to the equivalent official statistics from national offices around the world. My favorite sources that have compiled these links are OFFSTATS from the University of Auckland in New Zealand and the UN Statistics Division.

researchers at the Library of Congress upon request by members of Congress who need a deep and unbiased treatment of some issue of public concern. Topics can vary quite a bit, but sample titles include, for instance, Armed Conflict in Syria: Overview and U.S. Response; Protection of Trade Secrets: Overview of Current Law and Legislation; Unaccompanied Children from Central America: Foreign Policy Considerations; China and the United States—A Comparison of Green Energy Programs and Policies; Reform of the Foreign Intelligence Surveillance Courts: A Brief Overview; and Nanotechnology: A Policy Primer.

The tricky thing is that CRS reports are not readily available to the public—they are created for members of Congress. The protocol for an ordinary citizen to get one of these has been to ask one's representative for a copy. Fortunately, several sites on the web have emerged that have worked to compile as many of these reports as possible, make them browsable and searchable for the public, and permit free downloads. These sites include the U.S. Department of State, the University of North Texas, and Archive-It.

> **TIP: Use Google to Find CRS Reports!**
> You can find CRS reports through a Google search by following this format:
>> site:assets.opencrs.com "your key words"

Business Super Sources

As with government sources, one could easily fill a book with just the top business-related research resources. Still, there are a batch that stand out as substantive, information-packed sources that are most likely to be valuable to the broadest audience of business researchers.

Below are my selections, organized into key subcategories. I am not covering sites that are geared primarily for choosing stocks, making investments, and the like. As with the other sources listed in this chapter, you can find the specific URLs for each at the end of this chapter.

Note that some of the sites listed are derived from the government, whose top sources were covered previously, but I have chosen to place them here in one of these more specific subcategories.

- Advertising and Marketing
- Company Research
- Demographics
- Economics
- Finance
- Industry and Labor Research
- Market Research

Advertising and Marketing

Source: *The Ad*Access Project*
Source: The Emergence of Advertising in America: 1850–1920
These two sites represent two free searchable databases of advertising images collected and made available by the same institution. The Ad*Access project provides searchable images for over 7,000 advertisements printed in U.S. and Canadian newspapers and magazines between 1911 and 1955, covering five broad subject areas. The other collection is a browsable database of over 9,000 advertising items and publications dating from 1850 to 1920.

Source: *AdBrands*
This site provides news of recent advertising campaigns, profiles of leading advertisers by sector and geography, recent popular ads,

new campaigns and other information of interest to those following the global advertising industry.

Source: *Marketing Charts*
This site provides access to a collection of about 2,500 charts and
data files related to marketing, with a special focus on marketing in
the media industry.

Company Research

Source: *EDGAR (SEC)*
Search for public companies' registrations, financial information,
and other required filings on this site.

Source: *Company-Registers.info*
This site provides links and describes offices around the world where
companies must register in order to do business in that country.

Source: *Annual Reports Service*
Browse or search for the annual reports of 3,000 North American
and European firms and receive the reports by mail or electronically, at no cost.

Source: *Bloomberg Business Research*
Enter the name of a public or private company and get a timely
snapshot of key data such as sales, employees, recent news, products, and much more.

Source: *Index of U.S. Business Search Databases*
This browsable map-based directory surfaces and links the visitor
to sites of official state business registries around the country.

Source: *Mint*
Mint provides basic directory information for companies around
the globe. Users can search and screen companies by four categories: type of activity, region, size, and name.

Source: *Research Roundup: Business Filings Databases*
This directory provides links to corporate and business filing offices
and their searchable databases of filings for all 50 states.

Source: *Business Registries*
This is a collection of links, with brief descriptions, to official company registry sites around the world.

Source: *Find the Best*
Provides information on 30 million public and private companies, including descriptions, employee names and titles, size, ownership, competitors, products, contracts, and suppliers.

Source: *Glassdoor*
Find salary data, job interview questions, company profiles, ratings, and rankings of what it's like to work at thousands of organizations, submitted by current and past employees.

Source: *LinkedIn*
This extremely popular business social network provides profiles of companies, job openings, names and titles of current and past employees, analytics, and much more.

Source: *Rank and Filed*
A collection of tables, charts, and visualizations of key data culled from recent SEC document filings from public companies in the U.S.

Source: *Secretaries of State*
A listing and links to Secretaries of State offices in all 50 states, along with links directly to online services in those state offices that facilitate querying and searching its database.

Source: *Who Operates Where*
A searchable database with information about U.S.-based firms that operate in other countries; as well as non-U.S.-based firms that operate in the United States.

Source: *Global Brand Database*
This site allows users to conduct a search, either by text or image, of trademarks from 15 intellectual property offices and registration sites around the world.

Demographics

Source: *Business Analyst Online*
Business Analyst Online provides geographic-based data on consumers and businesses, generated and displayed in map form.

Source: *Social Explorer*
Social Explorer provides web-based tools so users can search and visually display demographic information of specified segments of the United States, individual states, counties, and census tracts.

Economics

Source: *EconPapers*
EconPapers includes over a million searchable working papers, articles, books, and other digital materials on economics.

Finance

Source: *BizStats*
BizStats provides access to financial ratios, benchmarking, and more.

Source: *Seeking Alpha*
Seeking Alpha aggregates and edits opinion, analysis, and recent news from 2,000 individual contributors on matters related to finance and investing.

Source: *Journalist's Resource: Economics*
This is a compilation of the most valuable and interesting news, articles, reports and studies broadly related to economics, which includes banking, jobs, workers, real estate, taxes, and other general business topics.

Industry and Labor Research

Source: *Industry News*
This is a collection of news and links for more than two dozen industries, ranging from advertising and aerospace to travel and utilities.

Source: *Industries at a Glance*
This site contains snapshots of national (and sometimes state and regional) data for more than 100 industries, organized by the North American Industry Classification System (NAICS).

Source: *ILOSTAT*
ILOSTAT provides annual and infra-annual labor market statistics for over 100 indicators and 230 countries, areas, and territories.

Source: *LEGOSH*
This database compiles the wealth of legislation in occupational safety and health (OSH) and serves as a snapshot of the current major national legislative requirements around the globe.

Source: *Working Papers and Technical Reports in Business, Economics and Law*
A listing with links to business and economics working papers and technical reports from universities and institutes around the world.

Market Research

Source: *Country Risk Reports*
A collection of short reports for 100+ countries around the world that quantifies and analyzes the economic, political, and financial risks of investing and doing business for each.

Source: *Free Report Library*
A collection of data-packed reports aggregating U.S. trade data. Specific topics include top import and export commodities by value; largest shippers, consignees, and carriers; trade statistics, and more.

Source: *Marketing Charts*
This site provides access to a collection of about 2,500 charts and data files related to marketing, with a special focus on marketing in the media industry.

Source: *MarketsandMarkets: Press Releases*
These are recent abstracts and summaries of the results and topline data of recent research reports published by MarketsandMarkets, a market research firm with corporate offices in Dallas and researchers based in India.

Source: *Market Potential Index*
A yearly updated chart that ranks the market potential of 87 countries around the globe based on several key indicators.

Source: *Market Research Library*
This is a searchable collection of the full text of U.S. government–written studies and analyses of hundreds of different products and services for countries around the world.

Source: *ReportLinker*
ReportLinker is a search engine that uses special software to scour the open web, including portions of the deep web, and indexes open-source market research reports and studies. Sites indexed include governmental agencies, trade associations, publishers, universities, and other selected entities that publish substantive market information.

Statistical

Source: *Statista*
Statista is a keyword searchable portal integrating over 1.5 million statistical pieces of data on over 60,000 topics from over 18,000 sources.

Source: *Aneki*
Aneki aggregates a great deal of data to surface world rankings on thousands of different topics, primarily related to places: countries, states, and cities. Aneki also includes ranking on topics such as jobs, diseases, sports, entertainment, and more.

Source: *Harris Vault*
A searchable archive of surveys and polls conducted by The Harris Poll all the way back to 1970.

Source: *Worldometers.info*
This site provides a stream of real-time, continually updated data on a wide range of social, business, and cultural metrics such as births, cars produced, forests being lost, tweets sent today, deaths from malaria, water being consumed, energy consumption, and world spending on illegal drugs.

Source: *Zanran*
A searchable collection of a wide range of statistical data.

Scholarly Databases, Theses, and Journals

There are a wide range of resources that stem from or are devoted to the academic community. Many of these references are open source or free-to-access scholarly journals and publications, or directories and databases of research-related materials and other materials by and for colleges, universities, and research institutes. Here are my favorites:

Databases

When doing online searching it's sometimes important—even necessary—to move away from searching the entire internet and to focus on a special, filtered set of articles, reports, papers, and other documents that are specifically geared for researchers. These include fee-based databases from companies such as ProQuest or EBSCO that we will discuss in the following chapter on libraries, but also include special academic databases that can be freely searched on the internet.

These scholarly databases contain thousands of articles published in peer-reviewed scholarly journals in disciplines ranging from anthropology to marketing to psychology to waste management, and are typically written by professors and academic researchers who are deeply immersed in their field and exploring the boundaries of new knowledge in their discipline. In addition to the journal articles, scholarly databases may include other academic materials, such as conference presentation transcripts, preprints and working drafts (see the sidebar) and other items of a scholarly nature.

From a researcher's perspective, accessing these materials provides several unique benefits: you'll find reliable research vetted by some of the best minds in the discipline, learn of the latest thinking in the field, and obtain the names of experts that you can track down and interview yourself.

There are some downsides to academic literature, too. Because the scholarly publishing process can be slow, sometimes what you read could have been written many months or even a year ago or more; sometimes academic writing itself can be dense and jargon filled, and the coverage may be too theoretical for your needs.

But there's no question that these free scholarly databases should be a component of virtually any research project. While there are several places on the web to do this research—the library databases we'll look at in Chapter 2, as well as certain open access sites described later in this chapter—there are two specific "super sources" that offer a comprehensive, powerful, but simple way to find these materials: Google Scholar and the Social Science Research Network (SSRN).

Source: *Google Scholar*

Google launched Google Scholar back in 2004, as a site where researchers could search the collection of thousands of peer-reviewed journals, as well as other scholarly documents such as technical reports, theses, certain books, and even a selection of web pages that Google classified as scholarly. While some academics and librarians have noted certain problems with Google Scholar regarding matters such as coverage, ranking methods, and other flaws, the fact is that the search engine has become a powerful and easy-to-use tool for conducting scholarly research.

Running a search on Google Scholar is not, on the surface, too different from doing a search on Google (see Figure 1.1). You enter your keywords, get back a list of matching items, and click on the items of interest to view them. But there are two important differences to keep in mind when searching this database:

- While many items that Google Scholar returns are PDFs of full articles or reports, others are only bibliographic citations or abstracts of the full piece. In order to get the entire article or document (full text) you will need to either get it from a library or link to the publisher's page to purchase it directly online.

TIP: Where's the Rest?
In some cases, Google Scholar won't have the full text of the item freely available, but if you copy the title of the item and then search for it on the open web, you might find a free version that someone posted on another site.

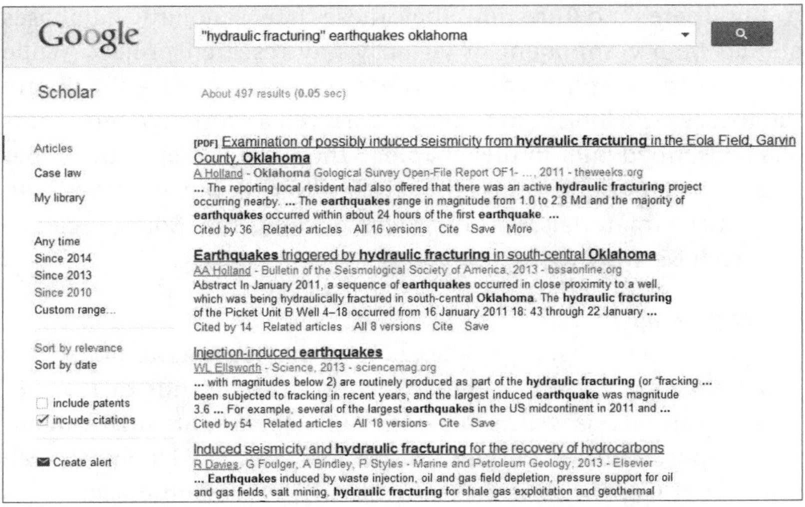

Figure 1.1 Results of a search on "hydraulic fracturing" and Oklahoma and Earthquakes on Google Scholar retrieves results from academic journals, documents, and proceedings

- The way Google Scholar ranks results is different from how it ranks its regular web searches. Here Google's algorithm integrates other criteria, such as how many times the paper has been cited by others and the prominence of the publication, following certain academic traditions in assigning a level of prestige to authors whose works are cited often as well as to the reputation of various publications.

Source: *SSRN*
The SSRN was launched in 1994 by five people who wanted to create a repository where professors, other scholars, and academic institutions could submit their research to obtain wide dissemination to others. Most of the hundreds of thousands of items in the SSRN collection are free and available to view in PDF (see Figure 1.2).

One interesting feature of SSRN is how it ranks its search results, with items downloaded most often getting the highest ranking. This rating system has even resulted in a kind of informal competition

A Few Tips for Searching Scholarly Literature

Conducting academic and scholarly research is not all that different than searching other literature, but there are some distinctions. Academic research itself has its own jargon, including the use of specialized terms to describe different types of publications. The following are some of the most common terms you're likely to come across:

- **Preprint:** A draft of a scholarly article, circulated to colleagues and others, typically before it undergoes the rigorous peer review conducted by a scholarly journal for approval before publication. Preprints may be accompanied with the phrase "submitted to . . ." or "will appear in . . ."

- **Working draft:** A work in progress. The author of a working draft typically solicits comments from peers to make progress toward a final report.

- **Open access journal:** A scholarly journal that makes its articles available free on the internet. The accepted definition of "open access" was established by the Open Society Institute and reads as follows: "free availability on the public internet, permitting any users to read, download, copy, distribute, print, search, or link to the full texts of these articles, crawl them for indexing, pass them as data to software, or use them for any other lawful purpose, without financial, legal, or technical barriers other than those inseparable from gaining access to the internet itself. The only constraint on reproduction and distribution, and the only role for copyright in this domain, should be to give authors control over the integrity of their work and the right to be properly acknowledged and cited."[1]

TIP: Click the Open Access Button to Ferret Out the Free
A download called "The Open Access Button" was created by two students, David Carroll and Joseph McArthur, medical and pharmacology students at Queen's University and University College, London. This slightly subversive research tool can help uncover free versions of journal articles you come across but can't access because they are kept behind a paywall. The "button" is a freely downloadable bookmark that works on all major browsers. When you link to an article behind a paywall, you then click the button and it will automatically search for the item on Google Scholar and on a repository of open access articles, and will even send an email to the author of the article. The project is supported by The Right to Research Coalition, a Washington, D.C.–based organization devoted to making scholarly research publicly available. The Coalition itself is supported by SPARC, the Scholarly Publishing and Academic Resources Coalition, an international alliance of academic and research libraries working to create a more open system of scholarly communication.

Figure 1.2   SSRN provides free searching of thousands of published and unpublished academic papers, conference presentations, articles, and other scholarly materials

among some university faculty as to whose work is downloaded most often, according to a *New York Times* article titled "Now Professors Get Their Star Rankings Too!" (Note that users of SSRN can alter the ranking method to be alphabetical or most recent if so desired.)

Another interesting feature of SSRN is the inclusion of various statistics that the site provides on the items in its database. For example, after clicking on an item the user can see how many times the abstract was viewed, the number of downloads, its overall download rank, and a "people who downloaded this paper also downloaded" feature. There are lots of other interesting features and capabilities of SSRN—the great thing is, it's free to use and search, so you can go and explore all these yourself!

Additional scholarly search engines include Microsoft Academic Search, Ingenta, and social media–oriented sites such as Research-Gate and Academia.edu, which include a search function for papers and works uploaded by its members.

TIP: Use Repositories

Sites like SSRN and others that collect open access documents, materials, reports, and so forth are typically called "repositories" of open access data, and there are many of these around the globe. A site called DOAR, which stands for the Directory of Open Access Repositories, lets users not only freely browse and find repositories, but also perform a keyword search of all the items contained in those repositories, and does so via a "custom Google search engine" allowing the user to employ the familiar Google search commands and limits to create a custom and precise search on these sources. A similar site, called Global Open Access Portal, also lists repositories, but organizes them into subject categories such as arts and humanities, science, social science, and so forth.

Theses and Dissertations

Less common but potentially valuable sources of information for researchers are masters theses and doctoral dissertations. For many years these works were only available on traditional fee-based databases, if at all, but with the growth of the open access movement they are increasingly available at no charge on a wide range of open access sites. Below are several sites where you can browse or perform a keyword search to find a relevant document. Note that the first site is a collection of repositories around the world that provide free access to theses, while the remaining sites are searchable collections made available directly by individual institutions.

Source: *Registry of Open Access Registries (ROAR): Theses*
Over 200 repositories of theses collections from around the world.

Source: *MIT Theses and Dissertations*
Over 30,000 selected digital and digitized theses from MIT, going back to the mid-1980s.

Source: *University of Toronto Research Repository*
Searchable work from the faculty of the University of Toronto.

Source: *University of Michigan Deep Blue Project*
Provides searchable access to "the best scholarly and artistic work done at Michigan."

Source: *CalTechAuthors*
A repository of over 25,000 research papers authored by Caltech faculty and other researchers at Caltech.

TIP: Try WorldCat
You can search for theses and dissertations on the world library catalog WorldCat (described earlier), by specifically choosing to perform an advanced search and then selecting "thesis/dissertations" in the pull-down box under the category of "heading." Note that, as a catalog, WorldCat will only alert you to the *existence* of these documents; in order to access them you will need to use WorldCat to locate a library near you that has a copy in its holdings and then either go to the library to access it or ask your local library if it can be borrowed via an interlibrary loan.

Ejournals

These days, an increasing number of scholarly journals are in digital form, and many of these fall under what is called "open access"—freely available directly to the user. That is a simplified definition, since the open access movement is actually a complex area with multiple types of open access (termed "Green" and "Gold"), but the thrust behind the movement is to support a faster, more accessible, and more flexible means of getting a scholar's work out to those who want it, relative to the expensive scholarly journals that academic libraries subscribe to. Open access publications may or may not go through the same rigorous editorial and peer review processes as do their more traditional scholarly brethren; the primary distinction is in how these publications may be accessed, shared, and utilized.

As part of this open access movement, several sites have created search engines, clearinghouses, directories, and other aids so researches can better find relevant open access journals and articles published in those articles. Here are the sources I know of and can recommend as worth trying:

Source: *JURN*
JURN is a curated academic search engine, indexing thousands of free ejournals.

Source: *JSTOR*
JSTOR includes more than 2,000 academic journals and thousands of monographs, and has digitized more than 50 million pages. (Note: In order to search JSTOR you either need to have an affiliation with a library or purchase a "JPASS.")

Source: *Directory of Open Access Journals (DOAJ)*
DOAJ indexes and provides access to over 7,000 scientific and scholarly peer-reviewed journals and is fully searchable.

Source: *Library of Congress E-Resources:*
  Business and Management
A listing and links to free ejournals that cover topics in business and management. Note that you can also navigate to higher levels of the domain to locate ejournals for other topical areas as well.

Open Access and Public Data Sets

In the age of big data, an increasing number of data sets are being made available for public consumption. This allows researchers to integrate and manipulate data in order to find patterns and gain new insights into whatever topic is being studied. Although not geared toward the layperson, for those who have some skill in using, manipulating, sorting, and understanding data these sets can provide valuable source material for one's endeavor, whether that involves analyzing health statistics, crime, business trends, social media usage, demographics, or some other topic.

What Exactly *Is* Big Data?

Other than being about the hottest business buzzword around, what exactly is big data? Big Data is one of those phrases that's somewhat imprecise, as you can find varying definitions from different sources; however, it is possible to come up with a reasonable and meaningful description.

I would say that the term Big Data can most usefully be defined as *the enormous amounts of numerical, quantitative, statistical, digital, and primarily unstructured data that is speedily being produced by all the different ways people, companies, processes, and objects are generating data.*

According to IBM, the world creates 2.5 quintillion bytes of data per day (www-01.ibm.com/software/data/bigdata). This data includes, for instance, user-generated data on oneself or one's company posted on social networking sites such as LinkedIn, Facebook, or Twitter; transactional and purchasing data collected online or via digital supermarket scanners; digital sensors for picking up weather, traffic, or other external data; digital images and videos; data generated via QR codes placed on objects; location-generated data via GPS-enabled phones; demographic and user preference data from search engines and apps; and so on.

But Big Data also has embedded in its meaning a reference to a *process*—that is, it implies not just the generation of this raw data itself but also the ability of super-powerful computers to crunch all this data in novel and interesting ways to uncover and display new patterns, visual graphs, and insights that could be used for making more informed and effective decisions. The tools, software, and strategies used to get to hidden data in an organization, as well as the process itself, is usually called data mining.

The types of new insights and potential enhancements in decision making that are promised, at least in theory, by big data and its proponents are seemingly limitless. Claims run the gamut of human experience and enterprise: better government policies for introducing new laws, regulations, economic and social programs; improved medical diagnoses, procedures, and best practices; better scholarly research; improved scientific understanding of phenomena by identifying previously hidden data; more accurate predictive models for organizations, governments, and companies; more efficient and more effective business decision making in areas such as target marketing, customer relations management, strategic planning, and possibly every other business operation.

What does this mean for today's researcher? While it's not likely that you will be generating big data sets yourself, you are increasingly going to come across charts, graphs, analyses, and summaries that were created via some kind of big data analysis. Sometimes these are very enlightening, as they reveal important patterns in whatever you were researching that are not easily or apparently detectible.

But good researchers need to watch out for two of the biggest pitfalls when looking at "insights" generated by a big data process. The first is the most basic principle that correlation is not the same as causation—just because, say, an analysis shows that people on Facebook are twice as likely as the rest of the population to be diagnosed with OCD, this does not mean that being on Facebook *causes* OCD. The second pitfall concerns determining how really *meaningful* are any coinciding factors that a big data analysis unearths. Keep in mind the "so what?" factor.

For example, if you see an analysis that unearths the fact that 28 percent of Amazon's DVD buyers make their purchases on Tuesdays—and that on those Tuesdays they buy 8 percent more documentaries than on other days—that should prompt your "so what?" response mechanism.

You can learn much more about what to pay attention to, and what to disregard, in Nate Silver's enlightening book on big data, *The Signal and the Noise.*

The following list includes three of the most popular sites on the web for browsing and searching for specific data sets.

Source: *Enigma.io*
Enigma.io provides access to over 100,000 data sources, many derived from the federal government, ranging from patent information to H-1B visa applications, federal campaign contributions, and many more. The site is fee-based and expensive, but a free trial is offered for new users.

Source: *Google Public Data Explorer*
This site is free and geared for those new to data analytics. Sets include the World Development Indicators, Global Greenhouse Gas Emissions, and the Global Competitiveness Report.

Source: *Windows Azure Marketplace*
This site offers a combination of free and fee-based data sets, ranging from California Commercial Properties in Foreclosure to Zip Code demographics.

Other Super Sources

Source: *The New York Times* Archive
The New York Times is a newspaper of record with historical significance. And that's why the ability to freely search its archives of over 13 million articles (back to its very beginning in 1851) and view

results is such a useful and important resource. While you can find information on anything considered newsworthy, you may find it of particular value for locating extensive obituaries on prominent persons. Note that to get full access you may need to be a digital subscriber or else search at a local library with a subscription.

Source: *Associations*
Professional associations can offer a bountiful harvest of information. They are staffed by knowledgeable and helpful people whose job is to provide information about their field to those who need it. There are thousands of associations, one for nearly every conceivable purpose and field of interest: browse or search and you'll find the Abrasive Engineering Society, the Antique Barbed Wire Society, the Glass Manufacturing Institute Council, the Dolphin Research Center, the Autism Research Institute, the World Cocoa Association, and the Flying Funeral Directors of America—for funeral directors that own and operate their own planes, of course.

TIP: Accessing Association Publications
Associations often produce reports and studies that are of interest to researchers. Many of these will be available for free on the web as downloadable white papers or PDFs. In other cases, they are only available to members of the association or are very expensive—and you may only need a single statistic or data point from just a portion of the study. Try contacting either the association's library or, if it publishes a magazine of some kind, the publication's editor. Sometimes the staffers at those departments won't mind finding the report and reading you the significant information you need. (Sales staff may only agree to sell you the entire study.)

Associations can also be a quick source of industry statistics and news. For example, if you want to find out how the sales of potatoes were last year, you need only inquire of the Potato Association of America or, if you prefer, the U.S. Potato Board.

How to Find: To find the name of an association that deals with your area of interest, a simple Google search with the name of the field followed by the word "association" will normally turn up relevant organizations. However, you can also use some standard reference directories to dig deeper and learn more about various associations that focus on your topic. The bible for this type of research is the *Encyclopedia of Associations*, published by Gale/Cengage. Nearly all libraries have a current edition. (Gale/Cengage also publishes companion association directories on international organizations, as well as local and regional associations.)

Source: *Conferences and Conventions*
Every day, hundreds of conventions and professional conferences are held around the country—the National Accounting Expo, the American Academy of Sports Physicians, the Beekeepers Convention, Computers in Libraries, and the Nuclear Power Expo, to name a few. These meetings are especially good sources of information for keeping up with changes in fast-changing subjects such as digital trends and technological advancements. The seminars and talks presented at these events typically reflect the state of the art in a profession or field. And if there is an accompanying exhibit hall for vendors, the latest and most interesting new products are often displayed as well.

How to Find: As with finding associations, the fastest and often most fruitful way to locate a conference of interest is via a simple Google search in which you input the topic you are researching followed by the words "conference" or "convention." And since many associations hold one or more national conferences, if you have already found a relevant association you will likely find the details on the upcoming meetings on its website.

Two major activities typically take place at these conferences: technical presentations by authorities in the field and product exhibits by vendors who set up booths to try to sell their wares to conference attendees. Although it is sometimes inexpensive or even free to visit the exhibition hall, it may run into the upper hundreds or even thousands of dollars to attend the information sessions. However, there are several strategies for tapping into the knowledge embedded in and the information presented at a conference without actually attending. Here are two such methods:

- Search for the name of the conference on Google and link to the main page. Then look for the program or agenda of the speakers. By browsing the program you can not only get an instant sense of what the hottest topics are in that field but also uncover the names and affiliations of experts you can later contact and interview as part of your research project.

- Speakers from past conferences sometimes make PowerPoints, videos, slides, or other documentation from their presentations available right on that site (or on social media sites like SlideShare or YouTube), allowing you to glean at least some of the knowledge from the event, even though you did not attend.

TIP: Getting Presentation Documents
If there was a presentation by a past speaker at a conference that looked particularly valuable and relevant for your research, but there are no PowerPoint files or other materials on the conference website, you may be able to find these on other parts of the web, uploaded by the speaker. Do a quick Google search on the speaker's name, along with the title of the presentation or the name of the event and see what comes up—you may find that the expert put the materials up on his or her own personal or professional site. If you still don't find anything, you may have luck simply emailing the speaker and seeing if he or she will share the documents with you directly. (See Chapters 7 and 8 on finding and interviewing experts.)

Locating Conference Bloggers and Tweeters

One of the great services that bloggers and tweeters have done for researchers is live blogging and tweeting the highlights of conference presentations. These people can be great sources for getting direct quotes as well as sometimes interesting color commentary, offering observations on matters not available from any official materials, such as the mood of the audience or presenters, reactions from audience, and other more subtle aspects of the event.

How can you find out if anyone was blogging or tweeting at an event you would have liked to have attended, or if someone will do so for upcoming ones? The best way is to see if there is any kind of official hashtag created by the conference organizer that was or will be used to indicate and organize social media commentary about the event. So, for example, on the main page of the 2014 RSA Cyber-Security conference the organizers told visitors, "To participate in Twitter conversations around RSA Conference, please add the hashtag #RSAC to your tweets." Not only that, the page had a link to all the tweets that included that hashtag.

Not all conferences are going to be so helpful and solicitous as to provide a relevant hashtag, but sometimes you'll be able to find it on your own simply by searching Twitter for the conference name and looking to see if a high percentage of posts about it included a certain tag or tags, which you can then use for future searches. Even if there is no tag, you can simply search Twitter with the exact name of the conference to find any relevant tweets.

> **TIP: Get in Touch**
> If you find a blogger or tweeter who seems to have done a great job in covering an event, consider contacting that person and interviewing him or her for more information regarding your specific questions.

Source: *Library Finder Guides*

Many public and academic libraries create print and digital research finder guides that list, and help patrons identify and find, the very best sources for certain common research areas, and most libraries have now put these guides up on the web. The UCLA library's finder guide research page, for example, offers guides to dozens of topics ranging from Africa and Applied Linguistics to Urban Planning and World Arts and Culture.

How to Find: Do a simple Google search on the topic you are researching and add the words "library research guide" and you will likely find more than one relevant webpage. (If your topic is very narrow, you may need to find a broader umbrella subject that includes your topic: for example, perhaps rather than "hydraulic fracturing" you may need to use the word "energy.")

Source: *Docuticker, The ResourceShelf, and FulltextReports.com*
I am grouping these three resources together because they all do such a great job at a similar task: finding and sharing some of the best, highest quality—and free—research-related reports and documents on the web. Each one is a bit different, though, and I've quoted directly from each one's own description so you can get an idea of each one's special focus.

DocuTicker is a professionally curated service that finds and collects abstracts from "grey literature," including reports in pdf published by government agencies, think tanks, NGOs, research institutes, and other public interest groups. You can subscribe to the free newsletter or conduct a keyword search of its archive. The vast majority of resources located by DocuTicker are free. A similar information-finding service, also published by the same company (FreePint, located in the United Kingdom) is the ResourceShelf which identifies and describes free resources available on the web, including databases, lists and rankings, real-time sources, and multimedia. Finally, FullTextReports, edited by prominent and well-known librarian and editor Gary Price along with his colleague Shirl Kennedy, calls itself "A top-tier research professional's hand-picked selection of documents from academe, corporations, government agencies (including the CRS), interest groups, NGOs, professional societies, research institutes, think tanks, trade associations, and more."

How to Find: Link to Docuticker, ResourceShelf, and Fulltext Reports.com directly.

Source: *The Wayback Machine*
Would you like to go back in time? Well, you can (sort of) on this site, as you'll be stepping back into the web of yesteryear. The Wayback Machine is a creation of the nonprofit organization Internet

Figure 1.3   This page retrieved via the Wayback Machine shows the front page of the September 15, 2008 *New York Times* at the height of the financial crisis when Lehman Brothers announced its Chapter 11 bankruptcy

Archive, whose mission is digital artifact preservation. It is an attempt to create a snapshot of as many public webpages as possible since 1996.

So you can key in the URL of any site—perhaps a newspaper like *The New York Times*, or a store like L.L. Bean, or any other entity with a website—and browse a calendar of dates for which the Wayback Machine has crawled the site and snapped a picture of it (see Figure 1.3). The site is not perfect for sure: you can't do a keyword search, not every site and not every date is captured, and results are occasionally spotty. Still, this can be an amazing resource if you are doing any kind of historical research and want to know how an organization presented itself and what its site looked like many years ago.

How to Find: Link to The Wayback Machine.

Source: *Museums*
There are museums for countless topics—antiques, whaling, theater, and much more—and many of these have libraries that accept

written, email, and telephone inquiries on subjects in their specialty areas. For example, The Paley Center (once known as the Museum of Broadcasting) in New York City, which has a holding of 150,000 radio and television programs and advertising broadcasts spanning back to a 1918 radio speech made by labor leader Samuel Gompers, has a library that will respond to reference questions on a limited basis. (Its full collection is open to the public and can be searched online, but viewing is only available to those who come into the library itself.)

TIP: Tracking Down Old TV Broadcasts
To find an actual video of a television news broadcast—and even check out a lending copy of what you find!—you can search the database of Vanderbilt University's Television News Archives, which contains broadcasts of ABC, CBS, NBC, CNN, and Fox News all the way back to 1968. The database contains over a million items. You can conduct an advanced keyword search, find abstracts of actual news programs, and then get the full program or relevant excerpt copied to a DVD for a minimal fee (see Figure 1.4).

How to Find: To find a museum that matches your subject of interest, you can do a simple Google search with your keyword followed by "museum" to see what turns up. Or you can conduct a much more focused search by using a print copy of the *Official Museum Directory*, which lists over 15,000 museums, planetariums, science and technology centers, art galleries and centers, aquariums, and zoological parks, and even includes a personnel directory for the institutions listed. You'll need to look at a copy in a library; and although the publisher does allow for online searching of the directory, it is only available for institutional and other paid subscribers.

One very famous museum with extensive resources on an enormous number of different subjects is the Smithsonian Institution in

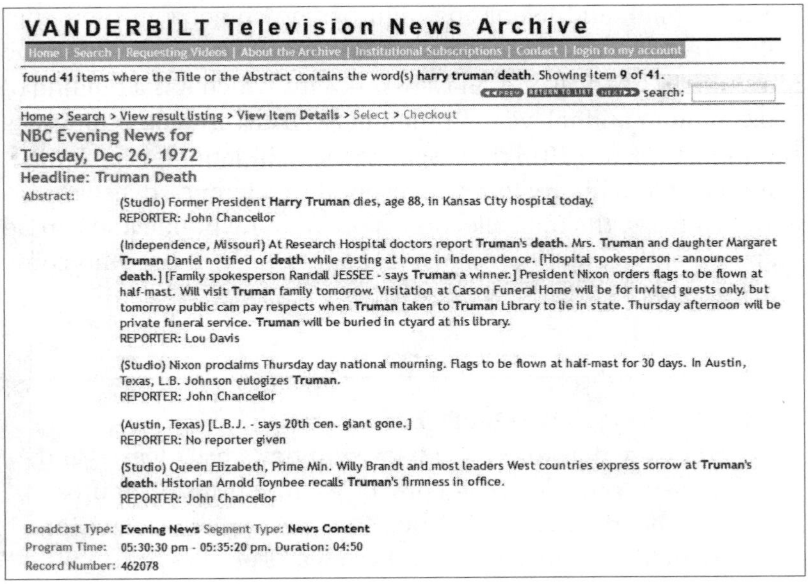

VANDERBILT Television News Archive

Home | Search | Requesting Videos | About the Archive | Institutional Subscriptions | Contact | login to my account

found **41** items where the Title or the Abstract contains the word(s) **harry truman death**. Showing item **9** of 41.

◄PREV RETURN TO LIST NEXT► search:

Home > Search > **View result listing** > **View Item Details** > Select > Checkout

NBC Evening News for
Tuesday, Dec 26, 1972

Headline: Truman Death

Abstract:

(Studio) Former President **Harry Truman** dies, age 88, in Kansas City hospital today.
REPORTER: John Chancellor

(Independence, Missouri) At Research Hospital doctors report **Truman's death**. Mrs. **Truman** and daughter Margaret **Truman** Daniel notified of **death** while resting at home in Independence. [Hospital spokesperson - announces **death**.] [Family spokesperson Randall JESSEE - says **Truman** a winner.] President Nixon orders flags to be flown at half-mast. Will visit **Truman** family tomorrow. Visitation at Carson Funeral Home will be for invited guests only, but tomorrow public cam pay respects when **Truman** taken to **Truman** Library to lie in state. Thursday afternoon will be private funeral service. **Truman** will be buried in ctyard at his library.
REPORTER: Lou Davis

(Studio) Nixon proclaims Thursday day national mourning. Flags to be flown at half-mast for 30 days. In Austin, Texas, L.B. Johnson eulogizes **Truman**.
REPORTER: John Chancellor

(Austin, Texas) [L.B.J. - says 20th cen. giant gone.]
REPORTER: No reporter given

(Studio) Queen Elizabeth, Prime Min. Willy Brandt and most leaders West countries express sorrow at **Truman's death**. Historian Arnold Toynbee recalls **Truman's** firmness in office.
REPORTER: John Chancellor

Broadcast Type: **Evening News** Segment Type: **News Content**
Program Time: 05:30:30 pm - 05:35:20 pm. Duration: 04:50
Record Number: 462078

Figure 1.4   Vanderbilt University offers free archives
of television broadcast shows back to 1968

Washington, D.C. Its specialties include art, history, air and space, zoology, horticulture, and marine life. Its website has a whole range of finder tools and database search services for researchers, and its reference librarians will accept reference queries from the public as well.

Source: *Ebook Collections*

There are several sites on the web that have made hundreds of thousands of ebooks available, making it easy to browse or search for the ones you want. Many of these focus only on freely down-loadable ebooks that are either out of copyright or are otherwise free to use. Others identify all ebooks; it's then up to you to either purchase it or find a local library where you can get a lending copy.

How to Find: Try any of these clearinghouses of ebooks: The Online Books Page (University of Pennsylvania); Ebooks on the Web (University of Buffalo Libraries); the Directory of Open Access Books; or the Open Library Project.

Source: *The Foundation Center*

If you are researching grants, how to write a grant proposal or other matters related to fund raising, you'll need to dig into the resources of The Foundation Center. The institute has created a searchable database of the contents of the Foundation Center's five libraries, called the Catalog of Non-Profit Literature, which consists of over 33,000 citations (65 percent of these include abstracts) of books, articles, federal regulations, research reports and other materials on fundraising, philanthropy, proposal development, and related topics of interest to non-profit organizations.

How to Find: The actual documents are available at one of the Foundation Center's primary libraries in New York and Washington, D.C.; and many are available at one of its three field office libraries in Atlanta, Cleveland, and San Francisco.

> **TIP: Learning More About Finding Donors and Funds**
> A set of advisory documents and guides available on the Web called Donor ID Techniques consists of a collection of documents and advisories on sources and strategies for finding donors and other individuals who could contribute to non-profits, universities, and other institutions that need to identify prospects and donors.

URLs and Chapter Note
Library Resources

Center for Research Libraries: www.crl.edu/content.asp?l1=1&l2=10&l3=14&l4=5 and www.crl.edu/content.asp?l1=5

CiteSeer: citeseer.ist.psu.edu

Hathi Trust: http://www.hathitrust.org

Library of Congress Ask a Librarian: www.loc.gov/rr/askalib

Library of Congress Reference and Research: www.loc.gov/rr

Library of Congress Searchable Databases: eresources.loc.gov

Library of Congress Virtual Reference Shelf: www.loc.gov/rr/askalib/virtualref.html

New York Public Library Articles and Databases: www.nypl.org/
collections/articles-databases

New York Public Library AskNYPL: www.nypl.org/ask-nypl and
www.nypl.org/ask-nypl/phone-us for phone numbers to ask
reference questions at the main branch

New York Public Library Research Guides: www.nypl.org/
collections/nypl-recommendations/guides

New York Public Library Schomburg Center for Research in Black
Culture: www.nypl.org/locations/schomburg

New York Public Library Science, Industry and Business Library:
http://www.nypl.org/locations/sibl#!

WorldCat: worldcat.org

Government Resources

Clearinghouses

Contact Your Government by Topic: https://www.usa.gov/contact
-by-topic

Data.gov: data.gov

Demographics: http://www.sbdcnet.org/industry-links/demo
graphics-links

Federal Agencies on Social Media: http://govsm.com/w/Main
_Page

FedStats: fedstats.sites.usa.gov

GPO Federal Digital System: www.gpo.gov/fdsys

MetaLib: metalib.gpo.gov

USA.Gov: usa.gov

USA.Gov: Business Data: www.usa.gov/Business/Business-Data
.shtml

Individual Sites

Agricola

ADAMS Nuclear Information: www.nrc.gov/reading-rm/adams
.html

Bureau of Labor Statistics Search: http://www.bls.gov/search/
osmr.htm

CDC Wonder: wonder.cdc.gov/

CIA Factbook: https://www.cia.gov/library/publications/the
-world-factbook/

Country Studies: http://memory.loc.gov/frd/cs/

Credit Union data: http://researchcu.ncua.gov/Views/FindCredit Unions.aspx

CRS Reports Archive-IT: archive-it.org/collections/1078

CRS Reports U.S. Department of State: http://fpc.state.gov/c18185 .htm

CRS Reports University of North Texas: digital.library.unt.edu/ explore/collections/CRSR/

DOE Research and Development Project Summaries

Economic Indicators: https://www.whitehouse.gov/administra tion/eop/cea/economic-indicators

Economic Report of the President: http://www.gpo.gov/fdsys/ browse/collection.action?collectionCode=ERP

Energy Citations Database: http://www.osti.gov/scitech/

Entrez: http://www.ncbi.nlm.nih.gov/gquery/

EnviroFacts: http://www.epa.gov/enviro/

Exporter Database: http://tse.export.gov/EDB/SelectReports .aspx?DATA=ExporterDB

Fatality Analysis Reporting System (FARS): www-fars.nhtsa.dot.gov/

FDIC datasets: https://www.fdic.gov/open/

Federal Business Opportunities: https://www.fbo.gov/

Federal Research Board: http://www.federalreserve.gov/econres data/default.htm

Federal Reserve Archive System for Economic Research: https:// fraser.stlouisfed.org/

Federal Reserve Economic Data: research.stlouisfed.org/fred2/

Federal Trade Commission: www.ftc.gov

Foreign Trade Statistics: http://www.census.gov/foreign-trade/ index.html

Global Legal Information Network: http://www.loc.gov/lawweb/ servlet/Glic?home

Government & Social Media Wiki: govsm.com/w/Federal_Agencies

Home Mortgage Disclosure Act: https://www.ffiec.gov/hmda/

Household Products Database: http://householdproducts.nlm .nih.gov/

Interactive Tariff and Trade Database: dataweb.usitc.gov/

International Energy Annual: http://www.eia.gov/cfapps/ipdb project/IEDIndex3.cfm

Library of Agriculture Decisions: http://www.dm.usda.gov/oalj decisions/decision-index.htm

Market Research Library: http://www.export.gov/mrktresearch/

Medline Plus: www.nlm.nih.gov/medlineplus/

National Center for Health Statistics Search: http://www.cdc .gov/nchs/

National Climatic Data Center Search: https://www.ncdc.noaa .gov/cdo-web/search

National Labor Relations Board Search: http://www.nlrb.gov/ search/cases

National Library of Medicine Databases and Electronic Resources: https://wwwcf2.nlm.nih.gov/nlm_eresources/eresources/ search_database.cfm

National Toxicology Program: https://ntp.niehs.nih.gov/

NIST Data Gateway: srdata.nist.gov/gateway/

O*Net Occupational Requirements: https://www.onetonline .org/find/

OFFSTATS: www.offstats.auckland.ac.nz/

ProQuest: Statistical Abstract of the United States: www.proquest .com/products-services/statabstract.html

PubMed Central: http://www.ncbi.nlm.nih.gov/pmc/

Search Copyright Records: http://www.copyright.gov/records/

Superfund Site Information: http://www.epa.gov/superfund/ sites/cursites/

The Information Bridge: http://www.osti.gov/scitech/

TOXNET: toxnet.nlm.nih.gov/

Trade Compliance Center: tcc.export.gov/

Trade Data & Analysis: http://www.export.gov/tradedata/

Trademark Electronic Search System (TESS): http://tmsearch .uspto.gov

TradeStats Express: tse.export.gov/TSE/TSEHome.aspx

TRIS: Online Transportation Research Information Services: http://www.trb.org/InformationServices/InformationServices .aspx

U.S. Bilateral Relations Fact Sheets: http://www.state.gov/r/pa/ ei/bgn/

U.S. Bureau of Labor Statistics: www.bls.gov

U.S. Census Bureau Economic Censuses: www.census.gov/econ/census/

U.S. Census Bureau Industry Statistics Portal: www.census.gov/econ/isp/

U.S. Census Bureau State Trade Data: https://www.census.gov/foreign-trade/statistics/state/

U.S. Census Bureau Statistics of US Businesses: https://www.census.gov/econ/susb/

U.S. Census Bureau USA Trade Online: https://usatrade.census.gov/

U.S. Census Bureau: www.census.gov

U.S. International Trade Administration: Data and Analysis: trade.gov/data.asp

U.S. International Trade Administration: Trade Statistics: www.trade.gov/mas/ian/tradestatistics/

U.S. International Trade Center DataWeb: dataweb.usitc.gov/

U.S. TradeStats Express: tse.export.gov/TSE/TSEHome.aspx

UN Statistics Division: unstats.un.org

USA Trade Online: usatrade.census.gov/

USPTO Search: http://www.uspto.gov/trademarks-application-process/search-trademark-database

Virtual World Trade Reference Room: http://www.trade.gov/mas/ian/referenceinfo/tg_ian_002086.asp

Business Sources

Ad*Access Project: library.duke.edu/digitalcollections/adaccess

AdBrands: adbrands.net

Aneki: aneki.com

Annual Reports Service: investorcalendar.com/research/index.asp

BizStats: www.bizstats.com

Bloomberg Business Research: http://tinyurl.com/ngwzhfo

Business Registries: investigativedashboard.org/business_registries/

Company-Registers.info: www.obchodni-rejstriky.cz/en

Country Risk Reports: http://www3.ambest.com/ratings/cr/crisk.aspx

EconPapers: econpapers.repec.org

EDGAR: www.sec.gov/edgar.shtml

The Emergence of Advertising in America: library.duke.edu/
digitalcollections/eaa/Global Brand Database: http://www
.wipo.int/branddb/en/

Find the Best: http://findthebest.companies.com

Free Report Library: http://www.datamyne.com/free-report
-library/

Harris Vault: http://www.harrisinteractive.com/Insights/Harris
Vault.aspx

ILOSTAT: tinyurl.com/ksqap94

Index of U.S. Business Search Databases: businessjournalism
.org/registration/llc/

Industries at a Glance: bls.gov/iag/

Industry News: www.headlinespot.com/subject/industry

Journlist's Resource: Economics: http://journalistsresource.org/
studies/economics

LEGOSH: http://www.ilo.org/safework/info/publications/WCMS_
217849/lang--en/index.html

Market Potential Index: http://globaledge.msu.edu/mpi

Market Research Library: www.buyusainfo.net

Marketing Charts: www.marketingcharts.com

MarketsandMarkets: www.marketsandmarkets.com/press
-release-2.html

Mint: mintportal.bvdep.com

Rank and Filed: http://rankandfiled.com

ReportLinker: www.reportlinker.com

Secretaries of State: http://www.coordinatedlegal.com/Secretary
OfState.html

Seeking Alpha: seekingalpha.com

Social Explorer: www.socialexplorer.com/pub/home/home.aspx

Statista: www.statista.com

Worldometers: www.worldometers.info

Who Operates Where: https://www.uniworldbp.com/template1.ph

Working Papers and Technical Reports in Business, Economics
and Law: http://www.loc.gov/rr/business/techreps/techrep
shome.php

Zanran: www.zanran.com/q/

Scholarly Sources

Academia.edu: academia.edu

CalTechAuthors: authors.library.caltech.edu

Directory of Open Access Journals: www.doaj.org

DOAR: www.opendoar.org/search.php

Docuticker: www.docuticker.com

Enigma.io: enigma.io

FulltextReports.com: fulltextreports.com

Global Open Access Portal: www.unesco.org/new/en/commu nication-and-information/portals-and-platforms/goap/

Google Public Data Explorer: www.google.com/publicdata/ directory

Google Scholar: scholar.google.com

Ingenta: www.ingentaconnect.com/

JSTOR: jstor.org

JURN: jurn.org

Library of Congress E-Resources: http://tinyurl.com/pslfgne

Microsoft Academic: Search: academic.research.microsoft.com/

MIT Theses and Dissertations: dspace.mit.edu/handle/1721 .1/7582

Open Access Button: openaccessbutton.org

Registry of Open Access Registries (ROAR): roar.eprints.org/view/ type/theses.html

ResearchGate: www.researchgate.net

Social Science Research Network: ssrn.com

The Resource Shelf: www.resourceshelf.com

University of Michigan Deep BlueProject: deepblue.lib.umich .edu/community-list

University of Toronto Research Repository: https://tspace .library.utoronto.ca/handle/1807/9944

Windows Azure Marketplace: datamarket.azure.com/

Other Super Sources

Directory of Open Access Books: www.doabooks.org/

Donor ID Techniques: http://majorgivingnow.org/expand/donor _id_techniques.html

Ebooks on the Web: libweb.lib.buffalo.edu/ft/EBooks.asp

Foundation Center: http://catalog.foundationcenter.org/

Open Library Project: openlibrary.org
The New York Times: www.nytimes.com/ref/membercenter/nyt
   archive.html
The Online Books Page: onlinebooks.library.upenn.edu/
The Wayback Machine: web.archive.org
UCLA Library Finder Guide: guides.library.ucla.edu/

Note

1. http://www.budapestopenaccessinitiative.org/read

Chapter 2

Libraries—Still Valuable in the Digital Age

Why Libraries?

"Why trudge off to the library when I have the internet at my fingertips, anytime and anywhere?" you may ask. Well, it's certainly true that you can go online for fast answers to a whole host of questions, but there remain many compelling reasons to go to your local library rather than your smart phone, iPad, or laptop.

Following are my top ten reasons why researchers should treasure libraries, even in the digital age, and visit their favorite library regularly.

1. Access to Books

This may seem obvious, but it can be easy to forget that at the library you can physically browse print books on shelves, find the ones you want, and then sit down and read or take them home with you. The internet does many things incredibly well—but one thing it does not do is provide the complete text of all books, particularly newer ones. Yes, Google Books certainly has scanned tens of millions of books—but you can only read the full text of those that are out of print and out of copyright (unless the publisher has provided permission). For the latest titles you are normally going to find only very short excerpts and limited samplings from selected pages. (That's why you can sometimes use Google Books to find the existence of a book, and then go to your library to read a copy or request a copy through interlibrary loan.) And while more and more people are enjoying ebooks (which, of course, you can also check out at your library), many of us still enjoy or even prefer books in hard copy.

2. Access to Magazines and Newspapers

Although many publishers do put the full text of their magazines or newspapers online, not all do, and those that do may charge a fee (this is particularly true for scholarly and academic journals) or prevent access to back issues. The library is still, then, a great place to go for magazines and newspapers, and for finding back issues of those publications. In addition, most libraries have a place where the most recent issues are displayed, which makes scanning them easier than searching on the web. For many people it is still harder to comfortably browse publications on the internet, or even in a digital flip format on a tablet, than it is to page through a print copy.

Furthermore, I have found scanning the covers of the magazines and journals displayed on library shelves to be an interesting exercise. By doing so you can quickly get a sense of the hot topics, notice interesting magazines that you might not have previously known about, and get a sense of how various media are covering the same topic. This kind of "meta-browsing" is quite difficult to do on the internet.

3. Access to Directories

As discussed later in this chapter, directories are invaluable tools for researchers, as they pull together related data on a subject and can provide leads for locating further information. Like books, complete directories—such as the *Encyclopedia of Associations*, *Research Centers Directory*, *Major U.S. Companies of Europe*, and so on—are not fully represented on the internet. Most are quite expensive—running in the hundreds of dollars or more—and they are not something you are likely going to buy on your own. So your library remains the best place to find and use them without having to purchase them or pay a search fee .

4. Access to Primary Materials

Although libraries (and other institutions, such as museums) are increasingly digitizing source material created originally in print— letters, maps, government decrees, etc. (see the section on The Digital Library below)—the number of primary source materials scanned into digital form and placed on the web still represents a tiny percentage of what is available at libraries around the world. As a result, you will often still need to physically go to a library to look at items like rare books, maps, manuscripts, letters, photographs, and other primary and special collection documents.

5. Access to the Internet

Getting access to the internet is no longer a big deal, since the vast majority of us have regular and reliable online access. Still, if you are in a location where a provider is unavailable, or you're traveling and don't have a smart phone with you, or if your home internet service is out for some reason, it's good to know that you can always go online by walking into the nearest library.

6. Access to Fee-Based Databases

As you probably already know, searching a database is a lot different than using a search engine like Google. Generally speaking, commercial databases provide access to focused sets of *highly filtered* information (e.g., newspaper articles, company financial data, articles in sociology journals, government reports) geared toward research purposes and offer sophisticated search capabilities. Unlike what you find on the internet as a whole, fee-based informational databases don't include advertisements, pornography, fluff pieces for getting clicks or other nonsubstantive data— and these resources are created specifically for those with serious information-gathering missions. Two of the most popular database vendors you'll come across in libraries are ProQuest and EBSCO.

7. Organized Information with Research Aids

Information held in a library is fully organized via a standard and consistent cataloguing method. Many libraries also create and distribute handy research handouts that clearly describe how and where to find the best resources for key disciplines and subject areas. All of which means that locating what you need at a library largely avoids the frustration that accompanies an internet search.

8. Personal Assistance

Not only can the research finding aids mentioned above help you find what you need, but so can the librarians, of course. Librarians are experts trained in the use and retrieval of information (most have a masters degree in library science) and are ready and willing to help you find what you are looking for. Think about it—for no fee at all, you can enlist the service of a trained specialist to help you find what you need and give you suggestions and ideas on other resources and avenues that you had probably not thought about. The antidote for the current malady of information overload is not some pseudo-smart software program, but a knowledgeable person—the librarian as the human filter.

Keep in mind, too, that recommendations and suggestions from a librarian are quite different from recommendations from a site like Amazon or a social media site. The latter work by algorithms and make assumptions about what you might want to look at—these are, no doubt, often very good assumptions, but they do not take into account your own larger, more subtle, and unarticulated research needs and context. The librarian is trained to do a reference interview with patrons and to ask the right questions to elicit the kinds of answers that will help them help you! Furthermore, the larger interest of online sites is not always clear—it may be to sell more books, get more clicks, or some other hidden motivation driven by profit, audience retention, or who knows what.

A librarian has only one mission: to help *you* discover what *you* want to best further *your* larger research project!

9. The Atmosphere

Sure, it's fast and convenient to look up information on your laptop while lying on your bed, or sitting at your kitchen table, or even when you're walking down the street with your smart phone—but are these the best environments for research? Maybe someone's playing music in the next room, or your dog's barking, or the TV is on upstairs, or someone is knocking at your front door. Contrast these scenarios to the library, designed to foster quiet study, reading, and information-seeking, and to be a place where patrons can sit at comfortable, oversized tables and desks, surrounded by books and art.

Not only is the medium the message, but so is the environment, and the message of a library's environment is "concentrate, think, reflect."

10. Community Activities

Although the primary mission of public libraries is to make information freely available, they also fill an important social and community need. If you haven't been to a library recently, step inside. Browse the bulletin boards. Look at the handouts. You'll find materials on community activities and programs ranging from free health education classes to career fairs, local transportation alternatives, upcoming lectures, and much more.

Some of these events and activities may be held right at the library, while other postings inform visitors of activities being held elsewhere. You'll also find information specifically about the history and culture of that town or region as well as material that's geared toward meeting the needs of the particular population that lives in the neighborhood (i.e., a library located in a largely Italian area should have books on Italian heritage; one located in a high-tech region will focus much of its collection on computing and emerging digital technologies). A library is a valued part of any neighborhood, and its role is to disseminate information that is going to be of value to members of the community.

Finally, here's another, admittedly subjective reason to visit your library. Personally, after spending several hours hunched over my laptop, entering commands into a search engine, and staring at tiny phosphorescent particles on a display screen, I welcome the chance to stretch my legs and walk through my lively urban neighborhood to the library. There I can see actual (not virtual) people, talk to a librarian, and run my hands across the spines of the books that are sitting on the shelves. It's just more enjoyable. A trip to the library balances my time on the computer and adds a richness to my day and research experience that I'll never find online.

The 20th Century Library

If your image of a library is of a dusty old place, then it's time to update your image. Many of today's libraries are sleek and efficient, filled with the latest communication tools and technologies, and beautifully designed. Some of my favorite modern libraries include the NYPL, the San Antonio Public Library, and the Rochester, New York, Public Library. Paris has built what some think is the state-of-the-art library—the Bibliothèque Nationale de France. I've been told that the Los Angeles and Cleveland public libraries are stunning, as is the "Book Mountain" library in Spijkenisse, the Netherlands. (You can see photographs of a collection of gorgeous libraries around the world by going to a site called Most Interesting Libraries in the World, compiled by the Swiss company Mirage Bookmarks.)

And speaking of stupendous libraries, it should be noted that in 2002 UNESCO completed a project to revive the ancient Great Library of Alexandria on a ten-acre site on the Eastern Harbor in Chatcy, near Alexandria University. Toward the beginning of the third century BC, the great library and a later "daughter" library together contained approximately 700,000 volumes. Sadly, the libraries were destroyed in a fire during a civil war in the third century AD.

The new library has a collection of about 1.6 million volumes, as well as a variety of high-tech information tools and resources

---

TIP: Getting the Most Out of Any Library

- If you've located a library that has the information you want, but it is not nearby, you can usually still get a certain amount of information and answers to some questions by calling or emailing. You'll find librarians to be very helpful people!

- When you go to a library, don't hesitate to ask the reference librarian for assistance. That's what librarians are there for, and by enlisting their help you can save yourself a lot of time and frustration.

- If the library doesn't have a resource you need, be sure to ask about interlibrary loan.

- Don't forget your own town library's reference department. After all, sometimes Siri is smart; other times, not so much. Whether it's the flying time from New York to Istanbul or the year the clock was invented, you can call, email, or message your library and a real human will help dig up that quick fact or answer you need.

including software for reading Arabic texts and digitizing manuscripts and making them available online.

Finally, if you really love libraries you might consider joining your library's Friend of the Library program. These programs offer some nice perks for a modest membership fee or donation—and of course it's a way to ensure your library survives and thrives.

Selecting a Library

There are three basic types of libraries: public, college/university (academic), and special (special libraries include business libraries). Let's look at each briefly.

Public Libraries

The best public libraries for information gatherers are the largest, usually the main branches of big city libraries, because these are most likely to contain the most extensive reference collections. It's here that you'll find the highest number of superb information sources described later in the chapter. If the only public library in your area is a very small one, you may want to look to one of the other types of libraries described in this section.

College and University Libraries

Academic libraries typically have more information sources than the average town's public library, and the majority of them are open to the public. An academic library's collection typically reflects the institution's majors and specialties, and thus is often your best bet if your research is on a topic that would be studied at such an institution, whether it be astronomy, management, law, or some other academic discipline.

> **TIP: How to Find an Academic Library**
> Contact the Association of College and Research Libraries, American Library Association, 50 Huron St., Chicago IL 60611-2795; (312) 280-2523.

Special Libraries

There are thousands of libraries around the country that specialize in particular subjects—farming, baseball, the environment, Asia, cooking, mass media, and countless other topics. Most of these libraries are open to the public, and even those that are not may still admit you if you explain to the librarian that you are working on a research project. Doing research at one of these special libraries, where you are surrounded by resources that pertain to the specific subject you're interested in, is like working in a veritable gold mine.

One valuable type of special library is the corporate library. A corporate library—or "information center," as they are increasingly called—contains a wealth of information on subjects related to that company's industry and specialties. ExxonMobil's library, for example, has extensive information on energy, while Boeing's libraries contain wide-ranging information on aerospace.

TIP: Identifying a Special Library

Contact the Special Libraries Association, 331 South Patrick Street, Alexandria, VA, 22314-3501; (703) 647-4900. Ask to speak with an information specialist or someone who can identify a special library in your area of interest. Or check a library copy of *The Subject Directory of Special Libraries and Information Centers*, published by Gale/Cengage, which lists thousands of special libraries.

Unfortunately, many corporate libraries allow access only to company employees. Even worse, in recent years some companies have either downsized their information centers or eliminated their libraries completely. But don't despair: Many corporate libraries survive thanks to smart management, and for those that do you can often get around an official closed-door policy.

For starters, once you've identified a relevant company library, call up the librarian, introduce yourself, and briefly explain what kind of information you are looking for and why. Let the librarian know your project is a serious and important one, and suggest that the library may be the best local source of the information you need. Describe what you'll want to do at the library and what types of materials you'll want to examine.

By taking a polite and informed approach, you may persuade the corporate librarian to let you come in and work at the library on a limited basis, or at least refer you to other useful resources. Be aware that when you visit a corporate library you won't be able to take anything out. And while you're there, try to work independently rather than impinging on the librarian's time, which is dedicated to serving the needs of the company.

TIP: Use Your Network
If you know someone who works at a company with a library you want to use, you may be able to gain entrance by using that person as a reference.

Finding a Library on the Internet

You can, of course, turn to the internet to find a specialized library, and the best way to do this is by consulting one of the many websites that provide a directory of libraries around the country or world. Many of these sites also describe libraries' holdings and collections, so you can know going in which specific subject areas and information resources they offer.

National libraries are particularly valuable, as they are created by governments to serve as a nation's central information source. Like the United States' national library, the Library of Congress (LOC), national libraries around the world typically collect all major publications issued in their respective countries. Some of the best places on the internet to search for and find links to libraries are:

- Libweb (lists over 8,000 libraries from 146 countries)

- National Libraries of the World

- The European Library (focuses on Europe and links to 48 national libraries of Europe)

- Wikipedia (its entry on national libraries contains links to over 200 national libraries around the globe.)

All-Purpose Resources: Oldies But Goodies

There are certain well-known, venerable, hard-copy research sources that you can find in almost any library that have retained their value even in the digital age. This section identifies and describes those that are of the greatest value to the widest audience.

It is true that most of the time a digital version of a work is more efficient and powerful than its print counterpart: with a digital resource, coverage is not limited due to the physical space constraints of print, it can be searched by keyword, it may be continually updated, and it can be made available anytime and anywhere. That said, for certain sources print is as good if not better than digital, and these are the types of resources I will be recommending in this chapter.

The print sources I include all share certain characteristics: they provide quick and efficient access to in-depth and substantive information, they are either not easily available or very expensive to access online, or they are actually more useful in print than digitally (typically because you can search further back in time, or because they offer multiple types of detailed indexes).

While one primary advantages of a print index or directory is the ability to go back many years or even decades, some publishers have created deep digital equivalents in the form of searchable archival databases; in such cases you get the benefits of both complete back-file coverage and the power and speed of keyword searching. Because some libraries offer only the print version of a given resource and not the database, or vice versa, it's good practice to be aware of your options.

There is another somewhat subtle but quite important reason to employ the library-oriented directories of newspapers and journals outlined in this chapter, and that is that they serve as a check on the specific sources you are most likely going to turn up when doing an internet search. As discussed in Chapters 3 and 5, search engines like Google generally favor the most popular sources, meaning that those most often linked to will be ranked higher in search results. This is fine as far as it goes (much more on this topic in Chapter 5), but it means that while you are likely to retrieve a lot of results from sources such as Huffington Post, *The New York Times*, *The Guardian*,

TMZ, or whatever matches the search engine makes to its index, you are much less likely to see articles published in small, niche, and lesser-known journals and news sites. (This is especially true for searches on popular topics.) The reality is that sometimes these smaller outlets are your ideal sources, if you can only find them.

By using an old-fashioned index and directory, you can bypass the ranking method used by the search engine and override this particular bias. You will gain a more rounded set of results than you would have received from a Google search—and that's a good thing.

Print Directories

The print directories covered here will help you find articles from newspapers, magazines, and academic journals. Note that many of them are also available through searchable databases.

Source*: Readers' Guide to Periodical Literature*
The *Readers' Guide* indexes articles published in over 300 of the most popular periodicals on popular topics including aeronautics, aging, astronomy, automobiles, biography, business, Canada, children, computers, consumer education, current events, education, environment, fashion, film, fine arts, food, foreign affairs, health, history, hobbies, home, journalism, leisure activities, medicine, music, news, nutrition, photography, politics, religion, science, sports, and television. Depending on the subscription in the particular library you visit, you can find articles in issues all the way back to the 1890s!

These familiar green volumes provide a quick way of finding articles published in back issues on your subject of interest. You may not always get "inside" information from articles published in these general-interest magazines, but they can still be good information sources. And because these periodicals are so popular, you can find back issues of many of them right there in the library.

Source: *Business Periodicals Index Retrospective*
This source indexes articles published in over 1,000 periodicals oriented toward business between 1913 and 1982. The scope is broad, ranging from advertising and marketing to real estate, business technology issues, finance, insurance, and much more. Almost all libraries have it.

This is an extremely valuable index if you are doing any kind of historical business-related research. Its name may mislead some people because the guide actually indexes periodicals that contain information on topics beyond the scope of what most people consider business. For example, it indexes articles from publications like *Aeronautical Engineering Review, Nursing Homes,* and the *Welding Journal.*

Many of these indexed publications are trade periodicals, covering a particular industry or specialized area in business, industry, or trade. Such publications generally provide more specialized and in-depth information than the popular magazines indexed in the *Readers' Guide,* but at the same time the articles are usually not overly technical or hard to read. This is a nice balance for the information seeker who is not technically oriented or an expert in the field but who still wants more than a superficial examination of a subject.

Special Periodical Indexes

Source: *H.W. Wilson Subject Indexes*
The Wilson Subject Indexes are multivolume series that identify articles published within many major subject areas. There are different series for different fields and disciplines (e.g., humanities, social science, science, art, business, education, agriculture, and law).

While most of the current coverage of the journals in these areas is available in up-to-date searchable databases, H.W. Wilson has published volumes of earlier coverage in its retrospective series. To use these indexes you consult the volumes devoted to your field of interest and look up specific subtopics. You'll find the Wilson indexes at medium and large libraries.

The trick when using these guides is to figure out which subject index to consult. What you need to do is determine which Wilson subject area your research topic falls under. For example, if you wanted to find out about growing tomatoes, that would be a food science question, and you'd check the *Biological and Agricultural Index.* If your subject were meditation, that would fall under psychology, and so you'd look in the *Social Science Index.*

The table that follows presents some samples of subtopics covered in various Wilson indexes.

If your area of interest is	The Wilson Index is
fire, mineralogy, oceanology plastics, transportation, and other applied scientific subjects	*Applied Science and Technology Index*
architecture, art history, film, industrial design, landscape design, painting, photography	*Art Index*
animal breeding, food science, nutrition pesticides	*Biological and Agricultural Index*
accounting, advertising, banking, economics, finance, investment, labor, management, marketing, public relations, specialized industries	*Business Periodicals Index*
curriculum, school administration and supervision, teaching methods	*Education Index*
astronomy, physics, and broad scientific areas	*General Science Abstracts*
legal information, all areas of jurisprudence	*Index to Legal Periodicals and Books*
anthropology, environmental science, psychology, sociology, archaeology, classical studies, folklore, history	*Humanities and Social Science Retrospective*
language and literature, literary and political criticism, performing arts, philosophy, religion, theology	*Humanities Index*

Table Wilson Indexes by Interest Area

TIP: Finding Searchable Databases of Periodical Indexes
Although in order to do archival research it is sometimes necessary to consult an old-fashioned print directory, in cases where you are concerned only with current literature you may find the equivalent *searchable database* in a library that provides access to the same high-quality journals indexed in the print directory. The following table lists the key directories discussed in this section and the name of databases where you can search them (and usually other sources on the same topic area). Note that these databases are primarily available from ESBCO, which merged with H.W. Wilson and makes them available on its EBSCOHost database system.

Key Directories	Searchable in These Databases
Readers' Guide to Periodical Literature:	Readers' Guide Full Text Select/Mega; Readers' Guide Retrospective 1890–1982; Readers' Guide to Periodical Literature
Business Periodicals Index Retrospective	Business Abstracts with Full Text; Business Periodicals Index Retrospective
Science and Technology Index	Applied Science and Technology Source/Full Text/Index; Applied Science & Technology Retrospective 1913–1983
Art Index	Art Abstracts/Art Full Text/Art Index Retrospective 1929–1984
Biological and Agricultural Index	Biological & Agricultural Index Plus
Education Index	Education Abstracts/Education Full Text/ Education Retrospective 1929–1983
General Science Index	General Science Abstract/Full Text
Humanities Index	Humanities Abstracts/Humanities Full Text/ Humanities Index Retrospective 1907–1984
Index to Legal Periodicals	Index to Legal Periodicals & Books/Full Text/ Retrospective 1908–1981
Social Science Index	Social Science Abstracts; Social Science Full Text; Social Science Index Retrospective 1907–1983

Table   Key Directories and Databases That Include Them

TIP: Spotting Hot Periodicals
Use periodical indexes to identify publications that are worth examining in depth. Take a look at the opening pages, where the indexed magazines and journals are usually listed. Reading this listing is a good way to identify the most important publications in your field of interest (and again, without the influence of a search engine's ranking algorithm). If you find one or more that seem to be right on the money in covering your topic, you can then, of course, still, go online to the appropriate databases and search for past issues there, or see what additional informational resources are available.

Magazine and Newsletter Directories

Sources: *Gale Directory of Publications and Broadcast Media (print); Magazines for Libraries (print; previously known as Katz's Magazines for Libraries); Standard Periodical Directory (print); Ulrich's Periodical Directory (print)*

There are magazines, journals, and newsletters covering thousands of different topics. The directories listed in the previous pages identify tens of thousands of such publications. The most comprehensive is *Ulrich's*, which provides information on over 300,000 periodicals, with a special focus on international publications and those geared for an academic audience.

There are, of course, many specialized publications being produced in the United States. Even if your topic is extremely narrow, there may be a periodical devoted to that subject. Let me give you a few examples. If you look under "Folklore" in *Ulrich's* you'll find *Folklore Center News*, and under "Motion Pictures" you'll see magazines like *Amateur Film Maker* and *Motion Picture Investor*, a newsletter that analyzes the private and public values of movies and movie stock. Under the category "Nutrition and Dietetics" you'll find dozens of publications, including *Jewish Vegetarian*, published by the International Jewish Vegetarian Society of London.

Back in the day—meaning pre-internet, of course—in order to locate the names of leading publications in a particular discipline, industry, or topic it was necessary to pull out and page through one or more old-fashioned print directories. Today, in the age of the real-time, social, and visual web, the best way to find leading publications is still, well, the old-fashioned way—through print directories! There are periodicals and newsletters covering tens of

---

TIP: Don't Forget Ejournal Directories
While the print directories already mentioned typically include ejournals, it's worth noting that there are free sites on the web that are specifically devoted to digital journals. Two that I recommend are the Directory of Open Access Journals and the Electronics Journals Library.

thousands of different subjects. The directories we've covered so far identify many thousands of magazines, newsletters, journals, and other periodicals, and virtually every library has one more of them on its shelves.

Directories are excellent resources for tracking down specific periodicals covering a particular subject of interest. The way these guides work is simple: you look up your subject, and the guide lists the magazines or newsletters published within the field. Each entry

TIP:
Use the *National Directory of Magazines* for in-depth qualitative reviews on magazines and other publications. Although this guide covers fewer publications than the others (about 5,300), and so does not cover the most obscure publications, it provides a superb analysis and review of the coverage and usefulness for those it does include. The directory is actually designed to assist librarians in deciding which magazines to obtain, so it is also an excellent tool for researchers who want to know which publications are considered the best in the field and how their scope compares with others.

TIP:
A couple of these directories can be searched online. The *Standard Periodical Directory* is searchable on a fee-based site called Mediafinder, while *Ulrich's*, along with *Magazines for Libraries*, can be searched on another fee-based database called UlrichsWeb. Gale itself makes most of its best-selling directories—ranging from American Wholesalers and Distributors Directory to Trade Shows Worldwide—available on its own searchable database, the Gale Directory Library. This database, which is only available in libraries, consists of the full text of as many individual Gale edirectories as a particular library has subscribed to.

typically includes the title of the publication, a short description, publisher, circulation, and sometimes additional information such as price, ad rates, audience, where it is available online, and more.

People Information

Source: Marquis *Who's Who* Series

The *Who's Who* volumes are the standard and most popular library directory sources of biographical details on people of various accomplishments. The best-known of these books is *Who's Who in America*, which lists facts on prominent Americans, such as their place and date of birth, schools attended, degrees awarded, special accomplishments, and current address. There are scores of more specialized *Who's Who* volumes, such as *Who's Who in Medicine and Healthcare*, *Who's Who in Asia*, and *Who's Who of American Women*. Virtually all libraries have *Who's Who in America*. Larger and specialized libraries have the other volumes.

One question you might have is, "Why bother consulting a *Who's Who* directory when I can look up a prominent person's name on Wikipedia?" That's a good question, and the answer isn't necessarily that the quality of a *Who's Who* entry will be any better than the one you'll find on Wikipedia, because the information that's furnished in these volumes is often provided by the biographees themselves, so accuracy will depend on their truthfulness. In fact, a good

---

TIP: Search a *Who's Who* Database or Purchase *Who's Who* Bios on Demand

Some libraries subscribe to the entire Marquis collection of over 1.5 million biographies. This database, which is updated daily, allows users to search by name and up to 15 other criteria including location and school attended, to name just a couple.

You can also link directly to the *Who's Who* site and search for the name of the person you are researching across all the directories. If you find a useful entry, you can simply purchase and download it for a low fee.

argument can be made that Wikipedia's many users, editors, and fact-checking capabilities will often provide more accurate information. But this will vary by entry. The main reason to consider using a *Who's Who* directory is simply that you may discover valuable information that is not available in Wikipedia.

Source: *Current Biography*
Current Biography is a monthly magazine with articles about prominent people in the news, in national and international affairs, the sciences, arts, labor, and industry. Obituaries are also included. At the end of each year the articles are printed in a single volume. An index at the back helps users find biographies during the current year and for a few years back. Medium and large libraries have the set.

This resource strives to be "brief, objective, and accurate, with well-documented articles." It may be more reliable than other sources since its editors consult many sources of biographical data, rather than relying solely on the biographees' own accounts.

A searchable database called Current Biography Illustrated, on the ESBSCOHost service, is available at certain libraries.

Source: *Current Biography Cumulative Index*
Biography Index scans thousands of periodicals, many books, and various biographical sources like obituaries, diaries, and memoirs to identify and index sources of information on prominent people.

Source: *Biography and Genealogy Master Index*
Biography and Genealogy Master Index is an index to biographical directories, providing information on more than 5 million current and historical figures. Over 1,700 current and retrospective biographical sources are used to index information on "figures from authors to scientists, from boxers to fashion designers" and "from Adam and Eve to Frank Zappa."

This source, then, will tell you whether there is a directory or publication that lists biographical information on a historical or well-known figure. For example, if you looked up Bob Dylan, you'd find that biographical sketches could be found in *Baker's Biographical Dictionary of Musicians*, *Biography Index*, *The New Oxford Companion to Music*, *Who's Who in the World*, and elsewhere. Once you've identified a biographical directory that will suit your needs, go to WorldCat (see page 4) to locate a library that holds a copy.

Source: *American Men and Women of Science:*
A Biographical Directory of Today's Leaders
Published annually, this directory profiles over 151,000 living scientists. This source is very useful for finding quick biographical information on prominent persons involved in the sciences. Data provided in an individual's entry includes birth date, birthplace, field of specialty, education, honorary degrees, current position, professional and career information, awards, memberships, research information, and contact information where available. Each year the publisher adds thousands of new profiles to keep this directory up to date. You'll find it in the larger libraries or in those that have a good scientific and technical collection.

Business and Industry Information

Libraries can be particularly valuable to people seeking business information. Specialized periodical indexes, industry directories, and special business guides can provide you with important facts about companies and businesses—without the access fees charged by many online business information sites. (Note that many more business information sources, not found in libraries, are identified in Chapter 1.)

Following is a selection of some of the leading and most broadly useful business sources found in libraries.

Source: *The Wall Street Journal*
You may have noticed that when you search the web and find an article from the *Wall Street Journal* you are unable to read it unless you become a subscriber. Well, there is another option; read it for free at your library!

Articles published in the *Wall Street Journal* are generally not too technical, yet they are in-depth and probing enough to provide very valuable information—and often exclusive and insider-type information not available from other news sources.

Most libraries keep back issues of the *Journal* in print (or, if further back, on a database or—horrors!—on the dreaded microfilm).

Source: *Company Directories*

A company directory is simply a book that provides a variety of look-up facts about the listed organizations. Leading company directories include:

- *Standard & Poor's Register of Corporations, Directors, and Executives*
- Dun & Bradstreet *Million Dollar Directory*
- *Hoover's Handbook of American Business*
- *Who Owns Whom*
- *LexisNexis Corporate Affiliations*
- *Major Companies of Europe*
- *Japan Company Handbook*

The information in a company directory typically includes data such as the year a firm was founded, the products or services offered, contact information, whether it is public or private, names and titles of top executives, total sales, number of employees, subsidiaries and branches, detailed financials if the company is publicly held, and more.

Before the web, these directories (as well as the corresponding searchable online company directory databases) were pretty much the go-to resources for facts on businesses and large organizations. They remain valuable today in that they are authoritative, free, and easy to use, but they are less useful than they once were, primarily because the data changes so quickly. The print directories are generally updated annually, and not every entry is necessarily going to be updated each year. So, if you use them—or even a professional database that includes entries from them—don't take the data as gospel, particularly when it comes to sales figures and employee names and titles. Confirm the information using online sources including the business social network LinkedIn.

> **TIP: Try Euromonitor**
> Many European company directories are published or distributed by Euromonitor, a UK–based publisher.

Source: *Business Rankings Annual*
Business Rankings Annual is a collection of thousands of citations of ranked lists of companies in various categories. This guide helps answer the question "Who's Number One?" in a certain field.

"Insider Directories"

Source: *Directories in Print*
Directories in Print describes over 16,000 different types of specialized directories, covering subjects such as banking, agriculture, law, government, science, engineering, education, information science, biography, arts and entertainment, public affairs, health, religion, hobbies, and sports. You can find this guide, published annually, at most large public libraries.

This excellent source includes an amazingly diverse range of specialized directories. (A directory is any kind of reference book that tells readers where they can find sources of information within a specific field.) Examples of the directories included in this "ultimate" directory: *Special Libraries of Israel*, *Bicycle Resource Guide*, *Major Companies of Europe*, *American Indian Painters*, *Index of Stolen Art*, and many more!

Source: *Research Centers Directory*
Research Centers Directory is an annual directory of over 14,800 university, government, and other nonprofit research organizations, think tanks, laboratories, and institutes. Major subject areas include agriculture, business, education, government, law, math, social sciences, and humanities. You'll find this guide in university and other academically oriented libraries.

The directory provides a wealth of information on who's conducting research on which subjects around the country. You'll find an incredible diversity of studies being conducted. Some examples of the research organizations listed in this directory include the Alcohol Research group, the National Bureau of Economic Research, the International Copper Research Association, the Birth Defects Institute, the Center for Russian and East European Studies . . . you get the idea.

I once used this guide when I was researching the topic of "rebuilding rather than replacing automobiles." By checking the directory, I found a research institute associated with a university in Detroit that was conducting a study on just that topic.

The directory is easy to use. You just look up your subject, and the directory refers you to relevant research centers. It provides each center's name, a contact person, the address, phone number, email, website, a description of the activities conducted, and the organization's publications. There is also a companion title called the *International Research Centers Directory*.

> **TIP: Use *Research Centers Directory* for Finding Think Tanks**
> *Research Centers Directory* is a good source for identifying and locating think tanks—institutions such as the Center for Democracy and Technology, the Heritage Foundation, the Brookings Institution, and other influential centers (often quoted in the news) that study public policy–related issues and publish their findings in reports or articles.

Source: *Foundation Directory*

The *Foundation Directory*, published by the Foundation Center and available in many libraries, is a guide that can help you find foundations offering funding and grants in your field. This guide is only one of many directories and publications published by the Foundation Center, which maintains information on more than 108,000 foundations, corporate donors, and grant-making public charities in the United States and over 3 million of their recent grants. It also supports a national network of library reference collections to make resources available for free public use. The biggest collections are located in New York City; Washington, D.C.; Cleveland; Atlanta; and San Francisco. These libraries provide important reference tools, such as sample application forms and the annual reports, tax information, and publications of foundations.

The Center itself publishes a variety of helpful information sources, including specialized directories that tell you where to get grants for projects that cover subjects like public health, the elderly, minorities, museums, and so on. You can even link to its site and, at no charge, search its Catalog of Nonprofit Literature, a database of the literature of philanthropy, updated daily, which contains over 30,000 bibliographic citations and abstracts.

Contact the Foundation Center directly for more information on its publications and collections.

Another library directory with similar information is the *World Guide to Foundations*. This print title provides data on over 40,000 foundations in 115 countries. Yet another useful source is the *Annual Register of Grant Support*, a guide to over 3,000 grant-giving organizations.

Online Catalogs and Archives

Finally, one way that libraries are integrating their offerings with the internet is by making their catalogs available for free online searching. Following are a few of the best sources.

Source: *Library of Congress Online Catalog*
On the Library of Congress website you can not only search the catalog of the Library of Congress for books, serials, manuscripts, maps, music, recordings, images, and electronic resources, but also link to specialized catalogs and tools provided by the Library of Congress, including its catalog of copyright registrations and ownership documents; an online catalog of prints and photographs; a broadcast and archival recordings catalog; and the National Library Service for the Blind catalog, which includes braille and talking books; and more.

Source: *Gateway to Library Catalogs*
Here's a site that not only permits you to search the catalog of the Library of Congress but also to search a wide range of library catalogs around the country, and even the world—from Aberdeen

University in the United Kingdom to the Zhejiang Provincial Library in China.

Source: *Libdex*
Libdex includes a listing and links to information about libraries around the world, including their websites and links to their catalogs.

Digital Libraries

An increasing number of institutions have gone several steps further and created "digital libraries," which consist of digitized versions of various primary sources from the library's collection. These materials could include documents like personal letters, governmental treaties, maps, audio interviews, photographs, movies, and other original source materials that could normally be accessed only by visiting the library. Even the Vatican, which has one of the world's most prestigious collections of old and rare precious documents, has digitized some of its materials and made them available on the web.

In the United States, the most prominent and best-known digital libraries are the theme libraries created by the U.S. Library of Congress as part of its American Memory series. This collection provides web access to a variety of rare American historical documents that previously could only be viewed in person at the library in the capital. The American Memory series consists of over 9 million items, including manuscripts, films, sound recordings, and publications in the Library of Congress's collection. Specific theme collections in the American Memory Exhibit include, for example, the following:

- Arendt, Hannah ~ Papers ~ 1898–1977
- Baseball and Jackie Robinson ~ Multiformat ~ 1860–1969
- Bernstein, Leonard ~ Multiformat ~ ca. 1920–1989
- The Chinese in California ~ Multiformat ~ 1850–1925
- Civil War Maps ~ 1861–1865
- Coca-Cola Advertising ~ Films ~ 1951–1999

- Lincoln, Abraham ~ Papers ~ ca. 1850–1865
- Louisiana Purchase ~ Maps ~ 1572–1902
- Presidential Inaugurations ~ Multiformat ~ 1789–2001
- Religious Petitions, Virginia ~ 1764–1802
- September 11, 2001, and Public Reactions ~ Multiformat ~ 2001–2002
- Washington, George ~ Papers ~ 1741–1799
- Woman Suffrage ~ Books and Pamphlets ~ 1848–1921
- World War I ~ Military Newspapers ~ 1918–1919
- World War II Maps ~ Military Situation Maps ~ 1944–1945

Dozens of other collections can be found on another part of the LOC site called Digital Collections. There you can find collections ranging from the Aaron Copland Collection and the Abraham Lincoln papers to Wright Brothers negatives and Yiddish American Popular Sheet music.

Many other libraries around the country and the world have been making parts of their physical collections available as digital libraries, as well. For example, the University of California, Berkeley has made its collection covering the life of anarchist Emma Goldman available.

The Boston Public Library's Digital Public Library of America is creating digital collections providing over 7 million items of historical significance from both recognized sources and ordinary people around the country. The collections can be browsed by date, topic, and other themes, and even searched by keyword. A small sampling of these resources includes the Golden Age of Radio in the United States; Leaving Europe: A New Life in America; and Staking Claims: The Gold Rush in Nineteenth-Century America.

The World Digital Library provides a visual time and geographic display allowing visitors to search for digital documents from a specified time period and a particular region of the world.

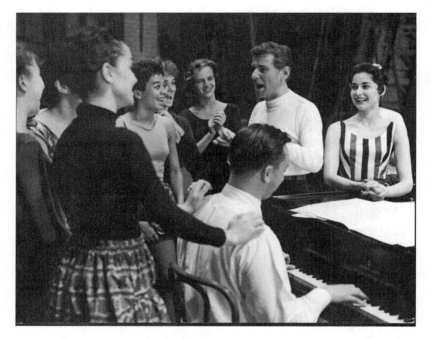

Figure 2.1 A photo of Leonard Bernstein with Stephen Sondheim at the piano, rehearsing music from the Broadway production of West Side Story, from the Library of Congress's Music Division

Finally, the New York Public Libraries Digital Collections has digitized over 800,000 items from its holdings for web users to browse, including photographs, audio, and other formats covering the arts, maps, birds, theater, immigration, social conditions, and more. Some of its specialized digital works include a collection on Jewish oral history; a Jerome Robbins Dance Division Moving Image Archive; the Thomas Addis Emmet Collection of nearly 10,000 handwritten letters and documents from America's founding, including a copy of the Declaration of Independence written by Thomas Jefferson; fashion drawings and sketches by Andre Fashion Studios; Music Theater Online—a digital archive of texts, images, video, and audio files related to musical theater; and a Theatrical Lighting database, to name just a handful.

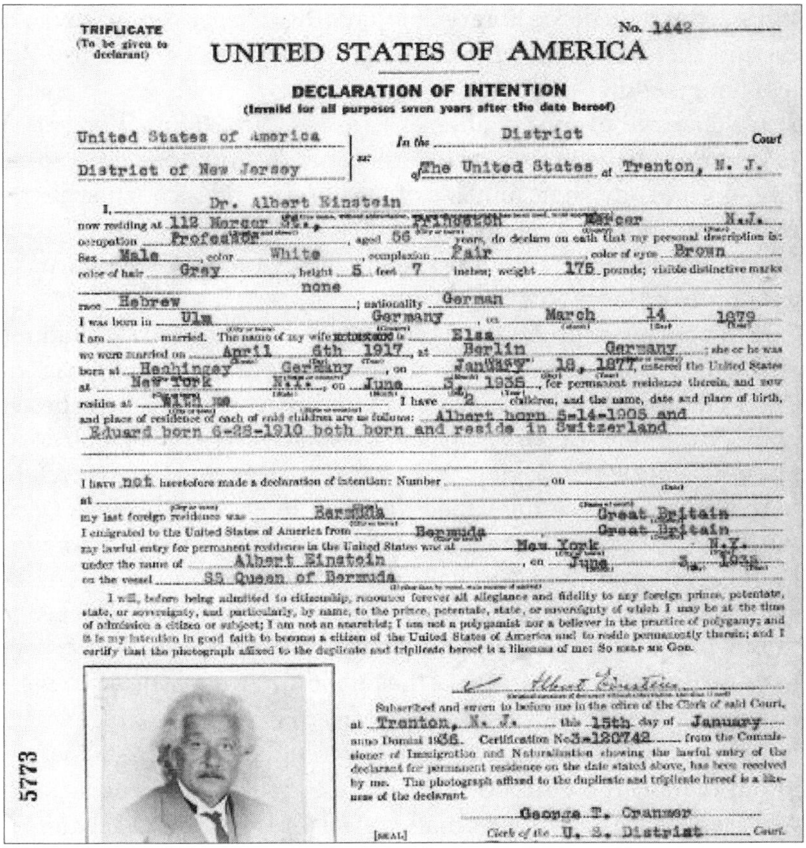

Figure 2.2   Albert Einstein's application to become an American Citizen is one of many thousands of historical images available from the Library of Congress's Digital Collections

The Future of Libraries

Walk into a typical American public library and you'll probably identify about three current core services: storing an underused circulating collection of paper books, ensuring community-wide access to Facebook on desktop computers, and sheltering homeless people.

—What Will Become of the Library?
Slate, April 2014

What *is* the state of the library in today's digital age? We can say that the internet has changed everything for libraries. We can also say it's changed nothing.

It's changed everything because, as we all well know, so *much* information has moved to the internet and is now available to us anytime and anywhere, outside of the library. And it's not just all the new sites, "born on the internet," like websites, blogs, and social media. Even older, traditional sources, such as books and journals, are now freely available on the web.

So it's changed "everything," then, because libraries have traditionally been warehouses for the traditional information containers of information, now rapidly shrinking in importance—pulp-based books, magazines, reports, etc. Libraries have served as the physical place where the public can go to obtain information, and therefore have been forced to rethink their missions and roles. Therefore, since the late 1990s or so, the library profession has had its work cut out for it, and continues to face real challenges—not the least of which is managing to stay relevant and vital while dealing with ongoing budget cuts.

But the internet can be said to have changed nothing, as well, because the *essential* mission of the public library—its *raison d'être*—remains the same, and that mission is *media-independent*. The broadest mission of a public library is to better enable participation in our democratic form of government by making the information that's necessary for self-governance available to everyone regardless of economic standing and ability. In the words of James Madison:

> A popular government without popular information, or the means to acquiring it, is but a prologue to a farce or tragedy, or perhaps both. Knowledge will forever govern ignorance, and a people who mean to be their own governors must arm themselves with the power which knowledge gives.

Mr. Madison's contemporary, Thomas Jefferson, called information "the currency of democracy."

That higher purpose of the library, then, does not necessarily depend on the specific form that information takes—print, online, or however it may evolve in the future. The job of the library professional, and the librarian (whose title may also change to reflect shifting roles) is to stay true to the mission while making the necessary adjustments given the state of technology, society, and other critical forces. In all cases, the library will be the organization that collects information based on a specific and predetermined standard and criteria, filters it, categorizes it, organizes it, then makes it readily available through whatever finding aids and mechanisms are deemed most appropriate and effective.

But, wait a minute. It's not quite that simple.

There's no discounting the fact that many libraries are underused, neglected, and underfunded, and in some cases may resemble the depressing image presented by the author of the *Slate* article quoted earlier. And it is certainly true that libraries are at a disadvantage in making the needed radical transformation. After all, they were built from the ground up to handle and manage one particular type of information—print. As such, a library's mind-set, so to speak, has traditionally been geared toward collecting, archiving, and displaying print-based information. And so a fairly drastic shift must be made—and indeed *is* being made—by libraries to make them not just storage facilities for print information resources but also active and vital cultivators, gatherers, harvesters, sorters, and distributors of information and knowledge.

What can and *should* today's state-of-the-art library be doing to remain relevant and vital in this age? That question has been and continues to be discussed, analyzed, and debated in and at countless library and information schools, conferences, journals, and symposia around the country and the globe, and it represents *the* existential challenge to the discipline of library science.

Certainly, providing community internet access isn't, by itself, going to cut it anymore as a reinvention strategy. And while libraries provide invaluable outreach services by giving users remote digital access to their powerful and expensive searchable in-house databases (some of which we will look at in the following chapter), that service does not motivate the researcher to visit the physical library. If anything, it makes it easier and more appealing to remain at home or wherever he or she is doing online research.

So what can libraries do to bring people into the library? While the form and shape of future library services are clearly beyond the scope of this book, among the innovations and new thinking that some far-sighted libraries are implementing today, or are considering, are:

- Making the library a more social space for collaborative working (at the Stuttgart, Germany library the first four floors are geared to social engagement, while the upper four floors are for books and "the stacks.")

- Implementing Maker Spaces, where patrons can use 3-D printers, create apps, and much more

- Offering the latest, most powerful hardware to provide the most compelling visual displays of information

- Making powerful analytical software available for performing intensive data analysis

- Providing self-publishing and print-on-demand technologies

- Redesigning the interior of libraries to make effective use of light, flow, space design, and the most effective furnishings to create optimal research and learning spaces

Various libraries—public, academic, and corporate, as well as other organizations for research and learning—are integrating one or more of these strategies to make their institutions places that people truly want to visit in order to research, study, collaborate, and work. In fact, one such library—the James B. Hunt Jr. Library at North Carolina State University (NCSU) in Raleigh, North Carolina—has integrated many of these strategies *and* come up with new ones. In many ways, then, the Hunt Library represents the state-of-the-art library for the 21st century.

Not only does this 221,000 square-foot facility—opened in April 2013—include lots of good old-fashioned books (about 1.5 million volumes) but it has integrated the latest and most innovative new design and technology features through its design, maker spaces, innovative use of automation, and the creation of Labs and Theaters.

For example, at the library's maker space patrons can create and then print their own creations via uPrint and Makerbot 3-D printers; the Teaching and Visualization Lab is a theater-like space with wall-size displays and high-quality audio where patrons can collaborate on complex problems. The library is designed to help its users "meet a variety of needs, including high-impact presentations; technology-rich interactive learning in small groups; large-scale, high-definition visualization and simulation; command/control room simulation; immersive interactive computing; game research; 'big data' decision theater; and comparative social computing." The Immersion Theater consists of 21- by 7-foot Christie MicroTiles in curved video display for adding and sharing content (see Figure 2.3). And a Game Lab supports the scholarly study of digital games.

The creators of the Hunt Library have even rethought the way books are found and retrieved. To locate a book patrons still search the online catalog, but rather than seeing only a textual print-out of matching books, the system displays images of the book on the shelf, along with images of other books located next to the targeted one. (This recreates a bit of that serendipitous browsing effect that

Figure 2.3   The James B. Hunt Jr. Library at North
Carolina State University is state-of-the-art, and includes
a wall sized curved video display

one usually gives up when searching for books online.) Once the patron decides he wants a particular book, a robotic device called Bookbot is engaged. Traveling swiftly through the closed stacks, Bookbot locates the desired title from one of 18,000 underground bins, retrieves it, and deposits it with a library staff member. The staffer holds it for the patron until he's ready to pick it up.

Many other libraries, large and small, are innovating to reinvent what it means to be culture's cultivator of how information is accessed and used. At the NYPL lab, for instance, experiments range from crowdsourcing old menus; to holding "hack" events that result in innovations like the creation of a computer vision technology (https://github.com/NYPL/map-vectorizer) that can identify building shapes from atlases; to designing a new discovery system to help users better find digital archives and manuscripts in the library.

All cool stuff, right? Very impressive, indeed. But can advanced technologies and tools, or beautiful reading and study rooms, or strategically designed collaboration centers and work–flow areas really make a library *the* go-to place for people doing research? Is this reinvention the answer that libraries have been looking for to bring patrons back and get them using the physical facilities again? The answer is unclear.

First of all, the vast majority of libraries have neither the funds nor the expertise of an NYPL or an NCSU. Secondly, even if the average library could take a page from NCSU's playbook, it's not possible to know with any certainty that a quiet place to collaborate and use the latest and coolest information technologies will be enough to bring researchers into the building. As Yogi Berra said, "Prediction is difficult—especially about the future." Yogi was right. We just don't know how this will all play out.

Someone who is in a better position than almost anyone I can think of to predict where libraries are headed is David Weinberger. David has served as co-director of the Harvard Library Innovation Lab and was a Fellow at Harvard's Berkman Center for Internet and Society. He is also the author or coauthor of several prominent books about knowledge and the internet, notably *The Cluetrain Manifesto*, which when published in 2000 was one of the very first works to explain how the internet was changing business, and virtually everything else. Over the years, I've been fortunate to have had several telephone chats with David, and each of those talks, without exception, has been thought provoking and enlightening. I recently had a chance to talk to him at some length on this whole "future of libraries" question.

Although David is a long-time supporter of libraries, he acknowledged right away that he doesn't often visit his own academic library; for one thing, he doesn't find its design or atmosphere particularly welcoming. But he notes that there are larger problems regarding using the library as our key source of expertise that go well beyond the attractiveness of the institution.

"The problem," David explained, "is that 'humans don't scale.' In other words, no single individual can be the best source for everything. The real knowledge," he said, "remains in 'the network' and there the intelligence embedded in a group of people . . . can outpace what individuals can know." (He explored this concept in detail in his book *Too Big to Know* [see Appendix B].)

David holds out hope for libraries, and he told me that what he'd really like to see libraries do to maintain value and relevance is to start engaging in activities such as the following:

- Providing spaces that provide the training and social space to teach patrons how to use the latest and emerging digital tools. This might include instruction on how to create professional-looking YouTube videos; using big data tools and techniques to better understand large data sets; using visualization software to make compelling presentations of research results; or even learning light programming to create custom big data applications.

- Helping users with what he calls "Presearch"—the preliminary exploratory research that's done ahead of time to inform the actual research process. Presearch can help researchers locate the proper area or "domain" of one's subject area, get the lay of the land of the discipline, so to speak, and create an effective research strategy.

- Connecting the knowledge of a neighborhood's librarians and citizens together to meet the information needs of the community. This could be done by incorporating citizen expertise into a searchable knowledge network. This would provide resources and links to expertise in the community, along with data on how often a given resource is used, by what type of user and for what purpose, along with feedback from those who used it.

[*Author's Note*: Some early efforts to make this happen have been carried out by the Toronto-based company Bibliocommons, which uses software called Bibliocore to connect the catalogs, books, resources, and expertise of libraries around North America, with an emphasis on enabling social interaction and patron engagement while doing so.]

The bottom line is that libraries still have work to do to ensure their place in the 21st-century information and research world. I, for one, believe there's too much at stake for them not to succeed.

URLs

Resources on Libraries

Google Books: books.google.com

Most Interesting Libraries in the World: miragebookmark.ch/most-interesting-libraries.htm

Association of College and Research Libraries: ala.org/acrl; Email: acrl@ala.org

Special Libraries Association: sla.org

Libweb: lib-web.org

National Libraries of the World: publiclibraries.com/world.htm

The European Library: theeuropeanlibrary.org/tel4/

Wikipedia: National Libraries: en.wikipedia.org/wiki/List_of_national_and_state_libraries

Directory of Open Access Journals: doaj.org

Electronic Journals Library: rzblx1.uni-regensburg.de/ezeit/index.phtml?bibid=AAAAA&colors=7&lang=en

Marquis Who's Who: marquiswhoswho.com/

Euromonitor: euromonitor.com

The Foundation Center: foundationcenter.org/newyork/

Library of Congress Online Catalog: catalog.loc.gov
Gateway to Library Catalogs: loc.gov/z3950/gateway.html#lc
Libdex: libdex.com/country.html

Digital Libraries

U.S. Library of Congress: American Memory Series: memory.loc.
gov/ammem/index.html
U.S. Library of Congress: Digital Collections: loc.gov/collections
University of California, Berkeley, Emma Goldman Papers: sun-
site.berkeley.edu/Goldman
Boston Public Library Digital Public Library of America: dp.la
World Digital Library: wdl.org/en
New York Public Library Digital Collection: digitalcollections.
nypl.org
Lucille Ball Marriage to Gary Morton: dbsmaint.galib.uga.edu/
cgi/news?query=id:wsbn40384

The Future of Libraries

What Will Become of the Library?: slate.com/articles/life/
design/2014/04/the_future_of_the_library_how_they_ll_
evolve_for_the_digital_age.html
Bookbot Demo: youtube.com/watch?v=Vaqd3P3vlSo
New York Public Library Lab: nypl.org/collections/labs
Bibliocommons: bibliocommons.com

Part II

Searching

Chapter 3

Search Engines, Precision Search Strategies, and Taming Information Overload

It wasn't too many years ago that only a small segment of the population—librarians, scientists, some journalists, and specialized researchers—knew anything at all about the concept of the online information search. But since the explosive growth and popularization of the internet in the early 1990s, we've all become searchers. We've come to take it for granted that we can call up our search engine of choice—which for the vast majority of us means Google—input a few words, and then, in a matter of seconds, view the answer to our query right in front of us. But it certainly wasn't always so easy to find information. And it's worth recounting here a very brief history of the online search and how we came to be where we are today.

How It All Began

Although search engines are quite new, the technique of querying electronic databases to find information has been around for many decades, and certainly existed well before the creation of the internet. Back in the 1940s, and continuing through the 1960s, the method for finding information stored in computer databases was a cumbersome process known as batch processing. The researcher (usually a computer scientist or perhaps an engineer) would first carefully formulate his or her information request, then physically hand off that query to a computer technician who would translate the request into computer language, using punch cards. Those punch cards were fed into the computer's input device to tell it what information to look for and retrieve from its database.

And then the searcher would have to wait for the response. The wait would not be a few seconds, nor a few minutes, but many hours or even days. The response would come back in the form of computer tape, which would then have to be translated into plain English for the researcher. And if that answer wasn't correct, or the question was not "understood" properly by the computer, the researcher would have to start all over, create a new search, and go through the process again. And, if necessary, again. And so on. And you feel frustrated when your search takes more than 5 seconds, right? Back in those days, scientists allegedly lamented that it was so difficult to find out what information already existed on a topic that it was sometimes easier just to start over.

By the late 1960s and early 1970s things got better, as developments in online information retrieval greatly sped up the process and the efficiency of computer searching. One of the key precursors of our modern methods of searching was pioneered by engineer Roger Summit and his colleagues at the aerospace giant Lockheed Martin. His team was given the assignment of making computer searching faster and more effective. Summit—who has been called "the father of modern search"—through trial and error and working with his team came up with the recursion search methods that we rely on today. The recursion process makes it possible for the searcher to view the results from his or her initial search and then immediately refine, update, and modify the query, run the search again, make additional modifications, view results again, modify again if necessary, and engage in this process as many times as needed.

The work of Summit and his team was so well regarded by Lockheed Martin's clients, which eventually included NASA and other governmental agencies, that the aerospace company decided to start up a new venture based on this newly developed search technology. That venture was eventually spun off and renamed Dialog, and became the leading provider of online information. Dialog served a broad range of professionals in government, education, science, law, business, and other fields who needed the ability to search massive amounts of literature and data in their field and get answers right away. (If you are interested in a comprehensive and scholarly examination of the birth and growth of the online search technology and industries, see *A History of Online Information Services, 1963–1976* by Charles P. Bourne and Trudi Bellardo Hahn.)

Dialog was not the only company that provided commercial online search capabilities during the 1970s. Other leaders during this time included companies such as BRS, Orbits, LexisNexis, DataStar, and Dow Jones. And since there was no internet to provide the connection to these services, customers had to set up a special dedicated phone line and modem to connect their computers directly to the computers of these information vendors.

The popularity of online searching continued to spread during the 1970s and 1980s to businesspeople, journalists, writers, and other serious researchers. Even *The New York Times* introduced its own searchable database of newspapers and publications in 1975, called *The New York Times Information Bank*, geared not for scientists or computer experts but for companies, journalists, librarians, and others with a need to search vast archives of literature. Despite the technological advancements, doing a search on a database still required training from the information vendors themselves, which included learning special computer commands and instructions that each system required in order to query its database.

Training was needed not only because it took skills and practice to create and run an effective search but also because online searching was so expensive. In fact, back in that day, searchers were charged on a per-minute basis, and depending on the specific database being queried, that per-minute charge could be $1, $2, or even $5—and on top of this per-minute fee, there would be an additional charge for each result retrieved and viewed or printed. It was not at all unusual for a single search to end up costing $25, $50, or in some cases, even into the hundreds of dollars. For this reason researchers spent most of their time creating and carefully constructing their search statement offline, with the goal of getting in and out of the database as quickly as possible to avoid racking up those high search costs. Add to this the fact that the majority of online searches at this point could only retrieve the title, a summary or abstract, and certain other descriptive data about the article—not the article itself—and you can see how different things were when it came to online searching.

Are you feeling grateful yet about how we search today?

To wrap up this mini-tour of online searching as it once was, when the internet expanded from its scientific, defense, and academic roots in the late 1980s and early 1990s to businesses, public libraries, and eventually to our homes, the major online database vendors like Dialog had to quickly adapt to the new world of cheaper online information. The companies adapted in different ways and with varying degrees of success. Some, such as BRS, CompuServe, GE, Delphi, and Prodigy, are no longer around. Others began making their services available through the internet, rather than via a dedicated line, and updated their complex search languages to more user-friendly versions.

The big professional online services are no longer the only game in town when it comes to searching computer databases, and some continue to struggle to remain viable and relevant in the internet age. However, they still play a critical role in providing the most robust and sought-after collections of valued information for select audiences. For example, LexisNexis (along with Westlaw) remains the go-to database for lawyers needing to search archives of citations, court rulings, and legal background information; Dow Jones's Factiva service provides thousands of timely, in-depth articles, reports, and data sets of value to businesses; Dialog, though much smaller today than it was years ago, continues to serve a wide range of industries and disciplines that need to quickly access filtered sets of high-value information on areas ranging from aerospace and chemicals to toxicology and water resources.

In addition, more familiar information companies, such as ProQuest (which today owns Dialog) and EBSCO, continue to provide powerful online databases to students, faculty, and businesspeople in libraries, academia, and other organizations that need access to millions of articles from scholarly and trade journals, leading newspapers, and other sources.

Now let's turn back to the internet and the development of internet search engines.

The Rise of the Search Engine

Early in the internet's history there was no effective way to find all the millions of files that had been uploaded to the network (webpages themselves were not part of the internet until the creation of the World Wide Web and the development of web-browsing software in 1991). There were some early efforts and rudimentary tools developed to assist internet users in searching and finding relevant files and discussions. The best known of these included the hierarchal menu navigation tool called Gopher and the FTP files keyword search system known as Archie.

When the World Wide Web began to take hold in the early 1990s, with its appealing graphics and hyperlinked pages, this new and revolutionary system for publishing on the internet quickly began to dominate what the public saw and was able to do online. Once again there was a need for some system or method to organize the quickly growing number of webpages and make it possible for a user to find the desired pages.

The earliest efforts to do this occurred in the early 1990s and took the form of organized directories of related webpages that grouped pages into categories and subcategories. One of these, called "Jerry and David's Guide to the World Wide Web," launched in January 1994. About a year later that directory evolved and changed its name to the now-familiar Yahoo! Yahoo!, along with a few other popular directories of webpages such as Webcrawler and Lycos, was of immense help in trying to instill some order and in organizing pages online, but these directories represented only a tiny fraction of the web—which of course was growing at a phenomenal pace. They were very helpful, but they did not provide the ability to search the entire web with one's own keywords or phrases to retrieve just what one needed.

By the mid-1990s the first true internet search engines were introduced. These operated on the same information retrieval principle as the existing professional online search services; that is, they offered the user the ability to input words and phrases to try and match those in a database. The big difference was that rather than searching a carefully constructed, consistently indexed set of related data compiled in a professionally constructed database, internet search engines were trying to make the entire internet one single searchable database. The problem was that there were no controls or consistency in what was on the internet—it was filled with advertisements, discussions, student papers, business reports, government data, abandoned websites, and so on. It was much more difficult to do an effective search of the internet than it was to search a standard professional business database.

Still, efforts were made to tame the web via a search engine. Some of the earliest popular internet search sites included products called Excite, InfoSeek, and HotBot. The problem with these and the other search engines at the time was that they really did not work. A web search using these Model T versions would typically return a jumble of unrelated items and webpages. If you were lucky, one or two might be somewhat relevant to what you wanted.

An alternative type of search system introduced at the same time, trying a different approach, was a site called AskJeeves. AskJeeves, which was launched in 1995, employed a butler metaphor and an accompanying illustration of a proper English servant that allowed the searcher to input plain English sentences, asking Jeeves to look for, fetch, and return what was requested from the web. And Ask-Jeeves was quite a nice and useful innovation for searchers, as it combined the advantages of a defined directory of preselected quality sites, an early version of natural language searching, a friendly user interface, and some search technology to do a pretty good job of bringing searchers what they wanted. It worked well about half or perhaps even more than half of the time—which was very good back in those days!

True search on the web—the ability to query nearly the entire web and bring back relevant and substantive results—was still not a reality. However, internet searching took a giant leap forward when in December 1995 the Digital Equipment Corporation (DEC) introduced its own search engine, called AltaVista. There were several reasons AltaVista worked so much better than previous search engines, but one key reason was that it was really the first to allow Boolean searches—the use of operators such as "and," "or," and "not" to create a truly precise search. This feature, along with coverage of a larger portion of the web, made AltaVista the search engine of choice for anyone who was serious about searching on the web, such as librarians, scholars, and business researchers.

While representing a great leap forward, AltaVista still had its flaws—some pretty big ones in fact. On the one hand, the results it returned were usually at least accurate—that is, the pages did contain the key words (along with any Boolean restrictions input) the searcher entered—a welcome advancement over what had come before it. But the search engine was still blind when it came to making a determination as to which of the results were really the best ones: which were advertisements, which were spam, which were old and outdated, which had only minimal information on the topic, and which ones were really substantive, valuable pages and worth highlighting at the top of the list for the searcher.

It's worth noting that during this time a nascent but soon to be significant new discipline was emerging called search engine optimization, or SEO for short. SEO is the art and science of creating and manipulating one's webpages to try to ensure that they receive placement closest to the top of a search engine's list of results. The reason for the development of this art/science was that by the late 1990s it was becoming increasingly common for websites to advertise or directly sell their products—this was something new! All of a sudden it became clear to marketers and others that to make a sale it was necessary to get search engine users to view their pages, and so a process of reverse engineering the factors that determined which pages get ranked the highest quickly became a very hot topic indeed.

Even in the late 1990s buying and selling on the web was still new and largely untested, but it became increasingly obvious that people were making more of their buying decisions based on their search results. Visibility of one's pages and site—meaning appearing somewhere in the first ten results returned—was quickly becoming a priority for businesses and anyone else who needed to be sure their sites were noticed. As time went on more companies began optimizing their pages for high placement on a search engine. But a lot of these optimized pages were just ads, fluff, or come-ons, and web searchers began having even more trouble sorting out the good stuff from all the promotional junk.

Search engines were unable to help the searcher separate the good stuff from the junk. Remember, this was never a concern for previous researchers searching a CD-ROM or more traditional databases, like a Dialog business research file or a ProQuest newspaper collection, as these databases were purely informational and each item entered into the database was chosen carefully by the librarians, indexers, editors, and others who worked at those firms to choose content that would inform the researcher. There was no motivation or real capability by the information providers to get high rankings in order to sell or persuade the researcher.

At this point a radical change occurred in research. No longer was it only a database editor or librarian who would determine what information a researcher would likely view from a search. Now a major role was played by the *intent* of the information creators themselves, whose interests were not always—or even often—aligned with the interests of the researchers. The question became, how could an automated search engine, without the benefit of human judgment, ever make the kinds of quality determinations needed to distinguish which items retrieved from a search are substantive and of most value to a researcher, and which should be filtered out, or at least ranked lower on a list? Most people assumed that this kind of evaluation could only be done by an expert, or at least a person who could apply some level of substantive assessment against a set of criteria. But that was BG (Before Google).

How Search Engines Work

It seems like a bit of magic, right? You link to your favorite search engine, enter a few words, and then in a blink or two of your eyes, displayed in front of you is not one but several, maybe dozens or hundreds or more, pages of information that answer your question or add to your knowledge of the topic. All done in a couple seconds or less and culled from billions and billions of pages on the web.

Well, it *is* pretty magical when you come to think of it, but let's expose a bit of how this process works so you can have a better understanding of what exactly happens when you run a search. This knowledge will help you better appreciate both the amazing power and the limitations of the internet search process. Here's what you need to know.

A search engine finds and organizes the web by deploying a special type of software called a crawler or spider. This software goes out to the web, finds and follows links, and creates a giant index of all the words on all the pages it encounters from its great web crawl journey. What this means is that when you search Google (or any other search engine), you are not actually searching the web "live," so to speak, but instead running your search against a very recently created but static index that the search engine created from its most recent web crawl. That static index is updated often, though depending on the search engine and how it classifies a particular site, webpages may be recrawled anywhere from nearly continuously to every few minutes to just a couple times a day or less. When the word or search string you enter matches a page in that search engine's index that contains those words, this is considered a match or hit, and that page will appear in the returned list of your results.

The ordering or ranking of those pages returned from a search is very important, of course, as most people will only look at the top 3, 5, or maybe dozen or so results retrieved. Each search engine has its own mathematical formula for determining how to rank matching webpages, but virtually all look at matters such as the frequency of the appearance of your key words (the more often they appear on a page, the higher the page's ranking), their placement (e.g., words near the beginning or in the title may get higher ranking), and other factors that relate to the popularity of any individual page, such as the number of pages linking to that page.

Google Rides In

Google was launched in 1998, and right off the bat the site seemed unusual. For one, unlike the other search engines at the time, Google's search page was not cluttered with lots of stuff—ads, links, promotions, and so forth. It was a nearly blank page sporting the Google logo, a search box, and really nothing more (not all that much different from what the Google homepage looks like today). For many searchers, frustrated with sorting through the barrage of junk, unverified collections of pages, and ads all over the web and feeling overwhelmed with the treasures and trash mixed together on the internet, the Google search page immediately provided a welcome feeling of clarity and calmness.

Figure 3.1 When Google first launched in 1998, it offered an appealing search page that was much more uncluttered than those of other search engines at the time

But the proof of Google's recipe was in its pudding. The amazing thing about Google was simply that it worked. In other words, if you entered words into the search engine, you would almost always get back a neat, clean list of substantive and relevant results. Hooray! This may not seem like much now, but it was certainly something to cheer about in the late 1990s.

And—fascinatingly—not only were the results relevant to the search, but somehow Google was able to figure out *which* pages it brought back to you were likely to be the *most* relevant and valuable—and then put those pages at the top of the returned list.

Wow. How did (and does) Google do this? While there are entire books and reports detailing the subtle factors that go into answering that question, the critical innovation that Google's founders came up with that provided this all-important capability was something it called PageLink. Simply put, this means that after Google determines which pages on the internet match one's search (see "How

Search Engines Work" above) it then applies its PageLink analysis to decide which of those pages should be ranked the highest. And that determination is based on what we could call a page's popularity, which Google defines and calculates based on how many other pages link to a particular page *and* how many sites and pages link to *those* pages, and how many link to *those* pages, and so on.

The premise behind this methodology is that if people link to a certain site or page a lot, and in the right context, then it is probably a good one. The analogy that's sometimes used to explain why this popularity method works is to imagine that you are visiting a town you've never been to before and you are hungry for lunch. As you drive down the unknown road, you come upon two restaurants; one is crowded and the other is empty. You'll almost always be better off if you choose the crowded one, based on the normally justifiable belief that it is probably crowded because people are gravitating toward the better restaurant.

Page links likewise serve as recommendations or tacit endorsements from others on the internet. While this may seem overly simplistic, in most circumstances it works quite well. In fact, it is not all that different from the way that the works of academics and scholars have traditionally been ranked through a process called citation analysis, which calculates how often any given scholar's work has been cited by peers. The more citations a scholar has, the higher his or her ranking and status. (This has other implications, too, such as the role of popularity in evaluating the credulity of certain sites and people, as discussed in detail in Chapter 5.)

The bottom line is that it quickly became clear among searchers that Google worked much better than its competitors, and it also very quickly became the search engine of choice for more and more people on the web. Of course, since that time Google has enhanced and refined the signals it looks at on the web for ranking pages, vastly expanded its search and advertising services, entered the business market, introduced its AdWords project, has been mired in various controversies related to everything from the data it collects on searchers to what it blocks, and has even set out to work on completely different endeavors, such as building driverless cars, developing renewable energy, and sending giant balloons around the world to expand the world's internet access.

But at its heart Google has been and still remains a search engine. And despite some disappointments in how it has evolved over the years for the searcher, it remains today the best general web search engine.

What's Next for Search Engines?

According to Microsoft's Stefan Weitz, author of the fascinating book, *Search: How the Data Explosion Makes Us Smarter* (Green-House Collection, 2014), the next generation of search will antici-pate what we want to find or do, prompt us with reminders, and even take steps to complete the tasks. The intelligence to do all this will be derived from crunching huge amounts of data about who we are and our past behaviors (e.g., our digital profiles), along with information about our current location and signals from digitally enabled objects. Stay tuned.

Getting the Most Out of Google: Power Research Strategies

All that being said, and while it's true that Google has an uncanny capability to retrieve just what you were looking for (sometimes even when you yourself don't know ahead of time what you want), there are still key strategies and steps you can take to make your Google searches even more effective.

Granted, Google does such a good job with its baked-in intelligence—everything from fixing spelling to automatically finding synonyms—that these tips can be considered more optional than required. But the best searchers also know how to employ the following methods to truly fine-tune their search results.

Basic Searching

The following tips and strategies have long been recommended for researchers who want to get the most out of their online searching.

- Figure out what you are really researching. Before you begin to create your search statement or go on the internet, it's a good idea to take a few minutes to think about what, exactly, you are looking for. Can you write it in a sentence? Are there other ways to describe what you are seeking? You won't get good results if you aren't sure of what you want to find.

• Try to identify nouns and noun phrases from your search and use those in your search statement. Search engines do best when they can "chomp down" on these types of words. They also work best on rare and obscure words, so try to avoid entering the most common words and instead be sure to include the most unusual ones.

• Although Google and other search engines are getting increasingly proficient at examining your search words and putting them into the best format, you can help ensure a more precise search by using these advanced search strategies:

  ○ If you are searching for a specific phrase, enclose that phrase in quotation marks. In other words, if you want information on how Big Data is changing the way market research is conducted, rather than entering the words

    using big data in market research

  instead enter

    "Big Data" "Market Research"

  Entering words within quotation marks ensures that *only* pages that contain the words as part of that specific phrase will be returned.

  ○ By default, Google assumes a Boolean AND (+) between all of the words or phrases you enter. So in the above search, Google will only return pages where *both* the phrase *Big Data* and the phrase *market research* are found.

    Use the Boolean OR operator if you want Google to understand that there is more than one word, phrase, or concept to describe what you are looking for. So, again, say you are looking for information on Big Data in the use of market research *or* in the use of recruitment. To instruct Google to do this, you would enter the following:

    "Big Data" "Market Research" OR Recruitment

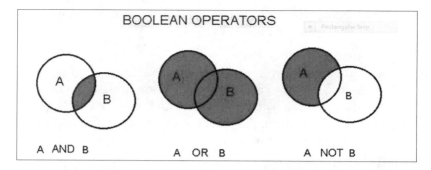

Figure 3.2 Boolean AND, OR, and NOT search operations

○ Finally, use the Boolean NOT (–) operator to *eliminate* sites that have words or phrases that are not going to be valuable for you and that you don't want to see it. So, for instance, if the above search was continually bringing back too many irrelevant pages on, say, IBM, you could rewrite the search statement to eliminate those pages by entering this search statement:

"Big Data" "Market Research" OR Recruitment -IBM

More Advanced Google Searches

You can instruct Google to return pages that are most likely to be substantive and valuable by using two very useful advanced search features: the site and filetype fields. The site field allows you to restrict results to those that originate from a certain type of domain. For example, restricting your search to .edu domains will limit results to those from schools, universities, research centers, and other educational sites, while restricting to .gov sites will produce results from webpages from local, state, federal, and other governmental agencies. These two types of institutions—educational and government—are typically more likely to provide substantive information (research results, data sets, etc.) than a commercial .com site.

Using the filetype field allows you to restrict results based on the file format of the item. For example, you can tell Google you only want to see results from PDFs, PowerPoints, Word documents, or other specific types of documents. Like the site domain restriction, you can use these format restrictions to increase the odds that you will get back more substantive and valuable results. PowerPoint, for example, is often the format used by people giving presentations at conferences, while PDFs and Word documents are often used by writers of research reports and white papers.

You can also combine the site and filetype together in one search to be even more restrictive.

There are two ways to engage these domain and file-type searches. You can either link to the Google Advanced Search (advanced .google.com) and use the readymade pull-down boxes to enable these searches, or you can input the actual search command words in the regular Google search page. (See the sidebar for the names of these and certain other advanced Google search filters.)

Google's Advanced Search Commands

The following filetype and domain prefixes can be used right on Google's main search page to enhance the odds of bringing back substantive information.

filetype: .pdf or .xls or .ppt or .doc. For example, the search: "big data" ethics filetype:.ppt limits results to pages in Microsoft PowerPoint

site: .edu or .gov. For example, the search: trends vegetarian "restaurant industry" site:.edu limits results to pages from an educational site

There are many other advanced Google search commands, but I find these two the best for obtaining the most substantive results.

Consider the use of the site search to limit a Google search just to one of your favorite websites. Google's site search not only permits you to restrict results to pages from educational, governmental, and other domains, as explained above, but also permits you to limit a Google search to a *single* website. This lesser-known feature can be extremely useful when you want to find out if a favorite site has published an article, blog post, or news item on a topic you are researching. You could just go to that page directly and run a search, but many websites do not permit a keyword search, or they offer a very incomplete or rudimentary search capability. So running a powerful Google search focused only on all the pages of that target site is a great work-around.

For instance, perhaps one of your favorite sites is *Wired* magazine's wired.com, and you have a very detailed research query but you *only* want to find results that were published on that topic on Wired.com. Say that query was to locate any article on the topic of privacy, the NSA, and Facebook that *also* included the name "Keith Alexander" but had *nothing* about Google. You can try to run this search on Wired.com but, as with most websites, the ability to perform an advanced, precision search is very limited and you'd be trying for a long time with very uncertain success. But in Google you could input a search statement such as the following to perform that sophisticated search just on Wired.com:

privacy NSA "keith alexander" Facebook -Google site:wired.com

What that search statement specifically tells Google to retrieve are pages that:

a. contain the word *privacy* AND MUST ALSO

b. contain the word *NSA* AND MUST ALSO

c. contain the exact phrase *Keith Alexander* AND MUST ALSO

d. contain the word *Facebook* AND MUST NOT

e. contain the word *Google* AND MUST HAVE BEEN PUBLISHED ONLY ON

f. Wired.com

You can see how valuable this feature can be for getting information specifically from your most trusted and valued information sources. (It can also help you with the information overload problem discussed later in this chapter.)

What about filtering search results by date? How can you ensure that the pages you retrieve are not going to be older than you want, or that they were published within a certain time frame? Or what if you *only* wanted older pages, which could be the case if you were doing more archival and historical research?

Unlike searching a traditional database, restricting web search results by date has always been a very tricky exercise. There are many reasons for this, including the fact that the definition of *date* itself on the web can be ambiguous. For instance, it could indicate when the original item was created, or when a site first put that page up on the web, or when the page was most recently updated, or even when the site was located (crawled) by a search engine. So you have to realize right away that searching by date is a rather dicey proposition.

That said, there are a few strategies you can use to help you filter by date. After you run a search on Google, you will see a small set of submenus under the search box at the top of the page of your results (see Figure 3.3). If you click the link "Search Tools" you will call up another set of links, one of which is labeled "Any time" and is checked by default. That means that your searches will return pages that were published anytime. But you will also see other options: past hour, past 24 hours, past week, past month, past year, or "custom range," where you can enter your own start and end dates. I have generally had good luck using this date-limit option from Google to restrict results by date. Note that after you create your date limit, you will also have the option of changing Google's normal default display method, which is "by relevance," to "by date."

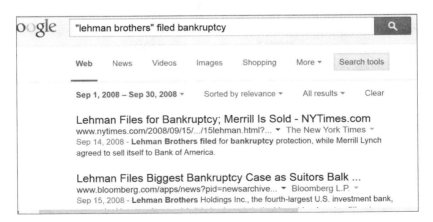

Figure 3.3 One of the most useful but lesser known Google features is the ability to limit results to a certain date. This search retrieved pages about Lehman Brothers just for the month of September 2008, when the company filed for bankruptcy

This can be helpful if you have a research query for which you need to see items ordered chronologically.

Another way you can use dates effectively in your web search is to follow the advice of blogger Amit Agarwal, who provides step-by-step strategies for using Google's advanced search functions to figure out the date when a page first appeared on the web. The steps are not republished here, but you can find them on his blog page.[1]

Special Google Search Tips

In addition to using Google's advanced features and capabilities to make your searches more productive, here are a few of my own personal strategies for getting the most out of my searches.

Use "Human Filters" to Get Top Results

When researching a topic, you will often discover that there is a particular writer, blogger, analyst, or expert who has the most interesting and valuable insights, and so you become particularly attentive to sites and sources where he or she is quoted. You can use that person's name to filter articles and other items on the internet so that a search will only retrieve those in which that person is quoted or mentioned, thereby serving as an indicator that that item is one you will want to pay attention to. Doing this not only helps you find results that have quoted your favorite authority, but also serves as a kind of quality filter to help you zero in on those sources that have passed your own kind of credibility test. In other words, those sites have a similar perspective regarding who is a valuable authority, and so you might assume that the article, blog post, or item will contain other valuable insights and mention other key people whom you'll want to follow or even contact yourself.

Here's an example of what I mean. In my own research on the topic of ethics and Big Data, I found that one person who I felt offered top-notch thinking and analysis was Kate Crawford, a professor and researcher. So to help find articles in which she is quoted or mentioned, all I did was enter the phrase

"Kate Crawford" "Big Data"

into Google to return those items that were about Big Data and included her name.

Of course, limiting results to just those that include a person's name is a very narrow search, so you need to also occasionally step back and conduct broader searches and scans to balance this ultra-precision search strategy.

Write the Answer You Are Hoping to Receive

This cool little tip was mentioned in the legendary cyber–guru Howard Rheingold's excellent book *Net Smart*, quoting Chris Heuer as the source for this idea. In the book, Rheingold quoted his strategy as follows:

> Knowing how to use advanced search can empower any searcher, but these technical competencies don't necessarily inform the searcher about how to find the information they want in an adequate context. What steps must be taken to turn searching and finding into learning and knowing?
>
> Chris Heuer teaches people to search through his social media club, and offers the good advice to "write the answer you want to get" when formulating your search query. For instance, I wanted to know how and why Thomas Edison (who championed delivering electricity through direct current), rather than his equally brilliant rival Nikola Tesla (who championed alternating current), ended up winning the battle for commercial control over electricity. The answer I wanted to get would complete the sentence "Tesla lost to Edison because . . ." so I entered that phrase (minus the three dots) into Google and Bing.

I have personally found this tip to be an excellent way of turning up the precise answer to a question. I've also found Google to be increasingly good at returning relevant results when a simple question is entered; for instance, "why is the moon red?" or "how do I get a passport?"

Use Google Images to Find Charts, Tables, and Graphs

One of the most common types of online searches is to locate tables, charts, and graphs. These high octane results are packed with valuable data that provides at an at-a-glance snapshot of key trends, series, and comparisons on your topic. A great way to find these is simply to run your search on Google Images. Because Google classifies tables and charts as "images"—at least when formatted as jpeg, bmp, or other image filetypes, as is typical—to pull them up all you need to do is enter your search terms and then hit Google's "images" link. One tip: because Google displays so many images on one page, it can be hard to read the headings and titles of the rows and columns as you browse down the pages of charts Google Images returns. So you'll want to enlarge the view of your browser, say to 150 percent, so you can read the text as you review them to more easily find the ones you want.

Beyond Google?

So far in this chapter we've been focusing on one search engine, Google, and I've explained the reasons for this focus. Google is not, of course, the only search engine out there, though when it comes to general search engines there really is only one other big name, and that is Microsoft's Bing. Bing is not much different from Google, in that it too does an excellent job returning relevant results, has advanced features and filters, and is very fast. There are some smaller differences, though, that could make Bing appealing more as a matter of personal preference than because it offers any truly significant additional capabilities. Perhaps the only somewhat notable difference is that Bing offers a certain level of integration with Facebook to connect searches with friends, but this has not proven to be any kind of game changer when it comes to doing good research on the web. (The use of social media sites and platforms as a research source is examined in Chapter 4.)

When it comes to talking about search engines, the interesting conversation is not always so much about Google, Bing, and other big names, such as Yahoo!, but what the smaller, niche search engines offer. There are many hundreds of these specialized search engines, and some can offer valuable alternatives, depending on the researcher's needs. Over the years I've kept a close watch on these, and below is a selection of my favorites. I've organized these by general topic category.

General Web Search Engines—with a Twist

Google, Bing, and Yahoo! are the big three when it comes to general web searching. But another that's worth mentioning is DuckDuckGo.

Founded in September 2008, DuckDuckGo works like a regular web search engine, with the difference that it does not track or share personal information. So it is an excellent alternative for those who are concerned about privacy. DuckDuckGo also offers a very clean interface, fast and relevant results, full Boolean and advanced searches, and a range of interesting little extras, or what DuckDuckGo calls "goodies," such as the ability to do quick calculations and lookups on a wide range of reference-type queries.

News Search Engines

News search engines don't index and cover the entire web, but are limited to sites and pages with recent news, and so include newspaper, magazine, and journal articles, sometimes social media posts and blogs, and other timely news-oriented reports. The best-known news search engine is probably Google's own News search, which can be engaged by clicking on the News link at the top of the Google

Figure 3.4 The DuckDuckGo search engine does not track users or retain their search history

search page. However, there are others as well that offer additional features and capabilities. Following are my favorites—not including "social" news sites such as Digg, which are covered in Chapter 4.

- **Topix.** Topix does an excellent job in filtering news searches (including traditional news sources, blogs, and other news-oriented sites) by geographic region. So, for instance, if you want to find news pages and bloggers that used the word *Obamacare*, you'd simply enter your zip code and then search on the word to find results only in your own region.

- **Yahoo! News.** Yahoo! News offers advanced search capabilities and the ability to filter results by source or time—both very handy news search options.

- **PRWeb.** PRWeb is an interesting niche search engine if you want to restrict your search to press releases. While not a comprehensive collection of all releases, it includes thousands of items, which can be filtered by one of several broad subject areas (e.g., automotive, computer, science, etc., and by subcategory, e.g., science/chemistry) and by date of release.

- **Trove.** Trove is another excellent news search engine that relies on people, not algorithms, to select the best news stories and create news streams on thousands of topics.

Specialized and Niche Search Engines

In addition to the more general and news search engines, there are scores of specialized and niche search engines. Following are a handful of examples to give you a taste of the range of search engines you might find useful.

- **Image and Video Search.** Most of us know the standard places to find images or short video clips. The most popular sites include, for images, Flickr, Google Images, and Picasa, and for videos, YouTube and Vimeo, among many others.

- **Scholarly Search Engines.** These sites search and return academic articles, papers, reports, dissertations, and books. Sites that I have used and liked include Google Scholar, Academia.edu, and ResearchGate.

- **Marketing and Business Search Engines.** There are search engines that provide results focusing on business topics such as market research, industry analysis, and business news. Note that although these are free to search, some will charge the searcher to download premium business resources such as market research and investment reports. Sites I've used and like include MarketResearch.com, Reportlinker, and Biznar.

- **Government Information.** There are many search engines that are focused on searching and retrieving sites from the U.S. federal government. One that I found to be particularly valuable and useful is called Metalib.

- **Demographic and Population Search Engines.** If you need to learn about the demographics of a particular region, find information on the U.S. population as a whole, or obtain business, geography, or other demographic data, the U.S. Census Bureau has several search engines on its main site. Another one I like is called CLR; while it's geared for real estate research, it includes neat and easy-to-read charts with demographic and profile information on the people that live in specified regions around the United States.

Other Search Engines

There are a whole host of other types of specialized search engines of potential value to researchers. For example, Noza.com is a searchable database of charitable contributions; GeoFeedia is a social media search engine that permits filtering and focusing on blog and other social posts based on several geographic factors. And Ebooks on the Web, created by the University of Buffalo library, searches multiple ebook sites from a single search box, by title or author, in order to locate literary classics and other books no longer protected by copyright.

There are scores of social search engines, too, such as SocialMention, Addictomatic, TweetBeep, and Topsy for searching and aggregating blog, Facebook, Twitter, and other social posts on the web. (Social searching is covered in detail in Chapter 4.) Ironically, sometimes the best of the new and niche search engines have a very short life span. What often happens is that they do such a good job that they are "discovered" by a larger company, purchased for their technologies which are then integrated into the larger company's products, and discontinued as free standing resources. This was the case with an excellent niche search engine called Blekko, which was acquired by IBM in May 2015 for integration into its Watson product.

Note that I have not included *people* search engines in this chapter—these are sites that claim they can help you find background information and an email address, phone number, or other contact information for someone you're trying to find. I am not including them because the majority of these are filled with errors and are typically misleading as to what is available for free and what you will need to pay for. That said, Zoomerang is much better than most, and a site called Skipease provides a gateway to several people search engines that have gone through some level of vetting and might turn out to be useful.

Beyond the Search Engine

So far this chapter has focused on search engines because that's how we all normally find information and do research on the web. However, it's important to point out that search engines themselves are not the only tool available for doing research on the internet. There are other finder tools that can be as useful, or even more useful, depending on the type of research you are undertaking. These include browsable directories and deep web resources.

Browsable Directories

As mentioned earlier in this chapter, the creation of browsable directories such as Yahoo! represented the first attempt to organize the web. These directories are still around and still offer value for web-based research. Although directories cover only a miniscule percentage of the web, their strength is that what *is* included represents a careful selection of a kind of "Best of" the web typically determined by a librarian or other subject expert and slotted into the appropriate category. This is particularly useful when you are beginning a new research project and want to be directed to a few relevant and valuable sources chosen by someone who has taken the time to select those sites. While there are many of these directory sites, two of my favorites are IPL2 (see Figure 3.5) and the Voice of the Shuttle. Unfortunately, while IPL2 remains an active site at this writing, as the book was going to press I learned it would no longer be updated.

Deep Web Resources

The deep (or "invisible") web refers to pages and portions of the web that *can* be accessed, but are not available, or at least not easily available, to search engines. There are several reasons portions of the web may not be findable by search engines. Deep web resources include sites with password protection, those with no outgoing or incoming links and therefore not findable by search engine crawlers, and sites where the data resides behind a firewall that can only be accessed by registered users or those who have special access. Some of these unfindable resources are actual searchable databases, and these represent the type of deep web resources of greatest value to researchers.

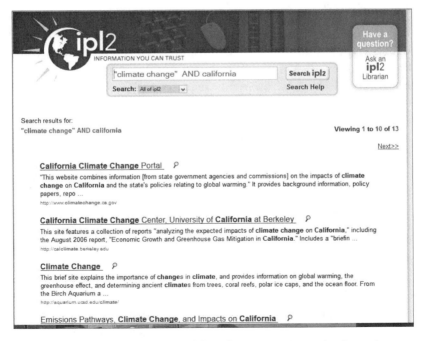

Figure 3.5 The Internet Public Library (IPL2) is a high-quality directory of pages on the web, grouped by subject

The good news is that there are methods for finding and searching these databases hidden in the deep web. One way is to use a specialized deep web search engine, which specifically goes out to find and query those databases if they are not password protected. While there once were several of these, they have mostly fizzled as a genre of search engine, and those that are still around are often unreliable. One that I can recommend for business-related deep web searches is Biznar, mentioned earlier in this chapter.

A better way to search a database hidden in the deep web is to find its name, link to that site, and find out what you need to do to run a search directly (e.g., register, sign up, get a free trial, etc.). Some of my favorite deep web databases are listed in Chapter 1. Note that many of these are government databases, as these represent some of the most useful collections of data for researchers.

The Heartbreak of Information Overload Syndrome

Do you feel anxious when confronting a list of tens of thousands of results from a Google search? Are you overwhelmed with the number of sources, sites, and options available for finding answers and information? Has your drive for creativity and productivity diminished as you flail about attempting to determine which source is worth your precious attention?

If so, like millions around you, you may be suffering from IOS: "information overload syndrome."

Okay, you won't be seeing any pharmaceutical ads on television for a little pill to help cure this newly named embarrassing ailment. But there is no question that as the number—and the variety—of options for finding information soars, so does our sensation of having *too many* choices, often resulting in paralysis. We don't know where to turn or what we should pay attention to.

You may think that information overload is a new problem caused by the internet and, more recently, by social media and all the related consumer-generated data. While it is certainly true that the internet and social media have exacerbated the overload problem, it's also a fact that lamentations over too much information have been going on for many, many years. You could trace the seemingly unprecedented growth of our information sources pre-internet to the middle of the 20th century, when an increasing number of books, journals, and governmental reports were being rapidly churned out (famously described in Alvin Toffler's classic book, *Future Shock*, published in 1970). Or you could go back much, much further to the explosion of scientific literature in the 18th and 19th centuries, or go all the way back to Gutenberg's invention of movable type in the mid-1400s.

And complaints about the *quality* of all the newly churned out information are nothing new either. Just as tweets, blogs, Wikipedia, and the like are condemned as superficial and vapid, the same kinds of criticisms have for years been leveled at whatever information sources happened to be emerging at the time. Even the first encyclopedias were disparaged by some as lesser, derivative sources. J. G. Herder, a student of Kant and a prominent figure in the German enlightenment, said this about the efforts by the French to manage their surfeit of print information by the creation of the encyclopedia:

> Now encyclopedias are being made, even Diderot and D'Alembert have lowered themselves to this. And that book that is a triumph for the French is for us the first sign of their decline. They have nothing to write and, thus, produce Abregés, vocabularies, esprits, encyclopedias—the original works fall away.[1]

More famously, the same kind of critique was leveled at the telegraph by Henry David Thoreau in *Walden*, who seemed to have foreseen demand for a 19th-century version of a celebrity tweet. Thoreau wrote:

> We are in great haste to construct a magnetic telegraph from Maine to Texas; but Maine and Texas, it may be, have nothing important to communicate . . . As if the main object were to talk fast and not to talk sensibly. We are eager to tunnel under the Atlantic and bring the Old World some weeks nearer to the New; but perchance the first news that will leak through into the broad, flapping American ear will be that the Princess Adelaide has the whooping cough.

So a bit of context is useful to understand that complaints and concerns over the quantity and quality of information are an old story indeed. And those criticisms will certainly continue to be leveled in the future against whatever new information modes and technologies are still to come.

Although concerns over information overload and quality are not unique to our time, that does not mean that the latest concerns have no validity. It's just that we need to dig a little deeper to figure out what the current problem is and what our solutions will be.

Let's begin by looking at these three questions:

1) What do we really mean when we say we are suffering from information overload?

2) What are the specific elements of today's information environment that are contributing most to the problem?

3) What, if anything, can (and should) we do about it?

Let's tackle these questions one at a time.

First, what do we mean by "information overload"? Some people have argued that the entire concept is an illusion. After all, one argument goes, when we walk into a library we are surrounded by thousands or even millions of books and other documents, but we don't feel overwhelmed or complain that there are too many sources. Where's that supposed information overload?

But just because we don't feel overwhelmed with thousands or millions of information sources in a library does not mean that the phenomenon does not exist in other situations. It simply makes the point that information overload is not something *external* but rather is best understood as a subjective sensation. It's the sensation of being overwhelmed or paralyzed when faced with deciding which of seemingly "too many" different sources and types of sources to consult.

The primary reason we don't normally have this sensation in a library is that the libraries have applied logical categorization and ordering schemes to make it easy for us to efficiently find what we want. But there are other, more subtle, factors at work as well. For one, physical items such as books, magazines, and newspapers on a shelf are, in a sense, "waiting patiently" for you and can be approached when you want them, then leisurely scanned and browsed. In addition, you have an expert—the librarian—close at hand, to help you find what you need if you're not sure where to turn.

Compare that process to what happens when you go to the internet to do research. There's *no topical categorization* of the billions of information sources, and they have originated from a huge range of *different types of entities*: research universities, news organizations, industry associations, bloggers, tweeters, government agencies, homemade videos, and so on. The *intentions* of the person or group who created a particular source can range from a desire to inform and educate, to a mission to convince you to support his or her cause, or to raise awareness of a new public concern. Or perhaps the source is designed simply to persuade you to purchase a product or service—forthrightly, indirectly, or via downright scams. Sources may purport to have published something for one purpose (to educate and inform, for example) while actually promoting a hidden and more narrow political agenda.

And unlike being in a library, where you can calmly approach a book, journal, or newspaper when you are ready, on the internet information comes "at" you. Whether through email alerts, new tweets, the continuous stream of real-time updated news or Facebook feeds, or the results of an internet search, online digital sources compete for your attention and clicks, sometimes employing absurd headlines and flashy multimedia to do so. It's natural that you are more likely to feel overwhelmed, perhaps even a little assaulted, in this environment and to experience that sensation of information overload.

These days the issue often isn't so much sorting out the bad and shallow information from the good stuff, as it was in the early days of the internet. Because the internet has basically become the default location for virtually all information storage, or at least references, for researchers today the problem now is also determining which of the many thousands of *good and useful* results to look at. Where does one start?

Taking Control

The good news is that because information overload is a *feeling*, dealing with it and ameliorating that frustrating feeling is within your control. You have the ability to improve your search approach as well as your overall research mind-set.

You can do so by following these three strategies:

1) Employ precision online search strategies and research tools to zero in on the most relevant and useful results from an internet search

2) Employ the right strategies for planning and managing your research process to improve your research productivity

3) Adjust your mind-set by maintaining appropriate and realistic expectations and monitoring what you are telling yourself in the course of your research.

Let's look at each of these strategies, one at a time.

Precision Online Search Strategies and Tools

Earlier in this chapter we examined some of the most effective ways to conduct a good online search. However, there are also a few search strategies of particular value for reducing your feeling of information overload. These primarily involve making your searches more precise so as to retrieve fewer but more relevant results. Here are a couple of my favorite strategies.

Before running a search on Google, think strategically about the words and phrases that can best be leveraged as effective filters. This means taking a few minutes to think carefully about what kind of results you want to find, and then crafting your keywords to ensure that you get the desired results and automatically screen out what you don't want or need.

Here is an example of how I employed that strategy when researching a recent article comparing competing vendors of Twitter search services; my goal was to locate reviews and comparisons of the various competitors. When I used the name of only one of those services—Topsy—in my search query, along with the words *comparison* or *review*, the search engine primarily retrieved pages from Topsy itself, comparing its service to others. There were also some press releases and trade articles reviewing that site. In another search, I entered the phrase "comparing twitter search services." Results from that search were pretty useful, but I still found that a high percentage of the items retrieved were too general and not precisely what I wanted—that is, a good comparison of the leading vendors.

So I gave it a bit more thought and decided that any review or comparison of those sites would naturally have to include the specific names of two or more leading Twitter search services. Topsy, Gnip, and TweetBeep were three of the big names, so any article that contained more than one of these names was likely to be some kind of comparative review or discussion rather than pages from a single Twitter search service. So I changed my strategy and entered a simple search statement with the three names, and that simple search worked well in retrieving only articles that reviewed or compared those (and other) leading Twitter search sites.

Another powerful strategy, mentioned earlier in this chapter, is to use the names of people whose work you have come to admire as a way to filter your searches. Remember that what you are doing

---

TIP: Good Newsle

Using a site called Newsle can help you keep up with your most trusted sources. This intriguing site operates like a personal social newswire, automatically alerting you when anything appears on the web that either was written by a particular person or is about that person. The site is free and easy to use, and is a great way to keep up with the latest works and ideas of your favorite human sources. And they don't necessarily have to be that famous either—it could be a businessperson, writer, great chef—anyone whose name might appear in a news article, blog post, or other informational site on the web (see Figure 3.6).

---

here is limiting the number of pages retrieved and increasing the odds that the results Google returns will be precisely on target.

So your mission, when turning to Google to do research, is to consider the following: What does your ideal result look like? Are there certain words—especially unique or unusual ones, such as proper nouns, specific phrases, or even names of people you trust and want to follow—that these pages would most likely contain? Then run a search on those terms.

Figure 3.6 Newsle alerts you to news, blogs, and web pages on people you want to keep up with and track

Keep in mind that you can also use specialized search engines to narrow results in a different way. For example, Google Scholar is limited to more substantive academic works, and the experimental site SearchPoint (see Figure 3.7) employs clustering technologies to filter and group search results into categories based on the most commonly occurring words and phrases surfaced in the search.

What about social aggregation sites such as StumbleUpon, Digg, TechMeme, and Memeorandum? These sites rely on a kind of wisdom-of-crowds (WOC) approach (see Chapter 5 for an in-depth analysis of the WOC phenomenon), whereby users click and promote news stories and sites in different topical areas, and sources that get clicked on the most move up toward the top of the list. While these kinds of sites are good for finding out what's hot now, and can provide interesting insights into what is currently (or recently) getting people's attention, I have not found them useful for in-depth research.

There are also web-based tools specifically designed to help manage and organize your web searches. My favorites are listed in

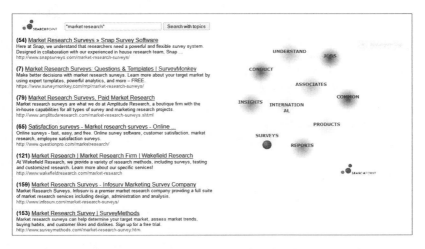

Figure 3.7 An alternative method for displaying results is to cluster similar results together, as provided by the experimental search engine SearchPoint

Appendix A, but two specific approaches worth calling out for dealing with too much information are the use of RSS Feeds and curation.

RSS to the Rescue?

While you may not have heard the term RSS (which stands for Really Simply Syndication as well as Rich Site Summary), there's a pretty good chance that you have already used RSS feeds to stay alert and informed on topics or sites important to you on the web. RSS, which has been popular since about 2004, is a technical term for news and information feeds that you can subscribe to on the web in order to receive updates from your favorite news sites and bloggers.

The way RSS works is pretty simple. Many blog and news sites include a little RSS button or link (often in orange) on their page. If you click on that button, you can then sign up to automatically have future news and posts from that site sent to an RSS Reader, which is software that allows you to browse, click, and read the content at your leisure. The major web browsers such as Explorer, Chrome, and Firefox all have a built in RSS reader, or you can use a standalone feed reader, such as Bloglines, NetVibes, or Feedly.

RSS can be convenient, and potentially a time saver, as it brings preferred information sources to you so you don't have to remember to track down the latest items yourself (see Figure 3.8). But RSS also has some drawbacks and is not an ideal solution for dealing with information overload.

One problem is that as you begin to subscribe to more and more feeds, you can soon begin to suffer from a feeling of "RSS Feed Overload," as hundreds of new items continually flow into your reader, creating a new pressure to keep up. The never-ending flow of feeds can make that feeling of being overwhelmed by information—even the specifically requested desired information—even worse. Furthermore, since RSS feeds work automatically—making them good alerting and "keeping up with" tools—they are a fundamentally passive approach to research. Finally, with the rise of certain social media sites—particularly Twitter—people increasingly rely on those feeds (updates, posts, etc.) from people in their own social network to alert them to interesting and important items, and as a result have forsaken RSS feeds.

My advice when it comes to RSS Feeds is to use them judiciously. Find perhaps five must-read sites, journals, or blogs in your field; subscribe to those feeds; check them when you can;

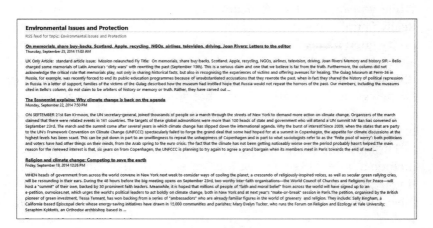

Figure 3.8 Subscribe to an RSS feed when you want news and information on specific high-interest topics delivered to you automatically. Environmental issues are the topic of the pictured feed.

and utilize these as a kind of personalized custom newswire to keep you up to date on the latest interesting news and analyses from your preferred sources.

Is Curation the Cure?

Curation tools are another way to keep up with new sites of high interest. These tools make it easy for anyone to choose a topic of interest—and that topic could be a person, social issue, company, place, or really any subject at all—and then create and publish a digital news "magazine" by aggregating interesting and relevant items on the internet. The magazine's curator carefully selects news, blog, multimedia, and social articles and posts on the chosen topic. Curation sites provide the user with a variety of free tools to locate the relevant items on the web about the chosen topic, filter for the most useful ones, add one's own comments, include images, and then publish the selected content and share with others.

One particularly powerful and popular curation site that I've used and liked is called Scoop.it. Topics curated by Scoop.it users number in the thousands, and range from Acadian culture to zookeeping. While Scoop.it's focus is on helping people become their own publishers, it also offers great benefits to researchers, since the "scoops" published by these curators typically represent a more refined set of online information sources than you would turn up using a search engine. Each of those digital magazine sites represents the focused work of an individual who took the time to use Scoop.it's tools to find the best sites and posts, organize them, identify each item and include a short summary or excerpt of the item, lay out the content and add images to make it attractive to read, and sometimes add personal commentary. In a sense, these curators represent a kind of community of amateur librarians whose mission is to find the best information on a topic, review it, comment on its value, and share it in an easy-to-use format. Scoop.it represents a very successful marriage between technology and human judgment. And it's all made available free, to anyone on the web (see Figure 3.9).

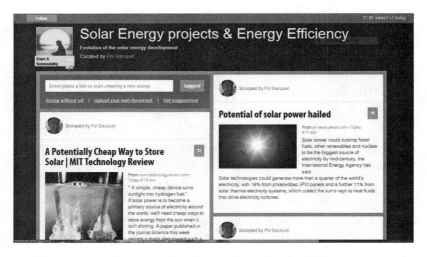

Figure 3.9   An example of a Scoop.it curator's aggregation
of recent online news items on the topic of solar energy

By tapping into the work of these curators, you are making use of other people's intelligence and labor to filter out the chaff and bring you the wheat.

So . . . how do you find the "scoops" in the field that you are researching? There are two primary ways: One, you can go directly to Scoop.it and run a keyword search on the titles of the curated pages hosted on the site, review the results for the scoops that appear most relevant, and subscribe to them; or, Two, you can do a Google site search on your topic, using the Google advanced search filters to limit the results to pages from the Scoop.it site. (See Figure 3.10 for an example of a Google search for Scoop.it publications on the topic of farmers' markets.)

Finally, it's worth noting that the concept behind Scoop.it isn't new. In fact, when Yahoo! was launched in 1994, it relied on the same idea—it created a site that filtered the web by employing librarians and subject specialists to find the best sites and organize them into topical categories. It's just that Yahoo! was created by a small centralized team, not thousands of users around the world; it could only organize web pages, it only listed the name of the page and a link, and there were no graphics or multimedia. Scoop.it and

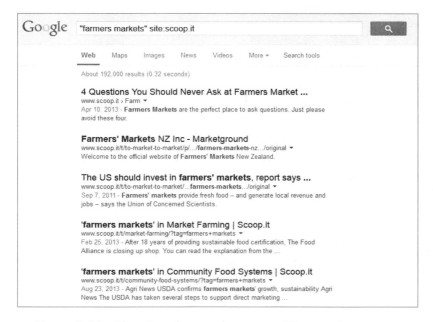

Figure 3.10   This Google search turns up "Scoop.it" curations
on the topic of farmers markets

other curation sites have helped bring digital curation into the age
of social media and the visual web.

Learn to Discern

While Arthur C. Clarke was making his statement on discernment
(see the Tip that follows) in the service of the *really* big picture—that
is, the need to pay attention to information that is going to make
humanity healthier, better our chances of survival, and enhance
our lives—we can also take that principle to a smaller scale and ask,
When immersed in data and sources, how do we apply discernment
to determine what truly deserves our attention?

While there is no perfect answer to that question, I have found
that the most valuable information is that which provides new
insight—it is something that elevates my understanding of whatever I am researching to a higher level. The best way to identify
information that leads to insight is simply to pay attention to your
own reactions when reading something. Does it give you an "Aha!"

TIP: Navigating the Age of Discernment

The late, great Arthur C. Clarke, scientist, futurist, and author of *2001: A Space Odyssey,* wrote about information overload. In an interview published in 2003 called "Humanity Will Survive Information Deluge" Clarke shared his take on what it means for us as a species and what we can do about it. He said,

> We are now faced with the responsibility of *discernment.* Just as our ancestors quickly realized that no one was going to force them to read the entire library of a thousand books, we are now overcoming the initial alarm at the sheer weight of available information—and coming to understand that it is not the information itself that determines our future, only the use we can make of it. (http://www.arthurcclarke.net/?interview=12)

Discernment is an interesting and telling choice of words. According to Dictionary.com, the root meaning of the word dates back to the late 14th century, from the Old French *discerner* (13th century) meaning to distinguish (between), or separate (by sifting), and directly from the Latin *discernere,* meaning to separate, set apart, divide, distribute, distinguish, or perceive.

Clarke's point was that it is now everyone's task—even our obligation—to use our capabilities to very carefully distinguish what information is worth attending to (and acting upon) and what information should be ignored.

feeling—providing new knowledge or understanding that gives you a deeper and better appreciation of the topic? If so, I'd say that this feeling is as good an indicator as any of what to pay attention to.

Productivity Tips

There are countless books, articles, and advisories on the best way to stay productive in your work, and of course there is no one best way to manage your time and work habits. That said, I do feel that a few basic productivity strategies can assist you in managing information overload when you are doing research. My suggestions are:

- Write down your research goal clearly and explicitly ahead of time. When doing so, try writing out the specific question that you want to answer from your research. This will help you focus your research strategy. Try also to break a larger research project into smaller segments.

- Set time limits on how long you will spend researching the different parts of your project. While the initial deadlines may be arbitrary, they can provide focus and help you avoid getting caught up in a loop of endless searching, linking, and reviewing; and keep you moving forward in your project. After all, as Shelley Hayduk, cofounder of The Brain Technologies noted in *The Secret to Digital Sanity*, "There is no beginning and no end to people's Facebook status updates, tweets, or Google news alerts." (*The Atlantic*, March 16 2011; http://www .theatlantic.com/technology/archive/2011/03/the-secret -to-digital-sanity/72550/) You can always come back to a section you felt you had not completely explored; the key is to keep moving forward and not fall into the rabbit hole of endless link clicking.

- Whenever there is something important you need to do, remember, or keep track of during your research, create some system that gets it out of your head and onto a document that you can review later. Getting things out of your head and into a paper or electronic document is a key productivity strategy of David Allen, the author of the *Getting Things Done* books.

- Identify a handful of your most trusted published sources and rely on those. While any such set will of course vary based on the topic and the researcher's own preferences, I personally have come to rely on one particular set of publications as trusted sources for the freshest insights on topics related to business, culture, and technology. These are *The Atlantic*; CBC radio (multiple shows); *The*

Economist; *The Globe and Mail*; *The New York Review of Books*; *The Nation*; *The New Yorker*; PBS and NPR (multiple shows); *Verge*; and *Wired*.

- Rely as much as possible on human filters to guide your research—see the search strategy outlined above as well as the chapters later in this book on finding, contacting, and interviewing people. Despite—or because of—the huge amount of digital information on the web, the most useful source remains other people.

Psychological Strategies

Remember that we have defined information overload as a sensation—the subjective feeling of being frustrated, anxious, and overwhelmed with too many sources, sites, documents, search engine results, and so on. Perhaps the ultimate solution to the problem of information overload is to acknowledge—and then change—this feeling. One way to do this is to through cognitive-behavioral therapy. The fundamental premise behind this form of therapy is that our feelings are derived primarily from our thoughts—what we are telling ourselves about a situation—and that often our thoughts about a situation are unnecessarily and unhelpfully dire and even irrational. Those dire thoughts produce intense, problematic, and unproductive feelings. Cognitive-behavioral therapy—or one well-known version in particular, called REBT (Rational Emotive Behavioral Therapy)—teaches people to closely examine what they are telling themselves about a situation, identify any thoughts that are irrational, unhelpful, or overstated, and replace them with more helpful and rational ones. This process will then, theoretically, help produce more healthy and productive feelings.

The basic principle behind REBT is fairly straightforward: we are disturbed not by things themselves, but by what we (silently) tell ourselves about those things—our thoughts about them. If you tell yourself that a situation is awful and you just can't stand it, your accompanying feelings will likely be dread, deep frustration, intense anxiety, and depression. If you reframe that phenomenon instead as unfortunate, inconvenient, or a pain in the neck, your feelings will still be negative, but they will more likely be those of resignation, disappointment, or annoyance, and not that same kind of debilitating intense anxiety.

So consider what you might be telling yourself (quietly and tacitly, if not out loud) when faced with lots and lots of information. Are you thinking thoughts such as the following?

- This is an impossible situation.

- I'll never get to all of those absolutely critical sources.

- It is terrible that I can't get to all of this.

- What a disaster it would be if I were to lose my job because I am not good at keeping up with the latest news and information the way I should.

If you have a tendency to think this way, take a minute to analyze how you are framing the situation. In this example, you have chosen to define the situation as impossible, and told yourself that you'll never get to it all, that all the information is critical, that if you don't get to it, it will be terrible, that you might lose your job as a result, and that you are no good at doing what you should be doing.

REBT trains clients to find, identify, and isolate this kind of "awfulizing" and catastrophic thinking. If you can examine whether what you are telling yourself is truly rational, reasonable, and healthy, and you find that your statements may not be rational or healthy, you can then determine whether there are other, more appropriate, realistic, and helpful ways to view the exact same phenomena.

For example, rather than describing the situation of having lots of incoming news feeds and sources with the anxiety-inducing word "impossible," wouldn't it be more appropriate to think of it as "difficult" or "challenging"? Then, rather than moaning to yourself that you will never get to it all, you can instead say to yourself that it's not humanly possible to get to everything, but you'll read the most pressing items whenever you are able to make the time. Instead of defining all the information as critical, it is more realistic to assume that most of the information would fall under the categories of useful, interesting, and important. And if you don't get to the information as soon as you'd like to, rather than defining the situation as "terrible" you could more realistically call it "unfortunate," but hardly a disaster.

The larger point here is that you have control over how you define and interpret events in your external world. You can apply that principle to whatever debilitating thoughts you are having about the amount of information you are dealing with as well.

Vendors will continue to crank out all sorts of new tools, sites, search engines, and features that will purportedly help us deal with our latest iteration of information overload. But technology problems are rarely solved by more technology. In fact, the irony is that because new technologies typically eliminate existing barriers to creating and disseminating information, they often result in *increasing* the amount of information available to us. A weariness to the flesh in any age!

So you can't rely on a technological solution to what is, ultimately and at its heart, mostly a problem of psychology and perception. And solutions to problems like this rest within you.

Note

1. "Why Google Isn't Making Us Stupid . . . or Smart," Chad Wellmon, *Hedgehog Review*, 14.1 Spring 2012.

Chapter 4

The Social Search: Tapping into Your Networks

What is a social search? And how is it relevant to you for doing good research? While there are a variety of definitions, I'd say that the most helpful way to think about social search is as an online search in which, instead of searching text, images, videos, surveys, or other digital content, you are seeking to gain knowledge directly from *people*. These might be people you are already connected to via a social network, or they could be people on social networks that you don't know but with whom you want to connect in order to tap into their knowledge.

In the context of the social search, it's useful to think of the word "search" in a somewhat looser and broader way. In a standard search—performed on a traditional database or on Google—you enter keywords and get a list of items or pages that match and are relevant to your search terms. A social search, in contrast, integrates a more casual browsing or listening process—I'll talk more about these distinctions later in the chapter.

Why bother doing a social search? What is special about this kind of research that makes it valuable, and what might it offer that you can't get from a standard search of traditional online sources?

The Emergence of the Social Search

To answer this question, let's take a brief detour to examine the initial excitement around social search and how it evolved over time. In 2007 Facebook and other early social networks were becoming increasingly popular. It soon became apparent that people on social networks were relying on their connections as a kind of personal news and information source. More and more users—particularly younger ones—relied on their social network connections to find out what was going on—what was new and interesting. They also began relying on their social contacts to help find answers to all sorts of questions; their contacts served as a kind of friendly, networked group of amateur reference librarians. Observers of the internet noticed this phenomenon and began discussing how the trend might impact research on the internet.

Some predicted that as we all became more connected, we would come to rely on our social networks as our *preferred* sources of news and information. Another prediction was that our social networks would do a *better job* of providing relevant and useful information than searches on the open internet, since our social contacts were people we knew and trusted, and they knew us.

Around this time, the popular blogger and previous Microsoft employee Robert Scoble wrote a post provocatively titled "Why Mahalo, Techmeme, and Facebook Are Going to Kick Google's Butt in Four Years," contending that "social graph searching," as it was then called, was going to be better than traditional searching. He argued that finding information from people in your social network is better since you will not receive spam, promotions, or other unwanted information from your contacts. Our networked contacts, the argument went, would serve as human filters to help direct us to what we needed to find out.

Over the years, as new social networks came and went and young people developed their own research habits, Scoble's predictions were *partially* realized. Many of us have, in fact, come to rely on our social networks to keep up with what's going on—if not about what's going on in the world, then at least in our local community, our communities of interest, or our circles of friends and families. And, as discussed later in this chapter, consumer social networks, such as Facebook and Twitter, as well as academic social networks, such as Academia.edu and ResearchGate, have proven to be useful for finding experts, tracking trends, networking, getting on-the-ground observational reports, and more. However, despite efforts by Facebook and other social networks to enhance their search capabilities, social networks have not presented any real challenge to existing internet search engines as a tool for research.

Twitter Soars as a Source for Researchers

Something did happen, though, that made human networked connections a more valuable way to find information: Twitter! Launched in 2006, the micro-blogging network, as it was first called, quickly gained momentum and users but was initially seen by many as an absurd communication platform whose users did things like post what they ate for breakfast. And while that perception is still prevalent in some circles, Twitter also began gaining respect as a platform that offered new and valuable ways to find information.

Emblematizing this change of perspective was a remark by Marshall Kilpatrick, a senior writer at the Read/Write website, in his article, "Twitter for Journalists." Kilpatrick said, "When I first saw Twitter, I thought it was the stupidest thing ever. Now, despite the length of this post, I find 140 characters plenty of space to communicate about almost anything."[1] *The Economist* soon weighed in with its own take on Twitter, explaining to readers that it is a medium that "favors observation rather than analysis."[2]

Twitter quickly evolved into a kind of personal newswire service, and despite its notoriety as a place for celebrity tweets and trivia, it became a platform where people could discover breaking news before it was picked up by traditional media. It also allowed users to hear about important developments, thinking, and ideas directly from people they knew and admired professionally and wanted to keep up with (see the section on "Twitter Searching" below that follows).

Twitter helped legitimize social networks as places to get news and information. At the same time, other social networks emerged that provided people with the ability to tap into the knowledge of individuals directly, including LinkedIn and the scholarly-focused social networks Academia.edu and ResearchGate, both launched in September 2008.

Those scholarly sites provided networking opportunities for academics, scientists, and serious researchers, allowing them to find out what others were researching, writing, or simply pondering. Subscribers to scholarly networks could also search other members' uploaded works and make personal contacts with other academics.

Finally, as more and more interesting and important discussions began occurring on social sites, companies and organizations began to realize that these authentic, grassroots, real-time conversations represented a new and unique source of insights and intelligence. These unprompted discussions could offer new insights for critical functions such as market research, marketing, brand management, public relations, customer service, reputation management, strategic planning, competitive analysis, and more. This, in turn, gave rise to the "social listening" discipline, in which organizations deploy software and social monitoring sites to search, track, follow, and analyze conversations on the social web to help them maintain a competitive edge.

Doing the Social Search

So despite Scoble's prediction, Google's butt remains unbruised. But it is also true that social networks, through their ability to make known and connect the knowledge of their members, have proven their worth for researchers.

The bottom line is that while social networks have not become any kind of *substitute* for traditional databases or internet search engines, they do offer researchers real benefits. Social networks can allow researchers to:

- Keep up with the works of a trusted set of experts in your field or from people whom you respect on the topic you are researching

- See newly released reports and documents by receiving alerts on unpublished manuscripts, articles, book drafts, and so forth from those in your network

- Encounter interesting observations and speculation by your trusted set of sources

- Find and connect with experts more easily so you can ask them your own questions and have a substantive conversation (See Chapters 6 through 8.)

Let's take a few of these leading social networks for a quick spin to see what you can learn on each and how to quickly zero in on what you need.

Academic Social Searching

For professors, scholars, scientists, and academic researchers, it's vital to stay abreast of what others in one's field are doing: what they are publishing, where are they speaking, what are they planning to research, and so on.

A social network designed specifically for academics to connect with others in their field is kind of a natural, and over the years networks geared specifically for scholarly researchers have emerged. The two big ones are ResearchGate (see Figure 4.1) and Academia.edu (see Figures 4.2 and 4.3). Both networks were launched in 2008, and while there are distinctions between the two, they serve the same primary purpose of allowing researchers to find other scholars' works and to share their own works so they can be found as well.

These networks function in much the same way. A new user creates a profile, including information about affiliations and research interests, and uploads any papers, articles, article abstracts, presentations, and any other documents the member wishes to share.

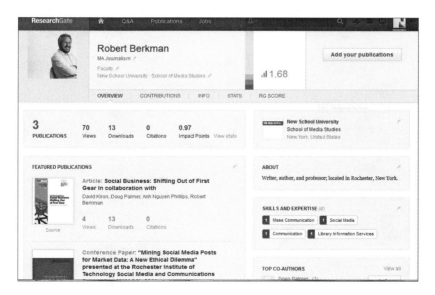

Figure 4.1   The profile of the author on the scholarly social network, ResearchGate

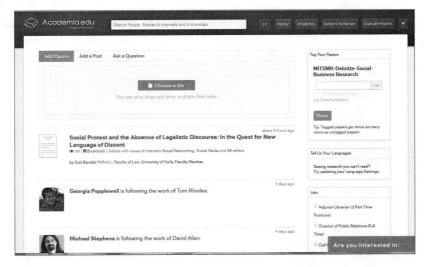

Figure 4.2 Academia.edu is another leading scholarly social network where users can share their work and connect with others in their field

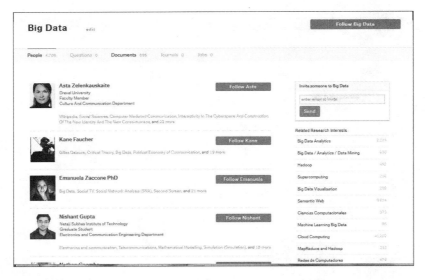

Figure 4.3 A search on "Big Data" on Academia.edu identifies scholars who have knowledge, credentials or shared work for that topic

The networks provide a Facebook-like status update feed, as well, where members can share what they are working on, pose questions, and comment on other members' posts. As with the consumer social networks, members may choose which users they want to follow and receive alerts from, in order to stay current on their latest work and most recent posts. Depending on the specific academic network, other features may include the ability to endorse others' skills and expertise, do literature searches, and join subject-specific discussion groups.

Although these academic networks are geared for and populated by scholars, anyone can link to the sites to search and discover who is doing what kind of interesting research. You don't have to be an academic or scholarly researcher yourself, in other words, to take advantage of these networks as information sources.

Twitter Searching

While many people use Twitter to keep up with friends, family, and celebrities, you can also use it to stay abreast of the activities, references, and even current thinking of people you think are the most interesting, insightful, and far-sighted in your field. This not only gives you some great food for thought, but also serves as a kind of early warning alert service to identify emerging trends that have not yet percolated up to the major media sources or even to the more niche online sources.

Given the ridicule that Twitter first endured—and often still endures today—it's surprising to many that this "silly" social media platform is probably the most valuable one for finding knowledge and expertise. Yes, it's true that the posts that tend to get the most media attention are snarky, controversial, or drama-filled "celebrity" tweets. Yet at the same time, Twitter is a place where important news often breaks first, and it has also become a platform on which one can build knowledge, stay informed, track trends, and learn from smart and insightful people around the globe.

As in that famous restaurant, you can get anything you want from Twitter's menu—there's lots and lots of fluff but there are also lots of nutritious items. There are, in fact, several ways that Twitter can increase your knowledge and add to your understanding of whatever you may be researching. These include the following:

- Keeping up to date in your field and spotting emerging trends, not only by following what the recognized leaders and experts in a field are tweeting, but also by following interesting people on the fringes

- Keeping up with the latest news and activities from companies, organizations, brands, and various movers and shakers in your industry

- Creating or joining a community of experts on a topic and moving from the role of observer ("lurker") to that of participant, to engage in interesting conversations

What's the best way to start finding and gathering all that expertise available via Twitter? I'd group your options into two broad approaches:

1. Passive approach: Follow key people and regularly browse and read their tweets.

2. Active approach: Conduct a keyword search on previous tweets from all Twitter users (who make their tweets public). Certain sites that permit keyword searching of past tweets also provide a keyword alert option and notify you whenever a new tweet is sent out that includes your keyword or phrase (these are identified and described below).

Let's look at the steps for engaging in both the passive and active approaches.

Passive Approach: Following Key People

The passive approach is the way Twitter is normally set up to work. You find someone interesting on Twitter whose tweets you'd like to read, link to their homepage, and click "follow," which insures that that person's posts will appear in your Twitter feed. You can find people to follow either by having Twitter find the accounts of people you already know (by inputting your email contacts), or you can have it suggest people to follow whom you don't know (here you scan Twitter's suggestions on whom it "thinks" you'd like to follow). Or you can use other means to find people to follow, such as noting someone's Twitter account on their blog or seeing a reference in a news article.

> **TIP:**
> To create a focused list on Twitter you click on the gear icon in the drop-down menu found in the top-right navigation bar, or you can go to your profile page and click on "lists" (see Figure 4.4).

What's a good way to go about finding and tracking key people on Twitter? Here is some advice I provided on how to go about doing this in a recent edition of *The Information Advisor*:

- Identify and list the 10 to 20 most important thinkers in your field or industry—people whose opinions you and your colleagues trust and respect. These are people whose work you make time to read, would arrange to hear speak at a conference, know are influential in your industry, have insights that you think are far-sighted, move the current conversation forward, are plugged in to insider

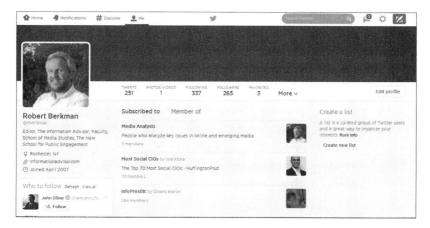

Figure 4.4   The author created three focused lists for following people on Twitter with a certain expertise

information, or are just extremely bright. They could be columnists, journalists, bloggers, analysts, professors, CEOs, or colleagues whom you find particularly insightful. Try to include fringe thinkers—people who are knowledgeable but whose ideas fall outside the mainstream, and whose views may seem unusual or sometimes even disturbing. Trends typically come from the fringes. The key is to create your own custom "trust network."

- Next, take your list and search for the names on Twitter (either via Twitter's own search function or by entering a name and "site: twitter.com" on Google). Follow them.

- Post a separate list of these industry experts and fringe thinkers on your Twitter homepage. (And note that many people on Twitter have made their own lists of trusted sources publicly available; if you find such lists that are relevant and valuable, piggyback on and subscribe to them.)

TIP: Find and Piggyback on Someone Else's Source List
To piggyback, click on "lists" when viewing someone's Twitter profile page. Select a list you'd like to subscribe to. Then click "subscribe" to follow the people on that person's list.

- Browse the tweets on your lists on a regular basis. When you do, note these indicators of emerging trends:

  ○ Patterns: Look for people saying the same thing, although not necessarily in exactly the same way. Look for retweets within your selective group as a good indicator of an idea that has gotten the attention and interest of those you follow.

  ○ Statements with passion behind them: anger, shock, glee, and so forth

  ○ Something that truly surprises you

○ Expert recommendations: Note when one of
   your trusted experts makes a particularly glowing
   recommendation of another source. Pay particular
   attention if he or she highlights one person, idea, or
   presentation from a group of experts. For example,
   one of my favorite analysts on citizen and networked
   journalism is NYU professor Jay Rosen. At one point he
   linked to his favorite presentation at a TED conference—
   which itself represents a highly selective group of
   people who have already been identified as having
   something valuable to say. When "*my*" expert highlights
   one of *his* favorite expert sources it's a powerful form of
   recommendation that's worth paying attention to.

TIP: Use Twitter to Leverage the Wisdom of Your Crowd
Although the trending stories on social media sites such as
Facebook often represent only the most dramatic or celebrity-
oriented news items of the moment, if you can find out what
is trending among your own select group of trusted sources,
those items are likely to be of particular interest to you. Twitter will send you an email letting you know what tweets your
own network is sharing most often. This can be a powerful
form of recommendation from people you trust, especially if
several of your connections are sharing the same item.

TweetDeck for Twitter Power Users

Finally, I would strongly recommend that you consider using a
Twitter dashboard application such as TweetDeck. TweetDeck provides a clean, at-a-glance scan of incoming tweets and offers simple methods for organizing and displaying different people and
topics you are following. It also offers the ability to search and filter
your incoming tweets.

Note that you can use TweetDeck as your general Twitter homepage by configuring columns for specific purposes. For example,

one column can display tweets from everyone you follow, while others can be devoted to more focused lists, and still other columns will alert you only when there is a tweet that contains a particular keyword or phrase.

For example, on my TweetDeck dashboard displayed in Figures 4.5, 4.6, and 4.7, you'll see that I set it up to display three columns of

Figure 4.5 Using the free TweetDeck dashboard helps organize different tweets from different people or themes I follow on Twitter

Figure 4.6 TweetDeck provides an "at-a-glance" display of incoming messages, new tweets on a designated keyword, and more

Figure 4.7   TweetDeck allows users to not only search for tweets on a certain word or phrase, but to limit results just to those tweets that initiated a high level of engagement

incoming tweets. The lefthand column in Figure 4.5 is equivalent to my regular Twitter homepage and displays the incoming tweets of everyone I follow. The second column displays only tweets that contain the word "hydrofracking." Note that I also limited this second column alert to show me only those tweets that have been retweeted at least twice; this additional limitation ensures that I only see tweets that are getting a certain minimum level of attention. TweetDeck also lets me add a sound or a pop-up function to alert me when a new tweet comes in. Finally, the third column displays the tweets from one of my focused lists, "Information Professionals."

TweetDeck is not the only free Twitter dashboard provider; others include HootSuite (which also provides a certain level of analytics) and Seesmic.

> **TIP:**
> Stay alert to observations or retweets from someone you trust that make you sit up and take notice, or provide an "Aha!" sensation. When that happens, you may have caught an early indicator of things to come.

Active Searching on Twitter

So far we've been discussing using Twitter as a more passive brows-ing and alert tool; once that initial setup is complete, you can sit back and wait for the tweets to come in. And that's a great way to use Twitter—as a kind of broad scanning platform. But there may also be occasions when you want to do an active, focused search of

> **TIP:**
> While the advanced Twitter search operators shown in Figure 4.8 can be quite helpful in making your search more precise, probably the most important one for avoiding "tweet over-load" and focusing your results is the hashtag (#). If you use the hashtag to search, you'll increase the odds that the tweets you retrieve don't include the word or phrase you entered in a passing or incidental manner, but rather that the tweeter has identified it as a key topic of the tweet. In other words, a search on the word "hydrofracking" will retrieve any and all tweets in which that word was used, even in passing, but a search on #hydrofracking, while it will return fewer tweets, should retrieve those that are *about* that topic (see Figure 4.9).

Twitter—in the same way that you might search a traditional data-base. Can you search all past tweets in the same manner?

The answer is yes, but with certain limitations. And you have a couple of options for where and how you conduct your searches. I'll focus on the two most popular and broadly useful Twitter search platforms: Twitter's own site and a third-party search engine called Topsy. While both permit deep keyword searching of the Twitter archive, they work a little differently.

Searching Past Tweets on the Twitter Site

You can search millions of past tweets, in near real-time, using the Twitter site itself as a kind of searchable database. You can then either enter your keywords in the main search box or use Twitter's advanced search operators to create a more targeted search.

Figure 4.8 lists all of Twitter's advanced search operators.

Operator	Finds tweets...
twitter search	containing both "twitter" and "search". This is the default operator.
"happy hour"	containing the exact phrase "happy hour"
love OR hate	containing either "love" or "hate" (or both)
beer -root	containing "beer" but not "root"
#haiku	containing the hashtag "haiku"
from:alexiskold	sent from person "alexiskold"
to:techcrunch	sent to person "techcrunch"
@mashable	referencing person "mashable"
"happy hour" near:"san francisco"	containing the exact phrase "happy hour" and sent near "san francisco"
near:NYC within:15mi	sent within 15 miles of "NYC"
superhero since:2010-12-27	containing "superhero" and sent since date "2010-12-27" (year-month-day)
ftw unit:2010-12-27	containing "ftw" and sent up to date "2010-12-27"
movie -scary :)	containing "movie", but not "scary", and with a positive attitude
flight :(	containing "flight" and with a negative attitude
traffic ?	containing "traffic" and asking a question
hilarious filter:links	containing "hilarious" and linking to URLs
news source:twitterfeed	containing "news" and entered via TwitterFeed

Figure 4.8 Twitter Advanced Search Operators. Twitter provides a wide range of advanced search operators to make a search more precise

After running your search, Twitter, as with other search engines, returns matching results. Figure 4.10 is an example of a Twitter search that combines two words (a Boolean AND search).

Note that at the top of its results page, Twitter provides the option to see all results or to limit the results to "top" tweets—based on

Figure 4.9   If you search for a word linked to a hashtag,
you are more likely to retrieve a tweet that is
"about" that particular topic

Figure 4.10   The result of a search for tweets that include
both the words "earthquake" and "hydrofracking"

metrics such as the number of followers, retweets, and other calculations. You can also filter results by type of media (e.g., pictures or images) and by tweets located "near you," among other options.

When scanning the results of the search, you can click on a tweet to read the full content directly on the tweeter's profile page, or choose to reply, retweet, keep it as a favorite, or click "more" to embed the tweet on your own website.

Note that Twitter often experiments and changes what it allows to be searched on its site, as well as its features and search functions. Depending on when you do your search, you may find a shorter or longer archive of past tweets and different types of filters and search options.

Searching Past Tweets on Topsy
Topsy is a social media search engine that was acquired by Apple in December 2013. As with the Twitter site, Topsy permits anyone to search past and recent tweets by entering keywords, but there are a few key differences. For one, Topsy focuses on providing analytics—graphs and charts displaying the frequency of tweets over time. It also calculates a "sentiment score," indicating whether tweets returned from a search were mostly positive or negative, and offers a different set of advanced search operators and filters.

You can see a sample Topsy search on hydrofracking in Figure 4.11, showing its calculated "sentiment score" of 39 (mostly negative, with 50 being in the middle) and a view of the frequency of tweets on that term over a 30-day period. By clicking on the

---

Tip: Be Cautious in Relying on Sentiment Scores
Over the last several years, many social listening and monitoring sites have integrated a "sentiment score," which purportedly identifies what percentage of posts about the search terms are positive or negative. While the technology behind this feature continues to improve, I cannot recommend these scores as particularly reliable; it's still too easy for the software to make errors and get thrown off by the many complexities and subtleties of human language.

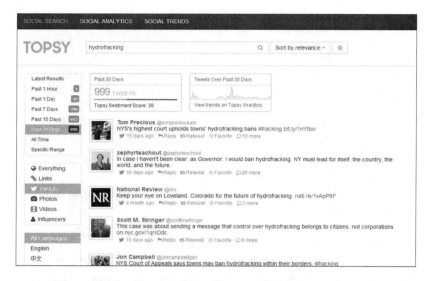

Figure 4.11 Topsy allows for searching on tweets and assigns a "sentiment" score that attempts to show whether the overall sentiment of a tweet is more positive or negative

"Tweets over past 30 days" frequency chart, you can identify specific tweets that occurred at different times during that period. In Figure 4.12, you can see that the greatest number of tweets on hydrofracking for the specified 30-day period took place on June 30, 2013. On that date, a New York State court ruled that individual localities have the legal right to ban the procedure within their boundaries.

There are other sites on which you can search past tweets, and two good ones I've used and like are SocialMention and Addictomatic. But you may discover that over time the lesser-known social media search sites are not particularly stable; they come and go, their features change, they are rejiggered, or subsumed by larger firms. Twitter's own search site and Topsy are two that should be around for awhile and continue to provide robust social search options.

Facebook Search

You may not know it, but you can search much of the content on Facebook, including information that Facebook members share

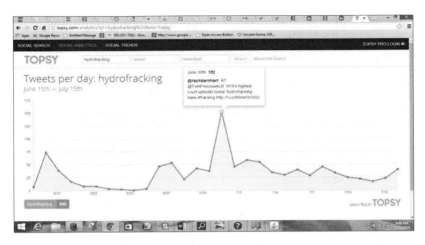

Figure 4.12   Searching Topsy for "hydrofracking" references occurring between June 15 and July 15, 2014 shows the highest number of tweets on June 30th

about themselves—where they live and work, things they like, with whom they are connected, causes and interests, relationships, and much more.

While Facebook is not exactly a go-to place for researchers, in March 2013 Facebook upped its game in the search arena by rolling out what it calls "Graph Search," a new function designed to offer a more robust search capability. What Graph Search offers is the ability for anyone to conduct a limited type of natural language/field search on the data that's been given up voluntarily by Facebook's approximately 1 billion+ subscribers. The data includes information directly from subscriber profile pages (gender, home town, and employer, for instance) as well as data derived from actions members have taken, such as joining a group or liking a page. The fact that you can now search and filter on these elements does make this social network one more potentially useful tool for today's digital researcher.

I'd venture to say that the vast majority of Facebook users rarely use the little search box that sits on the top of everyone's homepage. And why should you? After all, you generally find what you want on Facebook via your news feed, clicking on people's profiles, or perhaps joining a cause or group and seeing what the other members have to say.

When you are doing focused research, that little search bar comes in quite handy. But why bother searching Facebook? I'd say its potential value to researchers lies in the following:

- Bottom-up, experiential, and anecdotal observations and reports, particularly from activists and passionate advocates for a cause or issue

- Insights into emerging trends via insider group members' conversations, not reported in the wider media or elsewhere online

- Strong statements of particular viewpoints on contentious public issues, especially in Facebook groups

- Clues for finding and reaching hard-to-locate people

- Possible job search leads

So how can you use that search bar to find all these types of information? First, it's important to review a few basics about what you are actually searching and how the search function works. When you enter words into its search box, Facebook will try to match your words and phrases to those found in the key Facebook fields that are populated by user information. Those fields typically include a person's name, employer, group names, company pages, cities, and so forth. (Note that you are *not* searching the content on people's walls—Facebook has reportedly been working on trying to make this happen, but as of this writing it is still not possible.)

Items that match your search are displayed below the search bar, ordered by Facebook's own algorithm, which incorporates multiple factors but ranks highest those items that are the closest word match, are the most popular (for instance, have the most group members), are geographically near you, or to which you are connected through your friends (including your friends' friends). The result is an initial listing, such as the one shown in Figure 4.13.

Based on this initial set of results, you can either click on a particular item that is of interest to you or view all results, categorized by type, by clicking on the "see more results" link at the bottom of your list.

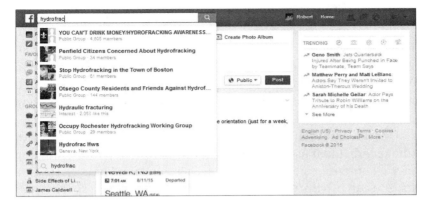

Figure 4.13   A keyword search on Facebook retrieves matches for a person's name, employer, group names, company pages, cities, and other elements in Facebook

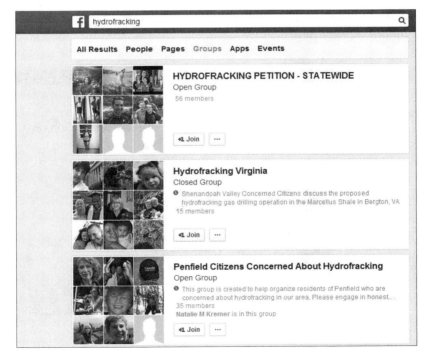

Figure 4.14   Facebook has retrieved a listing and description of groups concerned with the topic of hydrofracking

The returned listing groups results into Facebook's key categories—people, pages, groups, apps, and events—and you can click one type to view all entries under that category. See Figure 4.14 for all groups that were retrieved related to our hydrofracking search. Note that the third entry in this group, "Penfield Citizens Concerned About Hydrofracking," identifies a specific person who is among my Facebook friends.

One advantage of viewing groups that match your search is that, unlike individual user accounts, groups permit keyword searching of the content posted on their walls, as shown in Figure 4.15. This feature can be very valuable for drilling down to find a specific and narrow piece of data or concept, or to pinpoint some niche or unusual term not used elsewhere.

The bottom line is that Facebook offers some intriguing research possibilities. The most fruitful of these is the ability to locate people with whom we have what sociologists call "weak ties" (in Facebook's parlance, "friends of friends") and who have on-the-ground knowledge of or experience in the topic we are researching. Accessing

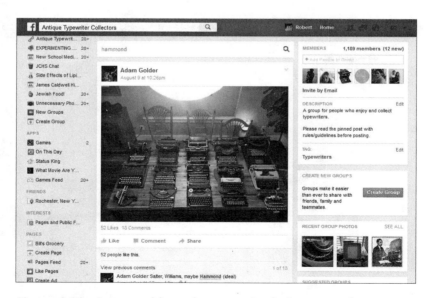

Figure 4.15   It is possible to do a search of all posts and comments on a Facebook group by clicking on the magnifying glass in the upper right hand corner of the group's page

bottom-up experiential knowledge is particularly valuable for topics that might be called activist- or cause-related, in which people invest their time, energy, and passion. I recently discovered, for example, that I have weak-tie connections to people involved in groups, pages, and events concerned with autism awareness, GMOs, and immigration reform.

If I want to, I can directly contact a person found through my Facebook searches by sending a direct message through the network. I might thus potentially gain access to someone who can inform me and answer my questions about behind-the-scenes, grassroots discussions on the topic or issue at hand.

Graph Search enables other interesting possibilities, particularly for recruitment, job hunting, and company research. Through Graph Search you can locate, for instance, friends of friends who live near an IKEA, or friends of friends who work at Google. And, again, it is a straightforward process to then use the "send a message" function to contact someone directly. Keep in mind that Facebook Graph Search is limited to information that people have chosen to make publicly available.

Searching Other Social Networks

Of course there are many social networks beyond Facebook, including visually-oriented sites such as Pinterest, Instagram, and Tumblr, which are harder to search because the primary posted content consists of images rather than text. Yes, you can search the tags and other metadata users may have added to describe a graphic image, but you'll surely run into terminology issues and inconsistencies.

There are businesses that are trying to do better brand tracking, research, grassroots market research, and market testing to get a deeper understanding of what their customers and potential customers are saying when they post a picture of the new kitchen mixer, scarf, or other recently purchased product, and technologies to make this happen are getting more sophisticated. For example, there is a fee-based service geared for businesses called Curalate, which daily compares tens of millions of images posted or shared on the web to its own collection of existing images, using a pixel-to-pixel mapping technology. Curalate is able to do this because it has established a relationship with Pinterest, Instagram, and other visual sharing sites so that when a user of one of those sites posts an image, Curalate can determine if the image matches one in its library, identify any brand or vendor, tag it as such, and make it retrievable for its subscribers.

What About LinkedIn?

Then there's the behemoth of business social networks, LinkedIn. LinkedIn has particularly interesting potential for networking research—finding people, of course, including tracking down someone who knows someone you know. After all, facilitating business networking was the reason LinkedIn was created. The site has an "advanced people search" function, available to premium (i.e., paying) members, that permits users to find people by a variety of criteria, including name, title, location, company, industry, keyword, and other elements,.

If you are already a member of LinkedIn and you are looking for an expert in a particular industry, or someone who knows a great deal about a product, you may already have someone in your connections who can make an introduction for you. But keep in mind that if you are not a paid premium member, LinkedIn only allows you to send a note (what LinkedIn calls "Inmail") to people on LinkedIn who have already agreed to be your contact (aka first-degree connections).

LinkedIn can be used for more than finding people. Of growing importance are groups and group discussions. You can search group conversations in LinkedIn by keyword and not only find relevant posts (see Figure 4.16) but also see the names and affiliations of the people who posted them—other potential expert sources to contact. And once you know where a person works, you don't necessarily have to try to contact them through LinkedIn's internal email system; you can look up the organization online and contact them directly (see Chapter 7 for tips on making contacts with experts).

My only caution with LinkedIn is that some of the posts are made by marketing and sales people who are seeking to establish their expertise and get buzz and attention. They might be experts, or

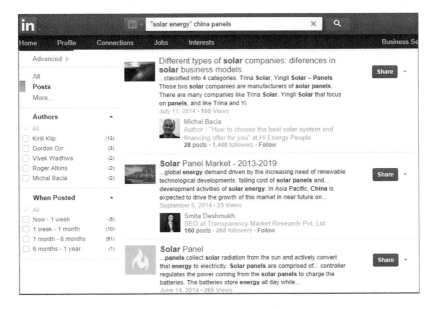

Figure 4.16 It is possible to search conversations by keyword on LinkedIn

they might be posting just for the sake of posting. Be sure to check out their background and experience before hitching your wagon to them.

In fact, verifying the credibility of social media content is the primary focus of the next chapter—so read on!

Notes

1. See readwrite.com/2008/04/25/twitter_for_journalists.

2. *The Economist*. A-twitter, January 31 2008 (http://www.economist.com/node/10608764)

Chapter 5

Truth, Lies, and Influence: Determining Credibility in a Trending Social Media World

A lie can travel halfway around the world while the truth is putting on its shoes.
— Mark Twain

Twain's observation about the speed at which falsehoods travel is even truer in the age of social media. Today many people, particularly those in their teens and twenties, get their news, information, and knowledge via social media and social networks—platforms that are fundamentally structured to facilitate the speedy transfer of information, valid or not, from one person to another.

Social networks such as Twitter and Facebook identify those news and information items being shared the most and then call them out as trending news (see Figure 5.1). Highlighting those items gives the topics even more prominence, increasing the odds that others will post and share them as well, thus boosting those topics' trending scores and making them more likely to be shared, ad infinitum.

In the age of social media, news, gossip, videos, clips, and commentary travel not just halfway but all the way around the world. But as Twain worried—how do we know if the information is believable?

What Is Credibility?

It is always worthwhile to examine the origin of the word behind a concept being explored. Discovering how a word was first used provides a deeper understanding of all that the concept encompasses—as well as what it does *not* encompass. The word "*credible*" is derived from the Latin root *credere*, meaning to

157

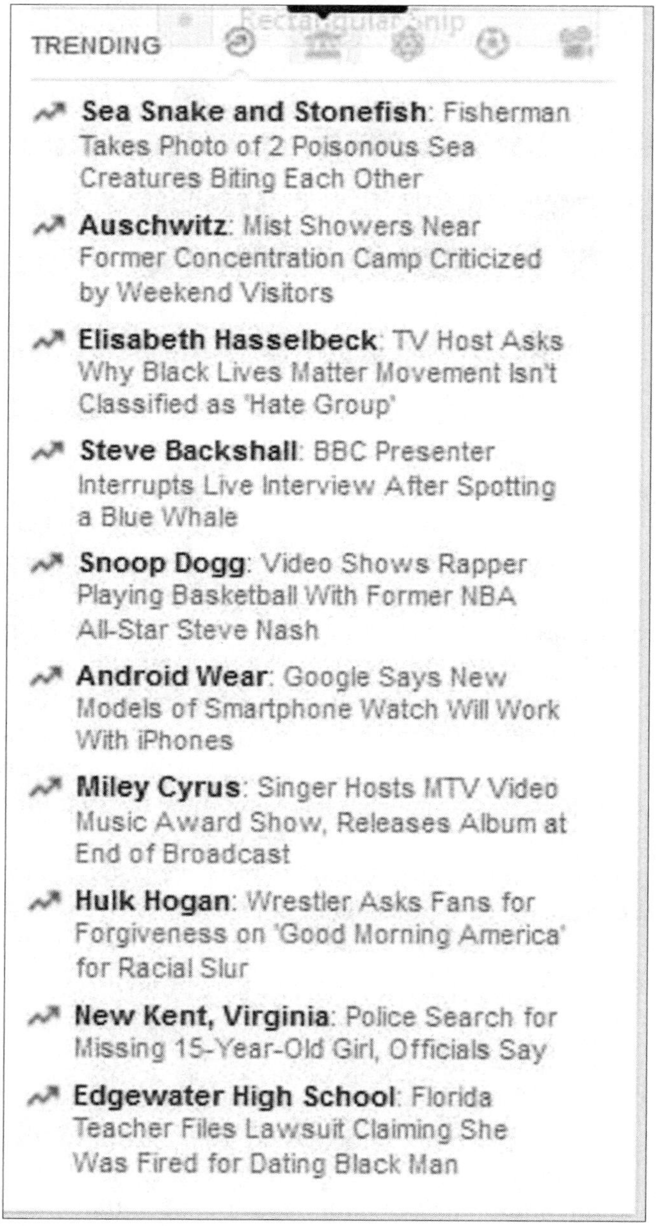

TRENDING

✎ **Sea Snake and Stonefish**: Fisherman Takes Photo of 2 Poisonous Sea Creatures Biting Each Other

✎ **Auschwitz**: Mist Showers Near Former Concentration Camp Criticized by Weekend Visitors

✎ **Elisabeth Hasselbeck**: TV Host Asks Why Black Lives Matter Movement Isn't Classified as 'Hate Group'

✎ **Steve Backshall**: BBC Presenter Interrupts Live Interview After Spotting a Blue Whale

✎ **Snoop Dogg**: Video Shows Rapper Playing Basketball With Former NBA All-Star Steve Nash

✎ **Android Wear**: Google Says New Models of Smartphone Watch Will Work With iPhones

✎ **Miley Cyrus**: Singer Hosts MTV Video Music Award Show, Releases Album at End of Broadcast

✎ **Hulk Hogan**: Wrestler Asks Fans for Forgiveness on 'Good Morning America' for Racial Slur

✎ **New Kent, Virginia**: Police Search for Missing 15-Year-Old Girl, Officials Say

✎ **Edgewater High School**: Florida Teacher Files Lawsuit Claiming She Was Fired for Dating Black Man

Figure 5.1   Facebook identifies news items being shared most frequently and describes these items as "Trending"

believe or to trust. When we talk about a credible source, we are referring to one that we can believe and put our trust in.

Of course we make decisions as to who has earned our trust all the time. Informally, we could say that in our day-to-day life a credible source (which could be a published item or a person) exhibits the qualities of accuracy and honesty. Additionally, a credible source does not intentionally hide any relevant interests or agendas, and is not unduly influenced by significant biases. Ultimately, a credible source has built up a reputation for accuracy and trustworthiness over time and has a track record of reliability.

Source Credibility in the Pre-Internet Days

Before the internet, of course, there were tried and true techniques and strategies for evaluating both published and human sources—and they are still largely valid today. While much of the rest of this chapter will focus on verifying the kind of social, viral, and real-time information we encounter on today's web, it's first worth reviewing the traditional of determining credibility.

Traditional Methods: Published Sources

Following are some key considerations when determining the accuracy of published data.

What Is the Type of Document?

There is a critical distinction between a *primary* and *secondary* data source. A primary source is an original document, such as a personal letter, photograph, or original government report. A secondary source takes the data from the original source, and is an account, such as a newspaper article. A concern with too much reliance on secondary sources is that they often omit the methods employed in collecting data and sometimes fail to reproduce significant footnotes or comments that may qualify the data in some way.[1]

What Is the Purpose of the Publication?

A source is suspect if it is published to promote sales, to advance the interests of an industrial, commercial, or other group, to present the cause of a political party, or to carry on any sort of propaganda. Data is also suspect when it is published anonymously or by an organization on the defensive, under conditions that suggest a controversy, or in a form that reveals a strained attempt at frankness.[2]

Are You Getting All Sides of the Story?

Try to determine whether the article, report, or book is presenting only one side of an issue when there is clearly more than one point of view. For example, an article that cites *only* the problems associated with, say, single-payer healthcare systems, without at least referring to potential benefits, could not be viewed as a balanced presentation. Such a piece may still be useful, however, for learning about the claims of those opposed to such a program, for finding out about other studies cited, and for obtaining leads for further research. The point is that it should not be used as the sole source of information.

Note that this issue of balanced coverage is tricky. It's not always easy to determine what constitutes balanced coverage. In fact, one can even make the case that presenting both sides of an issue is not always desirable. For example, when writing about a case of child abuse, does the best coverage give equal time to the abuser, to present his or her side of the story? These kinds of questions are thorny journalistic and sociological issues. Suffice it to say, *be aware* of whether a source includes all *reasonably legitimate* points of view on an issue, and if it is clear you are not, do not use that source as a definitive one.

Is the Author Trying to Subtly Influence You?

It's not enough to determine whether coverage of a topic is balanced; it's also critical to be able to detect the more subtle ways that an author may be trying to insert his or her views into a piece. Choice of words, placement of names, and other techniques can be employed consciously or unconsciously by the writer to influence the reader. For example, the choice between the following synonyms can connote different feelings and elicit different reactions.

Free enterprise	Capitalism
Persons incarcerated	Criminals
Mixed drinks	Hard liquor
Spiritually renewed	Born again
Stronger defense	More money for missiles
Increased revenues	Higher taxes

Even something as simple as the insertion of quotation marks or the use of a different word can subtly change connotations. For example, compare these two sentences:

John Doe, the company's director of public affairs, said that he was instituting the clean-up committee to make headway in cleaning up the environment.

John Doe, the company's director of public affairs, claimed that "helping the environment" was the reason he was instituting the clean-up committee.

By setting off Doe's words in quotation marks, the writer seems to imply that his remark should not be read as a fact; it almost seems as though the writer is winking at the reader. The word *claim* is another way to cast doubt on the speaker's trustworthiness. (Just as saying someone "*admitted*" something has different connotations than "*acknowledged*"). The writer could also have shown his or her skepticism by beginning the sentence with the innocuous words *according to*, which again would add a subjective element to the sentence, decreasing Doe's credibility.

Keep your antennae up and be attuned to these subtleties—again, if you detect that information is being presented in a slanted manner, it does not mean you have to disregard the material; keep an open mind and try not to let yourself be influenced by the *manner* in which a piece is written. You will need to make up your own mind after consulting a variety of different sources.

Is the Information Presented Logically and Is It Well Organized?
Are the data internally consistent? Are the conclusions supported by the evidence provided? Look for data presented in a well-organized manner, tables clearly labeled, and lucid accompanying explanatory

material. Typically (although by no means always), these elements reflect a well-thought-out study.

Is the Information Based on a Poll or Survey?
The quality of individual polls and surveys varies enormously. There is a science to accurate data collection that involves technical considerations such as sample size, rate of response, sampling and nonsampling errors, and more. It's important to find out how the information was collected (e.g., mail questionnaire or phone), who was interviewed, and the other details behind the study.

Polls and surveys that purport to measure people's views and behaviors are so fraught with hazards, in fact, that some observers believe that even the finest and most well-known survey organizations cannot overcome the great number of barriers to accurate reporting. For these reasons, polls, surveys, forecasts, and the like should be utilized by researchers only with a great deal of caution.

Dr. Jared Jobe, director of the Collaborative Research Program at the U.S. National Center for Health Statistics, noted that there are a number of areas in which polls and surveys can be misleading or inaccurate. The following are some of the most common problems:

- **Partisan sponsoring organizations.** Organizations that have a motive to manipulate surveys to achieve a desired result are obviously suspect.

- **Selection criteria.** By what mechanism and approach was the group selected? Was it a random sampling? The key point is whether the respondents were a *representative* sample of the particular population of interest. Jobe advises researchers to watch out for mail surveys, magazine subscriber surveys, and telephone call-in polls, because these are often biased by the fact that only persons with a particular reason for responding will answer the questions (those with extreme positions on an issue may be overrepresented).

- **Loaded questions.** Jobe's research has shown that people's opinions are greatly affected by the interviewer's tone, manner, and choice of words. Other studies have shown that people will provide different opinions depending on whether the words the interviewer uses contain positive or negative connotations. For example, according to one study, public opinion shifts if asked about favoring more spending "to aid the *poor*" compared to spending more for *welfare*. Responses sometimes differ even when alternative words are used that do not seem to be loaded. For example, some people may be less willing to approve speeches against democracy when asked whether the United States should "*allow*" public speeches against democracy than when asked whether the United States should "*forbid*" public speeches against democracy.

- **Placement of questions.** Question placement can affect the way people respond. For example, say a subject was asked whether defense spending should be increased by 10 percent. If he or she replied no, the subject might then be more inclined to say yes to a follow-up question as to whether the United States should increase defense spending by 5 percent. Had the respondents *only* been asked whether defense spending should be increased by 5 percent, he or she may have been more likely to have replied in the negative.

- **Asking for memories and recollections.** Jobe says that people are notoriously poor at remembering their past actions and activities.

- **Complex questions.** People will often answer questions they do not understand.

- **Vague questions.** Questions that are open to more than one interpretation obviously make for poor research results.

- **Sensitive questions.** Queries that ask people to admit to socially unacceptable behavior are less reliable. For example, people do not like to admit that they smoke.

- **Misleading conclusions.** Sometimes the survey process is fine, but the conclusions are misleading. For example,

Jobe cites the commercial that says "no toothpaste gets your teeth whiter." Such a claim can simply mean that the brand is not worse than all the rest.

The best way to guard against these problems is to get a copy of the actual questionnaire utilized and study it to try to detect any of these pitfalls. Jobe advises researchers to look at many surveys, conducted by more than one organization at different times. If these surveys generally reveal the same findings, then you can feel fairly confident about the results.

Also keep in mind what medium was used to collect the data, for example, if a survey was done by collecting views of people over a social network such as Facebook, Twitter, and so on. While the demographics of online social networks are generally more representative of the broader population than they once were, the types of people that populate a particular group on a network can still skew results. Look at the design, methodology, and sampling of these surveys particularly carefully.

Traditional Methods: Evaluating Experts

What have been the standard approaches for evaluating a person's credibility and knowledge when conducting interviews in person? Following are some tried and true strategies.

Signs of a Good Source

- **Peer recognition.** Has the source had anything published in trade journals or has he or she spoken at industry conferences? If so, that's an excellent sign, because it signifies recognition by peers. Peer recognition is one of the very best indicators of an authoritative source. If you don't know whether a source has written or spoken on the topic, there is nothing wrong with politely asking. Use your judgment when applying this rule. If an expert has made a brand-new discovery or just finished a research project, it may take time to be recognized.

- **Referrals.** How did you find the source? Were you referred by a recognized expert in the field or someone you felt was a worthy source? Good experts typically refer you to other good experts.

- **Repetition.** Does the source repeat things you've heard before that you know to be true?

- **Attentiveness.** Does the source pay careful attention to your questions and respond sensitively?

Sources to Beware Of

Next we'll look at several types of sources that should treated with caution.

The Biased Source

Bias is a tricky matter. The critical thing to be aware of is where a particular source is coming from. For example, is he or she a salesperson for a product, a political appointee, or a representative of a special cause? Take this into account when evaluating the information. This doesn't mean that people with certain viewpoints or leanings are not going to be truthful or accurate. It simply means that each person's perspective must be uncovered so that you know how to evaluate his or her information.

For example, once I was digging up information on how certain cities cut their energy costs by forming fuel-buying cooperatives. One of the people I talked to was the president of a regional association of fuel dealers. He told me that co-ops were a very bad idea; he said that although participants might cut their purchasing costs, they suffer in the quality of their service. I noted his objection seriously, but at the same time realized that because he represented a group of fuel dealers, his constituency would have the most to lose if this co-op idea really caught on. I decided to call the individual co-op members directly to find out if they had indeed encountered service problems. It turned out that none had.

You must also stay on guard against organizations that do not easily telegraph their biases. These organizations often have impartial-sounding names, but actually promote a very specific stand on an issue. For example, you locate an association innocently called Citizens for Energy Awareness. The name suggests that the committee merely wants to help spread information. But it's possible that the committee's sole raison d'être is to advance the cause of nuclear energy or alternatively, to ban it. To check for such biases, find out what kind of people the association is composed of. Are most of the officers of the Citizens for Energy Awareness executives at nuclear power plants? If so, you can guess why that organization has been created! Take a look at some of the organization's brochures and research reports. Do its studies and findings unfailingly reach the same conclusion and support the same side of a controversial issue? You might still get some good information from this special-interest group, but be aware that you will not get a balanced picture.

Another type of biased source that you need to be on guard against is the overly enthusiastic source. This kind of person is typically involved in implementing a new project of some sort. You're sure to get rave reviews from this person when you ask how the project is going. Nobody wants to express doubts about the success of his or her new venture, so you have to be careful not to take glowing reports as gospel. In the case of the fuel cooperatives, for example, the co-op members themselves may want to paint an overly rosy picture of their project. Probe for as many hard facts as you can. In cases in which you feel your sources have too many personal interests to be totally unbiased, try to supplement those sources with more disinterested experts. Again, in the case of the fuel-buying cooperatives, I would probably get the most objective information not from the fuel dealers or the co-op members, but from a government expert in the Department of Energy or another unbiased authority on fuel.

The Overly Narrow Source

Let's say you are trying to find information on crime trends in the United States, and you find an expert on supermarket shoplifting. You'll have to ask yourself whether that person's opinions go beyond his or her area of expertise and extend to overall U.S. crime trends.

The Out-of-Date Source

Are you looking into a field that is constantly changing? If so, you want to be sure that your sources have kept up with the changes. Try to find out the last time the person was actually involved in the subject. In certain fields—smart phone features and technologies, for example—information from only six months ago is dated.

The Too-Far-Removed Source
High-level sources with very broad administrative duties are often too far removed to provide you with the nitty-gritty details you need. For example, if you are digging up information on upcoming design trends in small automobiles, the head of the public affairs department of General Motors would probably only be able to give you the sketchiest and most basic information. You'd be much better off talking to design engineers to get more specific details. (Calling the public affairs office can still be worthwhile, if only to ask to be referred to a technical expert.)

The Unaccountable Source
One problem with speaking with someone relatively low on the company ladder, rather than with a high-level official accustomed to making public statements, is a lack of accountability. A firm's VP Communications or Public Affairs Officer may not give you the depth of detail you'd love to have on a subject, but she at least bears a responsibility for accuracy. That same firm's shop foreman, on the other hand, may speak openly, bluntly, and at length—but be sure to get those "facts" confirmed by other sources before relying on them.

The Secondary Source
Is your source a true expert or just someone who is reporting on the experts' work or reorganizing existing information? Secondary sources *can* be helpful, but they are not ordinarily as intimately knowledgeable about the subject as primary sources.

The Confusing Source
If the person only talks in technical jargon and is unable to communicate his or her expertise to you, you're not going to get much out of the conversation. Move on to the next one.

Evaluating Strategies
Here are some methods you can use to help evaluate your sources:

* Note the names of people who keep appearing in the articles that you read or are repeatedly mentioned by people you contact. When you see somebody's name mentioned or quoted often, from a variety of sources, it's

usually a sign that the person is a leader in the field and has something valuable to say.

- It's fine to ask experts for their opinion of other sources. Just be diplomatic about how you ask. One way is to ask if they agree with so-and-so's conclusions about the subject in question.

- Think about using certain sources as yardsticks. If you've spoken with someone you feel is a top-notch authority, you can measure other sources' responses against that person's.

- If a source makes a statement that arouses your skepticism, politely ask where the information comes from: His or her research? Hands-on experience? Something read somewhere?

- If you doubt someone's expertise, you can test the person by asking a question to which you already know the answer.

- Does the expert say something definitively that you already know is absolutely incorrect? If so, that is obviously not a good sign!

- Have you read anything the expert has written? I have found that the most useful experts to speak with are those that can write a clear, well-organized article or report.

- Does the expert simply repeat what everyone else says or does he or she have some fresh perspective on the issue? I've found that the truly superior experts can take an issue and not just describe the current situation, but also see further implications and add some new angles. The best experts provide insight into the underlying "why" questions, which lead to broad implications. For example, when I was researching the topic of publishing on the web, one of the best experts I spoke with early on told me that the *reason* web publishing was going to be significant was that before the internet there were two strong barriers of entry that made a mass-publishing operation difficult: 1) the need for a printing press, and 2) the need for some distribution mechanism, such as delivery trucks or a satellite system. The web eliminates the need for either of these, demolishes the barriers to entry, and therefore makes it possible for anyone with access to the internet to broadcast their information to a worldwide audience—and to do so virtually instantaneously.

- I've found that one intuitive way to evaluate an expert is simply to ask yourself after you've had your interview whether you feel satisfied.

Critical Thinking

Much of the advice given in this chapter could fall under the heading of critical thinking. Being a critical thinker is vital for a researcher. But what does critical thinking really mean?

Critical thinking means a number of things:

- Not believing something just because everyone says it's so
- Not believing something just because you have heard it repeated so often
- Not simply accepting the first opinion you hear

Critical thinking means constantly asking questions, probing, and digging deeply into a subject to learn more and more until *you yourself* are satisfied of the truth of the matter.

Critical thinking also means looking at bits of data, pieces of information, and bodies of knowledge and searching for connections and differences. It means sitting down and thinking hard about all that you've uncovered and trying to figure out what it all has in common. What are the threads that link the data? How do they differ?

What about the concepts of trust and faith? Can a critical thinker ever simply decide to believe what someone says just because he or she trusts a person's judgment? I think yes. However, the trust will be an *intelligently placed one*. The experienced researcher sometimes intuitively feels when to trust a source and when not to. But this is a very difficult call, and it may not always be possible to make a decision on whom to trust. But you can ask yourself certain questions to help you explore your gut feelings:

- Has the person proven himself or herself to be reliable and accurate in this subject in the past?

- Does the rest of his or her work show integrity?

- Does the person have an ax to grind in this case or does he or she seem unbiased?

When Evidence Is Not There

What does the researcher do when he or she does not find any hard evidence to support a claim or position? Must the researcher dismiss such conclusions or findings as unproven and therefore not worth accepting? Let's look at such a scenario.

Let's say I came across a scientist who claimed that his work and analysis showed that there was a strong link between levels of air pollution and the onset of heart disease. Say that currently the medical establishment had not proven any link between the two, and in fact, there was no evidence at all linking the two phenomena together. How would one evaluate the scientist's claims?

Obviously, few researchers are in a position to definitively determine whether this person's claim is valid. There are scientific methods of discovery that are performed extremely carefully under intense scrutiny to determine whether a reported phenomenon is indeed a reliable finding. However, you may find yourself in a position where you must make some kind of unscientific judgment on such a matter.

Although the judgment will be unscientific, it can still be of great importance, because it is this type of informal, unscientific, but rational judgment that can provide enough interest in a subject to get the gears in motion for scientific testing. There is lag time between the discovery of a phenomenon and its proof (or disproof), and the researcher can be a vital link in facilitating the movement from the stage of initial theory or discovery to the stage of proof. Furthermore, while the Web is famous for spreading wacky and unproven theories, you *can* get potentially useful "early warning" reports from ordinary people who have seen things not yet reported in the media.

Going back to the example of the link between air pollution and heart disease, what would you need to do to determine for yourself the likelihood that the theory is correct? There are a number of paths you could pursue. Start by answering these types of questions:

- What is the manner in which the person is presenting his or her findings? Is it in a sensational way, making claims

such as "revolutionary . . . fantastic . . . unbelievable," or
are the ideas presented in a more reasonable and rational
way? Does the author of the study provide advice on how
to best interpret his or her work, or does he or she just run
down a list of amazing benefits?

- Are there backup records available to document claims?
  If the research is very new, is there at least an attempt to
  carefully collect records and document findings for the
  future?

- In what types of outlets is the person choosing to publicize
  his or her findings? For example, does he or she advertise in
  the classifieds of *National Enquirer* and ask people to send
  in $10 to get his or her secrets, or does he or she approach
  the mainstream media or scientific community? What kind
  of audience is he or she trying to reach—a gullible one or
  one that will provide intense levels of scrutiny?

- Does this person make all of his or her records and
  findings open for anyone to inspect, or is much of it
  "secret formula" claims that will not be released?

- What else has this person worked on? Does the scientist
  show evidence of achievement in related fields? Is he or
  she respected by peers?

As you can see, most of these questions do not ask you to analyze
the actual claim itself but to look at relevant peripheral information
that can aid in making the judgment. And, of course, it is possible that
even someone who fits all the "right" answers will ultimately be
proven incorrect (or vice versa, but that is less likely). But you may
need to make a judgment call. Finally, your role as a researcher is not
to comment on whether the claims are correct, but on whether a phenomenon deserves serious scrutiny and attention from the larger
community. And this is no insignificant job.

Enter the Internet Age

In the pre-internet days, it was fairly straightforward to apply these
kinds of criteria for measuring credibility to our day-to-day information sources. Certain newspapers, magazines, radio broadcasts,

and television shows developed a reputation over time and could be evaluated based on their track record, editorial capabilities, oversight, and other factors. Most of us viewed these major media sources as fairly reliable, though certainly not perfect, sources of information on what was going on in the world.

So if you read something in *The New York Times* or *Washington Post*, or saw a story on the nightly news broadcast from one of the major networks, you knew that certain editorial filters were in place to give you a reasonably accurate view of the world. Sure, if you were a few notches to the left or right politically you'd be critical of the worldview of the news outlet, or what items it chose and how it reported the most contentious items. But overall, you generally felt that when you were given statistics or heard a piece of news, the information was at least accurate and verified.

The internet, of course, changed all that. By the early to mid-1990s, use of the internet became increasingly widespread, and the web made it more common for ordinary people to become their own publishers and even their own broadcasters.

As a result, the standard methods and criteria for assessing the credibility of our sources were no longer quite as useful. What we read and saw online did not typically go through standard editorial processes or checks. Those who were creating this information were ordinary people, not trained journalists or those working in a traditional newsroom.

Initially, everything on the internet was dismissed as garbage and unreliable. "Hah—where'd you get that information—off the internet?!" was a common derisive comment early on. But that dismissive reaction proved to be too simplistic. Sometimes the information was bad and other times it was good. It all depended. Librarians helped fill in the knowledge gap by creating all sorts of useful checklists for patrons and the interested public to use in evaluating unknown websites. These helped novice internet users check the origin of a website, determine the credentials of the author, figure out how recently the page was updated, and so on.

These checklists helped bridge the transition to the world of consumer-generated content, but were helpful only to a point. Things got more complicated when bloggers arrived on the scene in the mid- to late 1990s and began expressing strong opinions on politics, culture, technology, and countless niche topics. Bloggers often presented themselves as a more legitimate and honest alternative to what they saw as an unaccountable, out of touch, mainstream media (MSM) that was beholden to corporate and other powerful interests.

Welcome to Web 2.0

Bloggers began attracting a certain loyal audience who trusted these supposedly more authentic and transparent voices more than they did the major media outlets. For the advocates and users of the blogosphere, blogs were a welcome alternative to the major newspapers and broadcasters. To many, the traditional news sources represented an elite and arrogant club, unrepresentative of the public, whose claims to objectivity were a sham. Soon the internet spawned wikis and Wikipedia, citizen journalists, social networks, and a move by the younger generation to get their news and information not from traditional institutions, media, or authorities but from their peers—and often in near real time.

These were truly revolutionary developments in how information was being created and disseminated. They even spawned a whole new way to look at and use the web—it was no longer your older brother's internet. The new and improved internet was given the title Web 2.0.

That "2.0" suffix signified that this new web had transformed itself from the earlier static, one-directional set of web pages into a two-way conversational network, where the ruling ethos was transparency, openness, and authenticity. The notion of objectivity as an important—or even feasible—goal to strive for in reporting news and information went out the window, with a good riddance attitude. And perhaps the most important value inherent in the new web was a firm belief that a group knows more than any single individual. That philosophy helped spur the famous "wisdom of crowds" (WOC) meme, which I'll address in detail later in this chapter.

What We Gained and Lost

Stepping back a bit, what can we say we've gained—and what have we perhaps lost—in these new ways of creating and finding information? From the perspective of our ability to access a diverse array of credible and valuable facts, news, information, and knowledge, what has the conversational, social, and real-time web given us? And what has it taken away? I would say that we have gained the following:

- Instant facts and answers to straightforward questions

- A multitude of diverse voices that previously had no mechanism to be easily heard by many others

- Global news sources that are as easily accessible as local ones

- A new and sometimes powerful check on the mainstream press, particularly when a high-profile source makes an error, ignores something important, or is clearly biased

- Increased power of ordinary people, when acting as a group, to influence what is determined by the rest of us as noteworthy

From the researcher's perspective, we can say that this revolutionary transition in how information is created and found on today's social, real-time web has resulted in certain important losses too, such as the following:

- A decrease in the ability to exercise our "research muscles," since we can so easily get instant answers anywhere and anytime

- A decreased attention span and focus, especially when engaged in longer texts

- A lack of appreciation for the distinctions between different types of information sources

- An increased chance of falling into the trap of self-confirmation bias when performing research

- A diminished sense of history

- An increase in online news stories that are sensational, celebrity-oriented, scary, and "click worthy" due to their attention-grabbing capabilities. Furthermore, since legacy media imitate and take on the characteristics of newer media, this emphasis on choosing news based on dramatic appeal and emotional impact has been replicated in other media forms, particularly television news.

Several very insightful people have been able to articulate more about these losses. Nicholas Carr, author of *The Shallows*, has written about what happens to our abilities to perform a task when we rely so much on computers or other automated systems to do work and make decisions for us. Here's how he put it in the context of the impact of automation on pilots:

> The way computers can weaken awareness and attentiveness points to a deeper problem. Automation turns us from actors into observers. Instead of manipulating the yoke, we watch the screen. That shift may make our lives easier, but it can also inhibit the development of expertise. Since the late 1970s, psychologists have been documenting a phenomenon called the "generation effect." It was first observed in studies of vocabulary, which revealed that people remember words much better when they actively call them to mind— when they generate them—than when they simply read them. The effect, it has since become clear, influences learning in many different circumstances. When you engage actively in a task, you set off intricate mental processes that allow you to retain more knowledge. You learn more and remember more. When you repeat the same task over a long period, your brain constructs specialized neural circuits dedicated to the activity. It assembles a rich store of information and organizes that knowledge in a way that allows you to tap into it instantaneously. Whether it's Serena Williams on a tennis court or Magnus Carlsen at a chessboard, an expert can spot patterns, evaluate signals, and react to changing circumstances with speed and precision that can seem uncanny. What looks like instinct is hard-won skill, skill that requires exactly the kind of struggle that modern software seeks to alleviate.[3]

When we enter a couple of words into Google, browse through our Facebook or Twitter trending stories, or ask Siri to find something for us, we are not digging, testing, culling and sifting information, thinking, and engaging in the hard parts of searching for knowledge that engage our research muscles. And so we are not as likely to build and learn research skills and become knowledgeable researchers.

Fact, Fiction, Opinion, and Commentary

Unlike traditional newspapers, magazines, and broadcasters which tried to establish boundaries between news and opinion/commentary, the social web has few, if any, such boundaries. Facts, opinions, news, gossip, rants, user videos, research reports, and commentary all coexist without clearly defined boxes delineating what's what. Some have argued that this is a good thing, since after all, no information is context free and pure objectivity is a myth.

One consequence of the mixing of so many types of information is a loss of our ability to make important distinctions between factual news and opinion. That has implications, since, as the late senator from New York, Daniel Patrick Moynihan, purportedly said, "Everyone is entitled to their own opinion but not their own facts." No matter what one thinks about false objectivity, bias, flawed journalism, evidence, science, and how we form our beliefs, there is still a difference between facts and opinion. Furthermore, the traditional "wall" between advertising and editorial is crumbling online. Online news sites increasingly integrate "native ads"—advertisements that are designed to fit seamlessly into the editorial flow and may sometimes appear to be editorial content.

Probability and Proof

Not only has the social web made it harder to distinguish facts from opinion, there is so *much* information and opinion on the web that it has also made it easier for anyone to fall into the well-known psychological trap of self-confirmation bias. If you seek, ye shall almost certainly find!

Go to the web to see if anyone agrees with some pet theory or hunch of yours: could all that white pizza you ate last night be the cause of your dizzy spell? Isn't it weird how sinkholes happened whenever a drone flew over the area recently? Whatever it is you are wondering about, go to the internet, search on the keywords, and you will almost certainly find someone somewhere with a similar suspicion and belief. And when we fall prey to self-confirmation bias, we use whatever shreds of confirming information we turn up to "prove" to ourselves that indeed there *was* something to our suspicion after all! But most of the time, these "discoveries" are only a reflection of the power of large numbers—with billions of pages on the web, and who knows how many words, created by millions of people, probability theory indicates that there is a pretty good chance that some page, some place, created at some point, supports your pet theory!

And once you are convinced that you've found the truth, it may not matter to you what kind of actual evidence exists to dispute your theory or provide alternative explanations. According to research by Brendan Nyhan, PhD; Jason Reifler, PhD; Sean Richey, PhDc; and Gary L. Freed, MD, MPH on efforts to educate parents on the safety of vaccinations,[4] if we have a particular belief firmly in place, even when we are shown clear contradictory evidence we find ways to hold on to and justify our prior viewpoint, particularly if that belief is important to our view of how the world works. In fact, research has shown that showing someone disconfirming information can even backfire and serve to *increase* the person's belief in incorrect information. (This issue gets into the complex and fascinating topic of coincidence, conspiracy theories, and fringe beliefs, which I address later in this chapter.)

According to long-time information professional and author Reva Bash, we have also lost "history—the deep historical perspective." Basch explained this to me in a recent interview.

> Some great sources might perhaps be digitized but don't tend to surface in a casual search of the web. [In the past], it was easier to work our way down to esoteric journals and so on in the context of print and controlled bibliographic databases. That was a finite universe. When you'd exhausted the possibilities, you pretty much knew it. That's not the case anymore. Today you have to know how and where to check certain digital collections and historical sources. You have to know, or at least suspect, that they exist in the first place. And that takes a degree of expertise and sophistication about the research process that many users no longer possess.

Finally, another loss that Carr attributes to our reliance on the internet is a decline in our collective ability to concentrate and focus on longer bodies of work—research shows that our brains get accustomed to processing shorter bits of data and so it's gotten harder for us to maintain our concentration to read books or even get through long articles.

David Weinberger, a senior researcher at the Harvard Berkman Center for Internet and Society and author of several books on the impact of the internet on business, knowledge, and research, agreed that we should be worried about that trend. But he also told me that he believed that "it is hard to evaluate this impact in the long term."

> Just as our parents might have been concerned about some new ways we were thinking, and how it might impact a cultural value, today we, too, naturally seem to prefer our current way of thinking to new ways of thinking. So what I'm saying is that, yes, even though there does seem to be some evidence that we are now engaging in less long-form thought and reading, I don't think we can or should automatically assume that long-form thought must be the best form of thought. In fact, once we are on that other side of the divide, perhaps we'll say that long form actually held us back. Or not. Or maybe—and I hope this is the case—research will show us that there will be room for both types of thought, that in some cases we should apply long form, but in another, not so much.
>
> We've had a similar type of division of skills in our culture already. We have logical people who operate on a narrative of reason; and there are thinkers who make connections across multiple fields. So lots of thinkers, and different types of thinkers, is a good thing. There's no reason to doubt that in the future we will have multiple forms of thinkers—what may change, though, is that the long-form way may no longer be the dominant way. An alternative that is more loosely linked and not so sequentially logical and long form could become dominant.

What Hasn't Been Gained or Lost, but Simply Changed?

How else has the social web changed research? Weinberger says the web has also restored something, which he calls the "sociality of knowledge."

> Look at Reddit.com—a site where people can post links to posts on other sites, vote up or down on them, and engage

in what are often long conversational threads. The items that receive the highest votes get to the front page of Reddit. While there's lots of silly stuff there, it's also true that at its best, Reddit offers some great and thoughtful conversations on topics in history and science—sometimes with contributions from people with genuine expertise—and these include disputes, collaboration, and push backs. In fact, I've found some of the best treatment of some topics in history and science on Reddit.

But these conversations and discussion threads can be funny. The topic can be very serious, but there is a thread of silly banter here and there. It turns out that when you don't put knowledge through authoritative filters—which we've had to do in the past to get it onto our shelves—knowledge itself can include the funny and entertaining. We will bring our sense of humor, personhood, and a community to the discourse. We used to think humor was demeaning and distracting. But in a real-life conversation, say over dinner, even with a serious topic there will be laughter, and a sense of community.

So Weinberger believes that the social nature of the internet and our connections over networks is allowing the reintegration of knowledge into its full original human context—a context from which knowledge was artificially carved off and removed. That's a pretty thought-provoking idea. This reintegration of our sociality and knowledge may be having some unusual and important impacts.

Craig Silverman, a reporter and adjunct faculty member at the Poynter Institute, a journalism educational and research institute in St. Petersburg, Florida, addressed one impact. Silverman blogs at "regret the error," a site on which he reports on media errors and corrections, while also covering trends in news accuracy and verification.

Silverman has written on the challenges of doing verification in the age of social media. He told me that younger people may approach the production and presentation of sociality and information online with a loose and creative mind-set. "They may mix and play around with true and fake to express emotion," he explained, "posting information to convey feelings and not to convince someone that something is true." This emotionally driven and imaginative approach to producing new content, Silverman says, is just part of that generation's behavior.

This kind of experimental approach to creating new information by younger people has been a long time coming. Back in 2003 I wrote an article in *The Information Advisor* entitled "Are You Ready for the Wired Generation?" In the piece I shared some of the (quite prescient) observations of business and technology futurist John Seely Brown on how the upcoming digital generation was approaching information creation. To excerpt the article:

> Brown says that younger people are moving away from deductive linear/abstract reasoning to what he says is a notion of bricolage.
>
> Engaging in bricolage, Brown says, requires tinkering with the concrete and using tools ready at hand. For kids, then, these tools at hand are whatever virtual and digital objects are available. The rip/mix/burn process is an example of this kind of bricolage.
>
> Brown said that one must "tinker" in order to engage in bricolage, and this means it is necessary to be able to effectively make judgments in determining what to tinker with and use. This process involves re-creation, repurposing, and recontextualization of all types of media, sources, bits, and data. In a related point later in his talk, Brown also noted that kids also reason differently because they are constructing what he called "visual arguments" or non-linear narratives.[5]

Through this recap of what our new digital world has bequeathed all of us, we can see that as the late social and cultural critic and media professor Neil Postman once remarked, "all technology is a Faustian bargain." The social web has given us something valuable, but we have had to give up some things too. From a researcher's standpoint, our ability to access the wealth of information available on the internet is what we received in this bargain.

And even though we may have collectively agreed to give up something in this tacit bargain, what we've given up can to some extent be restored through education and information literacy. We can, in fact, apply a set of knowledge practices to help tilt the scales and cut our losses from the bargain. We'll use the rest of this chapter to learn how.

The Problems of Popularity

What does it mean to you when you come across someone on the web with a high-ranking Klout score, or someone with millions of Twitter followers, or a blogger whose site gets a high placement in a Google search? Do you give these people more credibility than those with lower scores? The fact is that, today, a calculated numeric score—whether based on incoming links, number of friends and followers, or some other network-driven metric—has become the de facto method for assessing the reliability of an individual source.

Did I say *reliability*? Perhaps I meant *authority*? Or maybe *influence*? No, we must be talking about *expertise*, right? Or does it really come back to *popularity*?

My point here is that our initial challenge is to first sort out the multiple, overlapping, and conflating words we use to try to answer the ultimate question: whom should I trust? Once again, before embarking on that endeavor, it is worth taking a short detour to better understand our terms and definitions. Here is some guidance on the origins of these various overlapping terms, according to one, ahem, "authoritative" source, Merriam Webster Online:

- **Popular:** Etymology, Latin *popularis*. From *populous*, the people, a people. Def 4:4 commonly liked or approved <a very popular girl>

- **Authority:** Etymology, Middle English *auctorite*, from Anglo-French *auctorite* (accent), from Latin *aucoritat-*, *auctoritas* opinion, decision, power from *auctor*. Def 2:2 a: power to influence or command thought, opinion, or behavior

- **Influence:** Etymology, from Medieval Latin *influential*, from Latin *influent-influens*, present participle of *influere* to flow in, from *in-* + *fluere* to flow. Def 3 a: the act or

power of producing an effect with apparent exertion of
force or direct exercise or command

* **Expertise:** Etymology, late 14c., from Old French
  expert and directly from Latin *expertus,* past participle
  of *experiri* "to try, test" (Source: Online Etymology
  Dictionary)

These definitions help us understand some useful and interesting
distinctions: **authority** has to do with an agent's ability to directly
exert power; **influence** can be exerted or flow indirectly and without
overt action, which could include people whose popularity gives
them a level of influence. Jon Kleinberg, a professor at Cornell University's Department of Computer Science, has explained that being
influential connotes *the ability to cause things to happen.*[6] Matt Galaway put it this way: "influence is really about watching the reaction
of the listener—not measuring the speaker."[7] **Popularity** by itself
cannot identify the impact of a person on who reads or listens to
them, and is more *passive* than authority or influence, in that a larger
group "bestows" the quality on an individual. And **expertise** refers to
one's ability or experience to "do" something.

What do these distinctions mean for you, practically, as a
researcher? For one thing, it is interesting to see that there are different measures and ways of assessing and rating a source's level
of trustworthiness and credibility. And these words are not the
only terms that we use as labels to decide whom to trust: we could
consider words such as reputation, reliability, and truthfulness,
too, among others.

But in today's social web, even though there are still many methods and measures for assessing credibility and trustworthiness,
the scoring system we have come to rely on is driven primarily by
just one of these factors: popularity. A source's score is nearly
always based on counting something (links, follows, trackbacks,
comments, etc.) flowing from a larger group to that individual.
And that has some real implications.

Popularity's History as a Credible Metric

Although it might seem that I am building an argument that evaluating a source by mere popularity is too shallow and narrow an approach to employ, the fact is that popularity has a distinguished and reputable history as a legitimate measurement of credibility. For many, many years the scholarly publishing world has applied its own popularity-contest methodology as one method for assessing the reputation of professors and other members of the academy.

Long before the internet, academics could and would be evaluated—both formally by university and tenure committees and informally by peers—by counting up how often their papers and articles were cited in *other* scholars' published works. A citation was seen as an important kind of endorsement of the value of that work, and the more frequently one's work was cited, the more the prestige of that paper or article would grow, along with the reputation of the author. And while not a perfect system (its flaws are still pointed out by academics), it has worked, and still works well enough to be accepted as *one* measure for assessing the reputation of scholars.

Popularity and Internet Search Engines
As we examined in Chapter 3, in the mid-1990s several competing search engines appeared on the web: a few of the most popular at that time were Excite, InfoSeek, HotBot, Yahoo!, and AltaVista. But web researchers had a problem. After a search on one of these engines, the results that were brought back were, more often than not, a mishmash of maybe relevant, often spammy, and frequently confusing randomly ordered pages. This forced the searcher to go on a long and tedious hunt through the list in the hopes of locating a valuable and relevant result.

Around the same time period, Stanford PhD students Larry Page and Sergey Brin were designing a new search engine and working to figure out how to make it more useful and accurate in surfacing the most relevant and valuable pages. Their insight was to look to the scholarly publishing world, where, as discussed above, a reference in a journal article to another scholar's work counted as a kind of endorsement. Google, the founders decided, would adopt and adapt that same method, with the difference being that on the web, what would count as an endorsement (and be seen as a proxy for the citation) would be when a site owner included *a link* to another page. That linked-to page would be given a boost in

Google's algorithm that determined page ranking for that particular search.

The search engine would then, like other search engines at the time, find pages primarily by examining pages in its index that matched a user's query words, but each of those pages would also be given a score based on the number of other pages that linked to it. The higher the PageRank score, as Google called its method, the higher a position that page would get in its results listing.[8]

That simple insight resulted in the first internet search engine that returned listings of web pages that were, for the most part, valuable, substantive, and relevant. Popularity as a metric worked—and in fact it worked extremely well.

This method of counting incoming links as a form of endorsement, and therefore as a proxy for relevance and credibility, was soon taken up by other search engines, though with some variations. For example, the now-defunct blog search engine Technorati also looked at incoming links as a way to rank bloggers, but chose to count only the number of *other bloggers* linking to a blog when ranking an individual blogger's authority. (Like Google, Technorati eventually updated and revised its ranking algorithm to include additional elements and signals to rank bloggers' authority.)

Finally, although we've seen how popularity as a metric to assess a source has been used in academia for ages, and is nothing truly new, it's still worth pointing out that there are a few key differences between how scholars apply this method and how it has been applied on the web. Perhaps the most critical difference is that scholars' works are cited by a much more selective group: *other scholars*. Another important difference is that in the scholarly publishing world there is little (though perhaps not zero) room to game the system. On the web, some people try to artificially manipulate their ranking upward by engaging in activities such as buying Twitter followers (yes, there is a market for that) or boosting their Klout score by engaging in strategic commenting on a higher ranking person's sites.

How Wise Is the Crowd?

So back to our original question: if someone (or some site, blog post, comment, etc.) gets a high ranking based on a popularity-driven counting method (which I will call here a "vote"), is that score a good indicator that this person's words are more valuable than those of someone with a lower score? Or that they know more or represent the best of whatever it is you are trying to learn about?

The answer is, it depends; sometimes it is, and sometimes it's not. Let's explore several circumstances.

When Popularity Based Scores *Are* a Useful Metric
There are various situations in which a raw score, derived by counting incoming links, followers, likes, or other popularity-based votes of endorsements *is* a reasonably good metric. These include the following:

- When the voting (links, follows, etc.) process that produces a score follows the specific conditions necessary to facilitate a valid wisdom-of-crowds process. I'll examine the WOC meme in detail later in this chapter, but, briefly, the term is used to describe the phenomenon whereby a large group of people can know more and make more accurate decisions than any single individual, even if that individual is an expert. However, a specific set of conditions must exist for this process to work well. Certain WOC-driven crowdsourcing processes that some organizations use to generate solutions to a problem, as well as Google's method of ranking pages based on the number and robustness of incoming links to a page, are examples of valid and effective applications of the WOC principle.

- When that ranking is performed by readers on comments made by other readers to an online news story as a means of complementing your knowledge about a news report or posting. For example, say there is an article published in *The New York Times* on a hot topic and 500 readers post comments. I find I can quickly complement the knowledge I learned from reading the story by reading the first few Readers' Picks selections, which list, in order, comments that received the most likes from other readers. The views of those highly ranked readers often add a different twist, voice, or perspective to the original article. I will often complement those Readers Choice rankings by reading a couple of the *New York Times* editor's handpicked selections, as well. I find that the combination of the original story, Readers' Picks, and *NYT* Picks ultimately provides me with a fuller understanding of the story. (I have also found that if a news item has been very widely circulated on Facebook and received hundreds or more comments, reading the most popular ones provides additional context, or at least a bit of insight into the audience's reaction to the item.)

- When you simply want to find sources or people that are well-known. Say, for example, you are in marketing or public relations and you want to find out which bloggers or tweeters have lots of followers so you can keep up with what they are posting, or to send your own publicity or marketing messages to them. In that case, a simple popularity-based ranking metric could serve your purposes just fine.

- When what you want to find is not a score that conveys a source's trustworthiness, credibility, or veracity, but simply "famousness" or "hotness" for the moment. That fame could be based on honor, notoriety, or just something unusual or interesting that has happened in the last couple hours or few minutes. On the web, whoever or whatever is getting the most attention, usually based on clicks, trackbacks, shares, tweets, and so forth, will be highlighted as trending—reflecting that entity's fame for at least the current 15 minutes.

When Popularity Falls Short

There are also several circumstances in which voting-derived popularity scores are *not* a particularly useful metric for finding the most knowledgeable or credible source on a particular issue. There is an inherent problem with popularity-based rankings on social media platforms, such as Klout scores or Twitter followers: people who are either too busy or who choose not to be active on social media may end up being penalized with lower scores. Even more troublesome is the fact that there are many people who engage in activities specifically to boost their scores, such as strategic commenting on high-ranking blogs, or tweeters who buy tweets to have a higher number of followers.

Another drawback with popularity as a metric is that very new sites or niche-based experts will not receive many links, comments, or likes, and so are not going to have, at least initially, as high a score as those that have been around for a while.

In addition, when you are searching for specialized hands-on *expertise*, popularity may not be your most reliable metric. If you want to know who the best doctor, lawyer, accountant, home builder, or septic pumper is in your area, while you might find some useful online recommendations based on ratings and rankings, offline word of mouth from someone you know personally still remains preferable and more trustworthy.

What About Consumer Rating Sites?

While this book focuses on finding information, not shopping, a huge range and variety of items are subject to online consumer ratings, and not just consumer products such as TVs and tents but informational items as well. So it's worth spending a little time discussing the trustworthiness of these internet-based reviews.

Marketers are well aware that the most valued kind of advertising or promotion is word of mouth. Studies show that a recommendation that comes from a friend or acquaintance is trusted more than any other type of advertisement or marketing message. So these online consumer reviews are powerful and influential.

And because they are so powerful, there is a lot at stake—specifically, money. Some vendors and third parties will churn out phony positive reviews for their own products and services and sometimes even negative ones for competitors. In fact, according to one researcher, fully a third of consumer reviews on the internet are fake.[9]

It will come as a shock to some people that this level of manipulation of consumer reviews is going on, but for me the interesting question is, could there be a way to distinguish the legitimate reviews from the phonies?

That question has gotten the attention of the academic community. Researchers at Cornell University, for example, analyzed real and phony reviews, and from their analyses they were able to identify specific words that were most likely to be found in fake reviews.[10] Another interesting study examined manipulated consumer reviews and discovered that when the first few reviews on a site are artificially written to be positive, it causes bias in the following reviewers so that they also write more positive reviews than would have occurred otherwise.[11]

These academic studies are intriguing and could eventually prove to be valuable in generating evidence-based strategies on how to spot fake reviews, and even the development of algorithmically based software to detect the likelihood of a suspicious review. (In fact, at least one already exists, called TweetCred, which I discuss later in the chapter.)

However, practically speaking it's probably more useful to consider how to best apply some reasonable conjecture, common sense, and intuition to try to determine whether a consumer rating is real or fake. Following are some general guidelines to help you make good judgments when looking at an item's overall rating score.

- Note whether there are there lots of reviews for the item or only a few. In general, the greater the number of reviews, the less likely that a small number of phony reviews can impact the aggregate score. That's why a site like TripAdvsor, which receives and then averages many thousands of reviews, is often so useful.

- Try to find out what interest—particularly financial—there might be in creating fake reviews for that category and adjust your skepticism meter accordingly. For example, there is little financial interest in pumping up positive ratings of, say, the tastiest recipes for homemade salsa, but there certainly would be for competing hotel chains.

- If you are mostly interested in learning the pros and cons of a reviewed item, consider ignoring the one- and five-star ratings, as these have a higher likelihood of being phony, and read the threes and fours to get more nuanced descriptions.

And when looking at any single review, ask yourself:

- Does the review site provide some kind of authority badge, indicating that this review was written by a person whose identity can be verified? If so, that's a big plus. If not, try to find out a bit about the person yourself, such as where else this person has written reviews. Sometimes you can click on a person's name to find his or her other reviews. Or, when it is worth your time and the reviewer has an associated name or handle, you can search that name online to try to find the other reviews yourself. If you can discover more about a reviewer, try to address the following questions:

  - How long have they been writing reviews? Someone who has been writing reviews for several years is probably less likely to be a shill than a brand-new reviewer.

  - What kinds of products do they review? The most suspicious are people writing very positive (or negative) reviews on a single product and doing so on multiple review sites. One trustworthy type are reviewers who focus on a specific niche (e.g., the person regularly reviews all types of newly released cameras) and also display a clear in-depth expertise on their subject and share lots of nitty-gritty details. But someone who reviews a wide range of products may be trustworthy too, as it may indicate that they are not shilling for a specific company. It's a tough call!

  - Another potentially useful strategy is to seek out and read other reviews by the same reviewer, in particular to see if he has evaluated something you have personally used and are familiar with. Does the analysis jibe with your own knowledge?

As I've already briefly noted, a lot of this discussion on whom to trust online relates to the whole WOC notion. Because this is a concept that's often misunderstood and misapplied, it's worth taking a close look at just what it is and then consider how to use it effectively as a research source.

Just How Wise Is the Crowd?

"The wisdom of crowds" (also referred to as "the wisdom of the crowd") is typically understood as the principle that large numbers of people on the web can answer factual questions more accurately and make better decisions than any one person—even if that person is an expert. But the phrase raises concerns; after all, how "wise" are the thousands of people who routinely post abusive or just plain odd comments on news and blog sites? And since when is "group-think" wise?

While there is a great deal of misunderstanding about what "the wisdom of crowds" really means, the term actually refers to something quite precise. Unfortunately, many commentators and even some good journalists don't really understand it, resulting in a great deal of confusion among the big crowd—all the rest of us. So let's look more closely at this principle, since once we understand it we can apply it to help us determine whom to trust on today's social web.

Empowered Groups

I think the best way to begin is to suspend discussion of the particular phrase for a moment and talk more generally about the internet's ability (via the web, digital tools, social media sites) to facilitate more powerful and influential group behavior. Clay Shirky, Associate Professor at the Arthur L. Carter Journalism Institute at New York University and well-known speaker and observer on the power of the internet, wrote about this phenomenon in his seminal 2008 book *Here Comes Everybody: The Power of Organizing Without Organizations*. In the book, Shirky examined how the new interactive conversational web (then usually called Web 2.0) and accompanying tools were making it so much easier for large groups of people to come together and coordinate their activities to share information, collaborate on group projects, and even engage in social action and work for social change—and do all these things without having any formal (or even informal) institutional affiliation.

(It's important to note that large groups could remotely share ideas, content, and data well before the social web, of course, in a variety of ways and for different purposes. Prominent pre-internet decentralized group endeavors included activities such as adding one's data to the DNA gene bank, sharing computer resources for SETI, and more. It's just that the networking capabilities of the internet, further powered by the social web, made it so much easier to do so—and greatly increased the influence and potential clout of the actions of dispersed groups.)

Underneath this very large umbrella of empowered online group action was a wide range of overlapping, diverse, and sometimes confusing terms used to describe the various ways the empowered social web–powered group activities were being played out. These included the wisdom of crowds, crowdsourcing, consumer-generated content, grassroots reporting, crowdfunding, prediction markets, groupthink, and other phrases you likely have come across at some point.

It's a worthwhile exercise to sort these terms out, because while they overlap, each refers to something different and each has its own rules that govern how and when they work. And—most relevant for this chapter and this book—each needs to be understood differently when it comes to determining information credibility on the social web.

Let's begin with the broadest relevant phenomenon, which is that the internet has enabled the creation of more *influential and powerful decentralized groups.* That was the focus of Shirky's book, in which he closely examined how the new two-way, conversational, and connected web and accompanying tools were enabling groups of people to come together—as the title says, *Here Comes Everybody.* Ordinary people, with no institutional backing, were now able to easily share information and ideas, and do things such as work remotely on a scientific project, document human rights violations by contributing to a collaboratively edited map, search for missing people and things, and even rally citizens to produce social change, influence the way a government operates, or change the government itself.

(While beyond the scope of this book, it's worth noting that although there is little doubt that bloggers, tweeters, and others on social media have played a role in influencing governmental policies or even helped create regime changes—most famously during the Arab Spring uprisings—few observers are convinced that online activity alone is powerful enough to truly change government policy, let alone a regime. Instead, effective social movements happen physically and on the streets. Social media can help facilitate and organize those kinds of on-the-ground activities, but they are not a substitute.[12])

This broader phenomenon of more empowered, networked group behavior itself is not inherently indicative of any kind of special accuracy, wisdom, or superior decision-making of the crowd (we'll get to that later). And while one can examine the circumstances that make a group's efforts more likely to be realized and successful, the fact is that groups form all the time over the web for countless purposes, and so this is simply a characteristic of our current networked life.

Crowdsourcing the Crowd

Some businesses, organizations, institutions, and even individuals looked at this phenomenon of the empowered online group and tried to figure out how to leverage it for a specific aim—that phenomenon is called *crowdsourcing* (the term is attributed to Jeff Howe, who wrote a 2006 *Wired* article entitled "The Rise of Crowd-sourcing"). Crowdsourcing activities leverage the online "crowd" to do things such as raise money for a cause (*crowdfunding*); help improve a product's design, features, or even shape its marketing campaign; or help solve a difficult business or social problem.

And although crowdsourcing and crowdfunding need to be done correctly to work, these activities have had many success stories. And while some criticize crowdsourcing as a kind of exploitation of the public's free labor when used by businesses to generate ideas from the online crowd, it has proven itself in the larger public realm. Examples include endeavors such as FoldIt, where in three weeks gamers were able to figure out the structure of a monkey virus retroviral protease (a protein-snipping enzyme), while scientists had not been able to solve that problem in a decade, and open innovation sourcing organizations such as InnoCentive, which provides cash awards to people who can present a viable solution to a social problem. One of InnoCentive's most famous success stories was a person who figured out how to separate the last traces of oil from frozen water in the Gulf of Alaska decades after the Exxon Valdez spill.

What Makes the Wisdom of Crowds Work

Now let's take a closer look at the so-called WOC—in many ways the most contentious and misunderstood of the aforementioned networked large-group phenomena. Some deride the concept altogether as a philosophy that dismisses the value of the credentialed expert. And while a discussion of the value of the credentialed expert today makes for an interesting argument, it's not what the WOC is about. So let's examine WOC in some detail to see if we can shed some light on what it is, what it is not, and where it plays a role for today's online researcher.

James Surowiecki, a writer for *The New Yorker*, is the person credited with coming up with the phrase. His book, exploring how and when large groups of people can be more accurate in answering factual questions or making decisions was titled *The Wisdom of Crowds*. In the book Surowiecki looked at problems ranging from simple ones, such as guessing the number of jelly beans in a jar or answering popular trivia questions, to more complex ones such as making predictions about future events or coming up with solutions to large social problems. He showed that large groups of people were more likely to come up with the right or best answer than an individual expert.

Surowiecki's most important discovery, perhaps, was the identification of four specific conditions that must be present for a crowd to act wisely (that is, to be more accurate, solve problems, or make better decisions). The conditions are *independence, diversity, decentralization,* and *aggregation.*

Independence requires that each person in the crowd is able to cast a vote or make his or her decision independently—with no knowledge of or influence on the actions of other people (as can happen, for instance, on consumer-rating sites where visitors can be influenced by previous ratings). *Diversity* means that the voting or decision-making group is not too much alike *Decentralization* means that there is no one overarching authority overseeing the process. And *aggregation* means that there is some process for calculating the group's final answer from all of the individual responses.

But it is important to note that while these four conditions must be present for the WOC process to work, Surowiecki did not answer the question as to *why* crowds can be smarter than an individual. That explanation was put forth by Harvard Felix Frankfurter Professor of Law Cass Sunstein in his book *Infotopia.* Sunstein, who is a prominent legal scholar and served as the Administrator of the White House

Office of Information and Regulatory Affairs in the Obama administration, explained in his book that the underpinnings of this phenomenon are mathematical and based on a key criterion: in order to be
wise, at least 51 percent of a group must be composed of people who
have the right answer. This mathematical principle is called the Condorcet Jury Theorem. It, too, has implications for when and how the
WOC principle works and when it does not.

The Condorcet Jury Theorem originated in political science,
where it was utilized to determine the probability of a given group
of individuals coming to a correct decision. The theorem states that
for any given group, the more people who know (and can express)
the correct answer, the more likely it is that the group will arrive at
the right decision. However, for the group to end up with the right
decision, more than 50 percent of the group must have that correct
answer; and the more people in the group that have the right
answer, the higher the probability of the accuracy of the group.
Expressed mathematically, the theorem is as follows:

> The assumptions of the simplest version of the theorem are
> that a group wishes to reach a decision by majority vote.
> One of the two outcomes of the vote is correct, and each
> voter has an independent probability p of voting for the
> correct decision. The theorem asks how many voters we
> should include in the group. The result depends on whether
> p is greater than or less than ½.
>
> - If p is greater than ½ (each voter is more likely to vote
>   correctly), then adding more voters increases the
>   probability that the majority decision is correct. In the
>   limit, the probability that the majority votes correctly
>   approaches 1 as the number of voters increases.
>
> - On the other hand, if p is less than ½ (each voter is more
>   likely than not to vote incorrectly), then adding more
>   voters makes things worse: the optimal jury consists of a
>   single voter.
>
> (Source: Wikipedia)

The implication of this theorem is that it adds *one more condition* to Surowiecki's list of four: in order for a group's answers to be

accurate, more than 50 percent of its members must know and provide the correct answer. And of course the corollary is true as well: when the group's members are mostly wrong the group as whole will be wrong as well.

What about that word *wisdom*?

The word wisdom is really a misnomer, as the process isn't about wisdom at all. Rather, what we are talking about here is more along the lines of "being more accurate"—that perhaps can be stretched to mean *smarter*, but *wisdom* is a stretch too far. A wise person is someone who has deep knowledge or experience, and can tap into his or her wisdom to make good decisions, provide meaningful advice, live a good life, and so forth.

So why was that word used? It's hard to say, but my guess is that the decision was probably made by the marketing folks at Surowiecki's publisher—"wisdom of crowds" does have a nice ring to it. But it's not the right word to describe the process.

How We Rely on the Wisdom of Crowds

In order to determine if and when the answers or decisions of a crowd are valid, it's important to look at the various ways group views are now being collected on the social web and apply the principle based on these varying conditions. In this way, we can understand the WOC principle not as something always and inherently right or wrong, but rather more or less applicable and useful, on a spectrum, depending on the circumstance and type of answers being sought.

WOC Conditions: Fully Present

It is rare that *all* of Surowiecki's four conditions—as well as Sunstein's fifth principle—are present to ensure that the group will definitely be smarter than an individual expert. One circumstance in which all factors could be present is when a person or organization consciously and carefully creates a crowdsourced project—either on the public web or privately—to generate ideas or solutions ahead of time. A dilemma arises here, though: how to ensure ahead of time that the requirement of the Condorcet Principle is met and more than 50 percent of the group will know the correct answer?

Companies sometimes do this kind of internal or external crowdsourcing by brainstorming projects to spur innovation. For example, the Swedish appliance company Electrolux wanted to come up with innovative solutions to a variety of problems and deployed its internal digital network to hold a crowdsourced "innovation jam," sourcing 3,500 new ideas and 10,000 comments. In an interview Ralf Larson, director of Electrolux's online engagement, told me that the entire company was invited to join and that they "had knowledgeable and skilled people to moderate and facilitate the event. Employees voted to select the top three ideas and several went immediately into the product development pipeline."[13]

WOC Conditions: Mostly Present
Google's WOC-based PageRank algorithm for ranking web pages works as well as it does because the voting—in this case expressed by linking—is done 1) independently, 2) by a diverse group of people, 3) in a decentralized manner, and 4) integrates a method for aggregating the votes (Google's own software). This is not to say that there are no attempts to manipulate the system through the creation of "link farms" to boost rankings or through other methods, but Google regularly monitors these and adjusts its system to try to prevent these gaming attempts from corrupting its process.

WOC Conditions: Only Partially Present
Comments on blogs and news sites offer a platform where anyone can voice his or her views, and opinions are very likely influenced by the comments made before them; therefore they do not represent a WOC activity. Similarly, promoting (up and down voting) others' comments or opinions on Facebook, YouTube, or news sites such as Digg can produce data that shows what is getting a group's attention, or what news or sites are hot at the moment, but there is no real independence of action.

WOC Conditions: Mostly Not Present or Not Applicable
In web-based or in-person live discussion groups, meetings, and forums a group of people (in-person or online) share their thoughts together as a group, may agree or disagree on an issue, and sometimes try to come to a decision. This method for arriving at a decision or agreement can either be a good one (say, if the facilitator knows how to bring groups to consensus) or possibly a bad one (if people are afraid to express their views due to fear, pressure, or other negative forces in the group), but has nothing to do with the WOC phenomenon. There is no independence of action (everyone knows what everyone else thinks or believes) nor is there decentralization of voting.

What about Wikipedia?

Does Wikipedia qualify as a valid wisdom-of-crowds site? From a philosophical standpoint, Wikipedia was created based on the notion that the group knows the most, and integrates the fundamental Web 2.0 tenants that knowledge is best derived from many voices, emerges from an ongoing conversation, is always evolving, and is not a static pronouncement from the head of a single expert. It also fulfills two of Surowiecki's conditions: diversity and decentralization. However, there is no true independence of action (everyone sees everyone else's edits); and there is a set of rules that contributors must adhere to (e.g., user edits need to reference published secondary sources, there must be neutrality of tone, etc.) so you can see that Wikipedia is kind of a special case.

And what about Wikipedia overall as a trusted source? While it is imperfect—suffering from issues that range from the occasional gross error to PR firms and others charging fees to create and edit entries—I have found it to be a very valuable resource, particularly for locating leads to other sources (I always scan the citations in the footnotes) and for coverage of obscure topics not written about anywhere else.

TIP: Doing Deliberation Right

If you are going to use a group to deliberate and arrive at a decision, you can take a few steps to avoid groupthink:

1) Get all points of view out and on the table before concluding which are correct or more acceptable.

2) Be sure everybody knows that disagreement is not only OK, but encouraged.

3) Make sure the culture of the organization rewards disclosure as well as disagreement.

At worst, group discussions can even turn into groupthink, which can result in disaster. In fact, the tragic case of the pressures that pushed NASA engineers to launch the Challenger on that cold Florida morning has become a standard case study used in schools to teach the perils of groupthink.[14]

WOC Conditions: A Question Mark

Can the WOC principle work to help with *value*-oriented questions of right and wrong, for which there is no factually correct answer? I asked Cass Sunstein that question some years ago in an interview. Here's how he replied:

> These are questions like should same-sex marriage be permitted. Those questions get into a more philosophical territory, but I will say that we can't exclude these questions from this process by saying they lack right answers, or else we will fall into the trap of relativism.

On a personal level, I have to say that I was not completely convinced by Sunstein's answer, and I imagine that there are more ways to look at this intriguing question. However, you are unlikely to have to grapple with this as a researcher. Your task will be assessing and verifying factual matters, not coming to any larger determination on whether proscriptive answers or decisions from a larger group represent an objectively better way to do things, make policy, or create a better quality of life.

When the Process Can Backfire

Based on the Condorcet Jury Theorem, the WOC process can also run into problems if group members are mostly poorly informed. This can be of particular concern when a group is asked to make a decision or answer questions that require specialized knowledge and expertise. This can occur not so much for commonsense applications (such as guessing the number of the jelly beans in a jar), or for popular culture questions, or when opinion counts more than factual knowledge (e.g., asking a group which news story is most interesting). But it can become troublesome for matters that require deeper knowledge or skill-based, hands-on experience. Say a popular political blogger posed the question to his or her readers, "Do you think it will be okay if I plant English lavender in clay soil in my cold climate?" In this case, the aggregated response of a group of that person's readers is not likely going to be, on average, more often correct than a single master gardener. And so we could expect that in this case the group would *not* perform well.

But, interestingly, if we created a group composed of master gardeners, that group could produce a valid WOC process in that an aggregated, independently cast, and decentralized response from a group of *skilled expert gardeners* (who together likely have a more than 50 percent chance of accuracy) will more likely to be correct than any individual gardener. (Ideally, that group of gardeners would also encompass some aspects of diversity as well in order to fulfill *that* requirement.)

There is one other exception to relying on the Condorcet Jury Theorem for assigning a high level of credibility to a group, and that is when the right or best answer to a problem is known by only a few—less than a majority, and what we can call "fringe thinkers." So for this reason, it's best to rely on the WOC principle when you are looking for answers on more accepted factual matters and not calling on imaginative or nonmainstream thinking.

Information Literacy Lessons from Information Experts

Most of what we have been discussing so far in this chapter is about building information literacy. Being information literate means understanding information sources and processes, so that you can be armed with the knowledge to make informed decisions on whom to trust and why.

While it might seem that the problem of discerning trustworthy from questionable information is a modern concern stemming from the internet and social media, the need to determine credibility is as old as the first human lie or error. Over the years, our information experts—academics, journalists, librarians, scientists, historians, and other scholars of research whose primary work includes ferretting out facts and truth—have developed tried-and-true rules and strategies that can still be applied to today's social and visual web.

Following is a compilation of what I feel are the most useful and important of these guidelines from journalists, librarians, and scholars, along with suggestions on how to apply the principles to today's social web.

Rule Number 1: Always Get a Confirming Source

This is probably the Golden Rule of journalism: don't believe something just because one site or source said it is true. Good journalists traditionally understand the imperative to obtain a confirming second or even third source before feeling confident enough to publish something.

On the Social Web: Getting a confirming source can be tricky because of the propensity of the internet to instantly replicate *all* information, good or bad. So getting an additional source should not mean finding another tweet that's repeating the same statement! It means finding two or more completely independent sources that are not just repeating the same statement. That requires a little more digging.

Rule Number 2: Go to the Original Source

Right after getting a confirming source, I'd say that the next most important journalistic rule is, whenever possible, go to the original source of the information so you can check it out yourself. There's no substitute for examining the original document, survey, report, site, or whatever was referenced by another person or site. This way, you yourself can see what is actually there and what is not, and how to correctly interpret it.

On the Social Web: Again, because so much content—blog posts, video snippets, tweets, and so forth—is simply repurposed and recontextualized, finding the original source of any content can be difficult. For tools and techniques, see the section on "Information Forensics" later in this chapter.

Rule Number 3: Build Your Own Knowledge First

It's harder to be fooled or misled on a topic for which you have already built a knowledge base.

On the Social Web: It's safer if you don't begin building your knowledge on a new topic from consumer videos, tweets, or other social sites. Go to the vetted and edited traditional information sources first, and get the views of experts and columnists, so you have a base of knowledge to assess the more freewheeling comments and observations you'll encounter on social media sites. This isn't to say that you might not find some credible and valuable information on the social web—you almost certainly will—but when you are first learning about a topic, the safer route for building your base of understanding is via more traditional resources.

TIP: Suspending Judgment

How should you assess information that you come across that doesn't jibe with what you already know about the topic? The late great scholar Jacques Barzun and his co-author Henry Graff advised readers, in their book *The Modern Researcher*, that you have a few options: accept the information because it is coming from a trusted source; dismiss it because it doesn't square with what you already think; ignore it; or do what the authors ultimately advise and "suspend judgment until more information comes out."

Rule Number 4: Engage in Probabilistic Thinking

Another bit of insight from Barzun and Graff is that "the historian arrives at truth through probability." Rarely can we be 100 percent sure of anything; more commonly, we come to believe that something is most likely to be true, or most likely not to be true. In most cases when determining credibility, you will ultimately need to make a decision as to whether a person, report, or argument is convincing or not.

On the Social Web: Be careful not to apply this useful rule to sites that rely on a voting up and down and WOC approach and conclude that the "best" comment, observation, video, and so on is the one with the highest number of votes or likes. As discussed earlier in this chapter, while this method has its merits, it is not foolproof, and its value depends on a variety of factors.

Rule Number 5: Consider the Experience and Expertise of the Source

When evaluating individuals' credibility, good researchers try to discover basic facts that shed light on their knowledge and experience. This includes factors such as their institutional affiliations, where they have spoken, written, and presented, who else has cited their work, whether they have any hidden biases or ulterior motivations, the currency of their information, and the manner in which they present their views.

On the Social Web: On social media sites you are going to encounter many people who are able to express their views and gain a following who do not have the traditional credentialed markers of expertise and reputation such as a PhD or having authored a book. As discussed above, on the social web factors such as the number of followers, high blog ratings, a high ranking on search engines, or a high Klout score can be seen as a kind of rough proxy for influence and authority, but you need to exercise the cautions outlined earlier as well.

Rule Number 6: Contact the Source Yourself and Ask Your Own Questions

Perhaps the best way to evaluate any individual person's credibility is to contact that person yourself and ask your own questions. Then you can assess their knowledge, responsiveness to your questions, openness, and other characteristics of a trustworthy source. Angie Holan, editor of *PolitiFact*, has advised asking this question when assessing a source: "Is there anyone who studies this topic who you respect who disagrees with you?"[16]

On the Social Web: People who blog, tweet, and share images and videos can typically be reached via social media sources such as Twitter, though it may take some work and experimentation to find the right method, such as email, a blog contact, or other avenue (see Chapter 7 for additional information). And when you do reach them, it helps to have some strategies to encourage a positive response (see Chapter 8).

TIP: Crowdsource Your Own Community

Here's a tip from NPR journalist Andy Carvin, widely respected as one of the earliest and smartest users of social media for his international on-the-ground reporting. One of Carvin's strategies was that when he saw a tweet that appeared to be newsworthy, but needed further verification, he would tweet that item to his own network of followers and ask for assistance in verifying it. See Figure 5.2 for an example of how Carvin employed his Twitter followers to debunk a claim that Israeli munitions were being used in Libya.

Note that leveraging ordinary people on social media to contribute to existing stories and suggest new ones is something that more and more journalists are trying. An experimental project called Bellingcat describes its mission as "uniting citizen investigative journalists to use open source information to report on issues that are being ignored," and crowdsources its community via a Twitter site.

Rule Number 7: Trust Your Gut

Back in the 1980s, Reva Basch, author of *Researching Online for Dummies* and *Secrets of the Super Searchers*, wrote about the "JDRL Factor." JDLR was an abbreviation for "Just Doesn't Look Right," the feeling one gets when some information, whether in print or

Figure 5.2   NPR Journalist Andy Carvin has relied on his
followers on Twitter to verify uncertain information

from an online database, simply seems off. Reva told me she first
heard that phrase from Don Ray, an investigative reporter, during
a presentation to a group of private investigators. Good reporters
and researchers of all kinds always have their JDLR antenna
attuned and notice when some piece of information just doesn't
seem right, and they subject it to an additional level of scrutiny.

On the Social Web: You'll certainly encounter outlandish claims
and remarks that will not sound right—the hard part may be

determining which ones *do* sound right. The bottom line is that although the various tools and strategies for assessing the credibility of information are important, much of all this ultimately boils down to trust. I discussed the use of trust in my 2004 book, *The Skeptical Business Searcher*, in which I wrote the following:

> In our daily business lives, we learn what sources—whether published or individuals—to rely on. These sources state something, and without going through an elaborate series of questioning or confirming, we put our trust in them. These sources have earned our trust, as they have proven to be reliable and trustworthy over time. We're usually not afraid to make decisions based on their advice. These types of sources are rare, and invaluable.
>
> On the web, of course, developing this kind of trust is a lot harder for several reasons. First, you often encounter new sources or experts for the very first time, and you have no history or background on which to base a good assessment. There are also fewer cues for judging the value of a person's opinion and knowledge on the web. In an office setting, we get to know colleagues and trusted advisors—how they behave in certain circumstances, a bit about their personal lives, visual cues and so on. All this helpful input is missing on the web. Instead, we have only the comments themselves and perhaps an accompanying website.
>
> So how do you come to trust a source on the web? In the same way that you do in daily life: over time or through a referral from another trusted source. Specifically this trust may occur after you spend time on a discussion group or social media site and eventually find that a certain person posts the most on-target, helpful, and insightful comments and suggestions to the rest of the group. Perhaps this person often has answers to your questions and you come to expect that he or she is going to be of help. This person can become a trusted web source.
>
> So the key, when doing any type of research on the web, is to build up a small but valued set of trusted sources. Then you can turn to them when you need help, and be fairly certain you'll receive quality information; this will help you avoid going through a questioning/checklist type of

procedure when you find information via a search engine or some other information hunt on the internet.

In the words of one well-known truth seeker, Bob Dylan, "If you want somebody you can trust, trust yourself" ("Empire Burlesque"). Remember that your own feelings about a source are your best guide.[17]

Finally, while not really a rule, one other factor that's worth considering when determining the credibility of a source is its accountability and the cost the source would incur should it become known that it was disseminating inaccurate information.

Here is what I mean. When a widely read news source—*The New York Times, Forbes,* or *The Economist,* for example—publishes something, if the information is wrong the publication will be held to account for its error by millions of sharp readers. That's one reason (though not the only reason) that high-profile publishers typically engage in careful fact checking, editing, and confirming to help ensure that what they put out there is correct. (Note that I'm not talking about larger issues here such as a news source's political perspective, biases, poor reporting, or any of the flaws that can creep into the fact-checking process or any of the other ailments that traditional and popular media sources can suffer from.)

So there is a definite cost in terms of reputation that a large news or media source (or even a widely read expert) is aware will be incurred for distributing downright bad information. As a case in point, consider the damage done to the reputation of *The New York Times* by Judith Miller's articles that were not critical enough of the Bush administration's claims of weapons of mass destruction in Iraq.

In contrast, lesser-known bloggers, people who tweet and upload video clips, and other people who share content do not incur such high costs for being wrong. Sure, someone might comment that they disagree or think that the information is dubious, but that's about it.

On the Fringe: Wisdom vs. Way-Out Wackies

There's a lot of strange and suspicious sounding stuff that goes around the web. Spend some time in the comments section of a news article, blog comment section, or even an old-fashioned web discussion board, and you'll hear from people who try to convince you of the reality of all sorts of unusual phenomena. Topics run the gamut from the connection between fluoride and neurological damage to secret plans by the government to stock up on bullets, malformed frog mysteries, conspiracies against raw milk drinkers, unexplainable animal mutilations, and of course concerns over vaccinating one's child.

And not only will you encounter unusual and hard-to-verify statements and beliefs like these, you'll also likely find people vehemently upholding their perspective, vilifying people on the other side as fools or malevolent, and seemingly ready to fight to the death to reject arguments, data, or evidence challenging their point of view.

So what's going on? And what should you do about it when trying to determine the credibility of some of the more outlandish claims? Now the fact is, things that sound incredible or unbelievable sometimes *do* turn out to be true, or at least worth considering—they just have not yet become more widely accepted. New ideas and thinking don't come from the mainstream but emerge from those on the fringes.

But is it possible to separate out the wackies from those wise ones who have a little extra insight and can see a little further? Perhaps not perfectly, but there are a few guidelines that I'll discuss in this section.

Facts vs. Opinions

First, it's worth saying a little bit about the whole matter of facts, beliefs, and opinions. A full discussion of epistemology, the nature of reality and how we choose what to believe as true, is a tad outside the scope of this book! However, I will offer a few casual observations on how we come to decide what to believe.

Most of us will concur that agreed-upon facts (e.g., yesterday the high temperature in Phoenix was recorded at 112 degrees) do exist, and not *everything* is up for grabs as a valid point of view. As John Oliver remarked in his comedy news show "Last Week Tonight," "You don't need people's opinion on a fact. You might as well have a poll asking, 'Which number is bigger, 15 or 5?' or 'Do owls exist?' or 'Are there hats?'"[18]

But things get trickier when we move away from discrete facts and start discussing the more complex matter of beliefs. A belief in what is true and correct is derived not only from observing or learning a set of facts, but also from a whole host of other complex and subtle factors such as one's life experiences, intuition, culture, parents, group identification, political affiliations, values, fears, and more. Remember in 1994 how shocked some people were when they saw videos of people in Los Angeles cheering the not-guilty verdict in the O. J. Simpson case? Well, for many of the poor non-white population that lived there, the larger controlling truth was about deep-seated beliefs and the day-to-day reality of oppression and control by more powerful groups, including the Los Angeles police and the justice system.

And we are all quite attached to our own beliefs, especially since our ways of looking at the world provide us with a sense of who we are and how the world makes sense. So, naturally, if a certain new set of facts or data threatens to force us to revise our worldview, we work quite hard to reject them. As Bertrand Russell noted:

> If a man is offered a fact which goes against his instincts, he will scrutinize it closely, and unless the evidence is over-whelming, he will refuse to believe it. If, on the other hand, he is offered something which affords a reason for acting in accordance to his instincts, he will accept it even on the slightest evidence.[19]

A more modern way to describe this phenomenon might be "truthiness," the word originally introduced by Stephen Colbert in October 2005 on *The Colbert Report*. The American Dialect Society then officially defined the term as "the quality of preferring concepts or facts one wishes to be true, rather than concepts or facts known to be true."

Research has shown people's inclination to work very hard indeed to support their beliefs. In early 2014, Brendan Nyhan, a professor of political science at Dartmouth, released the results of a three-year experiment involving more than 1700 parents who believed in the connection between vaccination and autism. Nyhan's experiment was to show those parents a wide range of scientific literature and various supporting narratives to see if the weight of this information would alter those parents' beliefs. The result was unexpected. "Not only were parents not convinced by the evidence presented, but for many of those parents, seeing that contradictory information backfired and served to *reinforce* the earlier belief.[20] (When I read through the more than 200 comments posted by readers of this article, a large percentage of those who believed in the connection between autism and vaccination angrily criticized and rejected the entire premise behind the research—which one could argue ironically proves the researcher's point.)

And not only does there appear to be a general human propensity to reject information that contradicts one's existing beliefs, as Bertrand Russell noted, but in the last 20 years or so within the United States there has probably been in *increase* in the distrust of others' differing views, even—perhaps especially—if the information comes from authoritative sources.

This rise in the propensity to reject others' views can be attributed to several mutually reinforcing factors: increased polarization of values within the country[21] and an increasing cynicism about the integrity of our institutions. Those institutions include corporations, educational institutions, the medical establishment, religious organizations, and of course the government—and government distrust is particularly driven by the corrupting influence of money. All this distrust has developed into a larger suspicion of pronouncements from those up on high, "the experts," and even what some might deride as "experts' so-called facts."

And it's hard to blame people for not trusting what our institutions and authorities say and do. Examples of misplaced trust abound. Weapons of mass destruction in Iraq; preventable fatal errors in hospitals; cover-ups for misdeeds at the VA hospitals and in the church, universities pushing certain student loans for self-interested purposes, doctors writing prescriptions for addictive Oxycontin, and the list goes on . . .

Another reason some people reject evidence and facts is that the disconfirming information could lead to consequences that the person simply does not like or does not want to happen. For example, some who dispute the reality of human-created climate change do so out of a concern that if that reality is accepted, it could (and probably would) lead to more government rules and regulation, which to those people would be anathema.

Of course it's not just conservatives whose ideology trumps facts. There are also some on the left who will reject, out of hand, data, evidence, or findings that could lead to what they perceive as undesirable changes in government policies, laws, or accepted social practices.

Finally, almost nobody—other than perhaps Socrates, who famously said, "I know that I know nothing"—thinks they are wrong. (Though, perhaps if challenged on his remark, Socrates might strongly cling to *his* core belief that he "knows nothing"!)

There's That Trust Factor Again

Ultimately, when it comes to deciding whether to believe something that seems outlandish, contrary to your own accepted beliefs—fringy, politically untenable, unheard of, or just weird— so much of it comes down to trust. And we all have different touchstones for whom and what we trust. Some trust *The New York Times*. Some trust their gut. Some trust results of careful scientific research. Some trust their own life experiences. Some trust their intuition. Some trust MSNBC. Some trust what their parents told them. Some trust Oprah. Many of us simply trust something that confirms what we already agree with or suspect is true.

The bottom line is that the matter of whom to trust is complex; there is no single way to determine who is trustworthy. However, in the following section entitled "General Principles and Truths" I share my own personal methods. Most of these are strategies and approaches that I don't explicitly articulate when I am evaluating the credibility of some source or person. Instead, I have integrated them to the point that together they produce a kind of internal level of confidence when I am reading something from an unknown source.

General Principles and Truths

Here they are—unpacked, articulated, and provided in list form.

1) Remain open to what others have to say—we don't
   know everything. Try to set aside and loosen up current
   beliefs when doing research. As someone once remarked,
   "research is a river—it takes you where it wants you to go."

2) Our current state of knowledge and understanding of the world has changed and is going to change. Just look at dietary recommendations. Before the 1960s, eating fat was fine. In the 1970s and 1980s it was considered the enemy of good health. Later, it was determined that some fats were OK and others were not. Today some researchers are promoting eating more fats overall. Since the best predictor of the future is the past, you can probably count on this current perspective to change again (and again and again) as we move into the future.

3) Utilize the critical thinking skills of the journalist and scholar: be open but also skeptical. Be open because we don't know everything; be skeptical because you need to apply some yardstick for resolving conflicting claims and coming to your own decision.

4) Understand and apply the notion of probability to serve as a check on jumping to conclusions on the larger meaning of a coincidence. Remember that when it comes to amazing coincidences we all have a tendency to remember the hits but forget the misses; and that, as my first-year probability professor told our class, "rare events *do* happen." Remember too that *sometimes* there *can be meaningful* coincidences—the odd and unexpected coinciding of events that are significant if they reflect some unseen, hidden, or yet-to-be discovered underlying force or reason creating that surprise. Again: open but skeptical.

5) What initially seems to be in opposition and contradictory does not have to be so; things are not always mutually exclusive and either/or. Natural climactic cycles occur AND man-made warming both exist; there is corruption in some medical circles but vaccinations are STILL most likely to be safe. Stay alert to false and unnecessary either/or dichotomies.

Evaluating Research Studies

With this larger perspective in place, following are four of my key principles and considerations when evaluating research sources, studies, and the credibility of unknown individuals.

1) Good science and independently conducted research is still our best (though imperfect) method and tool for understanding our world.

2) A single research study—no matter how good and scientifically conducted—is almost never the final word on the subject.

3) Whenever possible, consider research conducted outside of the United States. I like to read studies from the Scandinavian countries, Germany, and New Zealand. I generally trust these, as they are less likely to suffer from the corrupting influence of money or ideologically funded research.

4) What may seem wacky or fringe at one time can eventually gain acceptance as fact. A meta-analysis by researchers from the Harvard School of Public Health (HSPH) and China Medical University in Shenyang, for example, combined 27 studies and found strong indications that fluoride may indeed adversely affect cognitive development in children. Based on their findings, the authors suggest that the risk should not be ignored, and that more research on fluoride's impact on the developing brain is warranted.[22] (And in other news, Ralph Nader's conversations *were* secretly bugged by General Motors and the NSA *is* capturing the phone records of ordinary Americans!)

Evaluating Unknown Individuals

Asking the following questions will help you make better decisions regarding whom you believe and trust.

1) First, and most importantly, what, if anything, does this person have to gain or lose by convincing others of his or her views?

2) Who is this person? What work have they already done? What is their track record? Who has recognized their work or insights? Have they shown themselves to be a reliable and trustworthy source on other occasions?

3) Do they use logic and clear expression to make their points? Is their argument persuasive? The ability to

express one's views clearly is not a guarantee that the content expressed is accurate or true, but clear expression is a pretty good indicator of clear thinking.

4) Is the "argument" primarily an angry rant? And does the person seem to purposely bait others with outrageous remarks that are sure to inflame them, particularly when combined with personal attacks? If so, the person may be a troll—someone who frequents internet discussion boards solely for the purpose of stirring up trouble—and should be ignored.

5) When an argument or claim is far outside mainstream beliefs, what, if any, documentation or sources are provided to lend credence to the claim? Carl Sagan, making known his skepticism of people who claimed to have seen UFOs, said that "extraordinary claims require extraordinary evidence." While one might argue a bit with Sagan's requirement for extraordinary evidence, as opposed to plain old good evidence, some references to sourcing and documentation goes a long way in supporting one's claims.

6) Is the person passionate about their point of view? Passion is usually a good thing, as it means the person is truly invested and believes strongly in what they are saying. This can indicate that something important, but not attended to by others, might be happening. Such ideas should be listened to and given attention. If parents on a neighborhood discussion board start worriedly exclaiming that when their children play by a certain river they end up getting ill, these concerns need to be taken seriously.

7) Is the person open to conflicting views and discussing other points of view? Do they recognize where they could be wrong and are they open to other ways of looking at the issue?

Keep in mind that brilliant people can be misleading and rational people can be wrong.

Tools and Techniques for Assessing Social Data

As mentioned earlier in this chapter, Craig Silverman, editor of the Regret the Error blog, co-author of *The Verification Handbook*, and adjunct faculty at the Poynter Institute, explained how many young people today are motivated to create and post content primarily as a way to creatively express themselves and their current emotional state. So, reappropriating existing content on the web and creating a new composite of text and images satisfies a creative urge to express one's feelings and moods, while a strict concern over factual accuracy may be ignored.

But it's not just young people blurring the line between fact and fiction; this is increasingly being done by those whom we've all entrusted to make these distinctions: journalists! As the pressure increases on news outlets to highlight the most attention-grabbing items shooting around online, some of the most popular online news sites are defending the practice of eschewing fact checking and saying that their links are a form of "online performance art" and should not be taken as factual![23]

This phenomenon of prioritizing drama and the search for clicks has obvious ethical ramifications. According to the Society of Professional Journalists' code of ethics, the first obligation of its members is accurate reporting ("seek truth and report it" is the first element of the code). A lack of attention to accuracy has resulted in the circulation of hoax stories, some of which have even resulted in people making monetary contributions to people making false claims of hardships.[24]

When these kinds of stories start circulating and are shared by more and more people on the web, social networks such as Twitter and Facebook identify those topics as trending, thereby giving more prominence to those topics, increasing the odds that others will post and share them, boosting their trending scores ad infinitum.

This state of affairs has given rise to the need for a scalable way of separating the facts from the fiction, and has given birth to an emerging discipline known as information forensics. Information forensics employs digital tools, analysis, verification techniques, and software to probe, check, and assess the authenticity and determine the origin and flow of a piece of content on the internet.

Silverman told me that there are certain circumstances in which the problem of verifying is most acute:

- In times of crisis, when there is a great deal of uncertainly. When news is just coming out after some kind of disaster—whether natural or human created—the chances of bad information circulating are particularly high. "Because we all want to try to understand the situation," Silverman said, "we are predisposed to pass on rumors and we grab onto whatever information we find."

- Certain topics themselves, Silverman says, are ones about which you should "keep your radar up." These include issues that engage large diametrically opposed forces, involve money, have an importance attached to convincing people to look at the issue in a certain way, or have a history of misinformation attached to them.

I would also add that you should keep your radar up on topics that are extremely dramatic, involve personalities, seem bizarre and outlandish, or have strong political implications.

CSI Social Media

An information forensics approach to verifying content employs both tools and techniques. Let's take a look in some detail at what you can do right away when dealing with what is probably the most high-profile social media source of breaking news, dramatic images, and rumors: a tweet from an unknown Twitter user.

There are a few basic information forensics techniques you can use to begin probing an individual tweeter and his or her content after linking to the person's Twitter page. On the person's Twitter account you can find the following information:

- How old is the account?
  - Consider: A brand-new account could be suspicious; these are accounts most likely to create hoaxes.

- Who does this person follow? Who follows him or her?

  ○ Consider: Do those followed people seem credible?

  ○ What do they talk about? What are the interactions? Are they substantive and do they relate to the topic of the tweet?

  ○ The number of followers can be a good indicator of influence, but keep in mind that it is possible to purchase tens of thousands of Twitter followers for about $100.

- Who is the person behind the account? Try to track the person down and contact him or her directly to ask your questions and get your own sense of the person's credibility.

  ○ Is there an email, phone number, or company name?

  ○ If not, try following the person and seeing if you get a follow back. This allows you to send a direct message to the person. Otherwise, send a general tweet from your account, beginning with @personstwitterhandle in the hopes that he or she will see that tweet.

- Interrogate the actual content.

  ○ If the content under question is an image, use a site such as Google Reverse Image Search or TinEye to see if it is posted elsewhere. (see the Tools section in Appendix A.)

  ○ Find the history of that tweet by using the social media search engine Topsy, which allows you to search for tweets and sort by oldest tweet first. You can also put the exact text of the tweet into Google and sort by date. (In Google, restrict to tweets by preceding the tweet with the search command: site: https://twitter .com.) (See Figure 5.3) NOTE: The relationship between Google and Twitter is a volatile one, and over the years partnerships between the two have been established and dissolved, making it challenging for Google users to ascertain the depth of tweets available through the search engine at any given time, and how to search for them. I recommend an excellent site called

Figure 5.3 You can search past tweets on Google by limiting your search results just to comments posted directly on Twitter

SearchEngineWatch (www.searchenginewatch) to keep up with the changes that continue to occur with Google, social search, and new partnerships among search engines and social sites.

Technology Forensic Tools

There has been a growing interest in the academic and commercial research communities in developing algorithmically based software and big data statistical solutions to the problem of verifying and understanding social media. The products being developed are designed to probe a piece of digital content, automatically integrate some of the specific elements discussed above (the user's social connections, geographic location, number and nature of followers, etc.) and come up with an overall assessment of the likelihood that the tweet, image, or post is credible.

There is also a wide range of free, open-source social media verification tools available on the web to help users probe the accuracy, credibility, or origin of consumer-generated data. These vary quite a bit in terms of the type of content the tool is designed for (tweets, web text, web images, JPEGs from cameras, videos, etc.); what exactly it verifies (origin, if a composite, modified retweets, likelihood of accuracy, etc.); the methodology employed (examines keywords and metadata, geo-location analyses, compares to existing database of content, uses crowdsourcing input, statistical analyses, etc.); and what kind of information is provided to the user (whether the content is an original, a duplicate, or modified from an original; similar content on web). Some also offer special features such as the ability to compare the content directly with another version to highlight differences, creation of trust ratings, and so on. You can find a listing of the best-known digital forensic and verification tools and sites in Appendix A.

If you decide to try one of these tools, you should keep in mind that most are experimental and should be considered works in progress. While these tools are good for locating existing and similar matching text and images, I am more skeptical of their ability to do more subtle credibility analyses. But this is a very fast moving area, with a good deal of research money and support, and you can expect to see enhancements and improvements in this area in the near future.

TweetCred

While these kinds of information forensics tools are still in development, one product, called TweetCred, is available free as a Chrome Extension and in Beta. It promises the ability to make this kind of assessment and is available to anyone who wants to try it. Let's take a closer look at how it works and its potential for verifying Tweets.

TweetCred is an algorithm-based software product that works by assigning a credibility score of 1 (lowest) to 7 (highest) to individual tweets on Twitter (see Figure 5.4). That calculation is based on a wide range of signals associated with a tweet, such as data about the person who posted the tweet, associated external URLs, and other elements. I spoke in detail with one of TweetCred's developers, Patrick Meier, PhD, Director of Social Innovation at the Qatar Computing Research Institute (QCRI).

I asked Meier about the need for a tool like this, and he told me that it has to do with scale. That is, while it is possible for a single individual to carefully and manually interrogate and probe a small number of tweets (as outlined above), when one needs to sift, sort, and evaluate the veracity of millions of tweets, the process needs to be automated to apply those evaluation criteria to a much large number of items.

Figure 5.4   TweetCred uses a variety of signals to assign a "credibility score" to a particular tweet

TweetCred was designed to be used in this manner for a very specific type of user and application: to evaluate the disaster-crisis tweets that are sent by and to humanitarian workers, who may receive many thousands of comments and images during and after a natural or human-created disaster. Those engaged in providing humanitarian aid and making decisions on giving out aid and support need to be able to make quick decisions on which pieces of content that purport to show or describe the event are believable, and which are fakes, hoaxes, propaganda, or just erroneous.

So how does TweetCred figure out which tweets are most likely to be credible? It does so by employing machine-learning technology against large data sets of previous tweets sent during earlier humanitarian disasters, such as hurricanes, earthquakes, or events in war zones. It is then able to identify which specific signals are associated with the credible tweets and which are most often associated with false and inaccurate ones. By examining a training data set of more than 20 million tweets that had been sent out within this domain, Meier was able to identify elements such as user name, number of followers, types of links the tweet points to, and other signals to assign each item a probability of credibility score.

In total, 45 different elements were determined to be associated with credibility. These factors associated with credibility or non-credibility were first identified by two academic researchers who published papers describing their process and results.[25] For example, in one of the papers ("Twitter Under Crisis") researchers discovered that "false rumors tend to be questioned much more than confirmed truths." That bit of data led the authors to consider that people could be warned when an unusually high number of readers of a tweet were questioning the item.

As I noted earlier, although you can try TweetCred yourself, as of this writing it is not of much practical value. It is still very much a work in progress, requiring ongoing human input to better train its software, and it is limited to the domain of disaster tweets. However, Meier told me that there is no reason that the same premise could not work for other subject domains as well.

Fact Check Sites

There is a wide range of sites on the web that utilize a variety of human and automated methods to determine the veracity of a particular site, person, or claim. These include sites such as Politifact, which rates political claims on a scale from "true" to "pants on fire," and Snopes, which researches and investigates urban legends, political charges, or other dramatic statements that you might see in your email inbox or on an online discussion board.

Finally, there is a news site based in Dublin, called Storyful, that relies on social sources for its reporting and uses both traditional journalistic vetting and information forensic tools to evaluate and filter the consumer-generated news it collects before publication. Among other techniques to vet its items, Storyful examines the content's API to identify various elements, including date and location, and makes sure it is possible to definitively identify the person who posted the item.

Notes

1. Erwin Esser Nemmers and John Holmes Meyers, quoted in Gilbert A. Churchill, Jr., *Marketing Research: Methodical Foundations* (Hinsdale, IL: Dryden Press, 1987).

2. Ibid.

3. *The Atlantic*, November 2013, "All Can Be Lost: The Risk of Putting Our Knowledge in the Hands of Machines," http://www.theatlantic.com/magazine/archive/2013/11/the-great-forgetting/309516/.

4. "Effective Messages in Vaccine Promotion; A Randomized Trial," March 2014, pediatrics.aappublications.org/content/early/2014/02/25/peds.2013-2365.abstract?sid=4c82b05f-5ad9-4ab5-b91e-b187e909c237.

5. "Are You Ready for the Wired Generation," *The Information Advisor*, June 2003, 3–4, 6.

6. Robert Berkman, *The Art of Strategic Listening*, (Ithaca, NY: Paramount Press, 2008), 57–58.

7. Ibid.

8. This description of how Google ranks pages is a simplification of the search engine's initial PageRank methodology, which also examined other factors, such as the content surrounding the link on "page A" the number of page links (Pages B) coming into Page A and how many other pages Pages C) are inked to Page B and so on. Today Google integrates dozens of additional independent signals to determine page rankings, ranging from the user click-through rate, to the technical quality of the page, the depth of internal linking, the integration of other rich media, the amount of sharing on other social networks, semantically comprehensive writing, and more. Google also regularly revises and adjusts its ranking factors. For details, see http://www.searchmetrics.com/en/knowledge-base/ranking-factors/.

9. www.nytimes.com/2012/08/26/business/book-reviewers-for-hire-meet-a-demand-for-online-raves.html.

10. http://aclweb.org/anthology/P/P11/P11-1032.pdf

11. John Bohannon, Why You Shouldn't Trust Internet Comments, *Science* News, August 8 2013 http://news.sciencemag.org/technology/2013/08/why-you-shouldn%E2%80%99t-trust-internet-comments.

12. See, for example, "The Revolution Will Not Be Tweeted," Malcolm Gladwell, *New Yorker* Oct. 4, 2010.

13. Social Business Shifting Out of First Gear, research report 2013, MIT Sloan Management Review in collaboration with Deloitte University Press.

14. GroupThink, CRM Learning, November 8 2013 https://www.youtube.com/watch?v=SBw0ased8Sw.

15. Barzun, Jacques, and Henry F. Graff, *The Modern Researcher* (New York: Harcourt Brace Jovanovich, 1977), 109–112.

16. 8 tips for fact-checking from PolitiFact, Rachel Banning Lover, June 10 2014 www.journalism.co.uk/news/8-tips-for-fact-checking-from-politifact/s2/a557018/.

17. Robert Berkman, *The Skeptical Business Searcher* (Medford, NJ: CyberAge, 2004), Chapter 8.

18. Watch John Oliver and Bill Nye's brilliant take-down of climate change deniers, Sarah Gray, *Salon*, May 12, 2014 www.salon.com/2014/05/12/watch_john_oliver _and_bill_nyes_brilliant_take_down_of_climate_change_deniers/.

19. Bertrand Russell, *Proposed Roads to Freedom: Socialism, Anarchism and Syndicalism* (New York: Henry Holt, 1919).

20. *Effective Messages in Vaccine Promotion: A Randomized Trial*, Brendan Nyhan, Jason Reifler , Sean Richey and Gary L. Freed, *Pediatrics*, March 3 2014 http://pediatrics.aappublications.org/content/early/2014/02/25/peds.2013 -2365

21. Political Polarization in the American Public, Pew Research, www.people-press.org/2014/06/12/political-polarization-in-the-american -public/.

22. Impact of fluoride on neurological development in children Marge Dwyer, July 25, 2012 www.hsph.harvard.edu/news/features/fluoride-childrens-health -grandjean-choi/.

23. If a Story Is Viral, Truth May Be Taking a Beating, Ravi Somaiya and Leslie Kaufman, *New York Times*, December 9 2013 www.nytimes.com/2013/12/10/ business/media/if-a-story-is-viral-truth-may-be-taking-a-beating .html?pagewanted=all&_r=1&.

24. Report: Story of girl getting tossed from KFC hoax, Sean Murphy, June 24, 2014 www.azcentral.com/story/news/nation/2014/06/24/girl-tossed-from -kfc-hoax/11298409/;
    Video of Barack Obama speech circulating on the Internet was edited to change his meaning, Louis Jacobson, June 23 2014
    http://www.politifact.com/truth-o-meter/statements/2014/jun/23/chain -email/video-barack-obama-speech-circulating-internet-was/

25. "Twitter Under Crisis: Can We Trust What We RT?" Marcelo Mendoza, Barbara Poblete, and Carols Castillo. In *Proceedings of the First Workshop on Social Media Analytics*, pp. 71–79. ACM, 2010. "Predicting Information Credibility in Time-Sensitive Social Media," Carlos Castillo, Marcelo Mendozo, and Barbara Poblete, *Internet Research* 23(5) (2013): 560–588.

Part III

Experts Are Everywhere

Chapter 6

Identifying Experts: Who They Are, Where to Find Them

Despite the plethora of electronic information and answers now so easily available over the internet, finding and talking to experts and live people is *still* the most important part of the information-finding process, for all these reasons and more:

- Talking to an expert gives you the opportunity to pose questions and zero in on the specific issues that concern *you*. In essence, the information you receive from the expert is custom designed to meet your needs.

- If an expert makes a point that's confusing, you can ask a question to clear it up—not so easy to do with a magazine article or a website.

- When you talk to an expert, you receive the timeliest information possible.

- Talking to an expert is interesting and fun. You get the kind of live opinions and candid remarks not available from static published material.

- When you talk to an expert you are making a connection that could pay future dividends. Synergies happen!

In this chapter I'll look at different types of experts and share some tips and techniques for identifying the right expert for your information need.

First, remember that experts are everywhere. An expert is any-body who has in-depth knowledge about a particular subject or activity. Some experts are famous people—for instance, Jane Goodall or Andrew Weil—but the overwhelming majority of them are not well known outside their field. The experts you'll be talking to are most likely going to be businesspeople, government workers, technical writers, shop foremen, teachers, and other "ordinary" people with special know-how, skills, or background.

Here's a quick overview of a dozen of the best types of experts to track down and talk to. The pros and cons of each type are presented, along with strategies for reaching them.

Book Authors

Pros: Book authors typically have a solid and in-depth understanding of their subject. They possess a broad view of their field and can provide excellent background information.

TIP: Tracking Down a Book Author

The editor of a book can often help you contact the author, and you can often find the editor's name mentioned in the acknowledgments. If you don't find it there, call the editorial department of the publisher and ask for the editor's name. (If you cannot reach the editor, ask for someone in the marketing or publicity department.)

Will the publisher give you the author's address and phone number? Although many publishers have house rules prohibiting the release of this information, these rules are flexible. One key to getting the information is to make it easy for the editor or other staffer to help you. Be sure you have as much information about the book as possible: title, author, and date of publication. An editor at a major publishing house told me that her decision regarding whether to release information about an author often depends on *why* someone wants it. So think a little beforehand about whether your reasons for wanting to contact the author sound legitimate and important.

If you are trying to find the author of a paperback, check the book's copyright page (or the internet) to see if it was published first in hardcover. Given the way literary rights are licensed and sold, contacting the *original* publisher is usually going to be your most effective approach.

Cons: A book author may no longer be up to date on his or her subject. This can be especially true in fields that change very rapidly (such as digital technologies). Book authors can also be hard to find.

How to Reach: If you cannot find the person via an internet search, the standard approach is to contact the book's publisher, who will then forward your request to the author. You can also talk to the book's editor to ask how to best reach the author.

Magazine Staff Writers and Editors

Pros: Staff writers and editors of magazines and journals are typically nontechnical types who are easy to get hold of, easy to talk to, and very helpful. They usually keep up with developments in their field and are good at pointing out other places to look and people to contact for information.

Cons: While an editor or staff writer for a technical or trade publication may be quite knowledgeable about a field (such people have often covered a specific field for so long that they become experts themselves), newspaper journalists, writers, or editors of publications geared for the general public (*Time*, *Good Housekeeping*, etc.) may not be. True, they may write an article on a technical topic, but their knowledge of the field can still be somewhat sketchy—they are usually journalists first and subject experts second, and only learn about the subject through their contacts and interviews. But they can still be helpful sources. For example, I once contacted a popular magazine's staff writer about an article he wrote regarding the overnight delivery services industry. Although the staffer had a good working knowledge of the field, the real value of speaking with him was getting his referrals to the true experts in the industry, with whom he spoke when researching the piece.

How to Reach: When you read an article that's of interest to you, look for the writer's byline at the beginning or end of the piece. Then turn to the periodical's masthead (normally found in the first five pages of the magazine) and search for the writer's name. Contact the publication and ask to speak with that person. If the person is not on the masthead, he or she is probably a freelance writer. In that case, the editorial department of the magazine may be able to tell you how to make contact.

Another way to utilize magazine staff members as experts is to look at the masthead of a publication devoted to your subject of interest, and try to zero in on a specific department editor (e.g., technology editor or new products editor) who sounds as though he or she covers the kind of information you need. If you can't pick out a specific department editor but want to speak with someone at the magazine, ask to speak with the editor or the managing editor. If you are a subscriber, or at least a regular reader, it should help your cause to say so.

TIP: Zero in on the Best Expert
Take special care to note articles that are written concisely and clearly enough to be easily understandable for the non-specialist (i.e., you!). Chances are that the writers of these articles will be equally clear and enlightening in an interview or conversation.

Experts Cited in Periodical Articles

Pros: Virtually all periodical articles quote experts when examining an issue. For example, an article about a decline in the public's attendance at movie theaters, published in *The Hollywood Reporter*, will quote an industry expert on why movie-going is declining, what can be done about it, what may happen in the future, and so forth. This makes your job of finding a knowledgeable source easy. The magazine has already done the necessary research to find an expert and bring his or her opinions and expertise to its readers. All you need to do is make contact. Such people are typically leaders in their field and can be extremely valuable sources. They can provide you with a wealth of information and are one of my favorite types of expert.

Con: You may occasionally run into a very knowledgeable source who is not so adept at communicating his or her expertise. This can make for a confusing informational interview. If you encounter a confusing source, try to get the person to define any buzzwords or jargon.

How to Reach: When an article quotes an expert, the piece typically provides the reader with a name and professional affiliation. With that information in hand, you should be able to track him down.

Conference Speakers

Pros: People who are invited to present technical sessions at professional conferences tend to be leaders and innovators in their field. They should be intimately familiar with the topic of their presentation.

Con: Again, you may encounter a top-notch authority who is not particularly adept at communicating his or her expertise. Otherwise, there is no real drawback with this sort of expert.

How to Reach: You can find out where conferences are being held on a particular subject by checking a site such as AllConferences .com or 10times.com, by entering the name of your topic area with the word "conference" in Google, or by scanning the "upcoming events" column in a relevant trade publication.

TIP: Use Social Media to Follow Conference Speakers
Remember that you can sometimes keep up with what conference speakers are saying by following a blogger or tweeter who is attending the conference and is live blogging or tweeting from the event.

Federal Government Personnel

Pros: Many experts in government view sharing information with the public as an important part of their job. What is surprising to many is that government experts are sometimes the most helpful of all sources.

Con: If you don't have an expert's name, it can be time-consuming and frustrating to track down the person you need. If you do use the telephone, be prepared to be transferred around a bit.

How to Reach: See the government clearinghouses and databases listed in Chapter 1.

Association Staffers

Pros: As explained earlier in this book, people who work at professional associations can be one of your very best sources of information. They are normally very knowledgeable, helpful, and easy to reach.

Cons: An association executive might slant his or her remarks to advance the association's particular industry or cause. In addition, while some association personnel are true experts in their field, others are more oriented toward administrative or public relations work. Be sure you dig for the real experts. (Sometimes the true experts are not located in the association office itself, but work in private industry while maintaining a position with the association. It's fine to contact these people at their regular place of work.)

How to Reach: Simply do a quick Google search on the name of your topic with the word "association." You can also look up your subject in a library copy of the *Encyclopedia of Associations*.

Company Personnel

Pros: Whether it's the person who buys tomatoes for Ragu, or the employee in charge of computer keyboard quality control at Toshiba, sometimes only a specific person at a particular firm can provide the "inside" information you need. If you're researching a type of *product*, a good place to start getting information is a company that makes it. I've found that salespeople for manufacturers are more than happy to educate interested people about their product, and they don't mind if your questions are elementary.

Cons: It can be hard to identify the precise people you need to reach at a company, and when you do find them, some may be reluctant to reveal what you want to know. (See Chapter 8 for ideas on obtaining "sensitive" information.) When interviewing company personnel, you also have to guard against receiving information that's biased toward promoting their firm.

How to Reach: Enter the company's name and location in Google; or even better, enter the company name and a descriptive word or two that best describes what you want to research, and look for an article, blog post, or other information online that discusses that product, service, or innovation to see if someone from the company was quoted. Then you can search for that person's name. If this does not work, you can try to get the information you need by calling the company's public affairs or public relations office. If the people there don't have the answer, they should be able to connect you with someone who does.

> **TIP: Use Online Company Locator Sites to Get Through**
> Sometimes it can be hard to find the right contact information at a company you are trying to reach. Two sites that are geared specifically to surfacing the best contact numbers and methods are GetHuman and CorporateOffices.com.

Consultants

Pros: Some consultants are outstanding experts in their field who can provide a great deal of inside information, advice, and in-depth knowledge.

Cons: There are a number of disadvantages to using a consultant in a research project. First, it can be difficult to determine how good a particular consultant truly is (see Chapter 5 for tips on evaluating a source's expertise). An even bigger drawback is that unlike the other types of experts described in this chapter, most consultants expect to be paid for sharing their professional knowledge. This is understandable, because a consultant's livelihood is based on selling access to his or her expertise. However, few researchers are in a position to spend a great deal of money gathering information, and, as described elsewhere in this chapter, it is normally not necessary to do so!

How to Reach: To find a consultant, start by doing a simple Google search with the topic you are researching along with the word "consultant," and you'll come across both individual consultants and probably some online directories as well. To find others located nationwide, either check a library copy of *Consultants and Consulting Organizations Directory* (Gale/Cengage) or call a trade association of consultants, found by checking the *Encyclopedia of Associations*, and ask for referrals.

The Hands-On Expert

Pros: This is the person who actually performs an activity that you want to learn about—the fashion designer, master chef, computer coder, and so on. Such people understand the subject in the intimate and detailed way that comes only from hands-on experience. You can really get a sense of the nitty-gritty by talking with them.

Cons: These people's opinions will naturally be based on their own unique experiences. They are not like the journalist or industry observer who forms conclusions by gathering data from a wide variety of sources. You might receive a narrower, more limited view of the subject.

How to Reach: Sometimes a professional association can refer you to a member who is a hands-on expert. Or use your ingenuity. Ask yourself the question, "Who would know?" Let's say you want to talk to a top-notch auto mechanic. Try to figure out what type of organization would need to have such a mechanic on its staff. You could call up United Parcel Service, ask for the fleet department, then talk to the head mechanic. Or let's say you need to learn about custodial techniques and products. Maybe you'd call Disneyland's director of grounds maintenance. Hands-on experts are *everywhere.*

The Non-Expert Expert

Pros: The "non-expert expert" is simply another person who has had some personal experience with whatever it is you are researching. For example, say you were scheduled to have a hip replacement operation and were wondering how much mobility you'd likely have after the operation. If you can speak to one or more people who had the same operation, you will gain some useful information and get some helpful advice.

Cons: When you obtain anecdotal information like this, you need to be particularly careful in evaluating it for reliability and credibility. Obviously, it can be hazardous to draw broad conclusions from one person's personal experiences. However, if many people who appear to be trustworthy are telling you the same thing, you may decide that such anecdotal information is worth paying attention to. A full discussion of the uses of anecdotal information and strategies for assessing credibility is provided in Chapter 5.

How to Reach: One of the best ways to quickly and efficiently tap into the experiences, opinions, and views of non-expert experts is to post a message on relevant internet discussion groups or web forums.

College and University Faculty

Pros: Faculty at colleges and universities have a broad view of their areas of expertise, are accustomed to explaining things in a clear manner, often have published articles and conference papers to back up their work that are freely available on the web, and are relatively accessible. Some universities even provide the public with a listing of the names and areas of expertise of their faculty, making it quite easy to identify them.

Cons: Some faculty are extremely busy and can be difficult to reach. And although some stay on top of their field constantly, others may not be as up to date as they could or should be.

How to Reach: There are several ways to reach faculty experts. If you already know the name and affiliation of the person you want to reach, look for a faculty webpage associated with her institution. Such a webpage will often include contact information along with links to papers and presentations. You might also find a link to their syllabi, which can identify some of the critical issues in the discipline as well as important books, articles, and other resources. If you don't have the name of a specific faculty person, on the other hand, search Google on your topic along with the words "professor OR faculty" or "college OR university" and see what the search engine turns up.

Bloggers, Tweeters, and Other Social Media Users

Pros: Certain people who post on social media have built up knowledge of their chosen topic over many years. They have shared their views publicly over time and so can be assessed easily based on their past postings. They are also particularly easy to find and reach.

Cons: There is no credentialing and there are no barriers to posting on social media, and unless the person has already established his expertise in other forums, his authority and reputation are conferred only by his readers, followers, and others who engage with his work.

How to Reach: Popular bloggers' names will surface in a standard Google search, although tweeters are more easily found using Twitter's own search site (search.twitter.com) or the search engine Topsy.

In Chapter 7 we'll look at some additional ways to ferret out expert contact information, make contact with the right people, persuade them to speak with you, and prepare for successful interviews and conversations.

Chapter 7

Making the Connection: Getting Access to an Expert

How do you prepare for conversations with the experts? What's the best way to track them down? What should you actually ask? Here's what you need to know.

Getting Ready Beforehand

It's important not to contact an expert without first doing some preparation. One expert in library science who is frequently interviewed by researchers told me that if the inquirer has done some reading and checking around first, it makes her job a lot easier, and she can be much more helpful. Although it can be helpful to find and read something written by the expert you're about to speak with, it's not absolutely necessary. It *is* important, however, to have done some research on the subject first; without a grounding in

> **TIP: You May Be Helping the Expert**
> Think about any ways you may be helping the expert. For example, if the information you are gathering is going to be published or presented to a group of influential people, let the expert know that. If you quote or cite an expert, or include the person in a list of sources for further information, that may be helpful to his or her reputation or business. This point is especially important when you interview a vendor or consultant. These professionals normally charge for their expertise, but may share information with you freely in the hope of gaining new customers or prospects from among those who encounter your research. Give this careful thought in advance.

your topic, you won't know what questions to ask and may end up wasting your time and the expert's.

Before you contact any expert, take some time to think about how best to present what you're working on to her in order to encourage cooperation. What should be stressed? Is there anything that should be downplayed?

It's important to spend a few minutes thinking about the best kinds of questions to ask. Your questions should reflect the following:

- Matters that are confusing or unclear to you despite having read up on the subject

- Areas in which you need more detailed information

- Problems or subjects unique to your needs that have not been addressed in any of the sources you've already checked

Be sure to use this opportunity to probe for a deeper analysis of your subject, and to search for the significance of the information you've acquired so far. For example, if your research on the airline industry turns up the fact that "currently, corporations do not negotiate with airlines for volume discounts," you'll want to find out the reasons for this from the experts. If in your study of the economic problems of the aging U.S. population you discover that Medicare payments are going to be reduced, you'll want to dig out the implications of that policy once it is instituted.

Before contacting your expert, consider what kinds of queries will best draw on her area of expertise. Let's say you need to find out everything you can on the subject of tents. If you are interviewing a product design expert at a leading manufacturer, a question about the characteristics of various tent materials would be appropriate to that source's expertise. If the next expert you interview is an experienced camper, then a question about strategies for quickly setting up a tent might be productive. Of course, if you value a particular source's overall knowledge there is nothing wrong with asking questions outside his or her primary expertise. But it is important to carefully consider beforehand what a particular source's specialties are, and then try to zero in on them.

I recommend having a list of your questions in front of you when speaking to an expert. This will allow you to concentrate on what the expert is saying during the course of the conversation, rather than thinking about what you're going to talk about next. Additional questions are almost certain to present themselves while you are talking, but having that initial list is a critical aspect of your preparation.

TIP: Be Natural
While you'll have planned specific questions to ask your expert in advance, avoid sounding like you're reading from a list. If you can keep it conversational you may get more than you'd expected.

Selecting the First Expert to Interview

How do you decide which expert to talk to first? I've found that it's usually not a good idea to start with the leading expert in the field. It's normally better to wait until you've spoken with some other people. That way, by the time you speak with the premier experts, you'll know enough about the subject to ask your most incisive and probing questions, rather than basic questions you can have answered by other sources.

A good type of first source to contact is often the most basic. Just as a simple Wikipedia entry can help give you the basics on a topic and a foundation for determining how and where you need to dig deeper, start by interviewing a nontechnical person; for example, the author of an article that provides a clear and concise overview of the field. Learning and becoming confident in a topic will prepare you to speak with experts whose knowledge is deeper or more specialized.

Note Taking vs. Recording

The last decision to make before you talk to the experts is whether to take notes or record your conversation. This decision really comes down to personal preference. I prefer note taking on my laptop, as I can quickly jot down key points rather than have to work my way through a lengthy recording later to find them. Another reason I like taking notes is that some people get nervous knowing their remarks are being recorded, and may even hesitate to share certain information.

That said, if you are not quick at note taking and want to just relax and focus on the conversation, recording may be the best option. In that case, consider using a recording transcription service that will not only record the conversation but also generate a written transcript for you.

When taking notes, there are a couple of strategies you can use to ensure the best results. First, try not to make your notes too cryptic. Writing as if you are doing it for the benefit of another person will help you avoid desperately trying to decipher your own shorthand later. In addition, it helps to read your notes immediately after the interview—they'll make a lot more sense to you at that point than if you wait to review them several days later. During an interview you will rarely have the time to write full sentences; the time to fill in the gaps is immediately after the conversation, while the details are still fresh in your mind.

Making Contact

In today's hyper-busy, fragmented, and sometimes frazzled world, it's certainly no simple task to get an expert to pay attention to your solicitation for help, stop what they are doing, and take the time to respond to your request for information. As Economics Nobel Prize winner Herbert Simon has observed, "what information consumes is rather obvious: it consumes the attention of its recipients. Hence, a wealth of information creates a poverty of attention."

TIP: Try Contacting the Publication
If all else fails, don't forget that you can always call or email the publication, blogger, or other original source that quoted the expert and ask for the expert's contact information.

Because it can be challenging to get the attention of a busy expert, think carefully about your approach. Determine the best *means* of contact for a given situation—as discussed later in the chapter—and follow the strategies outlined in Chapter 7 for gaining cooperation.

TIP: When to Write a Letter

Remember personal letters? Yes, there are times when the "old-fashioned" method of communicating works best. In fact, an argument can be made that as a new mode of communication becomes increasingly popular (whether that mode is the phone, email, text messaging, tweeting, or something still to come) we eventually get overwhelmed with too many inputs from that particular medium. When that occurs, other supposedly passé methods such as phone calls and written letters can be very effective.

The general principle is to use whatever approach will stand out the most, get attention, and be least likely to get lost in today's information barrage. When email first became popular in the early 1990s, it became my preferred way of reaching people (including experts) because I found they responded quickly. Today, the danger is that with so many people getting swamped by email—both legitimate and spam—your message may not be answered at all. Phone calls, it seems, are becoming something of a novelty again and can produce good results.

Certainly, a letter sent by mail or courier makes sense if you are trying to reach a superstar celebrity, as without a personal connection (that is, you know someone) you are unlikely to get through via phone or email. When writing to an organization or business, an effective technique can to write to someone at the top. Such a letter will often be delegated to the appropriate office or individual lower down the ladder, where it may receive more attention having come from "above."

Finding Contact Information

What do you do if you've discovered an article that cites the perfect expert but doesn't reveal where he works or can be contacted? If you run into this problem, first search on the individual's name. If the name is a common one, append a keyword that relates to her area of expertise to help ensure you find the right person. For example, if you've found an article in which "Sally Jones" is quoted on, say, energy efficient residential heat pumps, search for her name along with a phrase such as "heat pumps" or "energy efficiency" and see what pops up. You may find her personal webpage, or perhaps a page from an institution she's associated with that provides her contact information, or at least additional leads.

Phone Calls vs. Emails vs. Social Media

As discussed earlier in the chapter, because so many people are pressed for time and stressed in their work, you need to think more carefully than ever about what is the best and most appropriate means of making contact: phone, email, social media, or even that old-fashioned letter.

The latest popular means of contacting someone is via social media, and while as of this writing this is often effective, it's clear that some of us are already getting more direct tweets or LinkedIn messages than we can handle.

What to do? Consider these tips for tracking down busy people:

- Set up an appointment to talk. Despite the problems of getting through via email, I still often find it the best way to reach someone. I often use email for my initial contact, even if only to set up a phone appointment. Suggest a couple of specific dates or date ranges to make it easy for the person to agree.

- If you do call someone and you're lucky enough *not* to get his voicemail message, don't assume that this means it is a good time for him to talk. Explain why you're calling and ask if you might be able to set up a phone appointment to ask your questions within a week or so.

- When you speak with an expert on the phone, keep your questions clear and succinct. And never read a lengthy list of questions! You don't want to run the risk of being confused with a telemarketer, or a survey taker from a market research firm.

- If you send an email, make sure the subject line is clear, inviting, and personal. But avoid being overly cute– you don't want it to sound like some kind of come-on, or spam, because many people (myself included) automatically delete such messages.

- You may need to make multiple attempts to reach a person—three or four times is not uncommon. Consider using more than one medium—phone and email, for example. When you send a follow-up email to a person who has not responded, change the header. I suggest simply adding the word "Resend" to the start of the header, which may alert the person if they missed the first one or meant to respond but never got around to it. Don't, of course, be a pest. (At least not *too* much of one!)

- An excellent strategy for gaining an inside track to a group of experts is to join a relevant online community, whether one of the traditional internet discussion groups, a Facebook group, or some other web-based affinity gathering. You'll be able to spot who the experts are and then approach them as a fellow group member. If you remain in the group long enough, and begin to make valued contributions, you truly will become a member of the community and will be able to tap into other members' expertise on a regular basis.

Sometimes you know *where* you're likely to find an expert—at a particular company or association, for instance—but you don't have a name. Here are some strategies for finding an expert in such cases:

- If you know the name of the department that can help you, ask to be connected with the director of that office. If you don't have a department in mind, ask to be connected with public affairs or public relations. Although a spokesperson there will probably give you fewer details than someone who works in the relevant department, you may still get some helpful information. Calling the public affairs or public relations department is also helpful when your inquiry relates to something that affects the company as a whole; for example, if you are trying to learn about a new product line or the closing of a branch office.

- When calling an organization's general phone number, be careful how you phrase your information request to the general operator. This person is usually very busy and will rarely have the time to help you figure out with whom you should speak.

Let's say you need to find an expert to talk to about new technologies in home residential lighting sources. An excellent information source would be a major lighting company, such as Philips. If you called the company headquarters' main phone number and asked the operator, "who can I speak with who can help me find out about trends in new residential lighting technologies?" you risk getting a discouraging, "Sorry, I don't know," or, if you're lucky, "I can connect you with someone who can take your name and address and email you some of our brochures." That's not exactly what you

---

TIP: Avoiding "Voicemail Jail"

One of the major frustrations of today's telephone communications is making a call and, instead of reaching a person, getting trapped in a series of voicemail prompts and menus. Pushing zero can sometimes work; other times this results in a maddening response along the lines of, "You have pressed an incorrect key. Dial 1 to return to the main menu." Arrgh!

To the rescue, I'm happy to say, is a cool little site called GetHuman, devoted to returning humanity to the customer service world. This site provides all sorts of valuable tips for consumers on getting through to real people, including the best numbers or number combinations to select when calling specific companies.

want, of course. Instead, try to help the operator by providing some guidance as to where to send you. For example, you might say, "I have a technical question on your latest lighting technologies. Which department can help me?" Now the operator can feel more comfortable connecting your call to the company's technical or engineering personnel.

Another strategy is to describe the type of person you want to reach by job function, for example, "I need to speak with the person in charge of selecting new store sites" or "please connect me to the director of your security operations." You can even try to guess the department you need; for example, by asking for "new product development" you may discover that the firm actually has such a department. Or, if you are fortunate enough to reach an informed and helpful operator, he may find and suggest a similar-sounding department—for example, "planning and development." If the suggestion sounds promising, ask to speak with the manager or director of that division. If the individual you reach can't help you, she may at least be in a good position to refer you to someone who can.

If you're calling a professional association, nonprofit organization, or public institution, there are certain departments common to many of these bodies that are especially fruitful information sources, such as the following:

- The in-house library. The reference librarian is an excellent source of information and can search published resources for you.

- The education department. This department is typically found in associations. Its role is to inform members and the public about the resources of the organization.

- The publications department. Here you can usually get an index of what the organization publishes, and sometimes what's about to be published.

There is one final important point to keep in mind when trying to make telephone contact with an expert you may not know by name: When speaking with the operator, administrator, or whoever else picks up the phone, don't be too quick to take "I'm afraid we can't help you" or "I don't know" for an answer. Often the problem is that you've reached someone who is not particularly knowledgeable about the organization's resources, or who doesn't understand what it is you're looking for. Try politely rephrasing your question—a couple of times, if necessary—or ask, "Is there someone else I can speak with who might know?" If this doesn't work, consider calling again later, when someone else may be manning the phones.

Finding Phone Numbers, Emails, and Social Media Contacts

Using Search Engines

If we know the name of a person, but don't know where to find him, the first thing most of us do is turn to Google, enter the person's name, and hope to pull up his current contact information. While this sometimes works, such searches often return pages where the person is mentioned but without the details necessary to reach him.

Here, then, are a few tips to increase the odds that your Google search will turn up email and other contact information on the target person:

- To find pages most likely to include contact information along with a person's name, try this search: the individual's name in quotation marks, plus the place where he or she is employed, or lives, or has some association with, plus words that are likely to be included in a webpage that includes contact information, such as "contact" or "email." So, for example, a search for Thomas Johnson at Chase Bank (chase.com) could simply be:

    "Thomas Johnson" chase.com contact OR email

- Particularly when doing business-related research, use Google's filetype limit command to limit results to PDFs, PowerPoint, Word documents, or Excel documents. (See Chapter 3 for details on this search strategy.) This technique can pay off because in many cases an executive's email address will not turn up on a webpage, but will be included in an association directory, conference speaker list, report presentation, or other non-HTML document or publication. In this case, you can construct a search string such as:

"Thomas Johnson" chase.com filetype:PPT OR filetype:PDF OR filetype:DOC OR filetype:XLS

You may need to experiment by adding and subtracting words until, with a little luck, you find the contact information you're looking for.

- Identify the email format for the person's domain. If you know where the person works, go to the organization's homepage and browse to try to find a page with email contact information for employees (likely pages include "about us," "our people," "news," and "press"). Note the format in which employees' names are listed (e.g., first initial of first name; last name; company domain or full first name; full last name company domain; etc.). Enter that name format into Google for the person you are trying to reach and see if you find a match.

  NOTE: Google technically does not recognize certain punctuation, and that includes the @ sign. However, as is often the case with Google, I have found that unexpected things can happen, and I have sometimes been able to retrieve results with that sign included. So it's worth a try.

TIP:
An intriguing and unusual site called "Email Format" is specifically designed to help web searchers find emails by surfacing and aggregating the most common email formats for people working at thousands of organizations. While the site is a bit mysterious (there is no obvious creator or background on the site) from my own tests it appears to be legitimate and accurate.

I have found that materials associated with professional conferences are a particularly useful source for locating an expert's contact information. Presenters often include their contact information in PowerPoint presentations and similar materials. To locate relevant conference materials, try searching for the person's name in Google along with the words "conference presentation." Then view the pages retrieved and link to the conference to see if it provides links to materials from the event. If not, you can see if the presentation was made available on another site by going back to Google and putting in the precise title of the presentation, along with the person's name and conference. SlideShare is one good source for finding conference presentations that include contact information for speakers and panelists.

Consumer People-Finder Sites

There are many consumer-oriented people finding sites on the web; among the most popular are Intelius, Spokeo, and Pipl. Additionally, there are scores of "free email lookup"–type sites that will

---

TIP: Try Sales Contact Finders

If your research is business- or professional-oriented, you might try sales contact finders for locating someone's email address. These sites are specifically designed for marketers and sales professionals searching for prospects, including contact information. Some of these services work on a trading basis, whereby subscribers can view desired contact information by adding their own (or others') contact information into the database. For that reason, these sites can be more reliable than "web scrapers" or other automated email finders that use algorithms and assumptions rather than data supplied by real people and businesses.

While sites like these come and go, two I've come across are worth checking out. Lead411 compiles phone numbers and email addresses for executives and managers. While it is an expensive service, a free trial will allow you to access a limited number of records. A similar site is Joe's Data, which provides descriptive information as well as the format used for employee email addresses at a particular organization. (The ability to view an available email address in its records is only provided to those who sign up for a free trial or for the full service.)

pop up as Google ads on name searches. I've found that such sites, generally speaking, are unreliable, offer little for free, and typically link searchers to a page requiring payment for more information. Use them at your own risk.

There is one popular people-finding site, however, that falls into its own category: ZoomInfo. This service utilizes sources and techniques that make it superior to other web-crawling sites. It offers a limited free trial of its services, and nonsubscribers may do an advanced search to find out if the name of a target person is in the database, retrieve a short snapshot about the person and their organization, and find out whether an email or phone number is part of the full record.

Note that having the format an organization uses for its employees' emails (e.g., first initial of first name, last name, company name. com) can prove to be helpful in trying to figure out someone's email address. In fact, there is a free browser extension called Rapportive that instantly displays social networking and related profile information for the person to whom you are sending an email (see Figure 7.1). While Rapportive was designed primarily as a kind of customer relations management tool to help sales, marketing, and customer

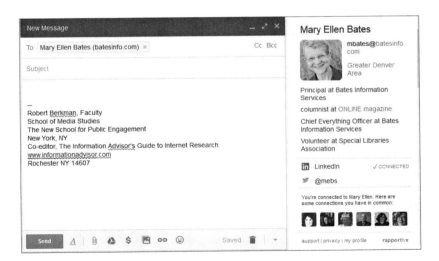

Figure 7.1 Rapportive is a free add-on extension to Gmail that automatically displays a snapshot and data about the person you are emailing based on their social network profiles

service people get background information on their prospects, it can also be used to verify email contacts for someone you are trying to reach. If you are guessing and testing someone's email address by using different formats or combinations, and for one of those guesses Rapportive displays a profile of the person, you will know you hit the right one.

Using Social Media

Whether it's a professional site like LinkedIn or a consumer site like Twitter or Facebook, it has become increasingly popular to make contact with people via social networking sites. Let's take a quick look at the available tools for making contact through these three leading social networks.

Facebook

On Facebook you use the search box on the top of the page to input the name of the person you are seeking and then review the names retrieved. If more than one person with the same name is retrieved, review the listings until you see one whose associated information (company, location, etc.) confirms—or at least makes it very likely—that this is the person you are trying to reach. You can then click on the name to link to the individual's Facebook page.

However, because you are not Facebook friends, you won't be able to send a direct message. You still have two options: you can either send a general message (which will be sent to the person's "messages: other folder") or you can request a friend contact. If you choose the latter, I recommend replacing the boilerplate Facebook friend request with a more personal message. (Note that after sending a message you can check your own Messages link on the left-hand side of your Facebook page to see if it was viewed, as Facebook will mark the message as seen once the recipient opens it.)

Twitter

You can use Google to quickly see if a person has a Twitter account by entering the person's name into Google followed by "twitter .com." Google will surface a Twitter page if she has an account; then you can click on the link and, as long as you have your own Twitter account, you can click to follow the person. If she follows you back,

Figure 7.2 Once someone follows you on Twitter,
you can send that person a private message

you can then contact her privately by sending a direct message as
illustrated in Figure 7.2. If she does not choose to follow you back,
you can still post a tweet from your account that begins with her
Twitter account to try to get her attention (for instance, "@kensma-
ters please contact me at my twitter account to explore a partner-
ship opportunity").

LinkedIn
LinkedIn's equivalent of email, called InMail, allows LinkedIn members, under certain circumstances, to send a direct message to
other members. Unless you have a paid account, your options for
using InMail for making contact with someone you don't already
know are pretty limited, since free members are only permitted to
send InMail to other LinkedIn members with whom they already
have an existing first-degree relationship (e.g., both parties have
agreed to connect). Strategies for connecting with persons you
don't know on LinkedIn include the following:

- Search for the name of the person you are trying to
  reach on LinkedIn's search bar. If that person is on
  LinkedIn, click on the name and retrieve his or her
  profile. Most LinkedIn members have a "connect"
  button under their name for other LinkedIn members

to request a connection. Clicking that button displays a standard boilerplate message, "I'd like to add you to my professional network via LinkedIn," that you can send to the target individual. Particularly if you do not know the person, rather than sending the boilerplate message, craft something more personal and explanatory.

- Sign up for a premium membership. Premium membership, which ranges from $20 to $75 per month, offers many additional features, including the ability to send InMail to all LinkedIn members (with a limit on how many can be sent based on type of premium membership). This option can vastly expand who you can reach directly. The premium membership is expensive, but under certain circumstances—for instance, if you are a journalist, if LinkedIn is running a special, or perhaps simply by requesting a trial—you may be able to get it for less for a short time.

Offline Searching

There are a variety of offline resources for locating email addresses and other contact information, including the following.

- **Executive Directories.** Because executive directories are compiled by humans, they are usually more reliable than similar resources that rely on web aggregation. An example is the *Leadership Directories* series of guidebooks, which is part of the Leadership Library. These directories provide names, titles, affiliations, and contact information for thousands of professionals in government, media, business, legal, nonprofit, and energy industries.

- **The Telephone.** In the digital age, it's easy to forget that the telephone remains a tried-and-true method for locating contact information. A call to the headquarters of the organization where the target individual works, with a request to obtain (or even better, to confirm) an email address, will often result in surprisingly successful results. If the entity is large enough to have a central operator, he or she will often simply look up the information and provide it to you right on the phone. Otherwise you can ask to be transferred to the particular department, or if need be, to Human Resources.

Chapter Websites

CorporateOffices.com
GetHuman: gethuman.org
EmailFormat: email-format.com/
SlideShare: slideshare.net
Zoominfo: zoominfo.com
Lead411: lead411.com
Joe's Data: joesdata.com
Rapportive: rapportive.com
Leadership Directories (A free trial can be set up at www.leadership
    directories.com/Requests/request_free_trial.aspx.)

Chapter 8

Talking with Experts: Strategies for Getting Inside Information

As discussed in Chapter 7, people *are* pressed for time and have become increasingly difficult to get hold of. But you should never assume that a given expert is not going to talk to you. Whether the topic is antique typewriters, the history of pizza, or Norwegian economics, experts and enthusiasts have great interest in their topic, and they enjoy discussing it. Remember, these people have devoted a large portion of their lives to learning about and exploring their field or passion. When someone approaches them needing information, they're almost always pleased to oblige.

Adding to their inclination to talk is the fact that no matter how mundane a subject may seem, there is always some kind of controversy that excites the experts. For example, I once discovered, in the course of researching the sexy topic of water meters, that an intense battle was being fought between those who favored plastic meters and those who liked bronze ones. The important point to remember is, you won't know unless you try. Always try.

Following are some specific strategies for approaching people you'd like to speak with, to smooth the interview procedure and encourage cooperation.

Presenting Yourself to the Expert

Okay, you've made a phone call and the expert you are trying to reach has actually picked up the phone and said hello. Now what? No, don't hang up. Here's what to do to get the conversation off to a smooth start.

Identify Yourself

You've got to first identify yourself—clearly and precisely—and explain why you are calling. You need to allay the natural suspicion most of us feel when a stranger contacts us out of the blue. Don't start off your conversation by saying, "Hello, may I ask you some questions about geothermal technologies?" Infinitely better is, "My name is Karen Johnson, and I'm calling from (hometown or firm and city). I'm currently collecting information on the benefits of geothermal energy (for a possible book, for a report for my firm, to learn about emerging careers, etc.) and I read your recent article 'Why Geothermal Is the Energy of the Future.' I wonder if I could have a couple of minutes of your time to ask a few questions . . .?"

It's helpful to explain your goals in asking the questions, as well as identifying the sources you've already checked or with whom you may have already spoken. The better the expert's understanding of why you're calling, the easier it will be for her to agree to speak with you. And you'll always have a more productive conversation with the expert who knows where you're coming from than with the one who is simply answering questions.

Ask the Expert if It's a Good Time to Talk

You don't want to interview someone who's in a rush to get it over with. If it's a bad time, set up an appointment for a phone interview at a specific time a day or two in the future. Doing so conveys the importance of your phone interview and legitimizes it. In fact, in many cases your best approach will be to make an initial call specifically to set up an appointment for a more formal conversation. If the expert wants to talk then and there, of course—and this is often the case—you need to be prepared to do so.

Be Serious, Get to the Point, and Admit Your Ignorance

You need to convey the fact that your project is important to you, that you've given it a lot of thought, and are well prepared. And because people are busy, let them know why you're calling within the first few seconds of the conversation. If you are new to the topic or unsure about how to approach it, it's good practice to *admit that to the expert up front.* It's fine to say something such as, "I'm just starting to learn about the subject, so I hope you'll excuse any questions that may seem a little elementary."

If the expert asks *you* a question to which you don't know the answer, simply say, "I don't know," rather than fumbling or trying to make believe you do know. Don't feel embarrassed or guilty that you don't know more—the whole idea of seeking information is to learn, of course. And once the expert knows you are a novice, he's more likely to explain concepts to you in layman's terms, avoiding topical jargon that may have you lost from the get-go.

Be Specific

This is quite important, especially at the beginning of the conversation. Suppose the topic you need to find out about is "the future of professional football in the United States." If you begin your conversation by posing such an overwhelmingly broad question, you're getting off on the wrong foot. That's too broad a question to address in a brief phone call, and your source will feel that she's been put on the spot. Instead, start off with a more specific question that can be answered more easily, such as "Do you think the recent spate of arrests of high-profile football players is changing the culture of the NFL?" or "Will increasing concerns about concussions impact the way new players are recruited into the league?" Even if these questions are not vital to you, they will serve to get the ball rolling, which *is* vital to the conversation. Later, toward the end of the conversation when a rapport has been established, you might throw in the broad "future of football" question. At this point, your expert is warmed up and is likely to be more responsive.

Follow the Expert's Lead

At the beginning of the conversation, let the source take the lead in directing the talk. If the person feels comfortable talking about something that's not exactly on the right track for you, show interest anyway. You can redirect the conversation to cover the precise areas you are interested in later, but it's a good thing you've got him talking.

Delay Tough Questions

Don't begin your conversation with questions that are likely to stump your source. If the expert's immediate reaction suggests you may have asked such a stumper, don't press for an answer. Drop it and go to another question. Later on in the conversation you can try bringing it up again, if it seems comfortable to do so. If you have questions that might be considered offensive, save them for the end, as well.

> **TIP: Don't "Survey"**
> Many people dislike surveys, but don't mind sharing their thoughts and opinions or on a subject. Make it feel personal.

Getting the Expert Interested

Everyone wants to feel important. You can help the discussion along by showing sincere appreciation and, later on, by letting her know that the information she's sharing is exactly what you're looking for. Another good way to get an expert to open up is to heighten her interest in what *you* are doing. Here are some strategies.

- As discussed earlier, consider in advance the ways the expert might benefit from talking to you.

- If you work directly for, or on assignment to a well-known publication or company, it helps to mention that. People often feel excited about being interviewed by a prestigious organization. This doesn't mean that experts always prefer talking to someone calling from a well-known entity. Some people are actually less disposed to do so, either because they would prefer to do a kind of public service and help out an amateur information seeker, or because they'd rather not have their remarks widely circulated. It's a personal preference that will vary among your sources.

- A good way to heighten the expert's enthusiasm is to let him know of any interesting bits of information you've come up with so far in your research. Some of what you've learned may be useful to the expert, supporting his own work. Similarly, offer to share your final findings with the expert. Remember, you're doing a lot of in-depth digging in his field; what you ultimately come up with may hold interest for him.

- Attempt to interest the expert enough so that she really wants to help you. For example, if you plan to ask an interior design consultant an art-oriented question, you may be able to gain her cooperation by suggesting that her input will ensure the viewpoint of her profession is represented in your research. Another approach is to appeal to the expert's ego. When you let a source know that your project is identifying leading experts in the field, it is very flattering, and many individuals will be happy to be included in that context. It's also a kind of compliment to ask for someone's ideas on a subject, especially if you mention that you'll be passing along those thoughts to others as expert opinion.

- Finally, ask whether your expert would like to be quoted by name or would prefer to remain anonymous. The ability to "name names" can be important to your research, but at times anonymity will produce the most open and honest responses.

> **TIP: Be Persistent**
> If your first few interviews don't go as smoothly as you'd hoped, don't despair. It's really a numbers game, and the process is such that some interviews will be great, some good, and some not so good.

Getting the Most Out of the Interview

There are several things that you should keep in mind during the actual conversation that will help you structure the interview in the most effective way.

Question Things

If an expert says something that doesn't sound right or that contradicts something else you've been told, ask for clarification. If an expert tells you matter-of-factly that so and so's theory on the link between attitude and illness is preposterous, for example, ask the expert *why* he or she does not believe it. What are the *reasons*? Questioning statements with a "why" instead of accepting them at face value is one of the very best ways to deepen your understanding of any subject. Don't let questions hang unanswered. Politely press for reasons and explanations.

Probe for Specifics

Try not to accept general, unproven statements. If an expert on computers tells you that Samsung makes the best smartphone on the market, ask him or her to tell you *why*. If you're then told that it's superior because the firm provides a better camera, ask *how* that camera is better. If the expert tells you that Samsung's camera is better because it has more capabilities than that of its competitors, find out *what those capabilities are*. To take another example, if an expert tells you that it would be extremely unlikely for someone to get sick from eating too much of a certain vitamin, ask whether it has ever happened; if so, what was the situation or condition that made it occur?

Ask for Definitions of Technical Terms

If the expert throws in any terms or buzzwords you don't understand, ask for definitions. Asking for explanations is nothing to be embarrassed about. It may be important for you to know the definitions of certain words, especially the standard terminology in the field. Explain to the expert that you want to understand the term precisely, but in layman's language.

Ask for Help

Early on in your project, you'll be trying to figure out exactly what you need to know to understand the field you are researching. You can enlist your experts' assistance in better defining what you need to find out. If you have a good rapport with an expert, you can ask that person to help you isolate the critical issues on which you need to become knowledgeable.

Let's say you're digging up information on the science of dreams and dreaming. Initially, you probably do not even know what the important issues in the field are and thus may not be sure what questions to ask. But an expert will know the issues. He or she may say something like, "Well, if you want to find out about the latest in dream research, you should ask experts about some of the recent findings in 'lucid dreaming' and discoveries about new methods for inducing lucid dreams." What you're doing here is asking the expert to tell you which issues are important in the field and what questions you should be asking other experts. In a sense, you are trying to learn the answer to the question "What should I be finding out?" And there's nobody better qualified to tell you than the experts themselves. (Because asking the question "What should I be finding out about this topic?" is somewhat offbeat, you should not begin your conversation with it; work it in once you've broken the ice.)

Stay in Control

You've got to keep your interview on track. Occasionally a source may think you are interested in an aspect of the subject that is actually not relevant to your research. He will try to be helpful, but may go off on a tangent and talk a blue streak about something that's not really of interest to you. Listen politely—and of course be aware that perhaps this is something you *should* be interested in!—but soon you'll have to rein the expert in by asking a question about something you *are* interested in. It's up to you to keep the conversation on course. You have a limited amount of time to devote to any project, and it's important to make the most of it. (As discussed earlier, at the very beginning of a conversation you may want to allow the expert to talk about almost anything for awhile, just to get the ball rolling. But at some point you'll have to get the conversation on track.)

Wrap It Up

At the very end of an informational interview, there are three very important questions you should always ask:

- Is there anything important we haven't discussed? It's possible that your source has some additional important information to discuss but hasn't mentioned it because you didn't ask. This provides the expert with the opportunity to talk about it.

- Do you have any published information you can email me? Often the expert has written articles on the subject or has collected some favorites and will share them.

- Who else do you recommend that I speak with? This is an extremely important question that you should be sure to ask all your sources. First of all, it's a quick and effective way to identify and gain contact information for another expert. Even more important, you now have a referral: someone you can cite when contacting the new expert. Be sure to let that person know that you were referred by the mutual acquaintance. If you leave a phone message for the expert, or send an email, it's worth mentioning the contact's name to encourage a reply. There's almost no better way to reach someone than through a direct referral like this.

  Another reason that it's so important to ask to be referred to other experts is that typically, the more people you are referred to, the more likely it is that you'll encounter specific and relevant expertise. Just as more general *published* sources can lead you to others that are more precisely focused, so it is with human experts. (Admittedly, this process can sometimes be a bit frustrating because it often results in your best sources coming at the very *end* of your information search—at the point when you'd hoped to be wrapping things up!)

TIP: Confirm Your Facts

The end of a conversation is a good time to clear up any confusing points the expert may have made during the discussion. You can use the time to confirm important facts, state or restate your understanding of the issues, and give the expert the opportunity to clear up any misunderstandings.

Staying on Course and Redirecting Focus

Throughout your interviews, it's important to stay on the course you've charted. To do so requires that you ask the right questions and direct your energies toward where *you* want to go.

The questions you pose to the experts will need to be continually examined, revised, and updated as your interviews progress. Some of your simpler questions will be answered the same way by every-one, and it won't be necessary to keep asking them. At the same time, you'll find that you'll develop new questions as you learn and move along in your research, and as experts bring up issues you were not originally aware of. You'll notice as you speak with your sources that the most important issues will emerge automatically as their conversation gravitates to the most critical matters. You'll then be able to incorporate these issues into your own list of questions and ask about them in your future interviews. Thus, your question-naire will be a flexible one, modified throughout your information search to reflect the major issues as you see them emerge.

If you come to a point where you start to be able to predict the answers from the experts, it's a sign that it's time to step back a little from the information-gathering project and assess where it's going. Think about whether your goals have changed since you began the project and, if so, how. Are there gaps in your information that need to be filled? Are there new angles to explore? Are there any new types of sources that you haven't thought about yet that should be approached? Take stock of where you are and how things are going.

> **TIP: Read Your Old Notes**
> Reading over the notes you've taken during interviews up until this point will stimulate you to think of new questions and fresh angles you haven't yet pursued.

Keep the "Big Picture" in Mind

At all times during your project, keep your ultimate goal in mind as your guiding force. Try not to get sidetracked into pursuing routes that have nothing to do with why you are conducting your informa-tion search.

Cracking the Tough Nuts

What do you do if you have a source who's really a tough nut to crack and it's important that this person share his knowledge with you? The great majority of experts *will* talk to you and give you the answers you need, but occasionally you will run into someone who is not so helpful. There are a number of possible reasons why an expert might be unhelpful. It could be you've called at a bad time. Perhaps the person is simply not the helpful type. There could be a competitive issue or conflict of which you are not aware. Or perhaps you've encountered someone who is protective of his knowledge and doesn't like to share it.

Whatever the reason, if you encounter someone like this, sometimes the easiest thing to do is abandon the interview and move on to the next one. As mentioned earlier, not *all* your conversations with experts are going to be perfect, so it's no big deal to drop a difficult one. However, if this is a truly critical source for your project, don't give up easily. There are some strategies you can use to turn a difficult interview into a productive one. In this section we'll examine ways to get through the rockiest interviews, including strategies for dealing with reluctant sources and difficult questions and topics.

Building Up Trust

A source who is unwilling to talk to you is often suspicious. Even if you've identified yourself clearly and explained why you are seeking information, she may still be suspicious of who you *really* are and what you're going to do with the information. From the expert's perspective, you are just an anonymous voice on the phone; you could be a competitor, or someone who's up to no good.

One strategy that can help allay suspicions is to simply stay on the phone and keep talking. Reveal more about yourself and why you're gathering information. Slowly, the expert will get a better feeling for who you are, and you'll become less anonymous and less threatening. As you reveal more about yourself and what you're doing, the unhelpful expert often loosens up and begins to talk.

Because a major concern for some experts is being misquoted or misunderstood, another way you can calm the fears of a suspicious source is by offering to send a copy of anything you write before it's published or presented to anyone. Some experts feel better knowing they'll have a chance to correct any errors and have some control over how they are represented. Their review can benefit you, too, serving as a check on the accuracy and completeness of your research.

Specific Problem Areas

Let's look at ways to handle some common interview roadblocks.

The "I Don't Have Time to Talk" Expert

What do you do if your source says he or she doesn't have time to speak with you? One strategy is to ask for just a minute or two. This will reassure the source that the whole morning won't be used up on the phone with you. But the interesting thing is that once this expert starts talking, he will often continue to talk for 20, 30, 40 minutes, or more!

Another effective technique in gaining cooperation is to ask the expert to tell *you* when he wants the discussion to end. If you give him control over the limits of the conversation, he's more likely to speak with you.

As discussed earlier, one very useful approach is to schedule a future day and time for a formal phone interview at the expert's convenience. This will allow him to budget some time to talk with you.

The "I Don't Know" Expert

How do you handle a source who is answering a lot of your questions with "I don't know" when you think the person really does know? Sometimes the "I don't know" syndrome occurs when an expert does not want to mislead you with an answer that's not precise. But often all you're really looking for is a general idea. If this is the case, try asking for a "rough estimate" or a "ballpark figure." This will take the pressure off your source to be exact and may yield the general information that you're looking for.

The Expert Who Will Tell No Evil

Sometimes in your interviews you may find yourself trying to understand the negative or unflattering side of an issue. For example, let's say you are interviewing a trustee of a college with a goal of learning about the school's most pressing problems. Or say you're interviewing a representative of the American Advertising Executives Association and you want to know why fewer recent grads are pursuing careers in advertising. In both cases, your sources may feel uncomfortable giving you negative information. In general, people prefer telling you the good, rather than the bad. It's safer, especially when one is representing a particular institution, product, or cause.

To make it easier for an expert to discuss negatives, ask for "the best points and the worst points" or the "strengths and weaknesses" of the matter in question. By asking experts to talk about—and indeed emphasize if they wish—the good, you allow them to dilute the bad, making it easier to divulge.

The "Too Smart" Expert

Occasionally, the leading expert in a field may be so intimately knowledgeable on all the details of a subject, and so aware of all the permutations that affect it, that he or she will have genuine difficulty answering basic questions. For example, one time I was writing a report on how companies can reduce their travel and entertainment expenses. One of the premier experts in the field answered many of my questions with, "That is too complicated a matter to respond to simply," or "There is no one answer to that question," or "It really depends on the situation." Although he was technically correct, he was unable to come down from his lofty plane and work a little to provide any useful input. If you come across an expert like this, stick with it. You should still be able to glean some good information from the conversation and get a feel for what the "big picture" looks like.

Obtaining "Sensitive" Information

In many information searches, it eventually becomes necessary to ask an expert about some controversial or sensitive matter. Although you'll be surprised at how often people will freely discuss this type of information, you'll want to have some strategies for getting as much cooperation as possible going in.

Don't Begin with Sensitive Questions

You should not begin your conversation with a controversial or sensitive question. This type of question is best situated in the middle of a conversation when the expert has warmed up a bit and is feeling more relaxed. It's also best not to end with a very sensitive question, unless you feel it is so sensitive that it may cause the expert to terminate the conversation.

Rephrase Questions

If you've asked a controversial question that the expert is unwilling to answer, try posing it in a different way. Let's say you received a "no comment" to your question, "Is Bill Jones next in line to be president of the National Restaurant Association?" You could then try asking something like, "Is Bill Jones considered a leading contender for the presidency?" or "Will Bill Jones be playing an important role in the association over the next few years?"

Go from the General to the Specific

You can lead up to the sensitive information with some more general questions. For example, once I needed to find out how much money, if any, a particular company saved by implementing a telecommuting program—that is, a system where employees can work from home via the use of a computer and an internet connection. Instead of asking directly how much money the program had saved for the company, I asked a series of questions: Overall, was the program a plus for the company? Did it save the firm money? Was it a significant amount? Roughly, about how much did it save?

Ask "Peripheral" Questions

Asking peripheral questions is a strategy you can employ to get bits and pieces of information that shed light on your primary query without tackling that query head on. To use the previous Bill Jones example, you might ask questions about the association vice presidency, past voting patterns, and so forth, in order to piece together a picture, rather than asking a direct and more sensitive question that the expert may not feel comfortable answering.

Ask for Ballpark Figures

When you need sensitive numerical information, you may find that it's easier for experts to provide rough estimates or a range rather than precise numbers. Another strategy for getting sensitive figures is to suggest a few numbers yourself to get a reaction. Often an expert won't volunteer the information but will respond to your estimates.

Ask for "Feelings"

You may find it easier to get an answer if you try to elicit an emotional response. Ask the person how he or she feels *personally* about a controversial topic.

Take a Position

Taking a position is an old news reporter's trick. Suppose you're trying to find out from an oil company executive whether there's any truth to the rumor that the firm is lowering its imports by 2 percent next year. If you bluntly ask the question, you're likely to get a "no comment." Instead, try taking a position on the question—state it as fact—and continue the conversation. In this case, you might say, "Since your company will be reducing imports by 2 percent next year, will there be a corresponding increase in domestic production?" Your source will have to bite his tongue to let your assumption go unanswered, especially if he fears you may later think you got the information from him! You may not get a definitive answer

---

TIP: Negotiate an Agreement

If you need to quote a source or write up sensitive information, you can often negotiate with the expert regarding how much or what type of information you are allowed to use. For example, although an expert may want her remarks to be off the record, you might ask to use only one particular statement made during the conversation. Many times you'll discover that the expert will agree to this. Similarly, you can negotiate exactly how you will identify the source. For instance, the expert may not let you use his or her name, but may be willing to be identified as "an employee of Jax Manufacturing in Boston, speaking under anonymity" or something similar. The more choices you give the expert, the more in control she'll feel, and the more comfortable she'll be in agreeing to *some* type of attribution. Fortunately, most of the time it's not necessary to work out attribution arrangements because all you really need is your expert's expertise and knowledge.

through this ploy, but you may get more information than if you asked the question bluntly.

Keep Your Conversation "Off the Record"

Sometimes an expert source won't mind talking about controversial topics but doesn't want to be identified as the source or see his remarks in print. If you believe this is the case, assure the expert that his remarks will be kept off the record, if he so desires. Most of the time, it won't matter to you if a source speaks confidentially or not—it's the information you're after.

If under no circumstances will your source divulge certain sensitive information you need, try contacting other people who may have access to the same information.

Offensive Questions

What do you do if you have a question or remark that you think may offend the expert? First, of course, always try to phrase your questions diplomatically to avoid insulting anyone. For example, if someone tells you, "It's a scientific fact that wearing wool hats causes baldness," you can express your skepticism politely. You might say, "Why do you think there isn't more widespread support of this view?"

Here are two other strategies to keep in mind. First, if you think a question is offensive enough to potentially cut off the interview, save it for near the end. Second, use another reporter's trick: pose the question in the third person. Don't, for example, ask, "Since you have never been invited to present your research results to the scientific community, isn't your information of dubious value?" Instead say, "Some people might say that since you have never been invited . . ."

Ethical Issues in Obtaining Sensitive Information

What do you do if you need to interview someone for information but do not want to tell the person who you are or why you need it? Sometimes this happens when you want insider information on a specific firm or competitor company—and the only place to find that information is by talking to individuals who work at that company itself.

This is an issue that professional researchers who conduct competitive intelligence (CI) have often grappled with. It's a tricky issue, because it revolves around the definition of what is and what is not misrepresentation. There may be gray areas in which the researcher does not out-and-out lie but is tempted to withhold the whole truth out of fear that such disclosure would discourage the source from sharing his or her knowledge.

What should you do if faced with this type of situation? First, give some thought to the following questions and considerations:

- Have you truly exhausted all public, published sources? As outlined in the book, there are scores of government documents, computer database records, trade magazine articles, and other public information sources available just for the asking. Be sure you have thoroughly researched all these potential sources.

- If you are sure no published information exists that can answer your question, try to identify people you can interview with whom you feel comfortable revealing who you are and the purpose of your project. For example, if you need to find out facts about a company's future strategic plans, you can obtain insights by interviewing Wall Street analysts, trade magazine editors, and other experts who don't work for the company.

- If the accessible sources do not have the information you need, ask yourself how vital it really is that you find that specific piece of information. Are there related data that could be helpful? Is there peripheral information from which you can piece together a picture?

- While you might think that the only way to get a piece of highly sensitive proprietary information is to misrepresent yourself, this is not necessarily the case. Say, for example, you need information on a competitive company. You just might find that if you call the knowledgeable source, are up-front, polite, and gracious, you may get unexpected cooperation. The source may be willing to help you for any number of reasons: he or she might have questions to ask you; the person may just enjoy talking; or perhaps he or she doesn't think what you are asking is particularly sensitive—who knows? The point is, don't assume you need to deceptive. As Mark Twain said, "When in doubt . . . tell the truth." You may be pleasantly surprised by the results!

If in the final analysis you are certain that the only way to obtain the information you need is by hiding who you are or employing a questionable cover story, ask yourself first whether it will be worth the possible repercussions. Following are my arguments as to why misrepresenting yourself—or even withholding relevant information (e.g., the nature of your research project)—is *never* advisable.

Self-interest
- Unethical research activity could eventually be revealed to others. How might this affect your reputation and that of your organization?

- Unethical data-gathering activities will eventually cause organizations to become so suspicious of researchers— with good reason—that sources of information will dry up. The job of the researcher will become that much more difficult.

- If there are no standards set in this area, you and your own organization can become targets for unethical information gathering.

Personal Ethics
Take a hard look to see if any research activity you are considering will violate your own personal code of ethics. For example, most of us would not consider telephoning someone and misleading them into sending a check for $500. But today, information is as valuable a commodity as money. We would all like an extra $500, but we recognize legitimate boundaries in how we obtain it. Don't the same standards hold true for precious information? You should put yourself in the other person's shoes and ask yourself how *you* would feel

if you were the target of the action you are considering. Would you feel that you were dealt with fairly?

Finally, it is important to remember that regardless of the constraints set by ethical guidelines, excellent research can still be performed by legitimate methods and by intelligent and thoughtful analysis of data.

Chapter 9

Wrapping It Up: Organizing and Writing up Your Results and the Expert Review

You'll eventually come to the point in your interviews when it is time to start winding down your information search. But there are a number of critical steps that still need to be attended to. Here are the things you need to know.

Knowing When to Call It Quits

How do you know when you've done enough work? Here's a guideline you can use: Be aware of when you can predict how the experts are going to answer your questions. As discussed earlier, when this first occurs, it's a good time to step back and redirect your focus. But if you've redirected once or twice already, and you can't think of any new paths to pursue, it's usually a sign that you've covered your subject well and you don't have to go any further.

Another sign that it may be time to quit is that you are putting in a lot of work but not getting much new information. When you reach this point of diminishing returns, it's probably time to wrap it all up.

One other rule you may decide to use: If you are approaching a deadline and you're out of time, you may have no choice but to quit! I've found that you need to budget something along the lines of 80–85 percent of your total allotted time for research and 15–20 percent for writing up the results.

Be aware, though, that typically the very best information in a research project comes toward the very end. The reason is that as you do more and more research, you naturally learn more and more about your topic. This then allows you to better define your project's scope and better refine your questions, and you get referred to people who have increasingly more of the specific type of expertise you seek. So don't wrap things up too fast if the good stuff is just starting to roll in. It's better to have completed an excellent research project that's a little late than a mediocre one that's in right on time.

Making Sure Your Final Information Is Accurate

After you decide to end your talks with the experts, the next critical step is to make sure you've covered your subject effectively and that the information you've gathered is accurate and complete.

The first thing you should do is to think back to your early expert contacts. Did you speak with top-notch sources at that early stage but not yet know what kinds of questions to ask them? Now that your knowledge of the subject is deeper and clearer, it might be worth going back to some of those people. Write an outline of your findings. Do gaps remain? If so, consider which sources you could consult to fill them.

Another step you might take at this point is to confirm the accuracy of certain discussions. Say, for example, that you spoke with an expert but you're not quite sure you understood the person completely. Jot down your interpretation of the conversation and send it off to the source for confirmation.

The next step is critical to the completion of the talking-to-the-experts process and making it really work. This is the expert review procedure, and it works as follows. If you are writing up your results, write a draft. If you are not writing up your results, write a rough draft anyway. Now go back and review all the different experts you've spoken with during the course of your information interviews. Select one or two who were especially knowledgeable and helpful— your very best sources. Get in touch with these people again and ask them to review your work for accuracy. Tell them that all their comments, suggestions, and criticisms are welcome. Be sure to tell the reviewers that they have indeed been specially selected. Ninety-five percent of the time these people will be flattered that you've singled them out, and they will be more than happy to take the time to read your draft. By all means insert questions in your draft noting points or conclusions you aren't completely sure of.

If you are going to write up your results, you will be acknowledging the assistance of your expert reviewers in the work; let them know you plan to do this.

Your reviewers will almost never ask for a fee to review your draft. A big reason for this is that you have been very selective in your choice of reviewers. You'll find that in any information-finding project you will always hit it off with at least a couple of experts along the way. The process is such that about 10–15 percent of the people you talk to will not be particularly helpful or knowledgeable, 60–70 percent will be quite helpful and provide you with very good information, and 10–15 percent will provide superb assistance. There is always that percentage of extra-nice experts who go out of their way to help you in any way they can. These are the people you get in touch with again to request a review.

I usually look for two or three reviewers, each with a different perspective. For example, after I wrote a report on the topic of microcomputers, I sent one draft to a computer programmer, another to a consultant, and a third to a vendor. If you know of an expert who specializes in only one aspect of your study, you can send him just that particular section of your work, but it's also useful to have at least one reviewer read and comment on the entire text. This sort of big picture review can help you avoid blind spots that reviewers of discrete sections will never notice.

There are two basic ways you can carry out the review process. One is to email the draft to your reviewers and ask them to mark it up and send it back to you. That's okay, but I prefer another approach. I recommend that you email the draft and ask reviewers to read it and mark it with comments, then *get on the telephone* with each of them, with a copy of your draft in front of you, and go over the draft page-by-page with the expert. This way you can ask the reviewers questions about any of their points that you don't understand, while also clarifying anything in your coverage that they may have questions about.

In essence, this expert review is completing the circle—the experts are now reviewing the expert information you've gathered. At this point, if you've done a thorough job, you're likely to feel like something of an expert yourself.

Note Taking and Organization

As mentioned previously, whenever you consult a written source of information or talk to an expert you'll want to take notes and keep your information organized. There are naturally many different approaches you could take to organizing information. I've found that the following method, while it may sound old fashioned, works quite well for the purpose of organizing a lot of unfamiliar information gathered from a multitude of sources.

Get a pad of paper, or open a blank page in your word processing program, and for the first batch of published information sources you consult (say, five to eight) write your notes in the pad or document, clearly marking at the top of each page the name of the source, where it can be found, and the pages consulted. After you've finished with this first batch, you should be knowledgeable enough to be able to define the key subtopic categories within your subject and fit all future information you collect—from both published sources and your talks with experts—into the categories you've established.

For example, let's say I'm trying to find out everything I can about the sport of ballooning, and, after reading and taking notes on a number of relevant articles, I've identified fifteen critical subtopics within the subject. These might include "purchasing a balloon," "setting up a balloon," "safety considerations," "fuel," and so on. My next step is to get a stack of index cards and write each subtopic on top of a different card. Then I'll go back to my pad and copy notes onto the appropriate index card. If one sheet of the pad contains notes about a number of subtopics (fuel, safety, etc.), but drawn from one source, I'll break up those notes into the relevant categories and copy them onto the appropriate cards. This will eventually result in my having a stack of cards, each containing information about only one subtopic, but gathered from a variety of information sources. In theory, all my future notes will fit into one of these categories.

As you continue to uncover information and become more knowledgeable about your subject, you may find that you'll need to modify the categories you originally created. Some subtopics may prove to be very minor and can be incorporated into a larger category. Or there may be additional categories to add as new topics arise that you hadn't considered early on.

This method of arranging information by subject, rather than by source, will make the final organizational steps simple. You can just shuffle the index cards until you're satisfied that the subtopics are arranged in a logical order. Whether you are planning to write up your results or make an oral presentation, you'll have an outline that's ready to use.

You may find it convenient to continue to take your initial notes on the large pad of paper even after you've created your index card categories. That's fine. Just be sure to copy the notes on the appropriate cards later.

As you can see, I'm pretty traditional when it comes to note taking; I still find shuffling pieces of paper and cards to be a convenient way to sort and organize notes. Of course, there are a wide range of digital note-taking products you can employ. A popular one among librarians and researchers is Evernote.

Writing Up Your Results

Here are some pointers to keep in mind if you plan to formally write up the results of your information search.

Sort the Gems from the Junk

As you read through all the notes you've taken—notes from magazine articles, government reports, talks with experts, and all the other sources you've consulted—you'll need to decide which pieces of information should be included in your report. How do you separate the valuable from the not so valuable? How do you decide which facts are important and which are useless?

Although this is a common concern among first-time information seekers, if you've done a thorough job in your search, you will understand the subject well enough at this point to know which information is important and which is not, relatively speaking. The following three guidelines may also come in handy:

- Pay particular attention to the information you've gathered and the notes you've taken during the last 10–20 percent of your project. As I've said before, the best information usually comes toward the end of a project, and you'll want to make sure that this information receives the highest priority when finalizing the scope, focus, and conclusions of your work.

- A critical question you'll need to ask about any piece of information is whether it is *relevant* to your investigation. Does it add value, shed new light, suggest a trend, or provide background on your subject? If a given piece of information does not advance your specific goals for the project, or fall within its topical focus, it should not be included no matter how interesting it may be.

- When evaluating your information, think about who provided it. Was it from a source you considered reliable or did it come from a biased or otherwise suspect source?

Be Complete

When you write up your results, don't leave the reader hanging. It's very important to fully explain your points clearly, preferably with concrete examples. A statement such as "the Model W skis are the best because they meet all important criteria" will only be helpful if you explain what the important criteria are. Anticipate the questions your statements will elicit from a reader, then do your best to address them.

Make Conclusions

A common question among beginning information gatherers is whether it is appropriate to state your personal opinion or make conclusions on a controversial issue. Let's say you've just spent three months learning all about the racquetball industry. You've spoken to club owners, association executives, sports columnists, and equipment manufacturers. You've read articles in leading trade publications and in the general press. As you read over your information, you begin to recognize that all indicators point to an imminent drop in the popularity of the sport. Are you qualified to state such a conclusion?

In most cases, I would definitely say *yes*—with a couple of small cautions. If you've done a thorough job digging out information on your subject, you are certainly justified in drawing conclusions and stating them. If you realize that the facts point to certain trends or add up to certain conclusions, you should state those conclusions.

In fact, findings like these are among the most important things that can come out of your research projects.

Now, although you can draw broad conclusions, it's best to quote the experts on factual data and opinions. Let's say you are doing a study on the fight against some rare disease. A statement in your report such as "this disease is not at all contagious" should be attributed to a particular expert, or at least preceded by words such as "according to experts I spoke with . . . ."

In any information-finding project, you are certainly permitted to step back, look at the big picture, and give your opinion. You should then indicate in some manner, however, that this is *your* conclusion. In the racquetball case, you could phrase your statement along these lines: "After investigating the industry and speaking with numerous experts in the field, this author believes the game will soon be decreasing in popularity. The major reasons for this, I've concluded, are . . ."

What do you do when there are strong arguments and evidence on both sides of an issue and you're not sure who is correct? I recently had to gather up two different perspectives on genetically modified organisms (GMOs). There were two distinctly opposing viewpoints: some political and organic-oriented groups were convinced of their dangers, while some scientists and investigative journalists claimed there was little or no proof of any health risk.

It was not totally clear—to me, at least—what the "answer" was regarding the safety of GMOs, at least at that point in my research. So in this case I would present the arguments of both sides as clearly as possible and leave it to readers to draw their own conclusions.

In many information searches you'll run into these kinds of gray areas; you'll want a simple answer, but there won't be one. That's okay. Just present the facts as you know them.

Whenever you write about a controversial or sensitive issue, be sure to ask yourself whether you are being fair. Fairness is pretty tough to judge, but I think the *Washington Post Deskbook on Style* defines it well. According to the book's editors, being fair includes the following:

- **Search for opposing views.** In other words, don't be lazy and accept the first opinion you hear. Get both sides of the story.

- **Be complete.** Don't omit facts of major importance. Otherwise, your reader will be misled.

- **Be relevant.** Unnecessary information will cloud an issue.

- **Be honest.**

To Quote or Not to Quote

People often wonder when it's necessary to attribute information to an expert or a written source and when it's acceptable to use the information without attribution. Although one wit claimed that "to steal ideas from one person is plagiarism; to steal from many is research,"[1] the general rule is that when you use somebody's idea or work, you must attribute it to that source. However, if somebody provides facts or general information that can be obtained from many sources (e.g., Death Valley, California, has the highest recorded temperature in the United States), it is not necessary to provide attribution.

What about obtaining permission to quote the experts you've interviewed? If you are writing a very sensitive piece, you can play it safe and specifically ask each expert for permission in writing, but normally it's not necessary. As long as you've identified yourself to the expert, explained that you are writing an article or a report, and made no off-the-record agreements, the expert should realize that you may use his or her remarks for publication.

Another common question regards obtaining permission to excerpt or quote published information. The general rule is that you may make what is called "fair use" of published materials without seeking permission. In general, fair use allows you to quote a few lines of a short article or a couple of paragraphs of a longer piece or book *with attribution* and without getting permission from the author or publisher. If you want to use more than this, you should send a letter to the copyright holder explaining precisely what information you want to use, where it is located, and why you want to use it. The great majority of the time, a publisher will *not* charge you for the use of the material but will require that you print a specific credit line. The publisher may also require you to send it a copy of the final work.

These general rules can help, but every case is different. Always use common sense, and, if you have any doubt at all about the need to attribute information or obtain permission to use it, err on the side of caution.

Meantime, if you run across a publisher that's unwilling to grant you permission to excerpt or republish its content, try to track down the author. If you can arrange to interview him or her, the same expertise that went into the published content will be made available to you without a hassle.

Libel is a much more complicated matter and a full discussion of the topic is beyond the scope of this book. It's worth noting, however, a concise definition that was published in the *Washington Post Deskbook on Style*: "Basically, a libelous statement is a published statement that injures a person (or organization or corporation) in his trade, profession, or community standing." Although traditional defenses against a libel charge have included "truth" (i.e., the information published was accurate) and "reasonable care" (on the part of the writer), it is impossible to generalize about this topic. The *Post* advises writers to again consider simply whether they are being fair. Did you give the party a chance to respond?

One final point. *Always* show your appreciation to the experts you speak with. If you can think of any way to help them or return the favor, offer it. And, if someone ever comes to you with an information request, remember how much you appreciated the experts who took the time to help you, and pay it forward if you can.

Note

1. Arthur Bloch, *Murphy's Law Book 3* (Los Angeles: Price Stern, 1982), p. 50.

Chapter 10

Troubleshooting: Typical Questions Information Seekers Ask

Some typical questions and comments I hear from researchers undertaking an information-finding project follow. Some of this will reiterate points we've already covered.

How do I know where to begin my information search?

There is rarely any single *perfect* place to begin your research. The Researcher's Road Map in this chapter should help you get started. The key is to get started on your research and begin learning about your subject. As you begin to gather information and understand your topic, this question will become irrelevant.

How do I know whether to use print sources or go online when starting my research?

It doesn't matter too much, though these days it seems that virtually all research can begin online. The basic rule of research stays the same, though: start off with basic sources and build up your knowledge gradually. Whether you choose print or electronic, your initial sources should be nontechnical and geared for the popular user.

I know that there must be some information on the topic, but I can't find anything!

It's extremely doubtful that *no* information whatsoever exists on your topic—especially in the age of the internet. One possible cause for not finding anything is that you may be unaware of the standard terminology used in a particular subject. For example, say you were researching the topic of "static electricity"—you would need to know that "electrostatics" is the standard scientific term for the phenomenon and that all indexes and materials will categorize the topic under that heading. Also, make sure you check as many sources as possible before you conclude there is nothing available on your subject. If you still cannot find anything, look up related or broader subjects. In the rare instance in which there is truly nothing written on your subject, it could mean you are onto something interesting, and the results of your research could add to the body of knowledge.

I've found some articles on my subject, but I can't understand them.

Don't worry. Continue researching the topic and look for articles written for a more general audience. If you can't find any, try finding a description in an introductory textbook or encyclopedia.

I'd like to call some experts, but I'm apprehensive about initiating contact.

You are certainly not alone! Just about every researcher is uncomfortable calling a complete stranger for information the first time. But think about it—you've got nothing to lose. Chances are the person is going to help you out, and if worse comes to worse and the conversation doesn't work out, you can always say "thanks for your time" and hang up. It took me almost two years of talking to experts before I felt really relaxed before making these kinds of calls, so don't be too hard on yourself.

I can never get hold of these experts—either they are out or they don't return my calls!

It's not that you can't get hold of them, it's just that you haven't made enough calls! The process of reaching experts is, to a great extent, a numbers game—call enough people and you will always reach at least a certain percentage. It's a time-consuming process, but it works! If the person is very busy, though, try calling her office, asking for an email address, and sending your queries that way. This makes it unnecessary for her to be available when you call and also allows her to respond when she has the time for it. Review the section in Chapter 7 on "Making the Connection."

I got the expert on the phone, but he talked so fast I don't think I got it all down.

Don't worry. Note taking is a skill, and you will improve with practice. After you speak with a number of people, you'll intuitively know how to capture the key points. And it really does help to read over your notes *immediately* after the conversation, so you can fill in gaps while the details are still fresh in your mind. If it looks like you missed something critical, call the person back to go over those issues again.

How do I know when to stop doing research?

There is no perfect time, but when you feel you can predict the experts' answers, have reassessed the direction of your project, and are expending a lot of research time but getting little new information, it's probably time to start wrapping things up. You can try writing a draft of your findings to see if there are gaps remaining that require additional research.

Help! I think I may have collected too much information! I'm swamped with articles, notes, and other data!

If you're overloaded with too many hits from a search engine, see the strategies I provided in Chapter 3. If it's just too much information on your topic in general that you've collected, your problem is probably not too much information, but not enough organization. Start going through your notes and begin categorizing each piece of information under a topic subheading; transcribe all related facts under each heading. This will make your big stack of information more manageable. Get rid of information that, although interesting, doesn't directly relate to the scope of your project or advance its mission.

I have conflicting information in my notes. How do I know whom to believe?

This is common—there is often more than one opinion on a subject. See Chapter 5 on evaluating information sources. Sometimes you may simply have to present both points of view and allow the reader to decide which to believe.

I really enjoy doing this kind of research. How can I find out about careers in this field?

I've been asked this question many times. There are a number of different careers that involve digging up and analyzing information, the most obvious and well-known of which is library science. Ex-librarians among others have started information brokerages or consulting businesses, selling their research skills to businesses and organizations for a fee. Other careers that involve a lot of research include certain types of journalism (such as investigative journalism), private investigator services, new business or product development, and market research.

After reading *Find It Fast*, you may feel overwhelmed by the sheer number of resources, strategies, and techniques it covers. Whatever you do, don't try to memorize the book. Just take a look at the Researcher's Road Map that follows to get a feel for the entire process, start some research at one of the "easy start" sources identified in Chapter 1, then go with the flow and consult the book for help if you run into problems. And remember the basics:

- The information you seek is almost certainly available for the asking.

- There are experts around who will talk to you and answer your questions.

A Researcher's Road Map: Project Planning and Source Selection

It can be confusing and difficult to know what type of source is best to use for what kind of research. This is a complicated matter, and there is no perfect solution. However, the following sections present two ways to make these decisions easier. "Project Planning" offers a step-by-step strategy for approaching a research project, and "Source Selection" presents what I see as the unique strengths of the major print, electronic, and other sources described in this book.

Project Planning

Although every information-finding project is different, in most cases the process of learning about a new subject follows a similar path. The trick is to build your knowledge of the subject by first using nontechnical sources and gradually proceeding to more advanced and technical ones. Any information-finding project I undertake generally goes through six steps, as shown in the table. While in practice these steps will overlap, I've found it useful to keep them in mind separately when planning my investigations.

1) **Define your problem**	Break your project down into its component parts. Determine why you need the information and what you plan to do with it. This will make your information search clearer to you and easier to conduct.
2) **Locate basic sources**	Unless you already have a strong familiarity with your topic, you'll want to obtain definitions and learn basic concepts. The best information sources to consult at this early stage are nontechnical ones that explain concepts and terminology in a clear and jargon-free manner. Sources can include periodicals geared to general audiences, reports published by the government for public consumption, Wikipedia entries, and consumer literature from product manufacturers.
3) **Obtain technical sources**	Now that you grasp the basics, you're ready to seek out more specialized information by digging into more technical material. Sources to check at this point can include trade publications, research center reports, and transcripts of conference presentations.
4) **Make a list of contacts and questions, then interview the experts**	When you've gotten all the information you can from published material, you'll want to begin contacting experts in order to fill in the blanks. During the course of your research and reading you will have been creating a list of experts; now, with your questions well defined, begin your outreach.
5) **Redirect focus and evaluate progress**	Now is the time to step back and review your progress. Compare what you've actually learned with what you decided you wanted to learn in Step 1. Make adjustments or redirect your focus, if necessary. Go back to earlier steps to fill in gaps, if needed.
6) **Write a draft and get expert review**	Get one or more experts to review your work for accuracy. Don't neglect this very important step.

Table   Six Steps for Project Planning

TIP: Talk to Your Authors!
When reading articles on your topic, conduct an imaginary dialogue with the authors—in other words, if what you read prompts a question, make a note of it. If you agree with something, note it; if you disagree, say why. This silent dialoguing and questioning spurs you to advance the authors' arguments and brings you to the next, higher level of discussion.

Source Selection

The list that follows is designed to highlight the special strengths and potential drawbacks of the major types of information sources discussed in the book. It can be useful for short projects or quick-answer research, when you don't need to consult many sources and are only looking for one or two to check.

Print Sources

Textbooks: Provide basic definitions and clarify terms. Useful for obtaining a basic understanding of complex matters—especially at the beginning of a research project. Drawbacks include a possible time lag in reporting news and movements in the field.

Reference Books: Statistical data, definitions, numerical data, and basic facts.

Nonfiction Books: In-depth coverage of a particular topic. Useful for obtaining a deeper understanding of complex topics. Drawbacks include length of time needed to get through and absorb an entire book during a fast-moving research project.

Directories: Lists, rankings, compilations, and addresses. Good for finding overviews, snapshots, and contact information for companies, magazines, products, etc. Drawbacks include the short life span of most directory data (use the most recent edition available).

Newspaper Articles: Coverage of events of local significance not covered elsewhere, with citations from experts; usually written in nontechnical manner. Drawbacks include occasional superficial coverage of complex topics.

Magazine and Journal Articles: More depth than newspapers. Best overall general research source. Also readily available electronically, which provides the advantage of searchability.

There are three major categories of magazine and journal articles: popular, trade, and scholarly. Popular magazines include those you would find on a newsstand, that appeal to the widest audience. Trade magazines are more specialized and are usually targeted to those working in a particular field or who have a special interest. Scholarly journals are typically written by professors and academics for other professors and academics. Although all these types of periodicals can be useful for researchers, trade magazines often balance depth of coverage with maintaining accessibility to the layperson.

Another category of print periodicals is the newsletter, which often provide highly-focused discussion and analysis of news and events in specific markets and industries. These are "insider" sources that specialize in practitioner-oriented coverage of the latest and most significant developments in the field. They are often quite expensive and are not as commonly found in libraries as other types of periodicals.

Electronic Sources

Professional Online: Sophisticated, powerful search capabilities; massive databases. Best for highly targeted searches of major and leading popular, trade, and scholarly literature, as well as government data and other highly focused, data intensive sources, including newsletters. Drawbacks include more complex search commands and occasional narrow coverage, and the lack of full text from certain journals.

TIP: Identify Keywords and Terminologies to Allow for More Precise Searching

As you are reading about your topic, note the key words and phrases that pop up. For example, if you are studying how businesses prepare for the future, you may discover such key phrases in the materials you've gathered as "forecasting," "strategic planning," and "anticipatory management." Use the keywords you come across to improve your search results.

Online Discussion Groups, Forums, Blogs: Excellent for locating experts and enthusiasts, up-to-the-minute developments in a field, and anecdotal reports. Drawbacks include a high noise-to-signal ratio and the tricky nature of evaluating the credibility of anecdotal reports.

Other Key Sources

Government and University Research: Free or inexpensive access to in-depth studies, often relating to issues in science, technology, or matters of public policy. Drawbacks can include difficulty finding what you need and the age of the study.

Associations: Free or inexpensive access to industry surveys, news, and overviews, as well as potential referrals to experts. Drawbacks include possible bias on the part of association personnel in favor of their membership demographic.

Experts: Customized, up-to-the-minute, live information. Drawbacks include the need to assess the expert's knowledge, credibility, and potential biases.

Which of the many information sources that we've considered will be best for *your* project? Unfortunately, it's almost impossible to know for certain which sources will turn out to be the most fruitful for a specific information-finding project until you begin digging in. In one case you may find that your best sources are research centers and museums; in another, a specialized bookstore and a trade magazine; and for other projects, a general internet search. The only way to know whether a particular source is going to pay off for a particular search is to try it. Look for as many relevant sources as possible—library resources, "supersources," federal government sources, business information sources (if appropriate), and, finally, the experts themselves—until you feel you've found what you're looking for.

This is not to say that you cannot make some educated guesses and choose sources that seem more likely to pay off. For example, if you need information on some very timely matter, it would likely be covered in a newspaper, wire service, or magazine; information on a more obscure scientific matter might be found at a laboratory, research center, or university. Similarly, a public-policy or consumer-oriented issue is likely to be covered somewhere in the federal government; an art-related issue covered at a museum, or perhaps a university; and so on. So you don't really have to fly blind. Read the descriptions of the sources in *Find It Fast* and use your best judgment to try to zero in on the ones that are most likely to cover your subject.

Appendix A

Digital Forensic Tools

There is a wide range of free, open-source social media verification tools available on the web to help users determine the accuracy, credibility, and origin of some consumer-generated data, or to perform other analysis and examination tasks to better verify unknown content. These sites and tools vary in several ways: what type of content the tool is designed to evaluate (tweets, web text, web images, JPEGs from cameras, videos, etc.); what it verifies (origin, composite, modified retweets, likelihood of accuracy, etc.); methodology employed (examines keywords and metadata, analyzes geo-location, compares to existing database of content, uses crowdsourcing input, performs statistical analyses, etc.) and what kind of information is provided to the user (if the content is an original, a duplicate, modified from an original, similar to content on web). Some also offer special or unique features such as the ability to compare content directly with another version to highlight differences, the creation of trust ratings, and so on.

If you decide to try one of these tools, you should keep in mind that most are experimental and should be considered works in progress. My own view is that while these tools are good for locating existing similar text and images, one should be skeptical of their current and near-term possibility to do more subtle credibility analyses. But this is a very fast-moving area, with a good deal of research money and support, and you can expect to see some enhancements and improvements in this area in the near future.

Here are some of the best-known digital forensic and verification tools and sites currently available.

CheckDesk: checkdesk.org/
   Employs journalists and sources to fact-check unverified reports; geared for journalists

Churnalism: churnalism.sunlightfoundation.com/
  Compares entered text to a large collection of press releases
Findexif.com
  Reveals EXIF information from digital cameras to determine
    origin of photographs
FotoForensics: fotoforensics.com
  Uses error level analysis (ELA) to examine whether parts of an
    image have been altered
Free OCR: free-ocr.com
  Extracts text from images
Geofeedia: geofeedia.com
  Free tool for location-based social media monitoring
GeoSocial Footprint: geosocialfootprint.com
  Tracks a user's location by combining user signals such as GPS-
    enabled tweets, social check-ins, geocoding, and profile har-
    vesting and provides a privacy warning to users if they can be
    tracked via their location data.
Izitru: izitru.com
  Examines metadata from camera JPEGs to verify if original;
    assigns trust ratings
Open Newsroom: plus.google.com/communities/1183071755019
87556985
  Storyful's open-source community on Google+ where journalists
    discuss the validity of breaking news
TinEye: tineye.com
  Uses image-identification technologies to determine the origin
    of an image and how it is being used

You can also keep up with newly appearing tools by linking to a
site called VerificationJunkie, which regularly updates new verification sites, sources, and tools.

Sources of Further Information

The following is a selected listing of my favorite books, magazines, journals, and associations that can assist you in learning more about research, finding information, and seeking knowledge in the digital age.

Books

General Research and Information-Finding Techniques

The following books are excellent basic texts for obtaining fundamental research skills.

Barzun, Jacques, and Henry F. Graff. *The Modern Researcher*, 6th ed. (Cengage, 2003). A classic book on the art of conducting research, including an analysis of the researcher's "virtues." Provides great food for thought on the problems, dilemmas, and challenges in the researcher's quest for truth.

Booth, Wayne C., Gregory C. Columb, and Joseph M. Williams. *The Craft of Research*, 3rd ed. (University of Chicago Press, 2008). A very thorough and detailed approach to conducting a research project. Topics covered include asking questions, reading critically, making good arguments, claims and evidence, drafting a report, communicating evidence visually, research ethics and more.

Brady, John. *The Craft of Interviewing* (Random House, 1977). Another classic—this one on how to conduct an interview. Aimed especially at journalists, this book provides strategies, tips, and advice on how to reach sources and then get them to cooperate with you.

Knowledge and Strategy

A wealth of excellent books are available that explain not just how to find information but also why information is important, particularly as a strategic asset in organizations. This discipline was once known as knowledge management, but with the rise of Web 2.0 and social media tools, today it is more likely categorized under the umbrella of social business or social enterprise.

Bernoff, Josh, and Charlene Li. *GroundSwell: Winning in a World Transformed by Social Technologies* (Harvard Business School Press, 2008). Li made a name for herself as a sought-after analyst on the internet and social media at Forrester Research, and she has been one of the most prominent analysts on the impact of social media on business. Here she and her co-author provide their take on what social media means for marketers, PR professionals, brand managers, and other businesspeople who have a stake in what the public thinks and says about their firm and its products.

Choo, Wun Chei. *The Knowing Organization: How Organizations Use Information to Construct Meaning, Create Knowledge, and Make Decisions*, 2nd ed. (Oxford University Press, 2005). According to Choo, a "knowing organization" possesses information and knowledge so that it is well-informed, mentally perceptive, and enlightened. Choo has written several outstanding books on information, knowledge, and organizations. He is particularly adept at looking at the nitty-gritty of the nature and strategic value of facts, insights, data, and knowledge from an information- and library-oriented focus.

Notter, Jamie, and Maddie Grant. *Humanize: How People-Centric Organizations Succeed in a Social World* (Que, 2011). This wonderful book explores how successful businesses are integrating social media tools and practices into their organizations—not only for enhancing efficiency and streamlining processes but also for enhancing employee morale and creating a more humane workforce.

Social Concerns and Technology Critiques

Along with the benefits that technology and the internet have brought all of us, there is, of course, a downside—the "Faustian bargain" that, as the late educator Neil Postman often reminded us, we all make with any new technology. The following works include both personal favorites and a selection of scholarly and probing works by some of the most respected technology analysts and social critics.

Birkerts, Sven. *The Gutenberg Elegies: The Fate of Reading in an Electronic Age* (Fawcett, 1995; paperback reissue with new introduction and afterword, 2006). Birkerts was one of the first widely published critics of life in a wired world. In this book he examines what will be lost in a culture where the printed word is replaced by electronic and virtual communications.

Carr, Nicholas. *The Shallows: What the Internet Is Doing to Our Brains* (W.W. Norton, 2011). Perhaps best known for his *Atlantic* magazine cover story "Is Google Making us Stupid?" Carr expands on his exploration of what digital information and the internet are doing to our brains and our ability to pay attention for long periods. It's filled with the latest scientific research and his own analysis of the impact, on young people and the rest of us, of spending so much time with short bursts of digital data.

Fuller, Jack. *What Is Happening to the News: The Information Explosion and the Crisis in Journalism* (University of Chicago Press, 2010). While this book is geared specifically for journalists, its fascinating premise and argument are relevant for any kind of researcher. Fuller looks to biology and evolution to explain why our brains are attracted to short, stimulating bits of information, and explores the implications for journalists and anyone who delivers information to a larger audience.

McChesney, Robert. *Digital Disconnect: How Capitalism Is Turning the Internet against Democracy* (New Press, 2013). McChesney is a prominent and respected professor known for his probing critiques of the media and capitalism. In this book he turns his attention to the internet and makes the argument that, rather than becoming the much-promised utopia for democratic discourse, the internet has instead been subject to the unrelenting forces of capitalism, and as a result has become a haven for commercialism, monopolies, and subsidies for the largest corporations.

Montgomery, Kathryn. *Generation Digital* (MIT Press, 2007). Montgomery, a professor in the School of Communication at American University in Washington, D.C., looks at how the younger generation uses communication and information technologies and how businesses are targeting young people as a new market. The book is authoritative, well researched, and scholarly, but still accessible to the lay reader.

Pariser, Eli. *The Filter Bubble: How the New Personalized Web Is Changing What We Read and How We Think* (Penguin, 2011). An important exploration of what happens when the internet becomes *too* personalized and search engines eliminate results that they deem irrelevant based on our profile, web search history, and other pre-existing assumptions about who we are and what we want to see online. Pariser outlines what we miss in an increasingly personalized digital world.

Postman, Neil. *Technopoly: The Surrender of Culture to a Technology* (Vintage, 1993). Postman is my favorite critic and author and I never fail to gain countless insights from his books. He had a penetrating mind and was a crystal-clear thinker, with a great wit and sense of humor. Because Postman was a longtime critic of technology, he is sometimes called a grouch or curmudgeon. But that's a misreading of his views and works. Postman's goal was simply to make sure we stop and think about what we are doing and that we do not march blindly and unthinkingly into a future that may have undesirable and unanticipated consequences. *Technopoly* was his primary work on the role of technology in society. He wrote several other outstanding and best-selling books, such as *The Disappearance of Childhood*, *The End of Education*, a series of essays in *Conscientious Objections*, and, his best-known work, a critique of television titled *Amusing Ourselves to Death*.

Media scholar and Fordham University professor Lance Strate, a former PhD student of Postman's, applied Postman's critiques to the current digital information age in a book called *Amazing Ourselves to Death: Neil Postman's Brave New World Revisited* (Peter Lang, 2013). The book also serves as a historical review of the media ecology discipline (media ecology examines the impact and relationship of media on society and culture) and offers a biographical overview of Postman's life and career. It's an excellent book that I highly recommend to anyone wanting a scholarly yet very readable speculation on what Postman would say (and what Strate does say) about the social media world we live in now.

Solove, Daniel. *The Future of Reputation: Gossip, Rumor, and Privacy on the Internet* (Yale, 2007). Solve is an extremely clear and knowledgeable writer. This book looks at how new ways of sharing what was once considered personal and private information are causing novel dilemmas and creating new social norms.

Internet and Social Media Verification Handbooks

As discussed in Chapter 5, the rise in social media has caused many in journalism, library science, political science, and other information-intensive fields to search for new ways to better verify the origin of socially generated news, videos, and other content. The two works that follow provide excellent strategies, tips, and sources for getting that job done.

Nieman Reports, *Truth in the Age of Social Media*, Summer 2012. Nieman Reports is the publication of the Harvard-based Nieman Foundation, which has the mission to "promote and elevate the standards of journalism." This special issue, available free online (http://niemanreports.org/issues/summer-2012/), contains several articles from editors and managers at news outlets such as CNN, AP, and BBC, on how they approach the verification of social media, citizen reporting, and other new forms of information. I highly recommend it for learning the latest methods that leading journalists are employing today to verify facts and information, ranging from crowdsourcing to the use of forensic analysis tools.

Silverman, Craig, ed. *The Verification Handbook*. Similar in mission to the above title, and edited by Poynter Institute's Craig Silverman, this guide is also free on the web (http://verificationhandbook .com/book/) and is a bit more of a practical verification tool and technique guide, with a special focus on helping emergency aid workers ferret out accurate data. The publication was sponsored by the European Journalism Centre, located in Maastricht, the Netherlands.

Digital Age and Culture Guides and Analyses

The following books are not so much social or cultural critiques, but rather are designed to teach readers how the digital age works and how to get the most out of the current information environment.

Baker, Stephen. *The Numerati* (Houghton Mifflin Harcourt, 2008). Stephen Baker is a reporter at *Business Week* magazine. His book looks at the increasing role and power of numbers in today's web world. *The Numerati* explores how web analytics, metrics, search statistics, internet user behavior measurements, and other analyses of quantitative data are being deployed to increase the capabilities of marketers and others who gather digital data for their own uses.

Blossom, John. *Content Nation: Surviving and Thriving as Social Media Changes Our Work, Our Lives, and Our Future* (Wiley, 2009). In this book, Blossom, founder and CEO of the information consulting firm and publisher Shore Communications, Inc., discusses what social media means for the larger culture, the publishing industry, politics, the media, and business.

Caldarelli, Guido, and Michele Catanzaro. *Networks: A Very Short Introduction* (Oxford University Press, 2013). A succinct, powerful, and scholarly review and explanation of the meaning and power of networks and network behavior, ranging from kinship networks to viral networks, and of course the type of network that's gotten the most popular attention: social networks.

Morville, Peter. *Ambient Findability: How What We Find Changes Who We Become* (O'Reilly, 2006). Morville was one of the first to examine the implications of a fully searchable world, or what has now come to be called the "Internet of Things"—the ability to find almost any object, anywhere and anytime.

Rheingold, Howard. *Net Smart: How to Thrive Online* (MIT Press, 2012). Rheingold has been writing and speaking as an internet and digital advocate for decades. Perhaps his best-known works are *Virtual Communities*, in which he explored what it means to build and be part of a community based on shared interests, and *Smart Mobs*, which demonstrates how collective action works online. *Net Smart* is one of the best treatments of what it means to live in the digital and social age, including a great chapter called "Crap Detection." The book reflects Rheingold's evolution from a *full steam ahead* digital proponent to his now more cautious, perhaps seasoned approach to being a smarter internet user and avoiding some of its pitfalls.

Shirky, Clay. *Here Comes Everybody: The Power of Organizing Without Organizations* (Penguin Press, 2009). Shirky is a professor and highly sought after speaker and consultant on the power of the internet. As examined in Chapter 5 of this book, his groundbreaking book explained how social media and the internet are allowing informal groups to form and collaborate to make a difference in virtually all parts of society. A must read.

Silver, Nate. *The Signal and the Noise: Why So Many Predictions Fail—But Some Don't* (Penguin Press, 2012). Statistician Nate Silver became something of a celebrity after correctly predicting the winner of 49 of the 50 states in the 2008 election by applying Bayesian probability theory and other strategies outlined in his book. It serves as an excellent introduction the proper use of data, information, possibilities, and probabilities in the service of distinguishing meaningful patterns from all the noise.

Suber, Peter. *Open Access* (MIT Press, 2012). A clear, informative, and enlightening examination of what open access is, what it is not, and how this movement to make more scholarly information freely available is important to researchers and culture at large.

Van Dijk, José. *The Culture of Connectivity: A Critical History of Social Media* (Oxford, 2013). I use this book as the primary text at the School of Media Studies at The New School for Public Engagement in New York City, where I teach an online masters course in social media. It's the most in-depth analysis and unpacking of the hidden and embedded assumptions, methods, and workings of social media and popular social networks I've come across.

Weinberger, David. *Too Big to Know: Rethinking Knowledge Now That the Facts Aren't the Facts, Experts Are Everywhere, and the Smartest Person in the Room Is the Room* (Basic Books, 2012). Weinberger is a clear and lucid thinker and writer on all things internet and digital. This book examines how our sources of knowledge and expertise are now embedded in the network, and what this means for business, science, education, and technology.

Weinberger, David. *Everything Is Miscellaneous: The Power of the New Digital Disorder* (Holt, 2008). Before the digital world, libraries and other entities that needed to keep track of information and knowledge needed to have one category in which to store each "object" for easy retrieval. In the digital age, there is no need to store a single copy, so there is no longer a need to create a single category. Information sources and other digital "objects," ranging from ebooks to an expert's webpage to a social movement discussion group, can be categorized in many ways, which helps people find them easily and form online communities around them. Weinberger deftly and compelling explores the profound consequences of this change in how we now find, use, and share information.

Magazines, Journals, and Newsletters

Most publications that focus on research and online searching are geared toward librarians and other information professionals. I founded *The Information Advisor* in 1988 for business research professionals, and remain co-editor for *The Information Advisor's Guide to Internet Research*, which provides sources and strategies for business, legal, academic, and other research professionals. The journal is published by Information Today, Inc. (also the publisher of this book), which publishes other print and digital magazines and journals for the information industry, such as *Online Searcher*, *Online*, *Computers in Libraries*, and more.

For those of you more theoretically inclined, I'd recommend *Explorations in Media Ecology (EME)*, an international journal dedicated to extending the understanding of media and media environments. It's published by The Media Ecology Association, whose mission is "promoting the study, research, criticism, and application of media ecology in educational, industry, political, civic, social, cultural, and artistic contexts, and the open exchange of ideas, information, and research among the Association's members and the larger community."

Finally, there are a handful of popular magazines that regularly publish insightful articles on the internet, the digital age, and notable information and communication technologies. My favorites include *The Atlantic*, *The Economist*, *The New Yorker*, *Salon*, *Slate*, and *Wired*. For radio fans, I'd highly recommend NPR's show *On the Media*.

Professional Associations

If you are really interested in learning more about research and information gathering, you should contact one or more of the following organizations. In addition to their regular member services, all publish various resources and hold regular conferences.

Association of Independent Information Professionals (AIIP) This organization's membership consists of independent information professionals (sometimes called "information brokers") who make their living doing offline and online information searches and in-depth research for a fee. This would be the group to turn to if you are interested in learning how to start your own information research and consulting firm.

Investigative Reporters and Editors (IRE) This organization is an excellent resource for learning how to gather information, interview sources, and perform online research. It publishes guides and puts on seminars and workshops to teach sources and strategies for uncovering a wide range of hard-to-find information.

Special Libraries Association (SLA) A leading and highly respected professional organization of librarians and information professionals who work in corporations, technical organizations, and various institutions outside the traditional public library. The SLA publishes regularly and puts on national and regional conferences.

Association of Internet Researchers (AOIR) A more scholarly and theoretical group, AOIR is a cross-disciplinary organization that promotes critical and scholarly internet research. It publishes conference papers, special issues, runs a listserv discussion, and holds annual conferences.

University Programs, Workshops, and Courses

If you are really serious about learning more about information, technology, research, and emerging forms of digital knowledge, you can get a degree in a related field. The closest traditional degree would be a Masters of Library Science (MLS), or a degree with roots in library science but expanded to encompass broader uses of information, such as data analytics, organizational information management, and information strategy.

Some schools that are well respected for their innovations in building on a traditional library science foundation and integrating current information age trends are the University of California, Berkeley School of Information, and the various consortia of "ischools," including the University of Toronto, Syracuse University, and Rutgers University.

About the Author

Robert I. Berkman is a professor, author, and editor who researches and analyzes trends on emerging communication and media technologies and explores their impact on business, education, and culture. His work is directed toward journalists, librarians, market researchers, media studies students, and others who have a need to understand the information ecosphere.

Berkman currently serves as a part-time assistant professor at the School of Media Studies of The New School for Public Engagement, where he has developed and taught online masters level courses on research methods, social media, big data, new media ethics, the social enterprise, and other media and technology topics. He is co-editor of *The Information Advisor's Guide to Internet Research*, a monthly international journal for business researchers and information professionals; a contributing editor and blogger for *MIT Sloan Management Review's* Social Business research project; a director and lead analyst at Outsell Inc.; and a country analyst for Euromonitor Inc.

Berkman is the author and coauthor of several books on research, the media, and the Internet, including *The Art of Strategic Listening* (Paramount Press, 2008); *The Skeptical Business Searcher* (Information Today, Inc., 2004); and *Digital Dilemma* (with Chris Shumway; Blackwell, 2003).

Berkman received his MA in Journalism from the University of Montana and his BA from the University of Virginia. He lives in Rochester, New York, with his wife, Mary.

Index

Italicized page numbers indicate figures or tables. Boldface entries indicate "Tip" boxes.

KIRKWOOD

12/10/2015